PRIVATE EYE

The Spies Who Loved Her, 2

KATRINA JACKSON

ISBN: 9781793323248

Editor: A.K. Edits

Created with Vellum

content warnings

graphic depictions of violence (shooting death)
graphic depictions of bodily harm
a racial epithet

Prologue

Kenny hadn't gone to college with many plans besides graduate and enlist. So when he'd scored in the top percentile on The Agency's recruitment aptitude test – disguised as a psychology final – it hadn't been hard to sway him away from the Army; he was still serving his country. Even if no one could know about it. Besides, The Agency wiped away all of his student loan debt once he made it through the probationary period. And as it happened, being a spy came naturally to the man who'd always been "the new kid." Some of his missions even felt like a cake walk compared to being the Asian kid enrolling in public high school in Columbia, South Carolina halfway through his junior year. If he could survive that, he could survive anything, he often thought to himself.

A bullet whizzed past his head.

Okay, "almost anything," he whispered to himself as he ducked behind the abandoned building and moved further into the alley where he was currently held up, with a team of Russian soldiers advancing on his position. The best aspect of his current location was unequivocally that his back was secure; the worst was that the large cinderblock wall behind him meant that he was effectively trapped.

"ETA?" he said into his comm unit.

Lane's voice was loud, too loud, in his ear, "I've got good news and I've got bad news."

Kenny rolled his eyes.

"Bad news, we're outnumbered," Lane started.

Kenny sighed and did another cursory check around the alley, looking for anything that might help him get out of this predicament. "I already know that. What's the good news?" he hissed.

Kenny heard the answer in his comm but also from up above. "The good news is that I brought some explosives just in case."

He looked up and frowned, "How the fuck did you get up there?"

Lane released the fire escape down to Kenny and motioned for him to climb up. Only when they were both inside the abandoned building did Lane answer him.

"So, funny story," Lane said.

Kenny rolled his eyes again. "Get to the point."

Lane clapped him on the shoulder and laughed, "These guys are idiots."

They moved to either side of a window at the front of the large empty warehouse he'd crawled into, looking down onto the street in front of the alley he'd just escaped. Kenny saw the ops team down below. They were dressed in all black tactical gear. It should have been difficult to see them except the geniuses hadn't been smart enough to shoot out the street light. Their guns were held at the ready as their leader motioned for them to advance just a bit further. There was also a large black van blocking the entrance to the alley.

They could have taken him down easily. But they were advancing, holding their fire, maybe even stalling for time. For what, he didn't know. And he didn't want to find out. Kenny realized how dangerous his situation had been, but he quickly suppressed the panic he felt, because he wasn't safe yet. His hand twitched and he almost reached for his phone.

Lane snapped his fingers and Kenny turned toward him. He signaled that they should head out. It was surreal on the street, eerie, too quiet. They looked left and right and waited quietly just in case, but the street really was deserted. Lane smiled at him and pulled a small pack explosive from his vest.

Kenny shook his head but Lane smiled wider. The other man was notorious for making a big mess when a small efficient advance would do. But as he launched out onto the street towards the mouth of the alley, Kenny had no choice but to follow. Technically, Lane was the senior agent and Kenny respected the pecking order, especially in the field.

They slowly made their way to the black van, their guns ready should anyone burst from it, but when they made it to the driver's side door, they were both shocked.

Lane turned to him, furious. "They didn't leave anyone in the damn truck," he whispered in outrage. "Fucking amateurs."

Kenny shook his head and kept his lips shut; he knew how much Lane hated dumb criminals. They didn't have time for one of his rants. Kenny covered Lane's back as he kneeled down to attach the explosive underneath the van. When it was armed, Lane gestured to Kenny to move across the street. They crouched into one of the many abandoned store fronts with a clear view of the alley's mouth.

"Can you fucking believe that?" Lane asked, a bit louder now.

Kenny shrugged noncommittally, trying to avoid being dragged into this discussion again.

"That is military protocol 101. In hostile areas and especially when you're *engaging* the enemy, you don't leave your vehicle unattended. How hard is that to understand?"

"Maybe they're not actually military," Kenny offered, a spark of a thought coming to him but disappearing.

Lane turned toward him and threw both hands out in exasperation. "It's also common sense," he yelled.

Kenny barely noticed the quick movement of Lane's thumb as he depressed the detonator. There was a three second delay before the van was catapulted into the air and fell back to the ground, landing on its side. Kenny flinched, but Lane barely moved except to shake his head. "Amateurs."

The blast caused a commotion in the alley; they could hear, but not see. The team was yelling and shooting at nothing or each other, trapped by the shell of the van, which was on fire and certain to blow at some point. Kenny frowned, maybe Lane was right; they didn't seem like the kind of Russian tactical team he might have expected.

Just then a member of the ops team squeezed out of the alley, followed by two others. One by one, they pulled the masks from their faces. In the pre-dawn darkness, lit only by a flickering streetlamp, Kenny recognized three of the corrupt Russian soldiers he'd been tracking.

This was supposed to be a simple reconnaissance mission for someone else's job; a quick in and out. But last night he'd run into Lane at an underground casino for the world's wealthy and corrupt. That was the first sign that something was wrong. While The Agency was notoriously, and understandably, cagey about all of the operations they were running, the one thing they were good at was providing their agents with a heads up if there was a possibility they might run into a fellow agent in the field on a parallel job. Agency protocol required agents be briefed about potential friendly encounters for their safety. It would be devastating for morale if an agent killed another. So when Kenny saw Lane at a blackjack table as he'd strolled toward the private poker rooms, his hackles rose. He only played one hand before begging off from his asset, claiming an urgent business meeting and rushed back to his hotel.

He'd had a strange feeling as if someone had been in his

hotel room so he made a hasty exit out of the service entrance at the back of the kitchens. He'd slipped past a convoy of Russian military vehicles just before they closed off a two-block radius around his hotel. When he called into his remote handler, she'd immediately redirected his call to Lane. They couldn't be sure if their covers were blown, but it was always best to assume they were vulnerable. They shut their ops down and were preparing to leave the country immediately when Kenny realized he was being followed. He'd tried to lose his tail and ended up trapped in an alleyway with one gun, one clip, and a wall too high to climb at his back. His cover had definitely been blown.

He raised his arms, took aim and put a bullet dead center in the forehead of one of the soldiers he'd been tracking. Within a few minutes, he and Lane had taken out all survivors and were searching their bodies for anything of use.

"Got something," Lane said. He handed a cell phone to Kenny. It had been damaged and wouldn't turn on. But it was the only thing they'd found, so Kenny pocketed it.

"What now?" Lane asked as he stood.

Kenny raised an eyebrow. "You tell me. My mission is a bust," he said, looking at the dead bodies around them.

Lane grunted and scratched at his salt and pepper five o'clock shadow. "There's no one here that I've been tracking, but that doesn't mean anything. These Russian fucks are so corrupt it's hard to know what they're up to and who knows what."

"So we should leave."

Lane nodded. "It's the smart thing to do." Then he turned to Kenny and smiled, "Kierra doesn't like it when I take too many risks. And Monica doesn't like it when I make Kierra sad." He winked at Kenny.

Kenny was a good enough spy that he knew his face hadn't betrayed his reaction. But the unexpected mention of Kierra caught him off guard and his mind immediately wandered to Maya. He felt his entire body clench with the urge to dig his own cell phone from his pocket.

"So let's scatter. Check in when you get wherever you're going," Lane said.

Kenny nodded automatically.

They walked away from the alleyway casually, but kept their firearms at their sides until all that remained of the explosion was the smell of charred metal. They were just on the outer edges of the business district. The sun had lightened the sky and the city was slowly coming to life around them. They separated without a word. Kenny headed east to the train station. He had a change of clothes, new identification, cash and other necessities in a locker there. He'd also memorized the schedule. If he hurried, he could be on a high-speed train out of the country within the hour. He didn't know where Lane was headed and he didn't want to know; just in case.

He felt as if he held his breath on the walk to the train station. He kept his head down and sidestepped the early morning crowd of delivery trucks and shop owners. He didn't let himself relax when he made it to the station or retrieved his stash from an old bank of lockers. He made a detour to the bathroom where he changed into fresh clothes that didn't smell like sweat, fire and gun powder. He also pulled the SIM card from his phone and washed it down the sink as he rinsed his hands. But he still didn't let his muscles loosen as he slipped into a seat in the quiet car or even when the train started moving.

He was at least half an hour outside of the city before he finally started to breathe normally again. Only then did he allow himself to pull his cell phone from his pocket. He looked around and made sure no one was looking as he extracted his personal SIM card from a secret compartment in his boot. He slipped it into his cell phone and waited while his information downloaded.

There were lots of things he could do to reestablish his link with the real world. He could text his parents or even call them. He could text Chanté. Hell, he could check his personal email for the first time in… months. But Kenny didn't do any of those things. Instead he tapped on the ChatBot app and swallowed an excited cry when he saw that bright green button at the top of Maya's avatar. He lifted his head and looked around the car, once again making sure he hadn't garnered any attention, biting his lips to stop the smile that wanted to spread across his mouth. The entire car seemed to be asleep thankfully. When he was satisfied that he was as anonymous as he could be, he tapped her avatar and requested a chat session. He fished a pair of headphones from his bag and plugged them into his phone. He waited patiently for her to accept his request. He agreed to her price. He finally let himself truly exhale when her face popped up on his phone screen.

She was lying on her stomach, smiling at her webcam. "Hi stranger," she said.

MasquerAsiaN
Did you miss me?

SHE NODDED BEFORE SHE SPOKE. "So much."

This was a terrible idea. It was too public. He had no cover. But he could already feel himself hardening in his pants.

MasquerAsiaN
Show me how much.

SHE DIDN'T BOTHER to ask for clarification; they both knew what he liked. She rose onto her knees exposing her soft, rounded stomach to him, her thighs jiggling gently as she spread her legs and sat back on her heels.

He looked around one more time and grasped his dick through his jeans. He couldn't do more than that and that was fine. Everything was fine as far as he was concerned. He hadn't been executed by the Russian military in an alley, he was on a train west, he had a cell phone that might give him some useful information about his failed op. And most importantly, Maya was slipping her hand over her belly and into her underwear.

Just for him.

MAYA USED to dream about her future while trying to survive graduate school. She imagined herself just a few years after graduation as a rising junior associate with the best office on one of the middle floors of a fancy high rise, a solid stable of reliable clients, the support of at least one equity partner and, most importantly, a savings account with actual money in it. She'd seen her MBA as a stepping stone toward the kind of life that would make her family proud and allow her to give back even a fraction of all that her mother had given her.

But those dreams had been pure fantasy. The idea of life in the corporate world was always better than reality; Maya had known that instinctively. Her deep unhappiness with her graduate program, her advisor and future job prospects made every day feel as if she were heading toward her own personal hell instead of the realization of her dreams. Maya hated the world of financial futures, trading was too cutthroat, and investment banking would only be a legitimate possibility if she could set up shop outside of the US, a possibility snuffed out almost as soon as the idea bloomed in her head; she couldn't bear to be so far away from her family.

But all of that anxiety about her future had turned out to be for nothing. During her final year of business school, Maya got a frantic phone call from her sister; their mother had died of a stroke. The eight-hour flight home gave her a chance to consider the state of her life as she tried desperately not to feel any of her grief. In the kind of cold assessment of one's life that always seemed to come too late, Maya found that she'd been wasting her time – and accruing an insane amount of debt – for a degree she wasn't sure she wanted. And life's responsibilities would no longer wait. Her mother hadn't been current on her life insurance payments. Her twin brother and sister were in their final year of high school. Her graduate cohort was full of absolute douchebags. And all of the pressure of dealing with the minute details of burying her mother and keeping her siblings together had suddenly fallen on her.

She arranged to take her final courses online and graduated a semester early because her mother hated unfinished tasks. While all of her classmates were starting underpaid internships, Maya found a 9-to-5 as a receptionist at an investment firm where she made just enough to keep a roof over her siblings' heads and make sure they graduated on time; trying and failing to fill her mother's shoes. It wasn't the life she'd been dreaming of, but if given the choice again, Maya would choose Jerome and Kaya in a heartbeat.

The unexpected year-long detour ended when Maya moved her siblings into their separate Midwestern college dorms and then moved herself back to New Jersey, since home technically wasn't home anymore. Her stomach had been tied in knots as she prepared to grovel for a letter of recommendation from her former advisor so she could get her life back on track. But one conversation with Dr. Browne had confirmed that the life Maya had been living was no longer an option.

But Maya was an optimist. She decided to be pleased that Dr. Browne had remained consistently useless when he informed her that he wasn't willing to write her any letters of recommendation because he was "no longer assured of her capabilities." She also took some comfort – as she'd walked out of his office and off campus for hopefully the last time ever – that he'd apparently *once* believed her capable. Her advisor's refusal to be a decent human being had been the final kick in the ass she needed to give up on the corporate world and chart her own path from the relative place of comfort that was Kierra's second bedroom. It was like their sophomore year of college all over again, except Maya couldn't afford rent for a couple of months and they had a kitchen – that neither of them used, because they couldn't cook.

And regardless of what her former advisor had to say about her work ethic, she'd immediately started applying for every position she was even kind of qualified for. She was broke, teetering on the edge of homelessness, overqualified and struggling to explain a year and a half detour on her resume without using her mother's death as a gotcha in interviews. She'd been very cautiously rationing the last $200 in her bank account when a flyer at the local community center caught her eye. A local religious group had organized a discussion on the ills of pornography and prostitution, especially the rising numbers of cam models. The talk was – not cleverly – entitled "Downloading Sin." Maya wasn't sheltered by any means, but she'd had to look up exactly what a cam model was and what they did. She threw the flyer away, used most of what little money she had left to buy a cheap webcam and hadn't looked back since. She knew immediately that she'd found her calling.

Maya loved every inch of her body and she had never shied away from showing it off. The rounded plane of her stomach, her slightly drooping breasts that ended in hard points when she was happy, every manicured nail, every light stretch mark, all of the white scars that attested to her lifelong clumsiness, even that small keloid on the back of her ankle – a constant reminder that you should never let a boy convince you to do anything, especially not jump out of a tree. Every perfect imperfection was hers. And apparently there was an audience very willing to log onto a chatroom and pay premium rates for the privilege of watching her touch herself exactly as she liked. It was a revelation.

But the highlight of her new career was Thursday nights. Thursday nights were her own personal treat. She couldn't stop smiling as she sprayed herself with her favorite perfume, a light floral scent that made her feel fragile and powerful all at the same time. Even though he wouldn't smell it tonight, she sometimes liked to fantasize that one day he would. Because Thursday nights were her regular, private chats with MasquerAsiaN.

Maya always tried to remember the screen names of her most active clients and MasquerAsiaN had distinguished himself immediately. Within a week of first popping up in her public room, he'd gone from a practical stranger to a regular client, chatting to her casually and mostly not sexually; his favorite topic seemed to be the books on her nightstand, just barely in view behind her. It took a lot to notice a stack of cozy mysteries when she was half naked on screen, so she'd started rotating the stack to pique his interest.

By the time he finally requested a private show, Maya had created a rough profile of him in her head; a list of information she'd unconsciously compiled and analysis of what it all meant. He was Asian, obviously. He chatted with her every day but at different times of the day and night, which led her to believe that he traveled a lot for work. He was probably in a relationship since, of all of her clients, he wasn't aggressive in his requests; he clearly wasn't hard up for any kind of sexual release. Although she also considered that maybe he was just a good guy. But Maya didn't have a great amount of experience with whatever one of those looked like, so there was a mental asterisk next to that tidbit. He also never haggled with her about prices and he always tipped her well above the app's suggested rate. Clearly he was financially comfortable.

The only part of this that should have mattered to Maya, Cam Model #2364, username: ThickaThanASnicka, was the financially comfortable part. MasquerAsiaN was exactly the kind of client cam workers dreamed of.

But Maya, the romantic, was unfortunately preoccupied by the way MasquerAsiaN always confronted the jerks in her public chatroom who asked her for the filthiest shit but never wanted to pay for it. Or the fact that he never forgot to ask how her day was as soon as their private chats started. Or that he sometimes paid her to just lie in front of her laptop's webcam and tell him a story. And she'd been on cloud nine after he remembered that marigolds were her favorite flower. But the best thing – the thing she wouldn't admit to anyone, not even Kierra – was the way her heart skipped a beat every time he asked her to call him 'baby' or 'sweetheart'; wanting her to pretend as if they were in a long distance relationship, instead of in the midst of a transaction. Maya could measure just how far gone she was over him – a man who always wanted to see her but never turned on his webcam so she could see him – by how much her heart swelled when she saw his username appear in her public chatroom. Even worse was that she'd started to think of Thursday nights as their date night – a time when they could jump straight to their private chat and just be together. Virtually.

ThickaThanASnicka has logged in.

SHE TRIED NOT to chew on her bottom lip as she waited for him to log on; she didn't want to disrupt her perfect lipstick application. Maybe it was the fact that they'd never met in person and he'd never let her see him, but those few seconds between when she logged in and MasquerAsiaN's request for a private session were always the worst. Her insecurities bubbled to the surface of her usually thick skin and she wondered if this would be the night that he didn't show.

But then he was there.

MasquerAsiaN has logged in.

HE SENT her a private video chat request immediately.

ThickaThanASnicka
Hi honey

MasquerAsiaN
Hi :D

MAYA WANTED to berate herself as her stomach flipped, but she could do that later. She'd been looking forward to this all day.

MasquerAsiaN
How was your day?

SUCH A SIMPLE QUESTION, with such a complicated answer.

Today she'd had to call Jerome and tell him that he was $50 from maxing out his monthly budget. And she'd fought with Kaya about failing a midterm. And then Kierra had announced that she was moving out to shack up with her bosses, which meant that Maya needed to find a new roommate ASAP.

But she didn't want to think about any of that right now.

ThickaThanASnicka
Better now that I'm chatting with you.

MasquerAsiaN
You probably say that to all the guys. ;)

ThickaThanASnicka
I say it to the girls too. :*

MasquerAsiaN
LOL

ThickaThanASnicka
How was your day?

MasquerAsiaN
Long and technically ongoing. I really should have cancelled tonight.

MAYA'S HEART plummeted to her stomach.

ThickaThanASnicka
But you didn't…?

MasquerAsiaN
I didn't. I wanted to see you.

ThickaThanASnicka
See me do what? ;)

MasquerAsiaN
Just see you.

MAYA COULDN'T STOP the surprised gasp that escaped her lips or hide the shy smile that spread across her face.

MasquerAsiaN
You're so fucking beautiful. I don't tell you that enough.

ThickaThanASnicka
You tell me that every Thursday. (:

SHE WONDERED if he could see the blush she felt spreading over the high points of her cheeks.

MasquerAsiaN
Like I said. Not enough.

ThickaThanASnicka
I wish you would let me see you.

SHE WANTED to take the words back immediately; she'd typed at the speed of her heart, which was apparently moving faster than her rational brain. The words were there, staring at her. The chat bubbles indicating that he was typing a response popped up and then disappeared. Maya kept the smile on her face, because that was Cam Model 101, but she felt as if she was dying inside. It seemed like an hour before he finally responded, but it couldn't have been more than twenty seconds.

MasquerAsiaN
I wish I could. But my job is sensitive.

MAYA WAS QUICK TO RESPOND, shaking her head and smiling.

ThickaThanASnicka
I understand. Let's pretend I never even typed that :)

MasquerAsiaN
It'll happen one day.

SHE DIDN'T BELIEVE HIM. But she wanted to.

MasquerAsiaN
This is terrible timing but I have to go.

ThickaThanASnicka
Okay. I'll refund this session. No worries.

MasquerAsiaN
I don't need a refund. You earned it.

ThickaThanASnicka
Lol I didn't do anything.

MasquerAsiaN
How long did it take you to get ready for me? Makeup, hair, lingerie? Lingerie that I really wanted to watch you take off btw ;) You earned every dollar.

MAYA COULDN'T HELP but laugh, which helped her fight back the tears she felt building at the back of her eyes.

MasquerAsiaN
But if you really want, you can do something for me.

ThickaThanASnicka
Anything.

THERE SHE WAS, typing too fast for her own good again. But her heart was beating so hard in her chest; foolishly anticipating all of the possibilities of things he could ask for. Things she would give him without hesitation.

MasquerAsiaN

I want you to think about me when you touch yourself
tonight.

HER SMILE WAS INSTANTANEOUS.

ThickaThanASnicka
I do that already.

IN FOR A PENNY, in for a pound, she thought to herself, as she pressed send on that message.

MasquerAsiaN
So do I.
Goodnight sweetheart.

ThickaThanASnicka
Bye, babe.

WHEN MAYA LOGGED out of their chat, she considered going into her public room, but she didn't have the heart for it tonight. She walked into her en-suite bathroom and looked at herself in the mirror. He was right, her makeup was worth what he'd overpaid. And more.

A single tear slipped down her left cheek.

"What a fucking cliché. Get a grip, girl," Maya said aloud

to her reflection. A half confession in the privacy of her bathroom to her mirror-self made her feel marginally better. But it didn't dull the disappointment she felt at not getting to enjoy their regular hour long session. She looked forward to it every week, maybe even more than he did. Even though she couldn't see him, there was something about fucking herself to his very specific directions that made her feel close to him. Whoever he was.

Maya reached for the packet of makeup removal cloths and slowly wiped the masterpiece she'd created for him away. And then she did as he'd asked: climbed into the shower and thought of him while she brought herself to a gentle orgasm with the small bullet vibrator she kept there for just such occasions. A small vibrator that was a gift from MasquerAsiaN in fact. The note attached to the package he'd sent to her P.O. Box said that he dreamt about using it to stimulate her clit while they fucked. She called that image to mind tonight; wanting him more than she could bear.

It was silly, she knew, to be the sex worker falling for her client. But it was too late to go back now. The only thing that ruined the beautiful warm glow of her post-orgasmic steam was that when she came, she wanted to call out to him. But she didn't even know his name.

one

Kenny pulled his car up to the wrought iron gate outside of Lane and Monica's house and base of operations. He pressed the intercom button and rolled his eyes when Kierra's voice greeted him through the speaker.

"State your business."

"You know why I'm here, Kierra."

"Refresh my memory," she teased.

"Kierra, this is my first day. Don't make me late."

"You're making yourself late, playboy."

Kenny let out an exasperated breath. "My transfer was approved so I'm here to join Monica and Lane's-"

"Super-secret spy operation."

Kenny looked directly into the camera mounted on top of the keypad. "Open the gate." He heard her giggle before the gate began to slowly open for him.

He parked next to Kierra's old Honda, which he recognized from the brief period when he was running surveillance on her for Monica and Lane. He climbed out of his car, smoothed his pants and sweater and headed toward the house. He was almost at the front door when it opened. Kierra greeted him with a smile. His eyes involuntarily scanned down her body, widening as he took her outfit in.

"Do you always dress like this at work?"

She gave him a blank stare and frowned, "Like what?"

"Like," he moved one hand up and down to indicate her body, "Like this."

Kierra looked down at herself and Kenny's eyes followed her gaze. Kierra was normally a good six inches shorter than him but in her very tall high heels, the top of her head came just about to his chin. From the ankle straps of her shoes to the hem of her very short black skirt, there was just miles of bare, smooth brown skin. He wondered if she could sit or bend over without flashing everyone in the room in a skirt that short. And then he felt like a perv for wondering. And then his eyes traveled over the almost demure thin long-sleeved, turtle-neck sweater – almost demure because it was very obviously see-through – and Kenny's eyes scanned over her black lace bra. He tilted his head back and raised his eyes to the top of the door frame.

"That outfit is an HR reprimand waiting to happen," he said.

"Well, as I'm the only support staff on site, I'll make sure to file your complaint about my outfit just as soon as you submit it. With all of the others," she added playfully.

His head tilted down, but he kept his eyes squarely on hers. "Have there been other complaints about your work attire?" Her smile made him instantly wish he hadn't asked that question.

She leaned toward him and stage-whispered. "Every night."

He groaned. She giggled. He wondered if this transfer was a good idea.

"Can I- Can I come in now?"

"Oh yeah. Absolutely," she said, opening the door wider to let him in.

Kierra closed the door behind him and motioned for him to follow her through the kitchen, into the pantry. In the small room, she turned to him and stretched her arm up to the second highest shelf. "Baking soda box," she said, pulling it down. "If you feel around behind it you'll find a lever." She then moved out of the way for him to do just that.

"All the way to the back...?" He asked and then he felt it. "Oh okay." He pulled the switch toward him and the wall at the back of the pantry began to open slowly.

"Et voila. Welcome to Command," she said, bouncing on the balls of her feet.

He worried that she might topple over. "Command?" he asked, with a raised eyebrow.

"It's her nickname. Just go with it," Lane said, his voice coming from the kitchen and startling them both. He appeared at the pantry door and leaned one shoulder against the frame. His eyes were focused on Kierra. "You got a minute?" he asked her.

Kenny rolled his eyes and looked away. He could feel the sexual tension arcing between them and he'd had enough of being in the middle of that in Berlin. "I'm going to go find Monica," he announced, slipping through the hidden door, not that they cared.

"She's in her office. First door on the left," Kierra yelled after him and then giggled and then moaned.

Kenny tried to forget that moan and walked quickly down the stairs. He entered a foyer that honestly felt too classy for a secret spy outfit. There were elegantly framed art prints on the black walls. Spotlights on the ceiling illuminated the small room and a single table at the farthest wall was topped with two orchids in a slim vase. The room felt better suited for the entrance to a modeling agency or just something less clandestine.

There were two hallways jutting off of the foyer to the east and west of the building. Kenny followed Kierra's directions and stopped at the first door in the east hallway. It was slightly ajar and he could see Monica inside sitting at her desk, writing. He took a deep breath to calm his nerves. This wasn't technically his first impression, but he wanted to present himself to her in his best light; calm and professional. He'd practically begged for this transfer; serving under Monica was a once-in-a-lifetime opportunity. She was a legend in The Agency and until now she'd never been willing to work with anyone on a long-term basis besides Lane. Kenny knew it was a huge honor that she'd approved his request. It meant that she saw potential in him. And he didn't want to disabuse her of that notion. He didn't want to let her down.

"Are you going to come in or do you plan to just stand there staring at me?" Monica asked without looking up from her desk.

He closed his eyes and shook his head. "Sorry, I um…"

She looked up then with one raised eyebrow. "Where's Kierra?"

He pointed toward the foyer and opened his mouth to speak, but closed it because the truth, "She and your husband are probably fooling around in the pantry," felt strange to even think, let alone say.

"I'm here," Kierra announced, pushing Kenny out of the way to stride confidently into Monica's office.

Kenny watched Monica's eyes glide over Kierra's body appreciatively as she walked around the desk and placed a stack of files in front of her.

"Is this Lane's doing?" Monica asked Kierra with a small smirk on her face.

Kenny stepped tentatively into the office. Kierra smiled and Kenny noticed that her lipstick was smudged. He looked away, not wanting to see any other signs of her encounter with Lane.

"Yes, ma'am," Kierra said. Kenny added the lust dripping from her voice to the list of things he wanted to forget. "He told me to tell you-" Kenny turned back as Kierra's voice went quiet to see her leaning over Monica and whispering into her ear.

When she was done, Monica stood from her chair. She walked behind Kierra and moved the hair from her left shoulder, exposing her delicate neck. And then she bent down to return the favor. Whatever Monica whispered to Kierra made her shiver violently.

"Do you two want some privacy?" Kenny asked. Which only seemed to make Kierra shiver even more.

It took a second before Monica moved from behind Kierra and crossed the room. Her cold, assessing eyes settled on him and she said very normally, as if she hadn't just been flirting with her PA in front of him, "No need. Come on. Let's get you up to speed on our new job."

Kenny shook his head and followed her out of her office, wondering again if maybe this transfer had been a mistake. They walked down the hall, past the foyer and into a boardroom on the other side of the underground structure. She indicated that he should sit in a chair at the long oval oak table and she moved to a small podium with a computer atop it.

"What do you know about the Mehmeti family?"

The question put Kenny's unease at being in the center of Kierra, Monica and Lane's situation for the past few moments to the side and conjured up another discomfort. He felt as if he was back at The Academy and walking into a pop quiz. He sat up a little straighter in his chair and began to recite everything he knew for sure and a few things he'd gleaned from intel on other missions about the Albanian crime syndicate.

"They have their hands in every illicit thing you can imagine," Kenny stated. "Political corruption, drugs, human trafficking. But they've recently started dealing in arms."

"Very recently," Monica agreed with a short nod of her head for him to continue as she tapped on the computer and the smart screen booted up.

"From what I can tell, the arms trade is the youngest brother Joseph's area. He started with a few transactions locally; barely noticeable. But there's been some speculation that he's started buying more weapons from Russian dealers and is looking to move into the US."

"Good," Monica said. Kenny had to force himself not to smile under her approval. "We've been chasing down some rumors about Joseph's American contacts. There are whispers that he has a connect in the Midwest and maybe even the US government. We thought for a while that there wasn't any validity to it; probably just Joseph boasting to raise his profile in the family. But two weeks ago we got confirmation of a deal with a white supremacist cell in West Virginia; purely by chance. The ATF was dispatched to intervene, but somehow Mehmeti found out about their plans."

Kenny was sitting at the edge of his seat.

Monica directed his attention to the screen. There was a spreadsheet with three columns there. He studied it. It took a few seconds to decipher the columns as dates, weights and IP addresses. But he knew not to assume. "What's this?"

"Transactions," Monica answered, giving him the barest amount of help.

"And the IP addresses?" Kenny thought he saw a ghost of a smile on Monica's face, but couldn't be sure.

Just then Kierra sauntered into the room, Lane on her heels, a coffee pot and three mugs balanced on top of a tray in his hands. Lane placed the tray onto the table and moved to a seat at the front of the room. Monica nodded to acknowledge his presence but began to answer Kenny's question.

"We know these are confirmed shipments of arms sales the Mehmeti family has brokered in the past month."

"Month?" Kenny asked, shocked. There were at least a dozen items on the list.

"Exactly. They're moving heavy weight and quickly. But we can't be certain of the exact kinds of weapons they're selling since the only information we have about the shipments is weight," she indicated toward the middle column, "and buyer." This time she pointed at the final column and Kenny nodded.

"Got it," he said.

"No, you don't," Lane responded, accepting a mug of coffee from Kierra.

Kierra walked to the podium, put a mug in front of Monica and turned back to the table.

"What am I missing?" Kenny asked.

At his question, Monica clicked one of the IP addresses and Kenny felt the air rush out of his lungs. He knew the website that popped up. Very well. His eyes darted to Kierra, whose hands were frozen over the third mug, her gaze fixed on the screen.

The ChatBot home page was a jumble of flashing text and large videos on loops of people in various shades of undress. It was the most popular cam site on the internet, with tens of thousands of channels offering a range of content, from daily lifestyle livestreams to the most hardcore sexual content and everything in between. With millions of unique hits an hour, even the smallest channels were finding audiences willing to part with every global currency – converted into virtual gold coins, the site's universal payment method.

"Why are you on ChatBot?" Kierra asked the question. Kenny noted that her hands were shaking.

"Part of the reason we had such a hard time tracking the shipments was because we were looking in the wrong places," Monica said, her voice all business.

"We assumed they'd be using the dark web. But they're clever," Lane added. "We compiled this list of shipments trolling through the public chatrooms on ChatBot."

"We think they're selecting random but popular models and then conducting the deals right out in the open. There's so much going on in the comments that it's hard to keep track of all of the conversations. And when someone is masturbating themselves on screen, who gives a shit about the two weirdos chatting in Russian?"

Kenny nodded. "It's smart."

"Very," Lane agreed.

"Are the models in danger?" Kierra asked.

Monica turned and gave her a sympathetic look. "No," she said in the gentlest voice Kenny had ever heard from her. "Your roommate is perfectly safe."

Kierra visibly relaxed. She turned to Kenny with a smile, "My best friend Maya has a channel on ChatBot."

Kenny smiled faintly, his tongue felt heavy in his mouth.

"He knows," Lane said over the rim of his coffee cup. "That's why he's here." He took a sip, his eyes dancing with mirth.

Kenny's eyes widened and his mouth fell open. Kierra's head swiveled between the three of them as she searched for an explanation. Kenny wanted to punch Lane in his smiling face but since Monica would probably punch him in return, he tamped down on that impulse with clenched fists.

Monica was the one who answered. "When Stepanov put the hit out on you, we had to dig into every part of your life to figure out any potential security risks, just in case. That included your roommate."

"You put my roommate under surveillance?" Kierra yelled, curiously, at Lane.

"We did not," Monica said as she turned to Kenny. "Kenny was supposed to investigate Maya's potential security risk, log it and move on. But you never moved on, did you, Kenny?"

Kenny's entire body felt hot. He wanted to completely disappear. Just cease to exist. But that wasn't going to happen. His chickens had finally come home to roost.

He'd always dismissed the warning at The Academy about getting too attached to surveillance subjects and assets, because he'd been so certain that he never would. The job was the job. But from the minute he'd logged into Maya's public chatroom and seen her – she was laughing and taking selfies, while her viewers looked on – he'd been hooked; completely mesmerized. He watched her for two days officially, confirming fairly quickly that she had no idea what her roommate did for a living and was actually very strict about not communicating with clients about her personal life. The likelihood that she was a security risk Stepanov could exploit was very low. He filed his report and moved on to the next potential threat in Kierra's file. But at home that night he'd sat at his desk with a cold bottle of beer and logged into cam model ThickaThanASnicka's public chatroom. He was already a few yards down a slippery slope and teetering on the edge of no return. But he couldn't make himself care.

For the past six months he'd been a regular viewer. At first he'd promised himself that he would just look, there was no harm in that. But then some asshole had been a dick to her, clogging up the chatroom with rude and derogatory comments and Kenny had cussed the guy out and reported his account for harassment before he could even register what he was doing.

Maya had thanked him, her face lighting up with a shy smile just for him, and he knew he was a goner. He'd started logging in every few days, deluding himself into thinking the way she bit her lip and grinned when she saw his screen name meant something more; or anything at all. Eventually he was logging in every day and he couldn't have stopped the growing infatuation if he'd wanted; which he didn't.

Sometimes he lied to himself that it had been innocent once. That he was just protecting Kierra and Monica, hell, even Lane. But that was bullshit. Logging into Maya's chatroom was his most selfish act. It was the only time in the day where all of his other responsibilities fell away. He quickly gathered all of his feelings of shame and worry and locked them away inside his chest and requested the first of many private sessions. He'd felt nothing but joy as he reached into his sweats, grasped his dick and stroked himself while she moved a bright pink dildo between her smooth thighs. Knowing that those smiles were actually – finally – just for him; that every time she touched herself was to please him. It was too late to save himself, so he didn't try. For months he'd refused to think any further into the future than the next Thursday and the Thursday after that; to the next time he could have Maya all to himself again. In just a matter of days, Maya became the singular focus of his fantasies. No matter where he was in the world, no matter the danger he was in, he never missed a Thursday night.

But something had changed since Berlin. His brain was filled with foreboding that this would all blow up in his face and soon. And apparently he'd been right. He hadn't expected his comeuppance to look quite like this. He'd assumed that the setting would be more memorable and – pathetically – that he'd be in a room with Maya, close enough to smell her perfume and, if she'd let him, touch her. Instead he was sitting in a boardroom watching the shrapnel of his career falling from the heights of his own hubris.

There really wasn't a way to explain himself besides the truth. He'd already tried out every possible excuse – hoping to come clean to Maya at some point. So he knew that any explanation he came up with sounded like bullshit. There was no artful lie that could make sense of this mess. Kenny flinched as he locked eyes with Kierra, the fire in her stare was so at odds with her normally bubbly personality.

"I couldn't help myself," was all he could think to say, pathetically.

And then Lane laughed, actually fucking laughed like this wasn't the worst thing that had ever happened to Kenny and his career wasn't over before it really began.

"I know that feeling," Lane said and took another sip of his coffee.

Kenny really wanted to punch him.

"CALM DOWN, SWEET GIRL," Monica said in that gentle voice again.

"Pervert," Kierra hissed at Kenny.

He wanted to point out that people in glass houses shouldn't throw stones and gesture broadly at the three of them, but he'd learned in Europe that Monica's reaction to people hurting Kierra was to swiftly introduce them to her fist or worse. So he kept his mouth shut.

He turned to Monica, "Why approve my transfer if you're just going to report me for fraternizing with an asset?" He tried to hide the hurt in his voice, but he wasn't sure how well he managed that.

Lane snickered. "Who said we're gonna report you?" he asked and pulled a very angry Kierra into his lap.

"If you're not going to report me, then why are you doing this?" Kenny pushed out of his chair and began to pace the length of the room.

"We've noticed something about the transactions," Monica said, again as if this soap opera was just business as usual.

Kenny turned to see her move behind Lane's chair and stroke Kierra's hair lovingly. She was still mad, but Kierra melted under her touch. Kenny watched the scene and wanted to turn away because it felt even more intimate than the flirting and it opened a well of longing inside his chest.

He'd never had that, but he wanted it. His job, however, didn't allow much time for a social life and he wasn't interested in dating another spy. But most tragically, his image of an ideal girlfriend had been refined over the past few months to exactly one person. He wanted that kind of closeness with a very specific cam model, who laughed when she climaxed, read cozy mysteries and biographies, and who wouldn't recognize him if he bumped into her on a city street.

"What about the transactions?" Kenny asked, tearing his eyes away from their tableau.

Monica seemed to have gotten lost in the moment and it took a second for her to regain her train of thought. "Joseph handles all of the negotiations personally."

"What?" Kenny asked, shocked again. He couldn't have heard that right.

"It's dumb as hell," Lane said.

"Why would he do that?"

Monica smiled a kind of feral smile that Kenny had seen before and it made him shiver in fear and awe. "Turns out Joseph chose ChatBot because he loves the site. It wasn't a genius move to evade detection, just convenient. He's in the chatrooms for hours most days, so why not get his rocks off and sell some illegal weapons at the same time?"

Kenny laughed at the beautiful absurdity of it all.

Monica continued, "Once we realized that, we went back and took a look at all of the cam model rooms he'd chosen and it looks like Joseph has a type."

Kenny felt a shiver run down his spine.

"No," Kierra said.

"Sorry, sweet girl. But Joseph likes Black women, the thicker the better. And your roommate is already on his radar."

Kenny felt his blood run cold and he clenched his fists. "No," he echoed Kierra in word and resolve.

"As far as we know, he hasn't done any deals in her chatrooms yet. He's only logged into her room a few times and for relatively short periods of time. But if she can get his attention we can use that. We can identify his buyers."

"Is that the mission?" Kenny's voice was hard, tight with anger. "Identify his contacts?"

"That's phase one of the mission, yes," Monica responded.

"What's phase two?"

"There's some evidence that if he really likes a girl, he'll ask her to meet him in person," Lane said.

Kierra jumped out of his lap, shaking her head.

"We'd like to bring Maya in as an asset and use her as a honey pot."

"Don't call it a honey pot," Kenny hissed. "Don't make it sound pretty. You want to use her as bait."

"No," Kierra said. "You can't do that. I'm saying no. She has a brother and sister who need her. Her mother died and she's all they have. She's my *best* friend. I'm saying no." She practically screamed that last word.

Kenny filed away those bits of personal information about Maya like the starving man he was and nodded his agreement. "I'm saying no, too," he said.

Lane sighed and rose from his chair. "We realize that this might be scary for you two. But first of all, this isn't your decision to make. And second of all, don't you want to know why we actually brought you here?" He posed the question to Kenny like he knew the answer. Like he knew every thought Kenny had ever had about Maya while she touched herself and talked to him in that deep sultry voice he loved.

Kenny squinted. "Why did you bring me here?"

Monica turned to Kierra. "Kierra's moving in with us."

Kierra scoffed, and Monica flinched, but she kept going. "And Maya is going to need a new roommate."

KENNY TRIED to walk with sure steps out of the conference room, but his back was aching from the built-up tension of the last few minutes. He shut the boardroom door behind him harder than he planned, but the slam didn't stop Kierra's yelling. She probably hadn't even noticed Kenny leave. The sound of her voice followed him down the hall.

He ended up back at the Command foyer and turned around in a circle. He didn't know where his office was located. He had no idea where to go. He took the steps up to the pantry and burst through the kitchen at a run. He sped through the living room and out of the front door. His heart was pounding and there was a slight sheen of sweat on his forehead. He walked to his car and considered hopping inside; driving as far away from here as he could get. But he didn't.

He pulled his phone from his front pocket and pulled up the ChatBot app.

There was a green light next to Maya's avatar. His thumb hovered over it. He shouldn't talk to her. Especially not now. But he knew that he would. Even just seeing her small picture had calmed his breathing.

When he logged into her chatroom, she noticed immediately.

ThickaThanASnicka
Hey stranger :D

MasquerAsiaN
Morning beautiful

ThickaThanASnicka
Is it morning where you are too?

HIS LIPS QUIRKED. He considered for a moment blurting out the truth, telling her exactly who he was and begging for her forgiveness. But he didn't. If Monica and Lane's intel was correct, then doing that would probably blow any chance they had to intercept the Mehmeti family's arms trade. But, as had been the case for months, his mission directive didn't top the list of most important things in his head. He didn't bare his soul for the simple fact that he couldn't handle being the reason she was sad or angry. It was a selfish impulse. And he didn't care.

MasquerAsiaN
I had a sudden urge to see your face.

BEHIND HIM THE front door opened.

"Kenny," Monica called.

ThickaThanASnicka
That's so sweet! Just my face…? ;)

MasquerAsiaN
If I had time, I'd want to see all of you. But I have to go.

ThickaThanASnicka
So soon?

MasquerAsiaN
Sorry work…

ThickaThanASnicka
: (okay. Have a good day sweetheart.

MasquerAsiaN
You too, beautiful.

"KENNY," Monica called out to him again.

He slipped his phone back into his front pocket, took a deep breath and turned back to the house. He followed Monica through the pantry silently. Back in the conference room the mood between his new bosses and their PA was decidedly chillier than when he'd arrived less than an hour ago, fresh-faced and excited to start working under Monica's tutelage. Back when he thought no one knew about his secret online relationship. He couldn't believe so much had changed in so little time.

Now Kierra sat in a chair as far away from Monica and Lane as possible, sullen. Monica and Lane stood ramrod straight at the head of the room, their eyes on her. Their gazes were intense and maybe even mournful. Kenny stood off to the side, too anxious to sit back down.

Lane took a deep breath and tore his eyes from Kierra. "Change of plans. Kierra is going to stay in her apartment until we've caught Joseph."

"Or longer," she muttered.

Kenny wasn't sure if he saw Monica's jaw tense or if he imagined it.

"Okay," Kenny said tentatively, wondering if maybe it would be that easy. "So what's the plan?"

"We're telling Maya everything," Kierra announced. She turned her cold-eyed gaze to him and repeated, "Everything."

two

Maya hopped onto the kitchen counter, her cell phone in one hand. Technically, she wasn't supposed to be online this afternoon. She'd put in a couple of hours on her channel this morning as she usually did on Tuesdays. A little sexy chat time, maybe a flashed boob here or there; nothing much, but just enough to keep her subscribers interested.

This was her half day off. She was supposed to be vegging out on the couch, watching the most recent episode of the Swedish mystery show she loved. That had been her plan all weekend long. But then MasquerAsiaN had logged into her chatroom for literally a minute and suddenly her plans changed. There was always something so beautifully disorienting about seeing his screen name on a day or at a time she didn't expect. It made her skin tingle and her stomach do flips and it was honestly the corniest thing in the world, but she couldn't help it.

She'd logged out of her chatroom at the regular time only to log back in on the secret account she used to check out her competitors' rooms and lightly stalk her favorite customer. She was about to waste the rest of her regular free day scrolling and refreshing the site, hoping desperately that he might appear again. Waiting for him like a lovesick fool.

Her front door opened and she sighed. "In the kitchen," she yelled to Kierra.

"Maya, can you come to the living room?" Kierra called back.

"I could, but I'm in the kitchen."

"Maya."

Her head lifted at the urgency in Kierra's voice. "Fine," she called back, jumping from the counter.

Their kitchen was a small hole of a room, with a half wall behind their sink and an overhang counter for a breakfast bar, so it only took two steps for Maya to see that Kierra wasn't alone. Her eyebrows lifted. She didn't have to guess that the tall man and woman standing behind Kierra like sentries were her bosses. She'd always wondered what kind of people could have piqued Kierra's interests so intensely that she'd essentially put her poetry career on hold to get them coffee. And seeing the Amazon's intense brown gaze and the easy, rakish charm of the man next to her put all of those questions to bed. Maya would have splayed herself on their desks every day for three years too if they'd looked at her with even half the intensity they were aiming at the back of Kierra's head.

Maya smiled at Kierra and wondered if this was the formal introduction to her best friend's boyfriend… and girlfriend. If so, it was about time, since Kierra was abandoning her to live with them. But Maya noticed the tension just at the corners of Kierra's eyes and the way her body was rigid, a clear indicator that she was pissed.

That's when she noticed him standing by the front door, as if he was too afraid to fully enter their apartment. Maya unconsciously held her breath as her eyes travelled down his tall frame. She sucked her bottom lip into her mouth as she took in his broad chest, lean waist and large hands. His very large hands. Her gaze traveled back up his body and she smiled at his strong, angular jaw and full lips.

"Maya, I have to tell you something," Kierra said.

Maya nodded absently and made eye contact with him. She almost smiled, her bottom lip still in her mouth. He swallowed hard. She did smile then, letting her wet bottom lip fall from between her teeth.

"Maya," Kierra said in that urgent tone again.

Maya reluctantly tore her eyes away from him and focused on Kierra. "What? Just tell me. Spit it out."

"Maybe you should come sit down," the man behind Kierra said in a not unpleasant Southern accent.

Maya raised one eyebrow at him. "I'll pass." And then she turned to Kierra. "Spill, short stack. You're scaring me."

Kierra took a deep breath. "So, first of all, these are my bosses," she said gesturing behind her.

Maya noted the way she emphasized the word 'bosses' as if Maya didn't know she'd been sleeping with them for months. They'd never talked about it explicitly, unfortunately, but Kierra had quit her job, pined for months and gone to an Irish writing retreat, only to come back and announce she was going back to her old job and moving in with her bosses because "the job is very demanding."

Maya looked around Kierra at the woman's solid hips and strong arms. Yep, she bet the job was *very* demanding.

"I guessed that," she responded.

"So you know how I've never said exactly what they did?"

Maya had to really think about that. Had Kierra never actually told her about her employers' job? Had Maya ever asked? Did she care? "Does it matter?" she asked honestly. "You're their PA."

"Fair. And it shouldn't matter except they're spies."

Maya put her hand on her hip and squinted at her best friend, roommate, and maybe future mental health patient. "Girl, what are you talking about?"

"They're spies. How else am I supposed to say that? Is there another word?" She shrugged and turned to the other three for help.

"I don't know. But try saying it in a way that makes sense," Maya replied, getting a little annoyed.

"They're international spies. Espionage. James Bond. Hell, Mr. Bean. Girl, what else do you want me to say?"

"Was Mr. Bean a spy?" Maya asked, ready to really consider that when Southern accent cut in.

"Not on purpose," he replied helpfully. The woman next to him rolled her eyes.

"Okay, well, why the hell are you telling me this? Whatever security clearance I need for this info, I don't have and I don't want." She made eye contact with Southern accent to underscore the point.

"Agreed," Kierra said. "And if I'd known that my job would put you in the middle of this, I wouldn't have taken it."

Maya noted that the woman's eyes skirted to Kierra and then drifted to the floor. Oh, Maya thought, they're fighting.

She backed away, waving her hands in front of her. "Well girl, you and your boos can take your spy drama to their house since you're about to move out."

"I'm not moving out actually."

Maya stilled. "Excuse me? I have been interviewing people for two weeks. What the hell do you mean you're not moving out?"

"That's why we're here," Kierra said in a small voice.

"What is why you're here? What is this entire strange ass conversation? Are you in danger? Do you need help? Blink once slowly for yes and I'll call the police right now," Maya said, holding up her phone.

"Alright," Southern accent said. "Here's the deal, darlin'."

"My name's Maya. Call me anything but my government name again and spy or not, I'll knee you in the balls."

The man by the door snorted softly and Southern accent turned to him, "Well damn if I don't like her already."

"Get on with it," the woman behind Kierra said.

"Alright," Southern accent said, "so the deal is that an emissary from an Albanian mob syndicate has been using cam models' chatrooms on ChatBot to conduct illegal weapons deals and we'd like to use your channel for a sting operation."

Maya laughed. "Is that it? Go ahead. Have fun. You all sound deranged, by the way."

"That's not it," the woman behind Kierra said.

"I'm sorry, what's your name?" Maya asked her.

"You can call me Monica," she said in a hard monotone. It was terrible timing, but Maya wondered if she used that voice in bed. And then she felt terrible for the inappropriate thought. And then she filed away a mental note to ask Kierra later because nosy best friend was nosy.

"Is that your real name or…?"

"It's unclear," Kierra answered.

"Girl, what have you gotten yourself into?"

"Also unclear," she replied sadly.

Maya wanted to go to her and hug her. She clearly needed it. But there was still so much happening. "And your name?" she aimed at Southern accent.

"Lane," he said simply.

"Oh okay, so yeah, these are fake names. Got it."

He rolled his eyes and let out a breath. The man by the door snorted another laugh that Maya realized she very much liked the sound of.

Lane said to Monica, "I can see why they're friends."

Maya rolled her eyes and turned to the cute one by the door. "And your name?" She made sure to arch her right eyebrow at him – which was incidentally her best eyebrow according to the woman who waxed her. She lowered her voice to a sultry whisper, which usually pulled anyone she wanted to flirt with down to their knees. Where they could be most useful.

His cheeks reddened and he swallowed loudly again. Got him, Maya thought in triumph.

"We'll get to him," Lane said. "Can we focus?"

Maya turned to him and frowned. "You want to use my chatroom? It's yours."

"We also need to use you," he said.

And maybe it was because she'd spent the entire morning thinking about MasquerAsiaN. Or maybe because she hadn't been fucked by anyone but herself in eight months. But Maya's mind suddenly conjured the dirtiest fantasy of all of them – Kierra too – in a pile on a big bed when Lane said "use you." She wanted to live inside that fantasy forever. Or at least longer than the two seconds Lane allowed.

"Not like that," he said. "Jesus, you and Kierra might as well be the same person."

"My ass is bigger," Maya said automatically.

"My titties are better," Kierra shot back.

"What the hell kind of-" Lane started, but Monica cut him off.

"The Albanian arms dealer has been in your chatroom a few times already. We need you to draw him there regularly so that we can put a sting in place."

"Fine. What do you want me to do? And how much are you going to pay me to do it?"

"Pay you? You don't-"

"Lemme stop you right there tall, gorgeous and menacing. I have student loans, credit card debt, barely any savings, and a younger brother and sister who still haven't learned how to budget. If you're not paying me, we're done." Maya started to walk out of the kitchen to underscore her point when Lane put out a palm to stop her.

"We'll tell you what we need you to do and then you tell us your price. How does that sound?"

"Like I'm getting out of debt," she said blithely, with a sarcastic smile on her face and a lift of her best eyebrow. She watched them all, including Kierra, smile back at her.

"I like her so much," Lane said to cute, silent and unnamed by the door.

"Alright, how do you want me to get your Algerian-"

"Albanian," Kierra corrected.

"Is that a different place?"

"I'm actually going to fight you when this is over," Kierra said in a playful, but disgusted, tone.

"Anytime, small fry." She turned back to Lane. "How do you want me to get this guy into my chatroom?"

"He has a type," Lane said. "Curvy and Black."

Maya stuck her hip out and smiled. "I am she."

"That you are," Monica said. "And that's why he's been visiting your channel sporadically. But he hasn't stayed because you're alone."

"Explain."

"He likes cam models with boyfriends. Couple play."

Maya pursed her lips and shook her head; her fleeting fantasies of financial freedom evaporating. "Well, I've got bad news for you, him and my bank account. I'm single."

"We know," Lane said and then he turned to look at the door. "This is Kenny."

Maya shook her head. "Oh no. You're cute and all, but every sex worker sets their boundaries and a pretty common one is that no one touches us unless we say a very unambiguous yes."

Cute and silent by the door began to shake his head as well. And then he finally spoke. "I don't have to touch you. He doesn't need the boyfriend to always be involved, he just seems to like knowing they're there."

Maya tried to ignore the way his deep voice washed over her like a shot of bourbon after the worst day. It made her nipples harden and her stomach clench. But still, limits. "So you'll just be there in the room with me while I'm showing off on my webcam?"

He nodded.

"Won't that be weird for you?"

Kierra laughed. But it was her angry laugh, the one Maya was used to hearing when she was supremely pissed and trying to keep her temper at bay. "Tell her," she ground out.

Maya turned to Kierra and saw that she was looking at Kenny with fury written on her face. She turned back to him, the question clear in her eyes and voice, "Tell me what?"

He swallowed. Took a deep breath. Ran a hand back and forth over his short, cropped hair and then finally spoke. "I'm MasquerAsiaN."

And then Maya was laughing, probably hysterically, shaking her head in disbelief. This was not how she'd planned to meet him. This was not the scenario she'd been dreaming about at all. She shook her head. "I don't understand."

"Tell her everything," Kierra hissed.

"I..." Kenny swallowed again. "A few months ago, Monica and Lane thought Kierra was in danger."

"She *was* in danger," Monica said.

Maya turned to see that she'd leaned forward, aiming her words at the side of Kierra's head. Kierra's face was pinched with pain. She closed her eyes briefly and looked away. Maya wasn't sure if whatever was going on with them was connected to MasquerAsiaN so she turned back to him.

His voice was shaky as if he was terrified. "I was supposed to just make sure that your cam channel wasn't a liability. I watched you for a few days and marked you as safe."

"Of course it's safe. I would be stupid to give any personal information about my life. Including Kierra," Maya said.

"I know. That's what I said in my report," MasquerAsiaN said.

Maya shook her head and reminded herself that his name was Kenny. "How long did it take you to confirm that?"

His cheeks reddened. "A couple of days. A week max."

Maya processed what he said, her brain whirring and trying to make sense of it all. And when she did, she was furious. Her jaw clenched, "You've been coming into my chatroom for six months. We've been having private video chats for almost as long."

"And what are those?" Lane asked.

Kierra shushed him.

"Was that part of your job?" She asked, trying to fight the pressure of tears in her eyes.

He shook his head quickly, "No. Absolutely not."

It was her turn to shake her head. "Then what the fuck is going on here?"

"I wasn't… I told you that I couldn't tell you who I was."

"Because he wasn't supposed to be in your chatroom. He couldn't tell you who he was and he never told anyone that he was visiting your channel, because he was breaking half a dozen rules to do it. Who knows how many rules he broke for the private chats."

"We won't know," Lane said, "until you tell me what those are. And in explicit detail, please."

"Lane," Monica said.

He smiled and shrugged, "I had to try."

"Why?" Maya whispered, her eyes trained on Kenny.

He shook his head and sighed, "Because you were so fucking beautiful and I couldn't stay away."

A few hours ago, that would have been the most romantic thing she'd ever heard. A few hours ago, she would have melted into a puddle to hear her favorite customer say those words. But something stuck in her head that ruined the moment.

"You knew who I was," she said. "You knew where I lived. You knew my best friend. You knew everything about me, but every time I asked about you, you gave me crumbs." As she spoke, the shock turned to anger, "You wouldn't even let me see you. Were you ever going to tell me who you were?"

"He couldn't," Lane said. "Not if he wanted to keep his job."

"I'm not asking you," Maya said, her eyes never leaving Kenny. "Were you?"

He swallowed again and shook his head.

"Fuck you," she screamed and turned to stomp down the short hallway to her bedroom. She slammed the door behind her. And then she turned, opened the door, and slammed it again. It felt good. She considered slamming it one more time, but then she remembered that she wasn't a child anymore and she paid rent here. This was her home. So she pulled her bedroom door open, and stomped back into the living room.

Lane arched one eyebrow at her but she didn't care.

She turned to Kenny and hated the way her stomach flipped at seeing his face after months of daydreaming about it. She hated that he was even sexier than she'd imagined. But she swallowed that attraction and glared at him.

He winced, "Let me explain."

"No," she yelled. "Out. Everybody get out."

Kierra opened her mouth to speak but stopped when she saw Maya's furious and determined glare. She held her hands up and backed down. Monica and Lane turned to Kierra, clearly expecting her to intervene, but she shrugged and looked away from them. Lane sighed and placed a hand on Monica's back, trying to usher her away.

"Maya, please," Kenny said.

"Abso-fucking-lutely not. If you want to talk to me, you'll pay for it. Now get out of my fucking apartment." She wanted to scream each word at him at the top of her lungs, but she fought to keep herself under control, afraid that if she didn't, she'd dissolve into tears. And she refused to give him the satisfaction. She didn't know him in person so she wasn't entirely sure, but she thought she could see the frustration on his face.

Good, she thought, it was only a fraction of what he deserved. He turned and pulled open the front door and stormed through it, slamming it behind him.

Maya reared back, her mouth opening in shock. She turned to Lane, who was slowly coaxing Monica toward the door, even though she clearly didn't want to leave. "Tell your little friend not to slam my door again."

Lane nodded, "Yes ma'am."

At the door Monica turned from his grasp and said, "Kierra," in a desperate voice that might have broken Maya's heart if it weren't already in pieces.

Maya turned to Kierra, who was turned away from them all. She was playing with her hair so that it covered her face, a move Maya recognized. She was instantly reminded of the first day they'd met, a week before classes started their freshman year of college.

Maya had said goodbye to her mother and siblings the day before when she'd hopped on a flight from SFO to Newark. She'd gotten all of her crying out on the plane and the previous night alone in her new dorm room. So she'd recognized the soft rise and fall of someone crying, but trying to hide it, when she'd spotted the girl sitting in the back of the orientation hall. She was sitting alone, turned away from the room, using her hair to hide her face. Maya had sat down next to that girl. She didn't speak, but she hoped that her presence was reassuring nonetheless.

Maya turned to Monica and Lane and the sadness in Monica's face made her anger evaporate. She'd assumed that Kierra was just fucking her bosses, but anyone who looked at her best friend the way Monica was looking at her now clearly loved her; or was well on their way to it. It made Maya's heart ache. Because she wanted that. She'd foolishly wanted that with MasquerAsiaN. Not that she'd ever admit it to another living soul now.

"Leave her alone," Maya said in a soft voice. "Give her space."

Monica didn't look at her or even acknowledge that she heard Maya's voice. But when she finally turned away, Lane caught Maya's eye. He nodded once, before softly closing the door behind him.

"How long have you known who he was?" Maya wanted to console her friend, but her own broken heart needed answers.

"They told me today," Kierra whispered, her hand moving, Maya guessed, to wipe her tears away. When she turned to Maya, her eyes were red. "I told them they had to tell you. It wasn't right."

"It wasn't."

Kierra sighed. "But if you'd asked me before today, I'd have said that Kenny seemed like a really good guy. If it matters."

Maya took a deep breath in and shook her head. She couldn't handle hearing that he might be the kind of man she'd been fantasizing about for six months. Not right now. "It doesn't."

Kierra nodded. "Tequila?"

Ah, Maya thought, now this was something she could deal with.

KIERRA WAS PASSED out on the couch. Like face down, mouth open, drooling and snoring. They had made a pact before the first tequila shot not to talk about the spies currently messing with their heads. Once, when they were sophomores, they'd gotten dumped on the same day. Tonight felt oddly reminiscent of that day and they leaned into the nostalgia of the moment. Apparently, a little bad dancing around the living room as they sang Chaka Khan songs at the top of their lungs and very much off-key was still the best way to momentarily cope with emotional drama.

When Kierra had passed out on the couch, Maya heaved a sigh that was equal parts exhaustion and relief. It was one thing to nurse her own broken heart and a completely different task to do so while her best friend was just as hurt. Maya felt at her breaking point. Finding out that the only person she'd allowed herself to open up to in a long time had been deceiving her made every shot of tequila she drank feel like torture. She'd tried to hide the few tears that leaked from the corners of her eyes as she danced around their living room, swiping at them so quickly she could pretend as if they'd never fallen. If Kierra noticed, she didn't say anything. And Maya didn't say anything when she saw Kierra do the same.

Maya threw the ugly quilt they kept on the couch over Kierra and walked to her bathroom. She took a short, hot shower, hoping to steam away her heartache. She stood in front of her mirror and wiped away the condensation to stare at her reflection as her mind replayed every dream about MasquerAsiaN she'd held secretly close to her heart. She brushed her teeth and imagined that all of those fantasies followed her toothpaste down the drain. She threw on a pair of boxers and a bralette, hopped into bed and pulled her laptop open.

The last place she wanted to be was in her chatroom. She actually had a hard and fast rule not to engage with any of her viewers while under the influence. She wouldn't have shown up to a day job drunk, so she wouldn't do it on her channel. But something drew her to the chatroom. Not something. Her heart.

His private message request came as soon as she logged in.

Her finger hovered the cursor over the red button to dismiss the window. She could see her chatroom moving quickly, her viewers excited to see her unexpectedly online.

But the only viewer that mattered was him. And she hated herself for it.

She accepted his request. The box prompting her to set her rates and time limit for their session popped up. She was feeling spiteful so she typed in an amount for half an hour that was triple her normal rate. Maya blinked when Kenny accepted her quote immediately.

MasquerAsiaN
I'm sorry

ThickaThanASnicka
You said that already.

MasquerAsiaN
I'll say it as many times as you need me to.

ThickaThanASnicka
I don't need anything from you but your money. And if you're just going to apologize, I don't even want that.

IT WAS EASIER to type the words than to say or mean them. Maya's heart was pounding in her chest. She wanted to cry. But she'd spent the last few hours stopping the tears building at the back of her eyes from falling by pure force of will. She wasn't going to lose that battle now in front of her webcam, where he could see. But after the surprise of finally seeing MasquerAsiaN in person and realizing she'd been deceived and three shots of very expensive tequila, she was growing too tired to fight off her own emotions. This was a mistake, she thought to herself. She was just about to end their session when his face appeared on her screen.

They'd been chatting online for months, but Maya's view of their conversations had consisted of a large window of herself and a white chat box. So when her own image shrunk to a small box in the upper right-hand corner and the larger window filled with his head and shoulders, a dimly lit room behind him, she didn't have the strength to stop herself from crying out. She'd literally been dreaming of what this moment would be like; to finally see his face fill her laptop screen. She hated him for ruining the moment now that it had arrived.

"Can you hear me?" he asked her slowly.

She rolled her eyes in response.

"I've wanted to do this for months," he said.

"But you were lying to me so you couldn't. Shame."

"I never lied," he said quickly, leaning toward his computer.

Maya took note of his five o'clock shadow, and the way his nose bent slightly to the left – her left – as if it had been broken at least once, and the way the light of his computer screen seemed to dance in his eyes, which she begrudgingly acknowledged were a beautiful brown; the same color of rich, wet earth.

"Everything I ever told you about myself was true," he said.

She laughed bitterly. "That's because you barely told me anything."

He opened his mouth to respond, but she cut him off with a raised hand. "I don't want to talk about this. So tell me what you're into or I'm leaving." She looked at the clock in the bottom left-hand corner of her screen as it counted down the time of their session. They were approaching the five-minute mark, which would take an automatic refund off the table.

Kenny took a deep breath and dropped his head into his hands.

Maya let her gaze wander over his large hands and long fingers and hated him even more because they looked as if they'd feel good inside of her. She licked her lips and realized that while three shots of tequila weren't enough to get her fucked up, when her heart and her pussy were at war, those were three shots too many. She moved her hand, ready to end their chat again, when he raised his head and their eyes met.

Her mouth fell open in a silent gasp.

"Okay," he said.

"Okay what?" She tried to sound bored, but at this point her feelings, her mind and her body were in the same building but on very different floors, so she hardly knew what she sounded like to his ears.

"Okay, I'll tell you what I want."

She sighed, assuming he would just start talking about his feelings again. Maya was fully unprepared for what he said next.

"I love watching you," he whispered, almost too low for her to hear. Almost. "But I want you to watch me for once. Is that okay?"

She nodded immediately and held her breath.

Her eyes widened as the camera angle shifted to his lap. And then they bulged out of her head when he lifted his hips and pulled his sweatpants down, exposing his dick to her gaze. He was semi-hard. He grasped his penis in a firm grip and started to stroke himself slowly. For her.

Maya clenched her thighs together and absentmindedly circled her hips. She wanted to touch herself, but she didn't want to give him the satisfaction. Besides, his long penis had claimed all of her attention and she didn't want to tear her eyes away for even the milliseconds it would take to reposition her body for maximum masturbation comfort.

So she watched his large fist glide up and down his shaft in sure, slow strokes, his palm sometimes covering the head. She watched his hard abs jump as his excitement grew. She chewed her bottom lip in anticipation. And then she moaned when a string of his saliva slowly descended into frame and landed on the head of his dick, his palm instantly using it to ease his movement.

Maya bit her bottom lip harder, trying to stifle the moan building in her throat, begging for release. She tore her eyes away from the screen just long enough to shove her hand into her boxers. She was happy he couldn't see her because she was fully incapable of caring about his months-long deception right in that moment. Her body and mind had been completely overtaken by her own lust.

"Faster," she whispered before the word even formed in her mind.

He complied and began to pant.

She rubbed her clit and imagined his head resting on the chair's headrest, eyes closed, his mouth falling open in ecstasy. She had become so good at imagining what he was doing at any given moment that it almost felt like second nature by now.

Her gaze was trained on the head of his dick, which had turned an angry shade of red that Maya felt she could relate to. She slipped two fingers into her pussy. She hoped he hadn't heard her squeak of surprise at her own touch.

But then he moaned and she had to close her eyes and clench her thighs tightly together again, her back tensing as the orgasm built and then finally washed over her in gentle waves.

Thankfully she opened her eyes just in time to watch his own orgasm overtake him. She tried to focus on the speed at which his fist seemed to cajole his release out in forceful spurts, landing on his stomach messily. She filed that beautiful sight away for later. But then she made a mistake. Her eyes caught on his other hand as it shakily rested over his heart, just barely in frame. She came again; a deep, shuddering moan escaping her lips.

Then she logged out of her ChatBot account, slammed her laptop shut and immediately and turned over in her bed to cry.

three

Kenny needed to focus. If he didn't make sure to keep his grip tight and his aim straight, he could shatter his wrists in a heartbeat. He punched with his right and then left gloved hands, stepped back and kicked the bag with the flat of his bare foot, dancing out of the danger zone of its sway.

He wore a simple pair of running shorts, the cool blast of the gym's air conditioning hitting all of his sweat-covered skin. He moved around the bag, skipping out of its orbit more than he punched, his eyes alert, his pulse pounding, letting his body distract him from his emotional pain; refusing to think about her.

Kenny's phone started ringing again from the floor at the edge of the mat. He ignored it. He'd been ignoring it all morning and all last night. He punched the bag low with his left hand, rammed his left shoulder into it and then pulled his knee up to connect with the bag at what would be about gut level for an average-sized man.

Someone cleared their throat behind him.

Kenny spun away from the bag and his eyes landed on Lane. He grunted and turned back to his workout.

"Well good mornin' to you too."

"Go away," Kenny said, a punch punctuating each word.

"Is that how you talk to your supervising agent?"

"I'm assigned to Monica, not you."

"Then is that how you talk to a *senior* agent?" Lane asked in a playful voice that infuriated Kenny.

"Why are you here?" Kenny had to grit his teeth together – grinding out each word – to stop from screaming. He was throwing a tantrum and in the wrong direction. He knew that. But he couldn't stop himself. He wanted to wallow in the mess he'd made of the situation with Maya alone. He wanted to punish his body until he couldn't stand so that when he went back to his hotel room tonight, he wouldn't be tempted to log onto ChatBot and watch her being beautiful and sexy and funny for her viewers; reminded of everything he could never have again.

"I'm here because the mission doesn't wait for your fucking feelings. You've got a job to do and if you want to impress my wife, you better get your shit together and do it."

Kenny was the son of two soldiers. His parents met in Basic and had been together ever since. They had exactly one child, reasoning that two active service soldiers could manage to raise only the one. There was some shuffling to his grand-parents' home amidst the regular transience of military life and the sometimes sticky situations that arose when both of his parents happened to be deployed at the same time. But through it all, he had had a stability that was rare for a child in his shoes, because his parents were meticulous in every part of their lives; everything and everyone in its place. It was a trait Kenny respected and had thankfully inherited. And it had always served him well in The Agency.

Kenny wasn't sure if Lane knew much about his past, but he was sure that the way his spine straightened gave some of that away. But Kenny couldn't help it; he believed in duty, responsibility and respect for hierarchy and Lane had cut right through the anguish and self-pity he was feeling to pull out those elemental parts of his personality.

He exhaled loudly. "She's not going to let me anywhere near her." The words felt like acid coming out of his mouth. "So unless you have another cam model for us to recruit, we're going to have to go back to the drawing board."

Lane just smiled. He shoved his hands into his pants pockets and nodded at the punching bag. "We have a meeting at Command in exactly one hour. I expect you to be there." He turned to walk away.

Kenny called after them. "Why did you come? Why not Monica?"

Lane turned back, the smile on his face not reaching his eyes. "You weren't the only one who had a bad day yesterday."

AFTER LANE LEFT THE GYM, Kenny halfheartedly swatted at the punching bag, wondering if maybe he shouldn't just leave and request a new assignment from The Agency and wait out his dismissal somewhere as far away from Maya as possible. But after a few minutes, he'd thrown his t-shirt over his head, slipped on his shoes, grabbed his phone and jogged the few blocks back to his hotel. Because training under Monica was still his professional dream. And – embarrassing as it was to admit to himself – a small part of his brain still hoped, foolishly, that if he stayed close to Maya… He couldn't even let himself finish that thought, it was so far out of the realm of possibility. But still, he buried it somewhere deep inside himself and held onto it with everything he had.

When he pulled up to the wrought iron gate outside Lane and Monica's house, he thought he would hear Kierra's voice again, but it was Lane who greeted him today.

"You're almost late."

"Sorry, traffic," Kenny said.

Lane's grunt was his only answer before the gate opened.

He didn't see Kierra's car in the driveway. He walked to the front door and tried the handle. He was just stepping inside when the gate began to whir as it inched open again. Kenny turned and watched as Kierra's car pulled into the driveway. As she parked, he felt his heart begin to beat faster in his chest, because she wasn't alone.

When Maya stepped out of the car, she avoided looking his way. Her gaze flitted everywhere but in his direction – toward the ground, the side of Kierra's car, back out onto the street.

But Kenny's eyes never moved from her. He felt just as he had yesterday when he finally saw her in person after dreaming about just that for months: complete and utter awe. She was everything he'd always thought she would be: smart, funny, quick-witted. She wasn't afraid to say exactly what she felt. And on top of all of that, watching her swivel between the surprises they brought to her doorstep while still exhibiting an intense care for her best friend made him slide just a few more inches under her spell. She was literally the woman of his dreams.

He also realized just how much of herself she kept from her viewers. He took his time studying her, noticing every detail, like the way she chewed on her bottom lip, which he'd come to realize she did a lot. Like everything she did, it was layered and context-specific. Yesterday, she'd done it, dragging him under her sway with a few simple, smoky words, as her teeth nibbled at the edges of her mouth, as if she was telling him he'd enjoy being able to do that. And he would. But today he watched as she pulled her entire bottom lip into her mouth, worrying it much like her nerves were probably worrying her. It felt like a condemnation and he internalized it, berating himself for being the cause of her distress.

He watched her walk around the back of the car and

hated himself for the way his gaze slid down her body. She was in black head to toe, the deep v of her t-shirt giving a perfect peek of her cleavage, while her joggers were just baggy enough to seem casual, and just tight enough to remind him that her hips were not small and would likely be the perfect size for him to grip when he was inside her. He also realized that he liked her in casual clothes, maybe even more than he did the sexy lingerie she wore during their cam sessions. He would like Maya in whatever she was – or wasn't – wearing. He still wanted her today as desperately as he had yesterday. Maybe even more.

He heard Kierra's voice, "You sure about this?"

Maya's eyes lifted to meet his.

There was a fleeting moment where Kenny's foolish heart thought he saw a softness in her gaze that he recognized; the same look she gave her webcam after she came, the giggle still dripping from her lips. But if it was there, it was gone in a heartbeat and her voice reached him easily across the distance between them.

"It's just business," she said. "And I need the money."

MAYA WAS TRYING NOT to fidget, but this was the strangest meeting she'd ever been in.

They were all sitting in a very normal boardroom that just happened to be located behind the pantry in Lane and Monica's middle-class, suburban New Jersey home. She and Kierra were sitting on one side of the table, shoulder to shoulder; them against the world as usual. Although their adversaries had usually been shitty professors or bill collectors, not the literal manifestations of their sexual fantasies.

Monica was sitting directly across from Kierra, her eyes laser-focused on Kierra's averted face. Lane stood just behind Monica's chair, leaning over her, his eyes intent on Kierra as well. Maya noticed the small movement of his thumbs across Monica's skin and her heart swooned.

She wanted that one day. And that was an inconvenient thought to have since she was expressly focusing on Kierra's drama to avoid looking in Kenny's direction. And he hadn't bothered to look anywhere but at her.

This was not how she'd expected this meeting to go when she'd sat at the dining room table eating breakfast with a hungover Kierra this morning. Somehow, in the cold light of a chilly fall morning, she'd thought that she could do this. She'd thought she could use the money they'd pay her to go about her business and crawl out of the mountain of debt she was just barely keeping at bay. She imagined the joy she would feel at being able to put a little money aside just in case Jerome or Kaya ever needed anything big.

She refused to think about him.

"Alright, enough of all this emotional staring," Lane said, cutting through the tension. "Who wants to hear my plan?"

Kierra and Kenny mumbled their acceptance while Monica merely dropped her eyes to her lap.

Lane walked to the front of the room and touched the screen. It whirred to life on a screenshot of Maya's public chatroom from about a week ago. She knew because she recognized her makeup and lingerie from that day. She smiled. She looked fucking great.

She heard Kenny fidget in his seat.

"Alright, so we captured this intel last week during one of Maya's broadcasts," Lane continued. He turned his eyes toward her and quirked an eyebrow up. "Great show, by the way."

She smiled and nodded her head primly. She could never turn down a compliment.

Kenny shifted in his seat again.

"So here," Lane tapped the screen again and it zoomed into the chatroom, "is Joseph Mehmeti."

Maya quirked her head to the side and studied the username and avi Lane indicated. "I don't recognize that name," she said.

"Makes sense. He's only been in your room less than a handful of times. But this," Lane tapped the screen again, "is another model he frequents a lot."

Maya sat back and crossed her arms over her chest as she studied the picture on the screen. She definitely recognized her. "That's LissXO," she said.

"That's her?" Kierra gasped, turning toward her.

Maya nodded and frowned.

"Oh," was all she said. And Maya couldn't blame her. LissXO was sexy as hell.

She was also Maya's closest competition. They'd started their channels at around the same time, they were both fat, Black models and were doing, at least for a while, about the same rate of business – if ChatBot's ratings could be trusted. But a few months ago, LissXO had shot up the daily popularity charts, leaving Maya in her wake. Maya was trying not to be infuriated but, as she'd whined pathetically to Kierra more than once, "what does she have that I don't have?" She was so ashamed of her own envy.

"Is there something I'm missing?" Lane asked.

Kierra clamped her mouth shut and Maya exhaled loudly. "She's my competition in my head."

"What?" Monica said, her first word in the meeting came out as a harsh whisper, which made Maya wonder if maybe this had been her first word of the day.

She turned to Monica and explained their one-sided competition. "She's at least ten spots ahead of me on most daily popularity rankings. I can only imagine what kind of money she's pulling in."

"What does that matter?" Monica asked the question in a tone of voice that Maya was used to. That tone of voice was code for "you just strip online" or "you're a whore" or "are you really taking this so seriously?" That tone of voice said Maya should be ashamed of what she did. That tone of voice refused to acknowledge that Maya was a fucking entrepreneur and that just because her product was her body didn't mean she wasn't running a small business. That tone of voice was why Maya hated talking to most people about her job. Not because she was ashamed. But because most people didn't have the range to understand it.

She took a deep, frustrated breath, trying to order her thoughts. She jumped when Kenny's voice interrupted her and he answered Monica's question.

"The daily, weekly and monthly popularity rankings are important. They're averaged at the end of the month, quarter and year. Channels with the best views are rewarded with financial bonuses. They also get prime placement on the home page if they make it onto the site-wide Top 20 chart. That obviously drives more viewers to their rooms and so on. If someone wants to make this a career, they should be worried about their competition."

Maya couldn't help but turn and gape at him. But for the first time he refused to look her way. He dropped his head and focused his attention on his lap. Maya turned back to Kierra whose mouth had similarly fallen open. When they made eye contact, Maya could see the words forming in Kierra's brain as her eyes began to soften, moving from shocked to gushy. Maya shook her head quickly. She still was not asking for any information about how good of a guy Kenny might be after he'd spent half a year lying to her.

She cut her eyes at him and her mouth fell open as they made eye contact.

He seemed sad.

She sucked her bottom lip into her mouth and turned away. It doesn't matter, she thought to herself.

"Well alright," Lane said, cutting the suddenly thick

tension in the room with his words. "I'll remember that. So let's just get to the plan, shall we?"

They all nodded, except Monica, whose eyes skittered across Kierra's face and then back to her lap.

"It's pretty simple, really. Hardly a plan at all," Lane offered, an easy grin brightening his face.

Kenny scoffed and shifted again. Lane ignored him. Actually, scratch that. Maya thought Lane's smile only widened at Kenny's annoyance. She smirked.

"We wanna start introducing Kenny to your room ASAP. You two," he gestured to Maya and Kenny, "can work out the particulars about what's allowed and not allowed." His gaze settled on Maya and he quirked his eyebrows at her again.

Maya pursed her lips and flipped him off with both hands, which made him laugh loudly.

"Anyway, there are some things I can't tell you or our sweet girl," he said, looking directly at Kierra for the first time since his presentation started. Kierra shifted in her seat and looked away. "But once you've got him in your room we'll meet again and work through any kinks. How's that sound?"

Maya cocked her head and said, "It sounds like we still need to discuss what you all are paying me?"

Lane clapped his hands and laughed. "Honestly, you really are great."

"How much do you want?" Monica said, lifting her head and making eye contact with Maya. Maya's mouth went dry and she was suddenly full of apprehension. How the fuck did Kierra manage not to burst into flames between Lane's charming ass and Monica's… everything?

She let out a harsh breath of air.

"She wants $40,000," Kierra cut in, drawing Monica's attention.

Maya's eyes widened at the figure. She could pay off all of her credit cards with that and still make a sizeable lump sum payment on her student loans.

"And that's only if this all stays online. If you want her in the field, her fee starts at an extra $10,000 and rises with the degree of danger scale per The Agency's civilian contractor rates."

Maya couldn't help the proud smile that spread across her face as she watched her friend – chin held high – challenge her boss and girlfriend, who was more intimidating than a team of football players.

"Any other requests?"

Maya shivered at the way Monica was looking at Kierra. As if she wanted to strip her naked and eat her for breakfast. Did the room feel warmer than a few minutes ago, she wondered?

"Since Maya works from home, you'll need to contribute a fraction of her portion of the rent, electric and internet since she'll technically be using those things in service of your operation. And since you probably want her to adjust her current broadcast and private session schedule, you'll need to pay her for any loss of income. She'll be happy to show you her records for that." Kierra turned to Maya and whispered, "You do have records, right?"

Maya scoffed, "Of course. I keep a very detailed spreadsheet of weekly, monthly and quarterly earnings."

Kierra nodded once and turned back to Monica. "And she needs a new webcam."

Maya held her breath as Kierra and Monica stared at each other. Out of the corner of her eye she noticed that Kenny's gaze was intent on the side of Monica's face. But when she looked toward the front of the room she saw Lane's eyes nearly glazed over in lust and she let out a harsh breath. Seriously, how had Kierra survived all of this? She felt as if she was going to melt into a puddle and she was only on the margins of whatever was happening here.

"I accept your terms," Monica said.

Lane clapped. "Well alright. So the mission is a go."

Maya couldn't contain the giddiness she felt, but she realized that Monica and Kierra were still staring each other down.

"Uh, would it be too much of an inconvenience if we spoke to Kierra alone?" Lane asked, inching toward the table.

Maya leaned forward, "Is that what you want?"

Kierra turned toward her, reluctantly dragging her eyes from Monica's. Kierra didn't technically need to answer. Maya could see her arousal all over her face; in her dilated pupils and soft pants. And honestly, after that negotiation, she was right there with her.

"I won't be long," she said in a breathy whisper. "Will you be okay?"

The fog of Maya's excitement cleared and she moved her head to look at Kenny, who had dropped his gaze back to his lap. She turned back to Kierra, forced a smile and nodded. "Yep," she said in a cheery voice that sounded strange to her own ears. "Take all the time you need."

Maya rose from her seat, nodded in Lane's direction, even though his attention was focused, as was Monica's, squarely on Kierra. She walked toward the door and out into the hallway where it was absolutely five degrees cooler. At least. But then she heard the door to the boardroom close and felt Kenny's presence behind her as sweat beaded at her hairline. She walked to the foyer, the sound of his footsteps following her. She turned toward him unexpectedly and his steps faltered. When he raised his eyes to look at her, she clenched her fists behind her back. How dare he be this fucking beautiful in person? She'd been underselling his potential in her fantasies.

"Maya," he started, but she cut him off.

"I told you I'm not interested in more apologies from you. It won't make me forgive you any faster. *If* I choose to forgive you at all," she added hastily. "If it's not about the… mission," the word felt strange coming out of her mouth, "then keep it."

He pressed his lips together and nodded. His hands disappeared behind his back and Maya tried not to notice the way his biceps rippled with that movement. When he spoke, his voice was all business and Maya belatedly realized that that was a bit of a problem as her nipples hardened.

"We should talk about how you want to play this for your broadcasts. My face can't be on screen."

"Wait, what?"

He nodded indulgently at her. "I'm a spy. I'm supposed to avoid being online in any traceable way. You never know who's in your chatroom," he said. Maya was happy he at least had the decency to blush before he continued. "If someone had a record of what I looked like or recognized me from another… encounter, my career would be over, and you could be in danger."

"Oh, okay. Maybe that makes sense."

He nodded again. "Besides that, I'll leave it up to you. Whatever you want, I'll do it."

She had to look away. She knew he was talking about the mission, but she also knew he hadn't chosen those words randomly. And she couldn't think about that now. In fact, she realized – as the clean scent of his cologne tickled her nose and stirred the lust she'd felt surrounding them in that boardroom – she couldn't even be this close to him. She didn't have the willpower.

She'd spent six months wondering if her interest in MasquerAsiaN was simply because of the mystery of his blank avi and his money. To find out it wasn't and that the attraction she'd felt online was only a hollow specter of what she could feel for him in person made her want to weep. She pressed her lips together and moved her hands to her overheated neck. She couldn't look at him. She was afraid she'd cry.

"Maya," he said again, in a gentle, beseeching tone as he inched a few steps closer to her.

She tried not to notice all of the different intonations of his voice. The direct, no-nonsense of his work voice and the soft pleading as he begged. She wondered what his laugh sounded like and if he ever growled when he came. She craved every new hitch of his breath as she tried to catalog the distinctions between who she'd thought him to be online and the man standing in front of her offline.

"Maya," he whispered, drawing out the two syllables of her name. He moved just a little bit closer. She could feel his body heat and she could have sworn she heard the pounding of his heart, or maybe that was her own racing pulse. She opened her mouth, unsure of what she might say. The sound of the boardroom door opening abruptly doused the heat building between them.

She and Kenny jumped away from each other. Maya swiped at her face and pulled her mouth into a smile just as Kierra came walking into the foyer.

She stopped and stared at them and gasped, her nipples very evident through her thin t-shirt. "I'm… I'm sorry, did I interrupt?"

Maya shook her head vigorously. "Nope. You ready to go? I need a… I'm ready when you are."

As she was asking the question, Monica and Lane appeared in the hallway behind Kierra. Maya saw Monica reach out and run one finger up Kierra's arm. She shivered.

"Yep, ready," Kierra said in a strained voice. "Let's go."

Maya turned quickly, ducking her head to avoid Kenny's gaze. His voice stopped them both in their tracks. "I should come over later so we can strategize for your broadcast tonight."

She should have said no. She should have said they could do that at a place that *wasn't* so close to her bed. But technically he was right. This entire mission hinged on getting him in her bed and convincing an Albanian arms dealer that he was supposed to be there. And as inconvenient as it was, she didn't want to say no. She'd been wanting him in her bed for what felt like forever. So she simply nodded and headed up the stairs without looking back.

Just as she'd made it to the top, Lane's voice stopped her and Kierra again.

"I think we should come over too," he projected across the foyer. "What do you think about that, sweet girl?"

Kierra mumbled something that might have been 'yes' or maybe 'please' and pushed Maya through the false wall into the pantry. They walked quickly to Kierra's car and shut the doors. They both exhaled loudly.

"Jesus fucking Christ I'm horny," Maya yelled.

Kierra was breathing hard and simply nodded.

"Is it always like that in there?"

A ghost of a smile touched Kierra's lips, which was all the answer Maya needed.

She turned to her roommate and touched her overheated arm. "You know I love you, right?"

Kierra turned a quizzical eye toward her. "Are you about to proposition me right now?"

"Oh my god no," Maya laughed. And then Kierra laughed. "I was just going to say that you don't have to be mad at your boos for me. You three clearly have a connection and you shouldn't jeopardize that on my behalf. You deserve to be happy."

Kierra grasped Maya's hand and squeezed. "Thank you." And then she gave her a wicked smile, "I'm still going to make them sweat it out a little bit longer. They get real desperate when I'm mad."

Monica gasped, "When did you get this freaky?"

Kierra smiled and winked at her. That smile turned to chagrin and Maya knew she wasn't going to be happy with whatever came out of her best friend's mouth next.

"I know you don't want to hear this, but I think Kenny might really like you."

Maya began to pull her seatbelt on. "Can we go home now?"

It was Kierra's turn to reach out and grasp her arm. "You deserve to be happy too. I think you liked him before you knew who he was."

"Well he lied to me, so before doesn't matter now. Does it?"

"Maybe," Kierra said and moved to pull on her own seatbelt. She turned the ignition to start her car but before she shifted it into gear she turned back to Maya. "I'm not saying you have to make it easy on him. You deserve to be mad." She leaned forward and whispered conspiratorially. "But if he's anything like Monica, he'll put in a lot of work to make it up to you. You deserve that too."

"Kierra," Maya ground out.

She put her hands up in retreat even as she kept talking. "All I'm saying is, how long has it been since you've let yourself be happy?" She asked the question as she shifted the car into gear, finally dropping the subject.

But it wasn't dropped. Kierra's question sat on Maya's shoulders like a heavy weight the entire drive home, because she knew the answer immediately. She hadn't been as happy as she was talking to MasquerAsiaN, or felt as alive as she did during those tense, angst-filled moments with Kenny in over two years. Since before her mother died.

debrief #1

Kierra used the few seconds it took Maya and Kenny to leave the boardroom to collect herself. She took slow, deep breaths and tried to pretend she couldn't feel Monica and Lane's eyes raking over her as they had been since the moment she and Maya arrived. The door closed softly.

"You have to talk to us, Kierra. This doesn't work if you don't."

She sucked in a harsh breath. She'd been prepared for Lane's dirty teasing or one of Monica's hard commands that shot straight to her nipples. But Monica's gentle voice that only marginally hid her hurt and the use of her real name was wholly unexpected and threatened to undo her. She raised her head and had to blink against the tears that sprang to her eyes. Monica's eyes were wary and vulnerable; scared. Kierra had never seen her look that way. It made her heart break as she realized that she'd been so wrapped up in her own hurt and fear for Maya that she'd lashed out at Monica and Lane without any care for their feelings.

"I'm still mad," Kierra whispered, even though it felt like a pretty hollow excuse right now.

"We understand," Lane said.

"You should have told me."

Monica sucked in a deep breath and pressed her chest forward to stretch her back. Kierra recognized the movement; it's what she did when she was trying to soften her words during a disagreement with Lane. She did it because she loved him and didn't want to say something she might regret just because they were momentarily at odds. Kierra *was* still angry, but there was something about watching Monica treat her with a care that she almost exclusively reserved for Lane that made her heart skip a beat. She bit her lips to keep from smiling.

When Monica spoke, her words were slow, her voice measured. The precision with which she chose each word stroked Kierra's skin like a soft caress. It was a different feeling than the excitement her normal tone of voice elicited. Kierra liked this new sensation.

"I'm not going to promise you that if this kind of situation came up again we would tell you classified information you don't have clearance for. You know we can't do that. It might also be dangerous for you if we did. If we lie to you about that now, the next time this happens we might not get past it."

Kierra nodded, but looked away.

"I don't want to jeopardize our relationship in the future to sweep this under the rug today," Monica said, her voice full of emotion.

Kierra knew she was right, but the truth didn't make her feel any better. She turned back to Monica and steeled her heart. "So where do we go from here?"

"Great question," Lane said in an excited voice that broke through the tension of the moment.

Kierra laughed as a tear fell down her face. She wiped it away quickly and turned to him.

He winked at her before he spoke. "Well, in the long term, we need to deal with your clearance issues. Have you made a decision on the Classified Materials Training program?"

Kierra nodded. "I've decided to do it. But how long will I have to be away?" The "from you" was silent, but she hoped understood.

"The training lasts one month." Monica's voice was lighter when she spoke. Kierra could discern the shift in her mood mostly because her frown had disappeared. Her mouth resettled into the comfortable hard line Kierra knew and loved. That, and the way her eyes were no longer mournful but once again filled with a depth of emotion when she looked at Kierra that made her skin tingle. Things weren't back to normal completely, but they were heading that way.

"Under normal circumstances, *we* would be able to train you on the basics. You'd only have to go to headquarters for intermediate testing and advanced certification," Lane offered in apology.

"But these aren't normal circumstances," Monica said, no apology in her tone. Just a dirty reminder of why they couldn't be trusted with one another as far as The Agency was concerned. It was a concession they made when they'd disclosed their relationship to the higher ups. If they wanted to continue working together, they would have to be audited – at some unknown point in the future – and any applications for Kierra's further training, pay raises, hell, even sick days, would be reviewed by HR with intense scrutiny.

Lane laughed. "Not normal at all. But don't worry, sweet girl, training is in DC. We'll just come down there with you. We've got it all figured out."

Kierra's brow furrowed, "Did you know I would say yes?"

Monica chuckled. Actually chuckled. Kierra and Lane turned to her with wide eyes.

Half of Monica's mouth lifted up into a grin, "You're too nosy for your own good. Of course you were going to say yes."

Kierra pressed her lips together, attempting to hide her smile.

"Okay, so once we're done with this current op," Lane said, "we'll head to DC for your training. Deal?"

Kierra nodded.

"Now to the most important thing," Lane said, his voice turning serious. "We still want you to move in with us."

Kierra cringed. Twenty-four hours ago she'd been ecstatic about finally being with Monica and Lane all the time, at work and after. It had been her fantasy for years and yesterday her dream had been close enough to taste. It tasted – unsurprisingly – like Lane gasping into her mouth, Monica's essence on his tongue. It was beautiful.

But less than a day later, she was full of fear; torn between the people she loved the most. "I- I can't leave Maya. This is all new for her. She needs my support."

Kierra saw the hurt in Lane's eyes and she purposely avoided Monica's gaze, knowing her sadness might tip her over the edge and she'd take those words back. But she couldn't do that. She and Maya were family. They'd been there for each other through their highest highs, lowest lows and so many bad hairstyles. She couldn't abandon her now. "It's just until we catch Joseph Mehmeti. I'll move in after. I promise."

They weren't happy, but they nodded, accepting her condition. Kierra exhaled loudly and stood from her chair.

"Okay," she said, suddenly nervous, but unsure why. "I'm going to… I need to get Maya home. She's got a broadcast tonight." Only as she began to walk toward the door did she realize that those nerves she felt in the pit of her stomach were just the physical manifestation of her body recognizing Monica and Lane's rising lust. Her reliable response to them made her steps shaky and her palms sweat. Lane wrapped himself around her back, one arm holding her around the waist. He kept her upright and steady as her legs gave out completely and a gasp escaped from her lips.

"We missed you last night, sweet girl," he whispered into her ear, following the words with his tongue.

Kierra moaned, her eyes closing involuntarily.

"Did you miss us?"

"No," she said. He grunted, tightening his grip and pulling her more forcefully back against him. He was hard. "I was sad and angry. Maya got me drunk. I passed out on the couch."

"You could have been sad and angry in bed with us. Taken all that energy out on us." Monica's voice was a gentle whisper that allowed all of the possibilities for just how she could have expended that energy to blossom in Kierra's mind.

When she opened her eyes, she saw Monica leaning against the door. Lane walked Kierra slowly toward her, the implication clear: she would have to go through Monica to leave. Kierra felt moisture pool between her legs.

As they inched nearer toward Monica, Kierra catalogued the other woman's arousal; her hardening nipples, the dilated pupils and the way her tongue kept darting out at the corners of her mouth as if she couldn't wait to taste Kierra. Her observations were accompanied by the soundtrack of Lane's panting breaths in her ear.

When they were within arm's reach, Lane grasped both of Kierra's hands as Monica opened her arms, welcoming the press of their bodies against hers. Lane moved Kierra's hands to Monica's shoulders, and her fingers dug into the hard muscle there.

"I'm still mad," Kierra repeated, rubbing herself between Monica and Lane shamelessly. Always shamelessly.

"Just because you're not moving in with us yet, doesn't mean you're not still welcome in our home. Our bed," Lane said.

"Very welcome," Monica whispered against Kierra's lips before she slipped her tongue into her mouth, swallowing the groan that burst from Kierra's mouth.

Kierra's hands caressed Monica from her shoulders to her breasts and then around her waist as Lane ground himself into her from behind. She wished their clothes weren't inconveniently in the way as they became a writhing mess of too many – and still not enough – arms and legs and mouths and tongues.

Kierra spread Monica's legs and settled her body between them. Monica broke their kiss to moan and Kierra planted soft kisses from her mouth down her neck. Lane reached out to cup Monica's head and pull her mouth to his, his hard penis settling into a slow and steady grind against Kierra's ass.

It would have been so easy to slip her hand under Monica's shirt, push it up over her head and feast – with her eyes and her mouth – on the soft mounds of her breasts. The rest of their clothes would come off easily. They could lock the door and make up for their very brief – but still too long – time apart.

Kierra knew Kenny would keep Maya company. He might even take her home. And then she and Lane and Monica could be as loud as they wanted. And maybe, the very tiny part of Kierra's mind not caught up in the way Monica's pulse tasted on her tongue thought, if Kenny drove Maya home, they'd talk and… something might happen there.

But Kierra's mind cleared. Maya wouldn't appreciate being abandoned to deal with the man who'd betrayed her – and, Kierra suspected, broken her heart – just so Kierra could bury her face between Monica's legs. Besides, Monica and Lane didn't deserve to get off so easy for keeping her in the dark about Maya's entanglement with Kenny.

She pushed away, sliding from between their bodies. Lane grunted. They grasped one another and turned to look at her. She waited until some of the lust cleared from their eyes before she spoke.

"I'm still mad," she said one more time, with a raised eyebrow.

Lane pulled Monica into his side. Monica reached to open

the door just barely wide enough for Kierra to slip through. Before she disappeared through it, however, Kierra's steps faltered as Monica moaned her name and the sound of their kisses followed her into the hallway.

Apparently she wasn't the only one willing to play dirty.

"Alright, let's talk details," Lane said, as soon as Maya and Kierra were out of Command.

Kenny nodded absently at Lane's voice, but kept his eyes trained on the door, where he'd gotten his last glimpse of Maya.

"Hey," Monica said, finally pulling his attention away. "Later."

She seemed less sad than she had throughout the meeting. He wasn't shocked by that. Berlin had taught him not to put too much stock in Monica, Lane and Kierra being put out with one another for long. Kenny nodded and followed her back into the briefing room. Lane was talking before he had a chance to sit down.

"Okay, now that we have a cam room, we're going to be one agent down while Kenny's… otherwise indisposed." Lane turned to him and winked, the dirtiest suggestions hanging in the air between them.

Kenny rolled his eyes and looked away, his face warm as he tried to hide his hunger at the possibilities. This was a mission, not his wet dreams. Well, it was a bit like *one* wet dream he'd had, but he pushed that memory aside. "So who are you calling in?" Kenny finally asked.

"We considered Asif," Monica said.

Kenny scoffed and met her eyes. "Unless the goal is to find the ChatBot server and seduce or destroy it, I don't see how he would be useful."

Monica smiled. "I agree. He's not right for this mission.

Well, not for this phase at least. We need someone with a little more finesse when it comes to computers."

Kenny was shaking his head before Monica could even finish speaking. Lane was laughing as he tapped on the smart screen and connected to the video chat app.

When Chanté's smiling face popped up on the screen Kenny felt a moment of ease that she looked like her old self again. The last time he'd seen her in Amsterdam, she'd been a shell of her normal bubbly self and he'd been afraid that the most recent instance of Asif's lack of care for her had sent her over the edge.

"Kenny," she squealed. "We're working together again."

Kenny exhaled loudly.

"Oh, don't give me that. You're excited. Just admit it," she said with a wink.

"No," he said. Chanté dissolved into a fit of laughter that sounded like bells tinkling. It made him smile reluctantly.

"This is cute," Lane said, which wiped the smile off of Kenny's face.

He sat up straighter in his chair. "Can we get back on track?" he asked Monica.

Her mouth was tilted in a fashion Kenny thought was maybe a suggestion of a smirk, but he couldn't be sure. She simply turned and nodded at Lane.

"Alright, so while Kenny makes his debut in the world of cam modeling-"

Kenny exhaled loudly again.

"You're gonna be a star," Chanté offered kindly.

"We'll," Lane gestured between himself and Monica, "be monitoring the chatroom looking for Joseph or any of his known associates. And you, little lady-"

"Loving this nickname," Chanté interjected.

"You're going to log anyone of interest and run down their location and ChatBot history. We need a complete digital dossier. Can you do that?"

"In my sleep. Or in the bath, like I am right now," Chanté said and suddenly the screen widened from just her face to her bare shoulders and bubble-covered chest.

Kenny groaned. "Chanté, we're having a meeting. Why are you in the bathtub?"

"Hey, I worked a long shift last night. I needed to wash all that glitter off and have a good soak. You try doing one of my routines and see how you feel the morning after." And then her face brightened. "Actually, how about you come to the club with me sometime. I have a few regulars who would *love* you."

Kenny dropped his head in his hands.

"Oooh, that might not be the best idea. He's in the middle of a… situation right now," Lane said.

Kenny lifted his head slightly to glare at Lane.

"Oh," Chanté said in a sad voice. "So Maya didn't take your online romance well?"

Lane laughed, "Not at all."

"Lane." Monica's voice was a hard reprimand. Lane coughed in a poor attempt to hide his outburst and shrugged in a kind of apology.

Kenny did not accept it and glared harder.

"I can't wait to meet her," Chanté said.

Her voice pulled Kenny back into the moment. "What now?"

"And I can't wait to see Kierra again," Chanté exclaimed.

Kenny stood up from his chair. "Where *are* you right now?"

"In our apartment, silly."

"Our… what?"

"Oh yeah, about that," Lane piped up, "You're moving in across the hall from the girls."

"Why?" Kenny asked, even though his brain had already moved forward in time to the possibility of running into Maya in the hallway or the laundry room. Flirting with her at the mailboxes. Asking her out on a real date. He felt like a fool. But his heart skipped nonetheless.

"Because we want someone close by just in case," Monica answered.

"Okay. And why is Chanté going to be my roommate?"

"Accommodations are technically part of my fee. And why not? It'll be like that study abroad trip to Nicaragua we took in college. Remember that trip, Kenny?" Chanté's face filled the screen again. She grinned at him and winked suggestively.

"Now this is a story I want to hear," Lane said.

"I'm curious as well," Monica agreed. Kenny turned toward her and now there was definitely a smirk on her face. "You're much more complex than I previously thought."

"That's my Ken Doll," Chanté said. Kenny cringed at her old nickname for him, which they'd both agreed she'd never use when they worked together. "He's an onion."

If Kenny had thought this day couldn't get worse, he was wrong. Maya wanted nothing to do with him, he was going to have to live with his preternaturally flirty best friend across the hall from her and Lane would never forget his nickname or let him live it down.

And right on cue, Lane doubled over in laughter as the words "Ken Doll" wheezed through his lips. Second worst day ever.

four

It was an unspoken best friend thing that sent Maya and Kierra on a cleaning spree as soon as they got home. They weren't sure when the others would show, so they disinfected and vacuumed at the speed of light. Kierra felt some added pressure that this would be the first time Monica and Lane would see her apartment for real. Maya pretended all of the pressure was solely on Kierra's shoulders, but she felt a similar – if unwanted – anxiety that Kenny would be in her home, in her room, in her bed. Her disappointment at his deception unfortunately didn't automatically erase the months of pent up anticipation about just this moment. She scrubbed and vacuumed while ignoring the butterflies in her stomach.

After a couple of hours, they looked at their apartment with satisfaction and then broke apart. Kierra went to wash the mountain of dirty laundry always cluttering the bottom of her closet, while Maya retreated to her favorite, relaxing pastime. In her bathroom, she put on her favorite true crime podcast, pulled the plastic tub of sex toys out of the linen closet next to her vanity and zoned out while she cleaned her work and personal toys, changed and recharged her batteries and organized her back-up bottles of lube by preference and flavor; finding comfort in the familiar protocols of work prep.

It was probably fitting that that's where Kenny found her.

He cleared his throat and she jumped at the sound. When she turned to look at him, she suddenly remembered that she needed to grab the vibrator she kept in the shower. The one he'd gotten her. Her throat constricted as her brain instantly remembered all of the times she'd used it wishing he was here with her, just like this. But *not* like this. And it made her angry all over again.

His face was red, his eyes avoiding looking at the collection of toys spread out over her bathroom sink. He cleared his throat again, "Sorry, Kierra told me to come back here. She didn't say you were…"

He let the sentence trail off, which made her irrationally angry. He'd been watching her fuck herself for months with a good portion of these toys, for him, but now he couldn't even look at them.

"She didn't say that I was what?" Each word was saturated with all of her annoyance.

"She didn't say you weren't dressed," Kenny said.

Maya looked down and was shocked to realize she was wearing just a tank top and a very small pair of panties, because she preferred to clean in as little as possible. She cringed and inched to the side of her vanity, trying to cover her basically bare lower half. "I uh… I was about to take a shower."

He nodded and backed away. "Yep, I'll wait in the living room."

"Thanks."

He nodded again and took two steps before turning back. His eyes were still cast down at the floor and his voice had lowered an octave or two. He seemed to be rushing to say whatever he wanted to say before he lost the nerve. "I won't apologize again. But I want you to know that I meant every word I ever told you." He paused, and Maya could hear her own heartbeat beginning to race. "You're absolutely fucking beautiful."

It took a few minutes after he left for Maya to drag her eyes away from the spot in the doorway where he'd been.

When she finally stepped into the shower, she could barely think straight, the scratch of her loofah over her body felt like a sensual torture. Her skin was sensitive, tingling. The sound of Kenny's voice telling her that she was beautiful had the same effect on her that seeing those words typed on the screen during their weekly chats usually did. She wished it didn't. She hated herself for it.

KENNY ALTERNATED between sitting ramrod straight on the couch and pacing around the small living and dining room area as he waited for Maya to come out of her bedroom. But no matter what he was doing, his brain was trying to connect the dots between seeing her very scantily clad in her bathroom washing every small to medium-sized sex toy known to man, remembering her using so many of those toys for his pleasure and then imagining her in the shower. The shower that was just behind the wall on the far side of the kitchen. The wall he was staring at right now.

He exhaled loudly and collapsed into one of the chairs at their dining room table. If his superiors had asked for his feedback, he would have told them that this plan was a terrible fucking idea. While Maya didn't seem to want anything to do with him, he still wanted everything to do with her. So it was probably not a genius plan to put him in the same room as her, to put him within actual arm's reach of the one thing he apparently wanted more than his career, but could never have. To be so close to her and not be able to touch her and talk with her the way he'd wanted would test every bit of his training and would surely wreak havoc on his mind. But his superiors had not asked for his input and right now the mission seemed to be the last thing on their minds. The sound of Kierra's giggle drifted through her bedroom door. Kenny groaned, tilting his head back to stare at the ceiling. Absolute torture.

Maya's bedroom door inched open and he rose immediately, standing at attention. She tiptoed into the living room, her eyes wary as they settled on him briefly and then skittered away.

"Where's Kierra?" The sound of another giggle, that turned into a moan, answered her question. "Ah. Okay." Maya hesitated, sucking her bottom lip into her mouth. Since she refused to look at him, Kenny took the opportunity to drink her in, that flash of her teeth as she chewed on her lip and, when she popped it back out, the slight sheen of moisture. Absolute fucking torture.

She turned back to her room and called at him over her shoulder, "Come on. They won't be as loud back here."

He probably should have said no. He probably should have turned and walked out of her apartment and sent an email to Monica informing her that he couldn't do this. But the soft sway of her ass and hips in a very small pair of boxers cut through all of his better judgement and he didn't care about anything else. This mission would fail and it would probably end his career. But if it meant he was able to just kiss the perimeter of Maya's orbit for a few days or weeks, it would be absolute fucking torture that was absolutely fucking worth it.

"SIT," Maya demanded.

Kenny was standing in her doorway as if he was afraid to enter her room. Which was kind of cute. She shook her head and pulled the large black bag from her closet. She placed it on the bed. Fuck cute, she thought to herself, trying to rekindle the anger she was supposed to be feeling, but kept slipping away when she looked at him. She wondered if this was a mistake as he stiffly settled onto the foot of her bed.

Maya started to second-guess herself. She didn't think she could go live on her broadcast tonight and touch herself for her viewers with him right there in the room with her. Scratch that. She could *absolutely* perform in front of him; she had bills to pay and – if she was being honest with herself for a fleeting moment – the thought of him being so close already had her wet.

But she was worried about the moment she shut off her webcam. After a performance, she was always keyed up, no matter how many times she came during the broadcast. Her body understood the difference between orgasms for work and orgasms for herself so she usually had to take a quick moment, call to mind *her own* fantasies, and give herself a gentle, selfish climax. And for months that fantasy had been MasquerAsiaN. In real life he was taller than she'd imagined, more built, hotter, with a light dusting of facial hair where she had imagined him clean-shaven. Even more beautiful. Her body's reaction to him was more intense than she could have dreamt and tonight, after she logged off, he'd be there. This sounded like a recipe for disaster.

"Okay so," she said, trying to focus on pulling her lights from the bag where she kept all of her equipment. "I was thinking that we start off slow. Nothing too flashy or kinky. And we keep it short."

Kenny turned his head toward her but watched her hands instead of her face. "Won't that piss off your customers? Your Tuesday shows are usually a solid hour at least."

Maya's hands stuttered. "Do you know my entire weekly schedule?" She refused to look at him.

She heard him gulp. "Just…just your public shows and our…Yeah," he said, ending on a whisper.

She wondered if his chest actually hurt at the realization that this Thursday would be the first Thursday in months they wouldn't chat together; because hers did. She turned away and began pulling the rest of her equipment from the closet while he pushed up from the bed and started pacing.

She took a deep breath. "They'll be alright. The newness of having my… you in the room will override their annoyance." She stood up straight and locked eyes with him. Her voice almost gave out, but she pushed through. "Actually, this might be a bit of a windfall for me." She smiled. She thought it was convincing.

"Enough to get you on today's popularity ranking?"

She sucked her bottom lip into her mouth and raised her hand to show him her crossed fingers. But his eyes were trained on her mouth, so she wasn't sure that he saw.

She wanted to kiss him. She thought she heard a faint knock on the front door. She let out a breath of air and walked to her bedroom door, wrenching it open. Maya stuck her head out into the hallway and waited, thinking maybe she'd imagined the sound.

"What's wrong?" Kenny asked.

"Shhhh," she hissed.

A tangle of moans seeped into the hallway from Kierra's room. "Jesus, I don't even want to know what those three are doing in there," Maya mumbled. She tried to feign a laugh but then she felt him behind her. Not touching. Just there. The warmth of his body licking at her bare skin like a tiny flame that would grow if only she would let it. She wondered why she hadn't put on more clothes.

There was another knock.

Maya pushed out of her room and down the hallway. She gasped when Kenny's hands wrapped around her waist. Or it might have been a moan. Fuck, she hoped it had been a gasp.

He pulled her back into his strong body. His mouth found her ear and she tried to swallow the moan that rose in her throat; she did not succeed. "I should get that. Just in case."

She should have asked, just in case what? But instead she closed her eyes and nodded, trying to sear the feeling of his hand on her soft middle and his breath on her ear into her memory. Is that his dick? Her eyes popped open, but he'd already moved around her toward the door. She saw his hands flex as he reached for the handle. She knew in that moment that unless there was an assassin behind that door who killed one or both of them, she was going to fuck Kenny, aka MasquerAsiaN, aka the man of her fucking dreams, who also happened to be a spy and a liar. It might not fix a damn thing, but she knew for a fact that it would be as good as she'd hoped it would be. And it would be absolutely worth it.

KENNY CURSED under his breath when he saw Chanté's face through the peephole of Maya's front door. He pulled it open just enough to stick his head out.

"Go away," he hissed.

She just beamed at him. "Nope, got a job to do. Let me in."

"Go away. I'll pay you double your rate."

Chanté arched an eyebrow at him. "Monica's paying me triple my rate."

"Fine, I'll pay you quadruple. Just go away."

Chanté reached out to cup Kenny's cheek. "I love you Ken Doll, but I know exactly how much money is in your bank accounts and what you're saving it for. I can't bankrupt you like that."

Kenny squeezed his eyes shut. "Stop hacking into my accounts, Chanté. I can't keep changing my passwords. And have you raised your rates?"

Chanté bounced onto the balls of her feet and gave him an impish smile. "If you need to know your current passwords just gimme a call, duh. And yeah, I raised my rates after that thing I can't tell you about in that place I was at that one time."

Kenny stared blank-faced at her.

"Well who the hell is it?" Maya's voice cut through his frustration at Chanté. She sounded annoyed.

"Oh my god, is that her?" Chanté squealed loud enough for Maya to hear.

Kenny exhaled and stepped back to open the door and let Chanté in. She pushed past him in her eagerness to enter.

"Maya," Kenny said, a pained smile on his face. "This is Chanté. She's handling the tech on this op." And then they were face-to-face. He sighed at the annoyance and confusion written plainly on Maya's face because he knew it would be no match for Chanté's endless enthusiasm and willingness to divulge all of his most embarrassing secrets.

WHEN KENNY PREEMPTED her opening her own door, Maya expected some big bad to come bursting through it. Instead, the cutest girl with the cutest voice ever, pushed into her apartment. Maya was confused.

"I'm so excited to meet you," Chanté said. "Kierra told me a little bit about you in Berlin."

"You know Kierra? Wait, when was Kierra in Berlin?"

"Oh," Chanté glanced at Kenny out of the corner of her eye.

He put his hands on his hips, exhaled loudly and shook his head.

"Um, I'm maybe not supposed to tell you about that. So let's just say…Maybe."

Maya laughed, "Alright."

"And also, you know, Kenny told me about you."

"Chanté," Kenny hissed.

She turned to him then and flung her arms out to either side. "Am I not supposed to tell her that either? God, what can I say?"

"Nothing. Let's try that for once."

Chanté opened her mouth wide and took in a large breath, clearly *not* okay with saying nothing. Maya cut into what she assumed was a very regular conversation between them.

"Let me guess, you're not a spy."

Chanté turned toward her, a big smile on her face. "Nope. I'm more like an independent contractor. Although some people call me an asset."

Kenny rolled his eyes at that. Maya caught the movement, but she didn't know what it meant.

"And you two have known each other for a while?"

"Oh yeah, we've been best friends since college. Way before this one signed up to The Agency."

"What Agency?"

Kenny clamped a hand over Chanté's mouth and the other cupped the back of her head, to stop her from answering. "My employer. You aren't authorized to know any more than that. And the background checks to get even the lowest level clearance is so thorough I'd know your third grade teacher's social security number."

Maya's mouth fell open. "Forget I asked."

Kenny nodded and turned to Chanté. "Can you for once stay on track?"

He moved the hand from her mouth slowly as if afraid of what might fall out.

She frowned at him. "I mean I can try, but I'm not making any promises."

Kenny smiled indulgently at her and moved his other hand from her head. "That's all I ever ask."

Watching them together did something to Maya's stomach and heart. It was like a gut punch to her resolve to keep this just business. A very inconvenient gut punch that kinda felt like lust.

Chanté turned to Maya, "I've got your new webcam. I thought we could set it up before your next broadcast."

"Sounds good. Follow me." She turned away from them and used those few steps to her room to try and settle her racing pulse with deep breaths. As she passed Kierra's door, she heard a woman's moan that did not sound like Kierra, so she assumed it was Monica.

"Oh my god, are they in there?" The "they" clearly understood.

"Yeah," Kenny grunted.

"Um okay. Maybe I'll just go say hi for a bit," Chanté said.

Maya turned to see Kenny grasp her by the shoulders and steer her past Kierra's door.

"We're staying on task, remember?" Kenny said in exasperation.

"Are all spies this freaky," Maya asked around a laugh.

"Oh girl, I wish. You all," she said gesturing toward Kierra's door and at Maya and Kenny, "are truly my people."

In her bedroom, Kenny stood awkwardly to the side, his back pressed against the wall, once again seeming unsure if he wanted to be there. Maya set up her lights and tried to ignore the pounding in her chest and between her legs in anticipation. And Chanté got to work setting up Maya's new top-of-the-line, state-of-the-art camera, with broadcasting capabilities. It cost thousands of dollars, which Maya knew because it had been sitting in her online wish list for months even though it was way out of her budget. The video quality alone would be lightyears ahead of her current camera; the one she'd gotten on deep discount when she'd first started modeling. Maya made a mental note to give Kierra the biggest hug ever, assuming she ever emerged from her room again. Which was an actual crapshoot.

"Okay, so what's the set up here? I know you're usually on your bed, so are we doing that still?" Chanté asked, all business.

"Uh yeah," Maya responded, shocked that Chanté had clearly done her research.

"You normally do a tight shot on you, but we'll have to widen our angle a bit for Kenny, right? Where do you want him?"

It was such an innocent and direct question and Chanté's meaning was quite clear. Where did Maya want Kenny positioned on the bed? But Kenny had once asked Maya that question almost verbatim and the implication had been very different.

MasquerAsiaN
Where do you want me to come baby?

ThickaThanASnicka
Everywhere

MasquerAsiaN
lol be more specific

ThickaThanASnicka
In every hole

MAYA STARTED CHEWING on her bottom lip, too afraid to look in Kenny's direction, especially not when she heard his gulp from across the room and realized that they must have delved back into the same memory.

Chanté fanned herself. "You two are very, very hot."

Kenny coughed and Maya cleared her throat.

"On…on the bed," she finally said. "I was thinking that he could recline against my headboard. That way we can angle the camera to just cut off his head."

"Good idea," Chanté said and turned to Kenny. "Well let's go."

He shook his head, "Um…"

"No, she's right. We need you in position," Maya said, her voice sounding much more sure about this situation than she felt.

"Exactly. If we don't get the angle just right, your career could be over," Chanté teased.

Kenny sighed. He shuffled over to the bed in his socked feet and sat just on the edge looking like he was ready to jump off any minute. Maya almost laughed.

"Seriously?" Chanté deadpanned. "Could you pretend like you've ever sat on a bed before?"

He turned to glare at her and Maya thought he looked adorable, she liked when they teased each other. She added that thought to the other inconvenient and borderline inappropriate ones cluttering her brain.

"Okay here," Maya said, climbing on her bed toward him. She saw his eyes widen as he watched her crawl toward him. "I want you in the middle." Chanté giggled. Maya gulped. She didn't mean for the sentence to come out like that; at least she didn't want to mean it like that.

Kenny scooted away from her touch, pressing his back against her headboard.

"Good, now spread your legs," she said as her eyes flew to the bulge in his pants and her mouth went dry.

When she raised her eyes to his, she saw the apology there. She lifted the right side of her mouth and shrugged in understanding. He spread his legs and for no reason that she could identify, she crawled in between them.

Kenny pressed the back of his head against her headboard and raised his eyes to the ceiling. His breathing was deep and slow. Maya became entranced by the bob of his Adam's apple and the length of his neck.

"So hot," Chanté whispered, pulling Maya out of the moment.

She turned around. Chanté was behind the camera, adjusting the angle on them. Maya recognized the tight feeling of her own hardened nipples.

"So did you and Kenny ever date?" Maya blurted out. Her eyes widened in shock. She absolutely had not planned to ask that question; it was none of her business.

Chanté giggled. "Never. But there was that one time in Nicaragua."

"Chanté," Kenny said, the warning in his voice made Maya's sex quiver. Ah, so that's what it felt like when everything a man did turned you on, even when you didn't want it to, she thought to herself.

"What happened in Nicaragua?" Since she'd already opened this dirty can of worms, Maya thought she might as well dive in head first.

Chanté sat on the bed and learned toward her. "There was a girl."

"Chanté," Kenny hissed.

"It's a good story, Ken Doll," Chanté giggled, her mouth dangerously close to Maya's.

Maya turned her head toward him. "Is that your nickname?"

"It's fitting, right?" Chanté asked.

For a second he seemed shocked, his eyes widening, and then he nodded.

Maya let her eyes scan Kenny's face, down his neck, over his broad chest, down each well-defined arm and settled in his lap where that noticeable bulge seemed to have grown. She licked her lips, chewed the corner of her mouth and nodded. "Yeah, I can see that."

Kenny gulped again.

Maya turned fully toward Kenny, still in between his legs, and crossed her feet at the ankles under her butt. She made eye contact with him and held his gaze. "So the girl?" she asked Chanté.

The bed moved and Chanté's mouth came very close to her ear, her soft breath rustling Maya's hair. "We were there on a study abroad. So was she, but from another school. We both liked her. And she liked both of us."

Maya sighed. She could see the broad contours of where this story was going. The part of her that felt betrayed by MasquerAsiaN didn't care about any of this, but the part of her that had craved every bit of information about him for months wanted this story and needed to watch what it did to him to have Chanté tell her.

"We flirted with her for like three weeks," Chanté continued.

"A month," Kenny corrected.

"Was it?"

Kenny only nodded, never taking his eyes off of Maya.

"So we flirted with her for a month. And then the night before we were all leaving, a bunch of us went out dancing. But the three of us left the club early and went back to the dorms."

Maya's sex clenched in anticipation. "And you had sex?"

"Hmmm, sort of," Chanté giggled. Maya smiled when Kenny smiled. "Kenny's like family. We agreed that that would be weird."

Maya turned to Chanté. Her eyes scanned over the other woman's face. She was really beautiful. "So it would be weird if you two fucked, but not weird if you fucked the same woman at the same time."

Chanté shrugged. "Everybody's boundaries are different." Chanté reached out then and smoothed a lock of Maya's hair behind her ear, trailing a finger gently along the outer rim. "What are yours?"

Maya's entire body felt like it was on fire. Chanté's lips were so close to hers. She could lean forward and taste her and if she was reading the look in Chanté's eyes correctly, she wanted her to do just that. But she didn't. "I don't share," she said to Chanté and watched the light dim in her eyes.

Chanté sighed mournfully. "Neither does Kenny. Nicaragua was the one and only time."

Maya turned to him and found him watching her with an intense gaze that made her pussy shiver.

And then her door flung open. They all turned toward it.

"Almost show time. We good in here?" Lane asked. He smiled and leaned against the door, one hand on his hip. "Well hello there, little lady," he said to Chanté, grinning at her like a Cheshire cat.

Maya looked at him. If it weren't for his tousled hair and bare feet no one would have known he'd just spent the better part of an hour doing whatever he'd been doing to her best friend and his wife.

"We didn't know you were gonna be here tonight."

"Who's here?" Monica said before she appeared by Lane's side.

"Chanté."

Their eyes laser-focused on Chanté and once again Maya wondered how anyone could withstand that kind of attention. She was already overheated and felt the urge to rub her thighs together to relieve the tension she felt in every cell in her body. And then Kenny's hand settled, gently on her knee. His touch was light, asking for permission. She shifted her leg to press more fully into his hand and he tightened his grip.

"Kierra will be happy you're here," Monica said. She stretched an arm out and Chanté jumped from Maya's bed and grasped it.

Monica was pulling Chanté into the hallway but she turned around. "Camera's set up. As long as Kenny doesn't slouch, his face'll be out of frame." And then she was gone. To Kierra's room, Maya guessed. To do god knows what. Maya shivered at the thought.

Kenny dug his fingers into her knee to settle her. She wanted to moan.

"The broadcast starts in twenty minutes," Kenny said to Lane.

"Don't worry. We'll be watching from the other room. If there are any problems, just call." He turned to smirk at Kenny and winked at her. "You two have fun," he laughed as he closed the door.

And just like that they were alone. Maya's entire body felt as if it was on fire. This was going to be the longest broadcast of her life.

five

Maya liked the routine of preparing for her Tuesday broadcasts. Making sure she had all the items she might need at hand: lubrication (lots of lube), her favorite small vibrators (internal and external), wipes for cleanup. The familiarity of it centered her. She was looking over the basket on her bathroom sink, flexing her fingers and wondering if she had everything she needed; and trying to ignore Kenny's presence and his nervous energy. She was failing.

Kenny was pacing the length of her bedroom. His limited range of movement kept him just in the frame of her bathroom door; in her line of sight. Every time he passed, he turned his head to look at her, quickly, shyly. She noticed. She pretended not to notice.

Out of the corner of her eyes she watched him stop, take a deep breath and walk toward her. But he stopped just at the door's threshold, his hands on either side of the door frame, his hard biceps flexed and straining the arms of his t-shirt. Maya swallowed to lubricate her suddenly dry throat. Kenny cleared his own throat to get her attention.

She raised her head to the large mirror behind her sink. They almost made eye contact in the reflection, but she shifted her eyes to his Adam's apple before their gazes could lock. She knew what her body would do if she looked him deep in his eyes. She could still feel his hand on her knee.

"I." He stopped, swallowed and started again. "I always wondered what you would be like just before and just after your broadcasts."

Her heart wanted to melt; she held her breath and refused to let it. Her sex quivered, completely out of her control. She was dreading "after," but looking forward to it as well.

"It's a job," she said, not that that explained anything. The underlying message was clear, "You were just a job." It was a petty barb. It was a lie she had to tell him, hoping she might be able to deceive herself.

He blinked and then pretended to smile, but it looked more like chagrin. She wondered what his smile looked like for real. She hadn't seen one yet but it was the one thing she'd fantasized about. For months, she'd fallen asleep while conjuring an image of what he might look like smiling – smiling at her – more times than she could count. Certainly more times than she would admit.

He nodded. "I'll go check in with Lane. I'll be back in a minute."

She nodded as he turned and walked away. "Don't be late," she yelled after him. The sound of her bedroom door closing was her only reply.

KENNY DIDN'T GO to Kierra's room.

He heard Chanté's giggle just as he passed. He walked to the front door, to the kitchen and back again. He just needed to move.

Kierra interrupted him on his third rotation. Her bedroom door opened and she slipped out, the sound of Lane and Chanté's laughter momentarily growing louder, before she closed the door behind her. Her legs were bare under an oversized button-up shirt.

Kenny stopped mid-step and stared at her. There was a smile on her face. He rolled his eyes.

"Oh, don't be grumpy. This is all your fault."

He ran his hands over his head, back and forth, and turned in a tight circle, his body buzzing with pent up energy and emotions he didn't know how to process.

Kierra tiptoed toward him. When she was close, but just out of arm's reach, she whispered, "Did you- Was it more than cybersex?"

He turned away from her and pressed his eyes closed. He could hear his blood pounding in his ears. He straightened his back and clasped his hands behind his head. "Does it matter now?" His voice sounded strained; every part of him felt wound tight.

"Depends," Kierra said in a light tone. He could hear the shrug in her voice and the sound of her footsteps as she walked away. "And that's what Maya said when I asked her."

He turned quickly, staring at her retreating back. He followed her to the kitchen. "Explain."

She turned and smiled at him over her shoulder. In the kitchen she pulled out a pitcher of water and a bowl of mixed berries. She frowned down at the bowl in her hand and lifted her head, "Does Chanté have any allergies?"

"Mild nut allergy. Don't believe her if she says she can eat peanut butter. She can't."

Kierra's eyes widened and she nodded gravely.

"What do you mean, depends?"

Kierra turned and pulled four water glasses from the cabinet by the fridge. "Depends on you, sir."

Kenny exhaled loudly. "Can you please just tell me what you mean? I don't have forever before the broadcast starts."

Kierra turned and pointed at the top of the cabinet to his right. "Can you grab that tray please?"

He exhaled a frustrated breath, but did as she asked.

"Okay, so here's the lowdown on Maya," Kierra said as she loaded the water, glasses and berries onto the tray. "She's got a hard shell, a soft heart and a big ass."

Kenny rolled his eyes. He knew all of this already.

Kierra perked up and turned to open another cabinet and pulled down a box of crackers and dried cranberries as she continued talking. "But I figure you know that already."

He grunted in agreement.

"But what I know you wouldn't have figured out while jacking off to my bestie on your computer," she said in a happy, non-judgmental voice that still made Kenny blush, "is that Maya has a firm no-second-chances policy when it comes to sexual and romantic relationships." She locked eyes with him then, clearly wanting to make sure he understood how important her next words would be. "If Maya was absolutely through with you, you wouldn't be here. Period."

"She needs the money," Kenny said automatically, the memory of her words from this morning echoing in his head.

Kierra laughed then and shrugged. "She gets by. And she's going to raise the rent on whoever takes over my room. That's why she's really pissed I'm not leaving. Every month I'm here she has to pay half the rent, not one third."

Kenny's head snapped to the side, "One third?"

Kierra picked up her tray and walked toward him. "Maya has a hard shell, a soft heart, a big ass, and the mind of a Gilded Age oil baron. She doesn't need this mission to get out of debt. And we certainly don't need you to help us. You're here because she wants you here. Even if she can't admit it yet."

Kenny's mouth fell open. Yep, this was definitely not the kind of information he'd gleaned, his eyes glued to his computer screen, watching her strip for him on video chat. But it made him hard nonetheless.

"Alright now move, this is heavy and the broadcast is

about to start," Kierra said irritably, but still with that smile on her face.

Kenny jumped out of her way and watched her walk back to her bedroom. At the door she turned back to him and nodded her head, "Hello, make yourself useful please?"

Kenny rushed forward. When he turned the doorknob, Monica's voice filtered through, deep but still soft. He watched the shiver rumble through Kierra's body. "Break a leg," she whispered. He didn't move as Kierra walked into her room and kicked the door shut behind her, slamming it in his face.

All he could hear was Kierra's voice on a loop in his brain.

You're here because she wants you here.

You're here because she wants you here.

He tried to stop his heart from blooming at those words, but it was too late. He hoped Kierra was right. He needed Kierra to be right.

MAYA'S HEART WAS FLUTTERING.

She looked at herself in the bathroom mirror. The sea moss green lace bodysuit she wore made her feel delicate and sexy. The plunging neckline made her breasts look amazing and perky, which was a feat because they only grew heavier and drooped elegantly just a bit more each year. She turned around and admired the way the thong made her ass look perfectly symmetrical, each cheek the same size, and round even though they absolutely were not. She swallowed hard and decided to change.

Kenny loved her in green. She'd made an unconscious mistake.

She was reaching for the bathroom door handle when she heard a knock on the bedroom door. She heard it creak open a bit and then open fully. He was back. And he was considerate enough to knock before he entered. Fuck, her heart had a field day with that one.

"Maya?" His gentle voice filtered through the bathroom door.

"I'm coming," she said. "Just get on the bed like before."

She wanted to rest – or maybe bang – her head on the door, but she couldn't jeopardize her hair or makeup for those sorts of dramatics. She wouldn't have time to fix any damage she did to the masterpiece she'd created. She closed her eyes and counted to twenty in her head while taking deep breaths, trying to slow the beating of her heart.

When she opened the door just enough to peek out into the bedroom, Kenny was standing next to the bed, his hands on his hips. His back looked broad and strong even through the fabric of his shirt.

She gulped. "What's wrong?"

He turned toward her and smiled. And she honestly wished he hadn't. She now knew what it was like to see his genuine smile aimed at her and much like every other part of him – excepting his relationship to the truth – it was better than she could have imagined. But apparently the universe was in the habit of giving her exactly what she wished for in the most devastating ways.

"I was wondering if I should take my shirt off," he said matter-of-factly.

"No," she blurted, stepping into the bedroom. "Not- Not this time." She knew for a fact that seeing even a millimeter more of his skin would compromise her desire to keep him at arm's length, if not even further away. She was shaking her head emphatically to get her point across, but her body was also quaking as his eyes raked over her, intent and hungry. Her skin became sensitive and she would have sworn she could feel every stitch of the delicate lace covering her overheated skin. The slightly painful feeling of her nipples hardening made it difficult to think straight.

She held her breath and he watched her body respond to him, his eyes settling on her breasts, which only made her nipples ache even more. She waited for him to apologize again or mention that he loved her in green or fall to his knees just because.

But once he'd drunk her in, he simply nodded. "Whatever you want," he said, in a voice that sounded deeper than before; thick. He crawled onto her bed. Maya's eyes flew to his ass and then shifted away.

She prayed to the universe to stop torturing her and just let her torture him… and her viewers.

MAYA HEARD Kenny's sharp intake of breath as she crawled between his legs and faced him.

She sat back on her heels, "Ready?" she whispered.

He nodded.

"Keep your hands to yourself," she ordered.

He nodded again. She was just about to turn when he spoke, "You can touch me."

She wished he hadn't said that.

She nodded and turned toward the camera, lying on her stomach. He groaned. She bent her legs at the knees and dangled them to one side. She checked the angle on her laptop feed and tried not to get distracted with the clarity of her new camera's output.

She pulled up the ChatBot website and signed in. Her public chatroom was a little slow, but not slow enough to worry. Her Tuesday broadcasts didn't make her the most money, but they were an integral part of her long-term business plan.

In Maya's research, there was very little logic to the kinds of ChatBot channels that hit the popularity charts. The streams ranged from hardcore sex to chatty rants to regular old day-in-the-life content, with models of all genders and presentations, of all races and in various languages. There was no clear path for a new model to follow, which she realized in the research phase of her early career. The one thing that seemed to be a general rule was that the best channels – those that saw steady growth – almost always had regular and consistent online presence, streams, chat shows, etc. It had taken a while to identify a schedule that worked, but Maya's Tuesday/Sunday broadcasts seemed to fit for her viewers, especially those who couldn't afford a private chat, but had a little bit of money to spend. She'd been on this schedule for at least eight months and according to her spreadsheet of broadcast stats, viewers and tips, her gross revenue had been increasing slowly but steadily month-to-month at first and, recently, week-to-week. So, even with the turmoil of finding out that her favorite client had been deceiving her still roiling in her stomach, she couldn't let it interfere with her business.

She typed quickly to say hi to her chatroom and smiled as the lagging conversation instantly picked up. Maya opened the broadcast box and checked the angle. It was perfect. Chanté really did have an eye for camera placement. Lying as she was on her stomach between Kenny's legs, her viewers would get a great shot of her chest and the rise of her ass in the distance, all in focus. Just at the margins of the shot and slightly blurry, was the suggestion of Kenny. His legs bracketed her body, the expanse of his chest and just the strong point of his chin and lower jaw. It was kind of romantic.

Maya moved onto her right side to clear his line of sight. "Is the angle okay?"

She saw Kenny nod on her laptop screen. He pressed his lips shut.

"We're not broadcasting," she said. "I'll tell you before I start."

"Oh. Okay. The angle is fine. It's good that I'm blurry."

"Yep. Chanté's kind of a genius."

"Tell her that. She loves compliments."

"So do I," she said enthusiastically, unsure why she felt the need to tell him that.

She saw his right hand flex. His grin broadened into a smile. "I know."

She turned back to the camera and took a deep breath. And then another. "Okay, in 3…2…1."

KENNY HAD BEEN TRYING DESPERATELY and in vain to send his brain anywhere else but here. He made a grocery list in his head, but he didn't cook, so energy drinks, protein powders and bananas didn't get him very far. He tried to think about tomorrow's workout, but somehow the word workout kept leading him to the dirtiest places and that was literally what he was trying to avoid. Because Maya's body barely clad in green lace was too much.

The soft globes of her ass kept fighting – and winning – in the war for his attention. He'd already catalogued the mole somewhere between her butt and her left hip, the faint remnants of a tattoo she'd clearly had lasered away, and every soft, beautiful dimple of cellulite from her ass down her thighs, he committed them all to reverent memory. Kierra was the poet, but Kenny had a halfway decent limerick composed in his head about the way the delicate swirls of the lace disappeared between her cheeks. He'd swallowed so many groans tonight, his stomach was full of longing, frustration and self-pity.

"Nope," Maya giggled, the sound pulling him out of his reverie. She was responding to the scrolling chat.

His head spun. Last Tuesday during this broadcast, Kenny had been at a safe house in Turkey, bleary-eyed from jet lag and stroking himself slowly back to sleep as he watched her.

And now he was here, Maya between his legs. Still, they might as well have been thousands of miles apart.

"You can't see him and at least for tonight, he can't touch me," she said in a breathy whisper that was still loud enough for the microphone attached to her camera to pick up.

He clenched his hands together.

"Hey babe," Maya said, over her shoulder. Kenny pressed his lips together. "They want to know if I can touch myself?"

He furrowed his brow. Why they fuck were they asking him?

And then she laughed and turned her torso toward him, her smile widened when she saw the confusion on his face. "Yep, I don't know why they're asking you either." She turned back to her camera with a smile. He saw her face on her laptop and bit his lips together. If he were in the broadcast, he would have given her every coin in his ChatBot account. And by the light chime that indicated when one of her viewers tipped her, a few of them agreed with his instinct.

But he only had a second to smile at their accurate appreciation before her legs widened and her hand appeared between her thighs from under her body. Kenny gasped as he watched her fingers lightly stroke her sex. His eyes were glued to her hand as she moved the small strip of fabric to the side and the bright pink of her pussy peeked through her brown lips.

She moaned.

Kenny stuffed his hands underneath his thighs.

She stroked herself slowly, up and down her sex, playing with herself the way he knew she liked.

The bed moved as she shook her head. He could hear the wicked smile in her voice. "You don't get to see," she said. "You thought my boyfriend could tell me what to do. Haven't I taught you all better than that?"

There was too much for Kenny to process. The way his heart yawned pathetically when she called him her boyfriend, as if he wasn't a fucking professional and this weren't all pretend. The playful annoyance in her voice as she corrected her viewers for perpetuating patriarchal bullshit – which was actually expressly forbidden in her room rules – as he'd seen her do numerous times before. He liked it every time.

But he couldn't quite process any of that as she slipped her middle finger inside herself. He only noticed the emerald green nail polish that clashed beautifully with her medium brown skin just before that finger sank inside her pussy. All of the blood in his body was rushing south to his dick. He felt the kind of euphoria that was usually a pretty good indicator of danger.

"I've got one finger inside myself right now," Maya announced to her viewers. "Who's going to make two fingers worth my while?" The chiming rang out.

His dick felt constrained by his jeans. He wanted to touch her. To tip her. To get her off. He wanted Maya. He always wanted Maya.

Her viewers tipped her to add a third and soon the room was quiet, save for the occasional chime of more money going into her account. Kenny and Maya's labored breathing and the gentle squelch of her sex as she curled her fingers gently in and out of her wet pussy soon overtook even that faux metallic sound. Her hips began to move to the rhythm of her pumping fingers. His world shrank to her fingers, her sex, her moans. This was the most perfect night he'd had in longer than he could remember. Kenny marveled at how different it was to see her from this side of the world. He noted all of the details he'd missed because of the static angle of her camera; the smell of her perfume and her aroused sex and best of all, as she got close – her hips grinding her clit into the palm of her hand– the small tremors in her thighs as her orgasm built.

Her left leg flexed and crashed into his shoulder, pulling the groan he'd been holding in from his lips. It was pathetic how much that contact undid him, his dick hardened even further, straining against his zipper. She pushed the ball of her foot onto her headboard, trying to get enough leverage to fuck herself harder onto her trapped fingers. It worked. They both shuddered as her fingers slid into and out of her sex faster, slightly deeper, those wet sounds louder in Kenny's ears. Her ankle and calf rubbed against his cheek as she rocked back and forth. His dick was pulsing and he knew that if this continued much longer he'd come in his pants like a fucking teenager.

Maya's head drooped to the bed as her thighs began to shake violently. Kenny had a flash of a fantasy, him fucking her like this, her head listing to the bed until she was screaming into her comforter, his name on her lips. But that was a fantasy. This was her broadcast and he knew she'd be pissed if she didn't lift her head to let her viewers watch her come. They loved to see that. He loved to see that. And it always raked in that last little bit of money they were holding in reserve.

He cleared his throat to get her attention. She moaned in response. He cleared his throat again and her head popped up just as she yelled out her release. She raised her hips slightly to free her hand and circle her clit.

And then she giggled. The giggle that he fucking loved. That he'd been dreaming about for months. That followed him into every one of his fantasies. That sounded even fucking better – melodic and crisp – in person, undistorted by technology and distance.

The chime of her tips sounded again.

He wasn't shocked that that giggle sent him over the edge, because she'd been training him for that over months and he'd happily allowed it. His back spasmed and his dick released in his underwear; untouched and unsatisfied. But it was a release nonetheless.

He finally tore his eyes away from her pussy, raising to look into the camera screen and saw her familiar, satisfied smile, her head propped up by her free hand. She smiled into the camera and wiggled a few wet fingers in farewell before she ended the broadcast.

Kenny's head fell back to the headboard. He was panting, his pulse was racing. He knew that he couldn't survive another broadcast like this. He couldn't wait until Sunday.

debrief #2

Kierra's room was silent but for the sound of all their labored breaths. Her skin felt warm. The soft cotton of her bra was chafing against her nipples and Monica's shirt felt oppressive. She was surrounded by the mingled smells of Monica and Lane's cologne on the shirt and on their bodies. Her head was swimming.

Not surprisingly Chanté was the first one to speak. "I think I should go home now," she whispered. "I've got a busy day tomorrow."

She leaned over and brushed her lips along Kierra's cheek. She stood from the bed on shaky legs.

"You sure you don't want to stay?" Monica asked, perched in a chair at the foot of Kierra's bed. There was a clear invitation in her voice. Kierra turned to her, knowing that the other woman would notice her arousal.

Chanté walked slowly toward the door. "No thanks. I like flirting with you all, but…"

She didn't finish the sentence, but Kierra knew Asif's name was probably right on the tip of her tongue. Kierra wondered if she thought it would be weird to have sex with someone – or multiple someones – she and Asif often worked with. And that made her wonder about her own feelings on the matter.

Chanté opened and shut the door quietly as she left.

"Well I am detecting a lot of sexual tension right now," Lane said around a chuckle that Kierra knew was choked with need. "What do you say you lay back and ge-," but she cut him off with a shake of her head. He sighed sadly.

"I told you. No touching me until I'm not mad anymore," she said, her eyes trained on Monica.

"You can't use this on us every time you're angry," Monica replied in a flat voice.

Kierra smiled. They'd shown up at her apartment hell bent on repeating this afternoon's seduction, but when she'd turned them down flat, she'd enjoyed watching Lane settle his head between Monica's legs while she touched herself. As a reward, she'd crawled on the bed and let them cocoon her between their bodies while they all drifted off to sleep for a short nap. She'd woken up hornier than ever, but she felt safe and less angry.

She probably could have let them have their way with her right then and there, but she loved how powerful she felt when they pined after her. She crawled across her bed toward Lane. He lifted his eyebrows in surprise and grinned. She reached out, grabbed his head and pulled his mouth to hers. She kissed him briefly, slow and gentle with a lot of tongue. Just the way Monica liked.

He laughed against her retreating mouth.

"We'll see," she said to Monica, and walked to her bathroom.

"You've created a fucking monster," Lane laughed. "A spoiled brat of a monster."

Just as Kierra closed the door she heard Monica's restrained voice grind out, "That's our girl."

Usually after a broadcast, Maya's adrenaline was so high she sometimes had the shakes. On those nights she couldn't do anything but grab her favorite vibrator and make herself come until she was just tired enough to wash off her makeup, shower and collapse into bed. Those were the good nights. But the bad nights were when nothing, not her toys or her fingers, gave her the kind of release she craved. On those nights she was forced to call to mind the fictional MasquerAsiaN in her head. She dreamt of using his hands and mouth and dick to get herself off. It got her there, but it wasn't enough. But now she knew that there could be worse nights. Nights when her on-camera orgasm was mild, just enough to rev her engines. Nights when her adrenaline hadn't even peaked and the real MasquerAsiaN was in her bed, between her legs. And she couldn't have him. This was definitely the darkest timeline.

After Maya closed her computer, she and Kenny were frozen, their ragged breath and the whir of her computer the only sounds filling the room. She lowered her left leg against his chest, he moaned. Who knows how long they might have stayed there just like that, but then they heard Kierra's door open and close. Maya jumped up and grabbed the packet of wipes from the basket with all of the equipment she hadn't used. Didn't need. She began to clean her hands, trying to hide how they shook.

Kenny's head was pressed against the headboard, his eyes lifted to the ceiling. His cheeks and ears were a bright red, his chest heaving. She had the sudden urge to climb back on the bed between his legs just to press her ear against his chest and hear what his heart sounded like; wondering if it was hammering against his chest like hers. It made her want to weep.

She cleared her throat.

He tilted his head forward and blinked rapidly. When he turned to her, she turned away. She pretended to look at her equipment as if she was considering dismantling it. The reality was that she was so horny she could barely remember what everything she was staring at did.

"Can I-" Kenny said and then stopped, swallowed. "Can I use your bathroom?"

She nodded and opened her mouth. The sound that came out was unintelligible as a word, but he got the hint. He walked delicately toward her bathroom and she realized that he'd come in his pants. He hadn't touched himself and they hadn't touched one another, besides that place where her leg rubbed against his face, which was apparently just enough contact for both of them. The point on her leg where his soft facial hair had touched still felt warm and sent little bolts of electricity shooting up her body periodically. It was too much.

As soon as the bathroom door closed, Maya grabbed the robe hanging on the back of her closet door and rushed out of her room. She needed space. She needed to be in an entirely different city, but she settled for the kitchen.

Her hands were still shaking as she washed them in the kitchen sink. Her mouth was dry, but she didn't trust herself enough to hold a glass. A door opened. Maya's heart stopped and she held her breath, but then Kierra appeared, a smile on her face and a tray in her hands.

It took a second for Maya to process what she was seeing. But when she did, "Did you have a fucking viewing party for my broadcast?"

Kierra stopped just inside the kitchen, the smile frozen on her face. "Would that be a bad thing?"

Maya threw up her hands and gestured oddly, spraying water on them both, still unable to string together a complex, coherent thought. She settled her hands on her hips and trusted Kierra to get the hint.

She did. "You're horny, huh?"

Maya just nodded.

"You like him, huh?"

Maya felt tears spring to her eyes and she turned away. "Liked," she replied.

Kierra made a noncommittal hum that Maya knew she reserved for when she didn't believe what someone told her. In that moment Maya hated Kierra for seeing her so clearly.

"Maya," she said in a gentle tone.

But then a door opened and Lane's loud voice preceded his and Monica's entrance into the living room. Maya wiped furiously at her face and hoped that when she turned back around she looked normal, whatever that looked like.

When she made eye contact with Lane he smiled. "Brava," he said, leaning toward her over the breakfast bar and winking.

Maya never could reject a compliment so she smirked and curtsied. He laughed.

Monica moved to stand just behind Kierra and leaned down to whisper in her ear. The tray in Kierra's hand began to shake, the glasses clinking together.

"You all right there, sweet girl? Need a hand?" Lane asked. Kierra glared at him and put the tray on the counter in front of her. But she didn't move away from Monica, in fact she might have leaned back into her. Maya tried not to dissect their behavior, hoping they wouldn't dissect her own frazzled movements any more than Kierra already had.

"Where's Kenny?" Monica asked, snaking a hand around Kierra's waist, her fingers slipping through the space between the shirt buttons.

"He's-"

"Here," Kenny finished, calling down the hall.

Maya sucked her bottom lip into her mouth and began to gnaw on it frantically.

When he stepped into view, Monica and Kierra shifted to allow him to join them in the overcrowded kitchen. They made eye contact for a brief minute and both looked away almost immediately. Maya's gaze crashed into Lane's. His smile was bright and he winked at her again. She wished he would stop doing that. She rolled her eyes and turned her head, focusing on the refrigerator, which didn't even have a magnet for her to pretend to be staring at.

"So," Kenny said in his deep, matter-of-fact, professional voice. Maya crossed her arms and wrapped her robe tighter around herself, hoping no one noticed her shudder. "Any action in the chatroom?"

There was a brief moment of silence before everyone, including Kenny laughed. "You know what I mean."

"We know," Monica said in a surprisingly light voice. And then it got serious. "Joseph Mehmeti was in your room just at the tail end of the broadcast. We'll only know if our bait worked if he comes back."

The reality that their plan might immediately return dividends seemed to sober them all.

"Okay, so what does that mean?" Maya asked in a small voice.

"For you," Lane said, "Nothing. You don't need to do anything different."

"What if he… what if he contacts me? What if he asks for a private session?"

"That's what we want."

"If he contacts you, you contact me," Kenny cut off Lane to say, answering her actual question. His voice drew Maya's eyes to him. His gaze was intense. Her throat closed with emotion. She nodded and shifted her eyes away.

"Who's in the TV spy movie now?" Lane mumbled under his breath.

"Lane," Monica barked.

Lane smiled and put his hands up in surrender. "Oops."

"Let's go debrief officially," Monica said. "We'll go across the hall and talk to Chanté about any flagged profiles."

"The fuck do you mean across the hall?" Maya asked, squinting her eyes at Monica.

"Oh yeah," Lane offered matter-of-factly, "Kenny and Chanté are moving into the vacant apartment across the way."

"The meth dealer's place?" Kierra and Chanté yelled.

"Uh… sure? We wanted you to have some backup close by, just in case."

Kierra moved out of Monica's hold to stand next to Maya. Her eyes were hard, her jaw clenched. "When were you going to tell me this?"

"Would you believe me if I said we forgot?" Lane asked.

"Not at all," she hissed.

But Maya didn't focus on them. She turned to Kenny and glared.

"I have orders," he said simply.

She rolled her eyes and was about to yell that if he was holding out hope for her to forgive him, keeping yet another thing from her was a great way to not achieve that goal. But he spoke before she could.

"But I would camp out close by even if I didn't have to."

The words died on her lips.

He nodded at her and turned to leave.

They stood in silence, listening to his footsteps and the opening and closing door. Maya was ready to yell just in case he slammed her door again. He didn't. It closed softly. She tried to be angry that he hadn't even given her an appropriate outlet for the emotion swelling in her chest; the inconvenient warmth she'd spent all day trying to keep at bay.

"Fuck," she breathed.

Lane chuckled.

Monica sighed, walking out of the kitchen. She turned toward Kierra. "I take it you're even more angry than before."

Kierra crossed her arms over her chest. "I wouldn't plan on even holding my hand any time soon."

Monica nodded and turned away. Maya could have sworn

her lips had tipped up on the right side of her mouth into an almost smile.

But Lane's smile was big and toothy. He nodded to Maya and winked at Kierra. "Sweet dreams."

When it was just the two of them alone in their apartment, huddled together in their kitchen, Kierra put her head on Maya's shoulder. "We're so fucked," she breathed.

"I wish," Maya replied irritably.

six

Maya was pissed. She put on her most boring outfit, black leggings and an oversized black t-shirt that hid the perfection of her hips and ass. She wrapped her hair in a plain head wrap and slipped the biggest pair of sunglasses she owned onto her face. She grabbed her biggest tote – which, if need be, she could use to cover the still visible part of her face. She put her ear to the front door, listening for any movement in the hallway. When she didn't hear anything, she peered through the peephole for a few minutes, staring at a blank wall. Finally, she inched the door open and stuck her head out into the hallway, looking left toward the former meth lab turned apartment of her former client, current fake boyfriend, and right toward the elevator. Everything was quiet, still.

She hurried down the hall and pressed the button to call the elevator a dozen times in quick succession. But she gave up waiting after barely thirty seconds and decided to take the stairs instead. She couldn't risk being in one place for too long or she might run into him. And since she wasn't sure if running into him would be a good thing or not, she thought it best to avoid him altogether. Out on the street, she pushed her sunglasses further up the bridge of her nose and walked briskly, eyes alert, to the grocery store. This was what her life had become over the past few days. Every time she left her apartment, she felt exposed, as if Kenny was hiding behind every shrub or around every corner.

When she'd agreed to help set a trap for this Albanian criminal, Maya had admittedly not thought it entirely through. She'd been so focused on watching her debt shrink and her credit score rise and all of the ways that would make her life – and Jerome and Kaya's lives, by extension – easier. She'd been thinking about the benefits in the far future and forgot to consider all she'd have to endure to get there. She ducked into the storefront of a closed design firm when she spotted a man walking out of a coffee shop across the street who kind of resembled Kenny. She lowered her sunglasses, squinted – made a mental note to go see her optometrist, geez – and realized that it wasn't actually him.

Normally, Maya was anal about thinking through all of the possibilities, but not this time. Of course she knew why she'd rushed past all of the particulars, even if she couldn't bring herself to admit it. But if she'd thought about what it would be like to be so close to someone she'd spent six months slowly opening up to – even though she knew she absolutely shouldn't – she'd have said no. If she'd given even a scrap of consideration to the perils of finally having the object of her internet affections reclining on her bed, a steely presence blanketing her barely clothed body and what that would do to her, she absolutely would have declined. But she'd said yes. Because she hadn't wanted the first and last time she saw Kenny to be red-faced and spluttering at her front door.

Although now she was holed up in her apartment feeling like a prisoner, terrified that the next time she saw him she wouldn't be able to deny her own desires. And he didn't deserve that. He didn't deserve to know how badly she wanted him still. He certainly didn't deserve to be forgiven even if her heart was pleading his case with every beat and her pussy was trying desperately to remind her of the way his dick had looked the one time she'd seen it, hard and angry. For her.

She exhaled as she entered the grocery store, feeling some relief that she'd made it to her destination with only the one close call. Relief that was quickly overtaken by annoyance. She'd forgotten her damn shopping list.

She spent the next twenty minutes trying – and failing – to remember what she'd come to the grocery store to get and then buying random things she passed that looked good instead. By the time her handcart was full of maybe one thing she absolutely needed, dish soap, and five things she definitely knew she didn't, including her favorite peach gummy candies and a paperback mystery she maybe already owned, she was more annoyed than when she'd arrived. She walked to the self-checkout line with a frown on her face.

The frown only deepened when she saw Kenny at one of the checkout lanes. She knew it was him, poor eyesight and all. She'd known him in person less than a week but she'd apparently seared his body into her brain so thoroughly that she'd recognize his broad shoulders and back that tapered into a lean waist, with a nice high, firm ass anywhere. Also the back of his head was cute. Or whatever.

She rolled her eyes and turned her back to him, hoping that he would pay for his – she peeked around him to see – bananas, energy drinks and brown rice, and leave without noticing her. She only let herself turn his way again once she'd scanned, bagged and paid for all of her items. She exhaled happily. He was nowhere in sight. She let her body relax as she walked out of the store, deciding that she could go without her sunglasses on the way home. Since it was actually a pretty gray day.

Just outside the grocery store's exit, she jumped in surprise.

"Do you need a hand?" His voice was deep and rich and, when she turned to face him, she was very unhappy to see that he hadn't shaved since Tuesday and his thicker facial hair was even sexier than it had been when they first met.

She exhaled angrily and gave up, extending her arms and her reusable bags to him. He took them both in one hand as if they weighed nothing, and given the size of his biceps they probably did.

He gestured toward her – their – route home, indicating that he would follow.

She squinted at him. "Don't look at my ass?" She'd meant it as a joke to alleviate her surprise and frustration and anger and lust.

But he moved his gaze slowly down her body and then back up to her face. "Whatever you want."

It was in that moment that Maya became sure of three things:

1. She wanted more money for this operation. She'd call it emotional hazard pay.
2. She needed to fuck Kenny soon. There was no way around it as far as she could see. It just had to be done, hard and fast and preferably all night long.
3. He'd still have to work for it.

She only thought of the fourth thing as they began walking toward their apartment building, his silent presence to her right, between her and the street, his eyes darting about, watching for threats. It was a devastating realization:

1. She really could have fallen in love with him.

KENNY DIDN'T KNOW Maya's schedule in the real world. He'd only done digital surveillance. So while he had a very good picture of her general nighttime routine from about 9pm until 3am, he had no idea what she did all day. And he was desperate for all of those details now that she lived just down the hall and he'd endured a frustrating Thursday night without her for the first time in months.

He'd spent the past three days trying not to pore over every millisecond from Tuesday night. He woke up just before sunrise as usual and went for a run, using his regular workout to canvas the neighborhood and get a feel for its character so he would have some baseline should a threat become apparent. Standard undercover protocol. He usually returned from his run and walked by Maya's door – with either a longing look or a determined forward stare, depending on his mood – just after Chanté got off her late shift at the local strip club. She was a featured dancer on a special, extended engagement; her usual cover. They ate breakfast and talked – about everything but the mission and Maya – before she started yawning and headed off to bed. He used that as his own cue to shower, change and head into the office – passing by Maya's apartment door one more time.

No matter how many times he came and went, he never saw her and only ran into Kierra twice; once in passing in the hallway after a run and once in Command while Lane and Monica were meeting with an asset offsite. It took him a couple of days, but he accepted that chances were incredibly high that she was avoiding him.

So when he saw her in the grocery store, chewing her bottom lip, deep in thought, as she absently swiped a box of gluten free pasta from a shelf, he'd had to take a few deep breaths in the breakfast aisle to calm his nerves. He considered – really considered – shadowing her around the grocery store. But as soon as the thought formed fully in his mind, he heard Chanté's voice in his head screaming "STALKER." And considering how they'd met and the hurt in her eyes when he'd revealed his online identity, he'd abandoned that dumb idea as quickly as it formed.

He'd headed to the self-checkout hoping to slip out of the store before she noticed him. Even when he turned to see her bagging her own groceries just a few machines away, he thought he could leave, take the long route home and spare her the confrontation she clearly didn't want. But back on the street he'd been unable to leave. He found himself rooted to the spot just to the right of the exit until she appeared.

"Do you need a hand?" he asked, legitimately shocked that his voice sounded strong and sure when his insides felt like jelly.

"Don't look at my ass," she said and he couldn't help but look her over. It had been so long since he'd seen her, actually these past three days had been the longest time in months. Her plain outfit was clearly an attempt to hide – from him – but there wasn't anything she could wear that would ever hide how beautiful she was from him. He would have noticed her in any crowd. He wondered if she realized that the leggings only accentuated her thick thighs and strong calves and delicate ankles. And while the shirt covered her butt, it also accentuated the shelf of her hips and nothing she wore would ever take away from how truly beautiful her breasts were. And even with the large sunglasses, currently perched on top of her head, Maya's face was beautiful, round, full, soft cheeks, plump lips, and her perfectly arched eyebrows that scrutinized and judged him and everything around him with a graceful lift. She was perfect.

"Whatever you want," he said. Her ass was wonderful, but not nearly the best part of her. Not by a long shot.

It was only a few blocks back to their apartment building. They walked in silence until Maya stopped him and rooted around in one of the bags he carried for her. She pulled out a small bag of gummy candy, ripped it open, and popped one into her mouth.

"These are my favorite candies when I'm stressed," she

said. Her jaw froze and he knew she wished she hadn't said that.

He could have pretended not to have heard her and let her off the hook, but he didn't. "I've never had 'em," he said. "I don't eat candy."

She stopped and turned toward him. "Say what now?"

He shrugged, "My parents didn't believe in candy."

"Who doesn't believe in candy? Candy is," Maya said in shock.

Kenny smiled. "They were both in the Army. They believed in balanced meals and no empty calories. No snacking. No candy."

"I-"

Kenny's smile widened and he chuckled at Maya actually at a loss for words. He'd never seen that before.

She shook her head and dug into the bag. "Can't have that," she mumbled to herself and then raised her hand to his mouth.

His eyes went wide but he opened his mouth to her automatically. He assumed she'd toss the piece of candy in when she reached a close distance, but she didn't. Her hand kept moving until she was placing the piece of candy directly onto his tongue, her fingers just grazing his lips. Kenny should have stopped there. He should have considered this a win he didn't deserve and couldn't have fathomed. Because it was. But he pushed his luck and closed his mouth to suck on her fingers as she slowly pulled her hand away.

She watched him chew on the candy as he watched her absentmindedly reach back into the bag, pull out another piece and slip it into her mouth. He wondered if she even realized she sucked on the same fingers he'd had in his mouth.

They both swallowed.

"So, what do you think?" she asked, her eyes still focused on his mouth.

He grimaced, "Too sweet for me."

She rolled her eyes and turned to continue walking. “No accounting for terrible taste,” she said, annoyed.

He walked beside her, closer than he had been, and leaned down to whisper into her ear. “Your fingers were the perfect amount of sweet though,” he said with a smile.

She didn’t turn to look at him, but he could see the grin on her face. “You don’t even know the half of it.”

He gulped and they walked the rest of the way in silence. Leave it to Maya to seduce him better than he could have ever seduced her.

seven

Kenny was trying to focus on Chanté's presentation but he couldn't. His left leg was jumping, he was gripping one hand in the other and his eyes kept drifting to the clock on the wall to his right. Every time he checked the time he made eye contact with Lane, who seemed to have one eyebrow permanently lifted to mock him, as if he knew what Kenny was thinking.

It was Sunday.

After running into her yesterday morning at the grocery store, she'd taken an even stronger grip on his thoughts. When they'd reached her apartment, she'd unlocked her door, grabbed her bags from him and slipped inside with a softly whispered "thanks." He'd gone straight down the hall and stroked himself furiously to a much-needed release, calling up every mental image he'd ever stored of her clothed and naked. But he only came when he remembered the feel of her fingers in his mouth. It was so pathetic.

For the past day, he'd felt restless, counting down the minutes until he could see her again. This morning he'd woken up, gone for his regular jog around the neighborhood, showered and dressed, the entire time consumed with that same feeling of anticipation that used to be reserved for Thursdays. Because he was going to see Maya today; not by accident and for longer than a walk from the grocery store.

She had a broadcast tonight. *They* had a broadcast tonight.

"Okay," Chanté's high-pitched voice cut through his mental meanderings. "Now that we're done with the boring stuff, let's get to the good shit."

"Great. You hear that, Kenny?" Lane said in a mocking tone.

Kenny refused to give him the satisfaction of acknowledgement.

Chanté smiled at him. "Don't worry, Kenny, I'll have you out of here in plenty of time."

"Let's stay on track," Monica said and Kenny was grateful for that, but he refused to look her way either. He was still too worried to face her. He was holding out hope that if he just didn't rock the boat or break any new rules then maybe she might still want to train him.

"Yes, ma'am," Chanté said in her standard purr. "So I've gone through all of the profiles we flagged during the broadcast."

Kenny felt everyone's eyes momentarily shift to him. His skin warmed and his dick twitched as he remembered Maya's smell, the sound of her moaning, that flash of pink. He refused to shift in his seat.

"We flagged twenty accounts," she tapped the smart screen and some ChatBot profiles appeared. Kenny recognized a few of the avatars as regular visitors to Maya's chatroom. "I discarded fifteen," Chanté said, tapping the screen to fill with the remaining five profiles. Kenny didn't recognize any of them.

He told them so.

Chanté nodded, "I figured. These two profiles had never visited Maya before." Kenny tried not to let his pride in Maya pulling in two new viewers show. "These three however have visited Maya's room sporadically. I crosschecked their viewer histories with Joseph Mehmeti's."

"And?" Kenny asked.

"Nothing. Sorry."

"Fuck," he breathed.

"But don't worry. You guys aren't paying me the big money for nothing," Chanté smiled. "I actually recorded the chat." She turned to Kenny and put her palms up. "Just the chat. Don't worry."

He blushed.

"Okay, so I went back through and I noticed that at the exact same time Joseph joined the room, two other users joined as well." She tapped the screen and Joseph's ChatBot profile popped up alongside two others. "Coincidence? Maybe. But I checked those accounts and guess what I found?"

"Chanté," Kenny warned.

She exhaled loudly, "Don't try and change me, Ken Doll. I like a bit of flair."

"A bit?" Monica deadpanned.

Chanté preened. Lane laughed. Kenny rolled his eyes.

"*Any. Way,*" Chanté said. "What I found is that those two accounts follow Joseph into every chatroom and have for the past four months. So I tracked their IP addresses which – if I can say was far easier than it should have been."

"Fucking idiots," Lane murmured with a shake of his head.

"Agreed. So anyway," she tapped the screen a final time and the two ChatBot profiles dissolved into mugshots and what looked like a precis of FBI dossiers.

"Well I'll be damned," Lane said as he and Monica leaned forward to scan the information in front of them.

Kenny couldn't help but smile as he did the same.

"Well, come on," Chanté said, and Kenny knew she was talking to him.

He turned to her and smiled brighter. "You did great," he said. Chanté clapped her hands together and blushed.

"Aaron and Malcolm Setter," Monica read.

"They're part of a fringe branch of the West Virginia Klan. They call themselves the Pendleton Patriots."

Lane scoffed.

"They've been under surveillance at least twice by the FBI in the past five years. But Pendleton County has a population of less than 10,000 and the city – which is a generous word in this instance – where they're based is so small, outsiders stick out like a dozen sore thumbs. So they manage to fly just under the radar and the Feds haven't been able to pin anything on them yet."

"Then how did they get in contact with a member of an Albanian criminal syndicate?" Monica demanded of all of them, not just Chanté.

"I don't know," Chanté said, a small quiver in her voice. "I'm pulling what information I can from the brothers' online profiles and banking records for them and their club. They have to be hiding money if they're brokering deals with the Mehmeti family. I'll find what I can."

"And I have a contact in the ATF," Kenny said. Monica turned to him with a raised eyebrow. "I'll see what he can give us."

She nodded and turned to Lane. He smirked at his wife. "I'll just sit here and look pretty while the young ones do all the work."

Kenny thought he saw Monica almost smirk, frown and then settle her mouth back to the hard line she normally wore. If she was going to say anything, the door opening behind them cut off her words. Kierra and Maya stood in the doorway and Kenny couldn't be one hundred percent sure but Kierra seemed like she was about to wreak havoc.

MAYA WOULD HAVE LIKED to have driven to Monica and Lane's house because Kierra was a terrible driver when she was angry. But Maya didn't know the route and Kierra didn't want to waste time giving her directions. So, she'd clenched her fists around her seatbelt praying to every god she could think of to let them make it there in two whole pieces. She'd had to run after a very determined Kierra through the kitchen, into the pantry and down to Command.

"I'm going to kill them," she muttered to herself – or Maya, it was unclear – just before she threw open the door to the briefing room.

"Hi, hello. Sorry we're late to the briefing you never told me about," she blurted out in a hard tone. "What'd we miss?"

"Well, good afternoon to you, too, sweet girl."

Kierra held up a hand. Lane quirked an eyebrow at her, his amusement at her temper evident. Maya didn't need to see Kierra's face to know she had focused all of her attention on Monica. Maya had been playing with a theory – when she was trying to distract herself from thinking about Kenny's mouth wrapped around her fingers – that every time Kierra had a problem, she laid it at Monica's feet. Lane might have been loud, and Kierra might have had them trailing after her like she was a piece of rare meat, but clearly whatever ship they were on was being steered by Monica.

"Hi Kierra. Hi Maya," Chanté said from the front of the room, with an excited wave.

Maya stepped from behind Kierra and waved back. "Hey girl. I love your hair like that," she said gesturing at the two cornrows on either side of Chanté's head that she'd accented with small metal baubles.

"Thanks! I like your dress," Chanté grinned as she ran a hand over her hairstyle lightly.

And Maya, shameless lover of compliments, grabbed the skirt of her dress and spread it out to best show off the geometric pattern.

"Don't you think that dress is so pretty on her, Kenny?" Chanté asked.

Maya's eyes crashed into Kenny's for the first time in just over a day. And like he had then, his eyes boldly drank her in.

"Beautiful," he whispered, more to himself than to Chanté or Maya.

She gulped.

"We need the room," Monica announced.

"No," Kierra said. "Let's keep going. We're smart. We'll catch up."

"Like I said, we need the room."

"Yep," Chanté and Kenny said in unison. Kenny jumped from his seat and moved aside to let Chanté walk past him and exit first.

Chanté whispered "sorry girl" to Kierra as she slipped out of the room.

Kenny stopped next to Kierra but looked across her to Maya. "You should come with me," he said matter-of-factly.

And maybe if he'd said 'us' she might have said no. Or if Kierra had been able to tear her eyes away from Monica, she might have had a reason not to say, "Okay," in a soft voice that seemed to make Kenny's jaw tick, which made her own pulse race.

THERE WAS an air of finality that Maya accepted as she walked into the hallway. She heard the briefing room door close and felt the vibration of Kenny's steps as he followed her into the foyer. Awareness of his body radiated from the soles of her feet, up her legs, swirled in her sex and made her nipples and scalp tingle.

Chanté met them in the foyer.

"Oh man, that's gonna be epic," she said, pointing toward the briefing room. "Wish I could see it." And then she tilted her chin up and looked at the ceiling. "Well, I could hack into the security feeds," she said but shook her head quickly. "Invasion of privacy. Not my forte. Well, unless I'm being paid. Or checking in on Asif? So um, does that mean we're done here?" She asked Kenny, who was standing just behind Maya.

He moved closer, his body still partially behind hers, their arms almost touching. "Yeah, probably."

"Okay good, I've got a shift at the club later and I need to go home and pick out my gear."

She turned to Maya, a big smile on her face. "You should come see me dance," she exclaimed.

Kenny cleared his throat.

"Maybe. We'll see. I'll let you know," she said and backed away hastily. At the top of the stairs she turned, "You two have fun." And then she was gone and it was just the two of them in the foyer. Maya could feel Kenny's body heat where they almost touched. Hear her own ragged breaths. She scrunched her nose. "Is that room soundproof?"

"Yes," he replied.

She turned to him, "Where's your office?"

He swallowed hard, which made Maya feel powerful. But she jumped as his hand settled on the curve of her back. That touch made her feel vulnerable in the best way possible. He steered her to the other side of the foyer, down a hallway.

She wasn't sure how many doors they passed, her entire attention was taken up by the heavy presence of Kenny's hand on her, the heat of it searing through her thin dress. At the end of the hall, he reached around her to push open a door. She crossed the threshold and stood in the center of the basically empty room. When the door closed behind them, she closed her eyes and sucked her bottom lip into her mouth. She listened to the sound of his slow steps across the room and around to her front. She knew where he was primarily by the way the hairs on her arms stood on end and moved to follow his body.

"Maya," he whispered.

She opened her eyes. He was so close.

"Tell me," she said, not even sure herself what she was asking him.

"Chanté identified two of Joseph Mehmeti's associates in your chatroom on Tuesday. They're members of a white supremacist gang from West Virginia."

Maya inhaled sharply.

Kenny's hands lifted but stopped just before they touched her. The part of her brain that wasn't consumed with fear was gleeful at the simple question in that gesture. She nodded. He ran his hands up and down her arms. "We think they're Joseph's US brokers but don't know for sure. We still need to gather more information. No one's going to get near you while I'm around."

She looked up at him through her eyelashes. They stood there, staring at one another, their breaths mingling. "This is so fucking dramatic," she said.

They smiled.

"I laid it on a bit thick. I'm sorry."

She swiveled her head to take in the room. "There's nothing in here," she said. She wished she hadn't said it when his face went from bright and open to wary and his hands fell away.

He shrugged. "I just got here. Haven't moved in yet. Maybe I…" He didn't finish the sentence.

She nodded.

"I know you don't want me to apologize anymore. But I really am sorry, Maya."

She pursed her lips together and pulled a slow breath of air in through her nose. She exhaled loudly, but whispered. "Were you really never going to tell me who you were?"

He scrubbed his hands over the crown of his head and turned away from her. She licked her lips, realizing she wanted to rub her hands over his head in that way, to run her fingertips across his lips, over his chin and down along the column of his neck. She wanted to be as near to him as she could get.

When he turned back toward her, he grasped his hands together in front of his chest and shook his head. "Never," he admitted.

Maya hadn't realized how much she'd been hoping for the fairytale answer. She wanted to hear that at some point he would have broken down under the weight of his deception and told her who he was. Hearing that that would never have happened hurt, much more than it should have for a man who was, until recently, just a blank gray avatar.

"I wish I could give you a different answer. But if I'd tried to tell you who I was without being able to tell you what I did," he grimaced and shrugged. "I would have had to lie to you forever. And lying to you for the past six months has fucking sucked."

Maya scraped her teeth over her bottom lip.

"You know I can tell your mood by how you chew your lip?"

Her eyes widened. She smiled. "What mood was that?"

Kenny's eyes lit up. "You're hurt, pissed." There was a long pause. Maya knew there was more coming, she waited with bated breath. "And horny."

Maya smiled her best, dirty smile at him. "Assuming you're right," she said, even though he was absolutely correct. "That doesn't mean that I've forgiven you."

"Good," he said, walking toward her with slow steps. "You should make me work for it."

Maya couldn't stop the breathy sigh that left her lips. Of course he would say something like that. The exact thing she'd been thinking since yesterday. MasquerAsiaN had always known the perfect words to dig right under her skin and stroke her into an excited frenzy. Oh, she thought, that's an idea.

She lifted her best eyebrow at him, "Work for it?"

He was right in front of her now. Their chests almost touching. She could smell the clean, barely-there scent of his cologne. "Just tell me what you want."

She lifted her chin, and her lips fell apart in a soft gasp that purposefully drew his eyes directly to her mouth. What she wanted was for him not to have lied to her for six months. What she wanted was for them to have met at some café or at a trendy, overpriced wine bar. But Maya's mother had raised her to be a practical woman who took control of her life even when everything seemed decidedly out of control. And wishing that she could change the past was an impractical endeavor that would lead nowhere, she had to deal with the here and now of reality. Or, she thought to herself, she had to make reality look like her fantasies. And she'd once had a very detailed dream about MasquerAsiaN that she could absolutely turn into reality. Correction, *they* could turn that fantasy into reality.

"You once told me you'd give your right arm to taste me," she said in a sultry whisper.

Kenny's face reddened. He stepped around her and walked to the door. Her head swiveled. She watched him turn the lock.

When he turned back toward her, it was Maya's turn to gulp. MasquerAsiaN had always seemed restrained, nowhere near desperate. He was precise and filthy directions accompanied by the sweetest compliments. But Kenny was reddened cheeks and broad shoulders, a tall strong body full of pent up energy. And he was currently looking at her as if he wanted to expend every ounce of that energy on her.

He stalked toward her, "I did say that. And I meant it."

Maya grinned at him and walked to his empty desk. He followed her, heat nipping at the backs of her thighs. She turned and her legs hit the cool metal, a nervous giggle slipped from her lips. "Seems extreme."

He leaned forward, the tips of his fingers touching the

hem of her dress. His perfectly manicured nails scraped up her thighs, taking her dress with it.

She moaned, wanting to scream that he was touching her, FINALLY. She put her hands on his shoulders and leaned into him for support. His hands moved around her body and cupped her ass. She gasped as he gripped her harshly and lifted her onto the desk. And then he lowered his long body to his knees, folded her dress up to her waist neatly and smiled up at her.

"I already know you're worth it."

KENNY WAS a serious child who had grown to be a practical man. He valued order and stability and had never willingly broken a rule in his life. Sure, Chanté had dragged him through a few ROTC infractions, but he'd rationalized those moments as necessary to keep her out of too much trouble. But then he'd stumbled into ThickaThanASnicka's cam room and never looked back as he hurtled through one ethics violation after another.

As he pushed Maya's thighs apart, rubbing his palms across the expanse of her smooth brown skin, he accepted that oral sex with an asset in his Agency office was just one more violation and he absolutely did not care. He groaned when the flash of her black underwear came into view. He put his hands underneath her knees to lift and spread her legs, exposing her panty-covered sex to his gaze. His eyes were glued to the apex of her thighs as her hand slid into view.

She rubbed her fingers up and down her crotch before peeling her panties to the side. Slowly. She ran one finger across her lips, small flashes of pink making his mouth water. He wanted to move her hand to the side and replace it with his mouth. But when he raised his eyes to look at Maya, her bottom lip was back between her teeth and her eyes were playful as she watched him.

She wanted him to wait.

So he did. He sat back on his heels and ran his thumbs along the sensitive spot on the inside of her knees. When she gasped, his eyes flew back to her pussy to watch her middle finger slide inside her sex, in and out as his mouth watered. When she had his full attention, she raised her hand to his lips, smearing her taste onto his mouth. He opened his mouth and she slipped her finger inside. He sucked her essence from her skin, wrapping his tongue around her digit.

"So what do you think?" Her voice was low, husky. He'd never heard her sound so turned on.

He hollowed his mouth around her finger, not wanting to miss a drop of her. He knew what she wanted to hear. Not that bullshit about her tasting sweet or like fruit or better than the candy she'd fed him yesterday. She wanted to hear that her pussy tasted slightly tangy, with a hint of salt and bright, and that he loved every note of her. But when she pulled her hand away he licked his lips and said, "I can't be sure just yet."

She didn't try to stop the smile from spreading across her lips. She moved her panties to the side again. "Well go ahead then."

Kenny had literally been waiting months for this. He didn't need to be told twice. He lowered his head between her legs, swiping his tongue up her slit to slowly circle her clit. When he sucked it into his mouth, Maya's hips bucked and he moved his hands up her thighs to grip her hips, keeping her in place.

She'd once told him exactly how she liked to be eaten, in excruciating detail, while he'd slowly stroked himself to a shuddering climax that left him gasping for breath, wishing he could call her name without it feeling weird. He remembered every detail of that chat and made sure he gave her everything she'd said she wanted; lots of firm swipes of his tongue and sharp suction on her clit. His fingers dug into her soft flesh, massaging her muscles and keeping her pressed securely to his mouth, except for when he pulled back so she could hear the wet slurping of his mouth, her favorite sex sound apparently.

Her gentle gasps and moans became louder right before she fully reclined onto the desk murmuring "oh fuck" and "shit" and "oh my god" like chants. Her thighs shook, starting with those gentle quakes he'd first seen on Tuesday and graduating to the violent spasms he was more familiar with. When she was close, one of her hands pressed against the back of his skull and her thighs clamped around his head. He pressed his mouth firmly against her sex, sucking intently on her clit. He was completely surrounded by her scent and her big, strong legs and the gentle encouragement of her hand.

He was so engulfed by her that he almost didn't hear the actual thing he'd been waiting all these months for. "Kenny," she screamed, as she came in a wet gush all over his face.

a brief debrief

Monica took several calming breaths and waited for everyone else to leave the briefing room. When Kenny lightly shut the door behind them, she finally spoke. "Are we going to have the same fight every day of this mission?"

Kierra shrugged, "Depends. Are you going to continue keeping me out of the loop?"

"If the loop is above your pay grade, yes."

Monica watched Kierra's nostrils flare.

"We can't keep having the same discussion over and over again, sweet girl," Lane said, trying to placate her with a gentle tone. "We handled this already."

"I thought we did and then you moved Kenny and Chanté in across the hall without telling me," she said, her hard eyes focused on Lane, but only for a second. She turned to Monica. "Was that information above my pay grade as well?"

"We forgot," Monica said.

"Bullshit."

"Well actually, I know it's hard to believe, but we really were going to tell you about that," Lane interjected.

Kierra raised both of her eyebrows at him. He stood from

his chair and put his hands out. "Hear me out. We went over to your apartment yesterday. Very professional like."

Kierra scoffed.

"And what were you wearing when you answered the door, Kierra?" He put a strong accusatory emphasis on her name.

She scoffed again but averted her eyes. Lane moved behind Monica's chair and began to massage her tense shoulders, trying to reassure her through touch that he could handle this. He could handle her. Which Monica knew was bullshit. No one could handle Kierra, unless she wanted to be handled. It was one of the many things they loved about her.

"I was washing clothes," Kierra said in a much smaller voice than when she'd stormed into the room. "I didn't have anything else to wear."

It was Lane's turn to scoff. "Try again."

She finally looked at them, her eyes skittering over Monica's face before lifting to Lane's.

Monica sighed. She had to remind herself that even though they'd spent three years pining after one another, they'd actually only been together for a few months. And while it would be easy and fun to react every time Kierra was put out with them, it wouldn't lead them anywhere but apart. They were still testing the boundaries of their relationship and working together made it hard to keep everything separate.

Monica patted Lane's hands. He stopped massaging her and backed away. She stood, her eyes trained on Kierra, whose entire body was taut with tension. The good kind.

"Come here, sweet girl," Monica demanded.

She pressed her lips together trying to hide the smile that clearly wanted to spread across her face.

When she was standing in front of them Monica asked her, "Are we still not allowed to touch you?"

Lane and Monica watched her internal battle flit across her face before she sighed. "Okay, maybe you were right about me not being able to do that every time I'm mad at you."

Lane nodded, "You should save it for when you're happy or you want something expensive."

She smiled at him and turned to Monica. "Go on. Touch me."

Lane grunted.

Monica resisted the urge to shake her head. It was the middle of the workday. They had the absolute worst timing; always hot and bothered at the most inopportune moments. She extended her hand and placed her fingers softly on Kierra's bare right shoulder, exposed by her loose t-shirt. She ran her thumb along just a bit of Kierra's collarbone.

"We need boundaries," Monica said.

Lane grunted again and snaked a hand around Monica's waist.

"We've been very lax about what we allow in the office. And that was fine when you were just our PA." She thought about that and corrected. "Actually, that was a bad idea then as well. But now it's even worse." Monica's thumb was skimming up Kierra's neck.

"What's the difference?" she asked in a breathy whisper.

"The difference is, before we thought this was all we had. Innocent flirting in the office."

"Innocent?" Lane asked, his mouth close to Monica's ear.

"Innocent for us," she corrected, tracing along Kierra's jaw. "But we don't have to play in the office anymore."

Kierra's eyes had been slowly clouding with lust, her gaze centered on Monica's breasts through her t-shirt. But her vision cleared and she squinted her eyes at Monica.

Monica moved her free hand to Kierra's other shoulder and squeezed. "We don't have to *only* play in the office." She moved her thumb to the corner of Kierra's mouth.

Kierra nodded and parted her lips. Monica slid her thumb inside, touching the tip of Kierra's tongue.

"But we need to keep work and play separate."

"Although right now that's a bit hard since your roommate is assisting us by getting herself off on our new recruit," Lane conceded.

"But all of our operations won't be like this," Monica replied. "So we need to do our best to keep all of *this*," she said, punctuating the word by pressing her thumb further into Kierra's mouth, "outside of Command as much as possible."

Kierra's tongue swirled around Monica's digit, she closed her lips and sucked.

"Besides," Monica continued, moving her other hand to Kierra's chest, grabbing her breast roughly through the thin material of her shirt. She raised an eyebrow when she realized that Kierra wasn't wearing a bra. Kierra sucked her finger harder and smiled. "Besides, just think of how wet you'll be at the end of the work day."

Lane sucked Monica's earlobe into his mouth as Monica circled Kierra's hard nipple with her thumb.

"So do we have a deal?" Monica began to slowly pull her thumb from Kierra's mouth. Kierra let her teeth grate lightly across her skin and smiled. Lane started chuckling into Monica's ear. Monica sighed. They both knew what was coming.

"Tell me what my clearance allows."

"We think Joseph Mehmeti is working with a group of US white supremacists. Chanté has leads."

"Maya wants more money."

"Not unless we need her in the field."

"Do I have to dress more professionally from now on?"

Lane answered before Monica could open her mouth, "Not unless you're looking to get fired."

Kierra's smile widened. She moved to press her chest to Monica's. "Then we have a deal," she said and grasped Monica's hips. She kissed her, rough with teeth, just the way Lane liked.

Monica held the sides of Kierra's face, letting her take

control for a moment, before pulling back and kissing her gently, suckling on Kierra's tongue slowly, rhythmically, never missing the chance to remind her that that was how she would suck Kierra's clit when she got the chance.

Lane's hands began to wander and Monica wanted to let them. She wanted to slip Kierra's clothes off and lay her on the conference table so she and Lane could make up for the time they'd been apart. But she was leading this operation and if she let it happen this time, they'd just cross the boundaries they'd just set as soon as possible and be in the exact same position tomorrow.

She pulled back from Kierra's mouth. Kierra whimpered at the lost contact. Their foreheads rested against one another's.

"Spend the night?" Lane asked.

Kierra nodded.

It still took a few minutes to disentangle their limbs. As they walked into the foyer Kenny and Maya were walking down the other hall toward them.

Maya smoothed her shaky hands down her dress repeatedly and Kenny swiped at his mouth. Monica wondered if they could be more obvious but decided to keep quiet because glass houses and all that.

"Everything all right?" Lane asked, because he'd never met an awkward moment he didn't want to run right in the middle of.

Kenny's cheeks flushed. But Maya squared her shoulders – which coincidentally only accentuated how hard her nipples were – and responded, "Everything's fine. Mind your business."

Lane huffed a laugh and turned to Monica, "If we need her in the field, I want *her* on my squad."

"Over my dead body," Kenny spat.

"This is like a trashy soap opera porn parody," Kierra laughed.

"I'd watch it," Maya nodded, trying to pretend as if she weren't looking at Kenny in her peripheral vision.

Monica rolled her eyes and turned to walk toward her office. After two steps everyone turned to her for orders. She sighed.

"Kenny, talk to your ATF source. Lane, we need a spoof protocol."

"What's that?" Maya asked.

"I'll tell you later," Kierra said out of the side of her mouth.

"Kierra, take Maya home. She has a broadcast to prepare for tonight." Monica ignored the shy looks Maya and Kenny turned toward each other. "And then you need to get back here."

"Yes, ma'am," Kierra replied. Monica nodded. That was the only time Kierra had ever said those words in a way that *didn't* sound obscene.

They were all still, staring at her.

"Go," she barked and everyone hopped to.

She was almost out of the foyer when she heard Maya whisper to Kierra.

"Jesus, that was hot as fuck."

"Mmmmmm," was Kierra's only reply, a sound that was somewhere between agreement and a moan.

Monica shook her head and pushed her office door closed behind her. If they managed to pull this mission off with all of this mess, it would be a miracle.

Lane was sitting at his desk when there was a knock at the door.

Monica didn't knock and Kenny didn't come to him for anything. And besides, he'd know Kierra's gentle knock anywhere.

"Come in," he called.

Kierra pushed the door open. Lane lifted his eyes from the report he was reading. She'd changed. He almost missed the tight jeans, that peek of her shoulder and knowing that she wasn't wearing a bra. But his eyes raked over her breasts, which were sitting high and just a bit fuller than he knew they actually were, in a crisp white button-up. He smirked as he took in her hips in a very professional, if a little tight, navy pencil skirt. He leaned over his desk to admire a very high pair of red heels. Red was Lane's favorite color on Kierra.

"So, are you back to work?" he asked as he let his eyes wander up her body.

"Yes, sir," she said in a husky voice that got a rise out of him, his eyebrows and his dick.

"What can I do for you?"

She smiled and bit her bottom lip. He didn't know exactly where her mind had gone but he knew that he approved wholeheartedly.

"There's a briefing in the boardroom in five," she said. Again, very professionally.

"Five minutes isn't a lot of time."

She inched into his office and pushed the door shut behind her. He sat back in his chair and watched her walk toward him in those heels and that skirt. Up close he realized that her shirt was not complete opaque. He huffed out a laugh.

She walked around his desk and he turned his chair so she could see what she'd done to the front of his slacks. He spread his legs wide and she walked to stand between them. She flattened her hands down her hips and thighs and hiked up her skirt just an inch. Just enough to bend a knee and rest it gently along his dick. While he was focused on that gentle pressure she reached over his desk and pressed the speaker button on his office phone. He knew who she was calling before she dialed.

"Yes," Monica's voice said.

"I've told Kenny and Lane about the meeting," Kierra said.

There was a moment of silence where Lane knew that Monica was weighing this particular challenge. They'd literally just decided to not do this, but Kierra liked to push Monica's buttons. Hell, Lane liked to push Monica's buttons, but even he would have waited a day or two. God, he admired Kierra's style. They waited – their eyes locked on one another – for Monica's response.

"I'm going to give you a choice," Monica said.

Her voice was hard. She wasn't angry, she'd expected this. But she was making herself clear. She would give them no wiggle room in the rest of her sentence. Lane moved his hips slightly, pushing his dick against the weight of Kierra's knee. She licked her lips.

"You can skip the meeting and fuck each other in Lane's office," she said and Lane sure liked the sound of that. "But neither of you can touch me for the next week."

Kierra's frown matched his own.

"You don't mean that," Lane said, turning to stare at his phone as if he could see her face.

"Try me," she said and hung up.

Lane sighed as the pressure of Kierra's leg disappeared. His dick throbbed. He stood and pressed a kiss to her forehead. She frowned up at him. "It was a good try," he said, before grabbing her by the shoulders, turning her around and following her out into the hallway.

They stopped in the open doorway of Monica's office. Kierra crossed her arms over her chest and frowned, sullen, as they waited. She raised her head and though her mouth didn't move they could both see the smile in her eyes.

"Good choice," she said to them both. "You won't regret it."

He threw an arm over Kierra's shoulders and pulled her against his side. "We know."

"I checked in on my connect in the ATF," Kenny said, standing in front of them in the briefing room. "He's running an investigation on the Pendleton Patriots."

"What do they know?" Monica asked.

"I don't know," Kenny replied.

"Then what the fuck was the point of the phone call?" Lane asked, his voice tight with annoyance and pent up sexual frustration.

Kenny rolled his eyes and aimed his answer to Lane's question at Monica. "My contact is a good agent, great investigator. He keeps his info to himself and only shares with others when they need to know and if it benefits his investigation. I didn't call to get details, because he wouldn't have given any. I just confirmed that he's a resource we can tap into if we need it."

"Can't hurt to ask," Lane muttered.

Kenny wanted to reply but he didn't, because whatever he was about to say would have been disrespectful. And Kenny had a strict respect of authority and protocol. Usually. Monica had realized that when they'd first met at The Academy. It was admirable, but in their line of work, useless. It was one of the reasons she'd rebuffed his transfer requests before now.

But when she and Lane had realized less than a month ago that Kenny was breaking any number of rules and jeopardizing his career to maintain a fragile online relationship with Kierra's roommate, Monica had begun to see Kenny differently. An agent who was more beholden to the rules than the mission was the kind of agent Monica trusted, but didn't want to work with for any longer than necessary. But an agent who wore their failures on their sleeves was an agent Monica could train. Neither agent was necessarily better than the other. But Monica believed that because the latter agent had already fallen, she just had to teach them how not to make the same mistake twice. The agent who had yet to realize that they were all fallible and corruptible was dangerous. Those were the ones who fell the farthest and the hardest. And she couldn't risk Lane or Kierra to that.

"Who's your contact?" she asked Kenny.

He turned and tapped the screen. A picture of a bald Black man with a bright, wide smile filled the screen. His badge photo looked more like a modeling headshot than ATF identification.

"I'm very interested in this," Kierra said.

"I agree," Lane echoed.

Monica and Kenny ignored them.

"Agent Lamont White. He joined a local police force after college and was recruited into the ATF after just two years. He's a rising star in the Columbus office. He's also well-respected, thorough and honest."

"How do you know him?"

"I was assigned to infiltrate the ATF for an op on Green Dawn."

"Who?" Kierra asked and then slapped a hand over her own mouth.

Monica turned to her and raised an eyebrow. Kierra mimed zipping her mouth closed, locking it and throwing away the key.

Kenny continued. "Green Dawn was a radical environmental group with cells in Canada and the US. They were loosely connected to other radical environmentalist sects radicalized after another Gulf oil spill on '02. They decided to save the planet by any means necessary and started wholesale manufacturing and selling meth from Cincinnati up to Windsor and east to Toronto."

Lane whistled, "That sounds really stupid."

"I don't remember hearing anything about The Agency investigating Green Dawn," Monica said.

Kenny shrugged, "Technically we weren't. A little-known

fact about Green Dawn was that their leader, the Supreme Being Wayland Evans-"

"The what?" Lane laughed.

"Wayland?" Kierra snickered.

"Real name, Jeremy Porter," Kenny continued as if he hadn't been interrupted.

"You mean he chose the name Wayland?" Kierra screamed and then put her hands up in apology when Monica glared at her. "Sorry. But Wayland."

Kenny blew out a frustrated breath of air. "Can I continue?"

Monica sat back in her chair and nodded.

"Anyway, the Green Dawn leader was also running the Midwestern leg of a human trafficking ring."

"From the Mediterranean," Monica said, remembering this particular op.

Kenny nodded. "So, we were working the human trafficking angle as part of a multi-agency task force and the ATF were pursuing firearms charges since the group had been stockpiling weapons for years. But like I said, Agent White doesn't share and kept dribbling information to us as if he didn't understand what a task force was supposed to do," Kenny said with a chuckle. "In the end, the only way to get what we needed reliably was to embed me as his new partner. We worked together for six months. The DEA took down the meth ring, ATF got their firearms cache, FBI closed down the human trafficking pipeline and Jeremy Porter went into hiding. But by then we had one of our agents in his inner circle and a few months later we took Porter down, dismantling what was left of Green Dawn."

Monica nodded. Yes, there was so much more to Kenny than met the eye.

"So your former partner has intel we need. How do we get it?"

Kenny shrugged, "Lamont didn't take my transfer well."

"Explain," Lane said.

"I'd worked it so that after the meth bust I'd be transferred. But Lamont and I had become friends and he called and emailed me. I couldn't respond. My silence made him suspicious and he got nosy." Kenny smiled and shook his head. "It took a few months, but he figured out that I work for The Agency."

Monica raised an eyebrow. "That's interesting."

"Very," Lane echoed.

"I can go to Columbus, but it's probably a sixty percent chance that he'll shoot me and a ninety percent chance he'll ice me out."

"We can't send you anyway," Monica said, bringing her hand to her chin. "We need you with Maya."

Monica appreciated the effort Kenny took to keep his body still. His reddened face, however, betrayed that struggle.

"What about Asif?" Kenny offered.

Monica shook her head and turned in her chair to face Lane. Her husband exhaled loudly.

"Of fucking course. I always get the goddamn white supremacists," he breathed.

"We can send you in as a… Marshal?" Monica asked.

"FBI would be better," Lane corrected.

"Agreed," Kenny said, reluctantly.

"What's our goal here, boss?" Lane asked. "Am I just getting the intel or do I have expanded parameters?"

Monica considered Lane's question. As his wife, she wanted to say that this was just an info grab. As the person who would have to deal with Kierra when he left and, god forbid, in the event that an elegantly gray hair on his head was harmed, she wanted to send Asif instead. But as his supervisor, the person directing this mission, and the person who understood Lane's strengths and weaknesses and desire for action, she knew the answer.

Monica sat up straight, her eyes on his and nodded. "If

you see an opening, I'm authorizing a full-scale dismantling of the Pendleton Patriots, retrieval of anything having to do with the Mehmeti family and any other domestic and international partnerships."

The smile that spread across Lane's face was almost feral. He looked like that tanned, sweaty college junior all over again. A bit grayer, but no less devastating.

"Not to interrupt this moment, or whatever," Kenny said. "But what's the point of taking down the Patriots if Mehmeti is still out there?"

Monica turned to him with a frown, "Mehmeti is still our main objective. We need to get him into a private session with Maya so Chanté can try and hack his computer and we can finally trace his IP address."

"So what are you gonna do to make that happen?" Lane asked smugly.

Kierra's muffled laughter filled the quiet room as Kenny's blush spread across his cheeks and ears.

"Go home and get ready," Monica said to Kenny. "Meeting adjourned."

eight

"Mmmhmmm," Maya mumbled into her cell phone. "For real?"

She was talking to her little sister about… well she wasn't actually sure. The phone call had started as their weekly check-in, which Kaya preferred to terminate after about twenty minutes. Jerome liked to tell Maya nearly every detail about his life – although recently their hours long conversations tended to revolve almost exclusively around his Chem I lab partner. Jerome clearly had a crush on him, but he had yet to name it as such. But Kaya liked to give Maya the quick and dirty run down on her classes, the professors she hated ("all of 'em") and any notable highlights from her dating life ("the dude was trash but the wings at the dive bar downtown are the best I've ever had").

That was Kaya's usual pattern, but for some reason she wasn't sticking to it today. Their check-in was nearing an hour. Maya was trying to figure out how to gently nudge her sister toward getting to whatever she was tiptoeing around so she could get ready for tonight's broadcast before Kenny showed up. She exhaled a soft breath, her body beginning to warm just from thinking his name.

"What?"

"Hmmm? Nothing. Nothing," Maya said hastily, embarrassed that she'd actually given herself away so easily. "Girl, just say what you're trying not to say, please." She blurted the words out partially to change the subject, but also because she really did have a schedule to keep.

Kaya took a deep breath and exhaled right into the phone. Maya rolled her eyes.

"Okay, so I'm dating someone," Kaya said in a rushed whisper that Maya almost didn't hear.

"Huh?" Maya asked and turned the volume up on her phone. "Speak louder."

"Ugh," Kaya huffed. "I said I'm dating someone." She yelled the sentence directly into the phone. Maya pulled her own phone away from her ear and turned the volume back down.

"Why is that news? When aren't you dating someone?"

"Are you calling me a ho?"

Maya laughed. "The irony," she mumbled. "No, dumbass. I'm saying that your motto since you were seventeen and mom finally let you date was 'never waste a Friday night alone or pay for a meal'."

"My wisdom," Kaya deadpanned.

"So, what's special this time around?" Maya asked. There was a pause, the silence on the other end of the phone stretching and stretching. Maya pushed her worry about her schedule to the side, sat up in her bed and really focused on her sister.

"I don't know, I just… like them," Kaya finally replied in a soft voice. Maya knew she was smiling.

"Okay, that's good." She used her gentlest, encouraging voice, a poor imitation of her mother. "Is there something else you want to tell me?"

Maya was chewing on her bottom lip and she assumed her sister was doing the same. It was a family habit.

"Nope," Kaya said definitively. "That's it. Just… I like them, okay?" She tried to imbue her voice with its normal attitude, but Maya knew her sister's voice well enough to know that what she was actually asking was, "Are you going to judge me?"

"It's perfectly okay. I'm happy you're happy. And I look forward to meeting your bae."

Maya pressed her lips shut and hoped that Kaya absorbed those words.

"Ugh, you're old. 'Bae' is washed. Keep up," Kaya said, all traces of her previous vulnerability gone. "You're on the internet way too much to not know the terminology."

Maya rolled her eyes, "Shut up. But anyway, speaking of the internet, I have a broadcast I need to prepare for."

"Oh shit, my bad."

"Don't apologize. I always have time for you to tell me how played out I am."

"Washed," Kaya screeched. "Do I need to start sending you updates?"

Maya laughed. "Please do! Love you, Kai."

"Love you too, Mai."

Maya hung up the phone and fell back onto her bed. She tried not to wonder what her mother would have said to her little sister in this situation. She'd spent the first six months after her death second-guessing every decision she made – every hug, every dinner – because she knew her mother would have done it better. It had pushed her to the brink of a nervous breakdown. She tried instead to focus on what she thought she'd done right. She'd listened to Kaya. She made sure she understood that she loved her unconditionally. She left the door open for the future. That had to be enough.

Her phone beeped. It was a text message from Kierra.

Sleep over at Command.

MAYA SMILED.

Sounds dirty.
You and your boos back on the same page?

KIERRA SENT HER A WINKY EMOJI.

We're gonna be.

MAYA SENT HER AN EYE ROLLING EMOJI.

Don't rub it in, tiny terror.

THE CHAT BUBBLES POPPED up and disappeared twice before Kierra finally sent a message.

Ok don't kill me, but maybe give Kenny a chance?

MAYA TYPED 'NO' but her thumb hesitated before she could send it. Kierra sent another series of texts in the meantime.

He likes you.
You like him.

MAYA BLEW out a frustrated breath as she typed.

That's not enough. Doesn't fix anything.

KIERRA HAD CLEARLY BEEN EXPECTING that response.

Well whatever he did to you in his office had you smiling like the Cheshire cat on the way home so…

MAYA RESPONDED with her own winky emoji.

The man gives great head.

SHE WAS TRYING to change the subject. Again. But Kierra wasn't nearly as suggestible as Kaya.

I bet he does.
So was it just head or could there be something between you two?

MAYA CHEWED ON HER LIP.

idk
I really liked him when we were chatting online. But it was all lies.
I don't really know him.

KIERRA'S RESPONSE WAS QUICK. Maya knew she'd been waiting for just the right opening to give her two cents. She was actually surprised Kierra had been able to wait almost a week. It had to be a record for her.

Then get to know him.
You already have to get...close for the mission.

MAYA ROLLED her eyes as she typed.

Now is not the time for your corny jokes.

KIERRA SENT BACK A LAUGHING EMOJI.

You right. My bad.
Look I'm just saying, get to know him.

Maybe you like him.
Maybe you don't.
Maybe he has terrible taste in music.
Maybe he has a big dick.
Give love a chance.

MAYA SCRAPED her teeth along her lip.

I'm ignoring give love a chance.
You're compromised.

KIERRA TYPED.

Fair.

MAYA SENT A THINKING EMOJI.

Alright.
I'll give him a shot.
lbr I've been wanting to do that anyway.
Even when I was really pissed.

KIERRA SENT A TOOTHY SMILE EMOJI.

Really happy you're finally admitting that to yourself.

KIERRA SENT A BROWN FINGERS-CROSSED EMOJI.

Really hoping he likes to read and has a big dick.

MAYA SENT some laugh cry emojis.

He absolutely has a big dick.

KIERRA'S RESPONSE WAS IMMEDIATE.

WHAT?!!

MAYA LAUGHED to herself as she sent a brown peace sign before turning her phone off. She stood from her bed and walked into the bathroom. She looked at herself in the mirror and realized that corny as she was, Kierra was right. Even though he'd lied to her, directly and by omission, she could tell that what little he'd revealed about his personality had been the real deal. And while she had no idea if they had anything more than a few months of pent up sexual energy between them, she owed it to herself to find out for sure, because it had been years since anyone made her feel the way Kenny did. And she knew she'd regret it if she didn't see this through.

After two years as a cam model, Maya didn't get butterflies in her stomach much anymore; not since she'd discovered that so many men were terrifying. So when she felt the flurry of nerves hit her as she stepped out of the shower, she knew that it was all Kenny. And she decided to let herself lean into those feelings for once.

KENNY CAME HOME from Command and jumped straight into the shower. He wrapped his towel around his waist and walked back into his bedroom. His steps faltered when he noticed the clothes laid out on his bed.

He texted Chanté.

I don't need your help.

IT TOOK her a few minutes to respond. He assumed she was at the club, although he wasn't sure when her shift started. Or maybe it already had.

Yeah. You do.

HE WAS PACING the full length of their living room by this point, his stomach in knots.

It's not a date.

CHANTÉ SENT him an eye roll emoji.

Duh.
That's why I went for casual.
Don't forget cologne.

HE TYPED, deleted, and then typed a few replies, but didn't send any of them. He couldn't figure out how to express that this was business – for Maya and Lane and Monica, who he knew would be watching tonight's broadcast from Command. But he had finally admitted to himself while Maya was coming and shuddering on his tongue that he actually didn't give a shit about the mission. If it came down to having a real shot with Maya or keeping his career, she won.

He'd gone through the motions the rest of the day, touched base with his ATF contact, and even sat through another strategy session with Lane and Monica – with Kierra taking notes – for when Joseph finally made contact. But he'd done it all while wishing he was still back in his office on his knees for Maya. And how was he supposed to tell his best friend that? Apparently he'd waited so long Chanté figured it out on her own. She was good at that.

Too much silence.
Overthinking?

KENNY NODDED and then remembered to type.

Yes.

CHANTÉ CALLED him and he exhaled. This would be easier over the phone.

He accepted her call and put the phone to his ear. "Hello."

"Alright, so here's what I need you to do for me, Ken Doll. You're freaking out 'cause freaking out is what you do best."

"Chanté-"

"Shh, we don't have a lot of time. Accept that I'm right and let's move on."

Kenny gave her an angry grunt, but kept his mouth shut.

"You fucked yourself by lying to her. The only way to make this right is to demonstrate that you want to start over. You've gotta convince her that from here on out, you'll tell her nothing but the truth."

"And you think that'll work?"

There was a longer pause before Chanté answered him. He could tell by the sadness in her voice that she'd been thinking of Asif. "Positive."

"Chanté-," he started, but she cut him off again.

"Not right now, Kenny," she said in a weary voice that made him want to fly to wherever the fuck Asif was and shoot him in the arm. "Let's just focus on you, okay?"

He scrubbed a hand over his face and exhaled. "For now."

"Okay great," Chanté said, her bright tone returning. "So, put on the tank top, gray sweatpants and no underwear. And spray on that cologne I like, byeeee." She hung up before he could respond.

As Kenny walked back into his room he tried to clear his

mind. He pulled deep breaths in through his mouth and expelled air out of his nose as he pulled on a pair of briefs, regardless of what Chanté recommended, and sprayed himself lightly with the cologne Chanté liked – which was actually a scent Maya once told him she'd smelled in a store and loved.

He turned at a knock at his front door.

He should have taken the time to pull on at least a pair of pants. But he grabbed his gun from atop the dresser in his room instead and walked cautiously toward the door. When he looked through the peephole, Maya's face took his breath away. And then he realized that she was in her robe.

He wrenched open the door and pulled her inside.

"Hey," she whined.

He poked his head out and checked the hallway.

He slammed the door and turned on her. "What are you doing in the hallway in your robe?" She didn't answer him; her eyes were glued on the gun in his left hand, which was aimed safely at the floor. "Oh, sorry. I wasn't sure who was knocking," he said. He walked to the cheap dining table to his right and put the gun down carefully.

"And it might have been someone that you'd need a gun for." It wasn't a question. He could see her putting all of this together in her head. He liked to watch her think, he always had, even before their first private session. He knew she'd agreed to help them with this mission much too quickly; surely faster than he liked. There were things she wouldn't have had time to consider. And clearly the reality that there might be guns involved was one of them.

"I've never been around guns much," she admitted in a small voice.

He nodded. "I'll do my best to keep them away from you as much as I can."

She looked up at him and nodded, a ghost of a smile touching her lips.

"Why are you in the hallway in your robe, Maya?" he asked again in a gentler voice.

"I was getting ready. But I wanted to talk to you before the broadcast and I didn't have your number."

"Technically it's classified."

Her eyes widened. She opened her mouth, closed it and nodded.

"What do you need to talk about?"

She took a deep breath and shoved her hands into her robe's pockets. "About this afternoon. Well…" she started chewing her bottom lip and all he could feel was terror that she regretted it and the intense need to throw on his workout clothes and go for the longest run he could manage. "I don't know if I can forgive you for lying to me. But there's clearly something between us."

She seemed to be considering what to say next. She furrowed her brow in confusion and her mouth turned down into the cutest frown. It was also an expression he'd never seen on her face before, because when she was on camera she made sure *not* to frown. He drank it up and was speaking before he knew what to do with himself.

"Have dinner with me?" He said it in a rush and then pressed his lips together.

Her eyes shot to his and that frown became a gasp with the slightest upward tilt on the right side of her mouth. "Are you asking me on a date?" As she spoke her mouth lifted into a bright smile that took his breath away. He couldn't speak so he nodded instead.

She pulled just the corner of her bottom lip between her teeth and he gulped down the groan in his throat, which made her smile widen.

"Alright," she whispered.

He exhaled and smiled but ducked his head to hide it from her. "Don't," she said walking toward him. "I like the way you smile. I used to dream about what it would look like at night."

She stopped just shy of pressing her body to his, a shocked look on her face that she'd admitted that.

Kenny put one hand against her cheek, his thumb running across her smooth skin, something he'd always wanted to do. They stayed like that, staring at one another in the silent realization of a fantasy they'd apparently both had before. It was a beautiful moment and then it got better.

She pulled away from him and opened her robe. His mouth went dry. Maya was wearing another bodysuit. He hadn't known what to do with her outfit on Tuesday. He'd assumed it was a coincidence that she was wearing his favorite color and lace – a combination he'd made sure to tell her was sexy as fuck on her dozens of times. But he kept telling himself that it must have been an accident. Nothing else made sense.

But this bodysuit was not an accident. Because this bodysuit – orange, with a mix of leather and mesh, with lace accents – was his favorite. He'd told her that once and she'd never worn it in her public broadcasts or chat sessions again. She'd once gasped "only for you," while fucking herself into a stupor. Just for him.

This was no coincidence.

"Let's go get our rocks off on camera, shall we?" She posed one leg on the ball of her foot to show off the smooth brown skin of her inner thigh, bit her bottom lip and winked at him. "I might even let you touch me again."

He groaned as he felt his dick harden in his boxer briefs, which he only remembered in that moment was all he was wearing. Maya's eyes traveled down his body, amusement dancing in her gaze when they made eye contact again.

"Okay, let me just go finish getting dressed," he croaked.

The smile that spread across her face was wicked and dirty and fucking perfect.

"You're finished," she said decisively. She brushed past him, making sure that their shoulders touched. "Come on, babe." He happily followed her out into the hall and back to her apartment, half naked and deliriously happy.

KENNY WATCHED as Maya rifled through her basket of dildos and toys and lube for the third time. She'd already checked the angle of the camera at least four times – adjusting his position on the bed the tiniest bit each time to make sure that his face was hidden – and checked her laptop's connection to its charger twice.

"Are you always so obsessive about this?"

She looked up at him and smiled, a real genuine smile. "You only need to run out of lube once in the middle of a broadcast while trying to get the biggest dildo you own into your pussy before you learn that you can never be over-prepared," she replied.

He licked his lips and nodded. "Got it."

She crawled onto the bed and began to move toward him on her hands and knees. He didn't know where to rest his eyes, on her breasts or her mouth or her eyes.

Her eyes, sparkly and mischievous, won.

"Kenny," she moaned his name. Not like she'd moaned his name when she came earlier. That moan was unrestrained joy. This one was dangerous. He loved it.

"Maya," he croaked.

She straddled his legs and crawled up his body, resting her ass right on his growing erection. He crossed his arms over his chest so that he didn't actually touch her and groaned.

She leaned down and breathed the words directly against his lips, "Do you want to touch me?"

Their eyes were locked. "Yes."

"Where?"

His laugh sounded half-crazed to his own ears. "Everywhere."

"Good." She sat up straight and bounced on his lap.

"Fuck," he breathed.

"So here's what I'm thinking. We need to get this Algerian"

"Albanian," Kenny corrected.

She lifted her eyebrow at him.

"Sure, Algerian, whatever," he acquiesced.

"We need to get him in the chatroom but the real goal is to get him in a private session, right?"

"Yes," Kenny replied, wondering if it would be rude to ask her to either grind against him so he could be fully incoherent or get off of his lap so his brain could return to normal functioning. But Maya didn't show any intentions of moving so he kept going, his words coming a bit slower than normal. "If we can get him in a private session, Chanté thinks she can hack his computer and we can find his contacts that way."

"Why can't she do that in the chatroom?"

"He's got an IP scrambler. We'd have to sift through everyone in the chatroom to find the one he's using before she can even try and get into his computer."

"But if his is the only computer besides mine," she said.

He nodded and tried to sit up straighter, easing the delicious pressure of her ass on his dick. "The longer the session the better."

She moved her ass back onto his dick, frustrating his efforts to ease his distress. "If you can do that then you wouldn't need me in the field, right?"

He nodded.

"Okay, good. The money sounds great and all, but I've decided that maybe it's not worth it."

He looked up at her, his entire body feeling light with relief. "I agree."

"Okay, so I think we've gotta give him a good enough show that he can't help but ask for a private session."

"Well yeah, that's what we're doing," Kenny said.

She smiled down at him indulgently. "Oh babe," she said and he tried not to let himself get caught up on that one word. He failed. But at least he tried. "Watching me fuck myself with my fingers for a few minutes is like, step zero point five on my channel. You know that."

He gulped. Did he ever.

"But the way I get you all to fork over the extra money for a private show is to give you almost everything you want but then stop right before the threshold. So when I targeted you-"

Kenny spluttered, grabbed her hips and deposited her onto the bed next to him.

She giggled.

"You didn't target me. I asked you for a private session because I wanted one."

"I know. I did that."

"You did what?"

"Oh wow, you really don't know, do you?"

"Know what?"

She crawled off of her bed and spoke while she walked around her room. "The last broadcast I did before you asked me for a private session, I set the scene for you."

"It was a public session," he reminded her.

"I know. But it is entirely possible to address a crowd but only speak to one person." She brought his attention to a familiar stack of books on her bookshelf. "You always noticed the biographies on my bookshelf, so I chose these. I wore that green baby doll see-through thing you loved."

"With the lace over your breasts," he said, remembering.

She swatted at his legs until he moved them so she could sit in front of him. "I angled my pussy away from the camera, instead of head on if you will, because you always like a bit of mystery. And when I came, I laughed right at the camera," she said with a wicked smile on her face.

"Because that's my favorite part."

"You always hated when I would cover my mouth when I came."

His mouth fell open in shock. "So you conned me," he laughed.

She smiled. "I have an MBA and an undergraduate degree in marketing. Of course I conned you."

"Fuck, you're perfect," he said and stretched his arms out to pull her body toward him.

She crawled back into his lap happily. This time he tentatively placed his hands on her hips and squeezed the soft flesh there. She rewarded him by grinding into his cock.

"You really should have been at the briefing earlier," he whispered, looking up at her adoringly.

She smiled down on him, arched one eyebrow and leaned down to whisper against his mouth again. "Underestimate me at your own peril."

And then she licked his lips. Kenny groaned in response and Maya wasted no time in pressing her mouth to his. He smiled as she slipped her tongue into his mouth, sliding against his and then retreating. He sucked her bottom lip and was surprised to feel her shiver against him. His teeth scraped gently along her tongue and she giggled.

"You have no idea what your laugh does to me," he said. It wasn't the first time he'd said it, but she was usually reading his words.

This time she ground her pussy into him and he gasped. She took advantage of his shock to kiss him deeply again. "No, I get it. It's technically my job to get it," she said.

Just then her phone alarm started blaring. She sagged against him, and he wrapped his arms fully around her.

"That's my ten-minute warning," she said. "We should get in position."

He pressed a soft kiss to her shoulder. Her alarm kept blaring but neither of them moved for a minute or so. It was an unexpected moment of calm.

Eventually Maya pulled away and crawled out of his lap. She leaned across the bed to grasp her phone and turn off the alarm. When she turned back to him she had that dangerous smile on her face again. "I think we should try another position."

He frowned, "Do we have time to reposition?"

"Correction, I'll reposition, you just stay where you are, okay?"

He nodded and spread his legs. He kept nodding as she crawled between them and leaned over her laptop, her ass high in the air directly in front of him. He was still nodding, when she sat back, her laptop mirrored this time on the TV at the foot of the bed. This way they could read the text from their new position. He didn't stop nodding when she reclined against him, her back to his front, the perfect angle for her viewers to watch her play with herself and for him to see across the planes of her body.

But his head finally stilled – his entire body stilled – when she stopped just before starting the broadcast, turned to him and whispered, "You can touch me this time."

back at command

"Alright, I've got coffee, water, sparkling water," she turned toward Chanté to make sure she knew that was for her, "popcorn, pretzels and a really nice charcuterie platter I picked up at Whole Foods. Do any of you want anything else?" Kierra turned to the briefing room toward Chanté, Monica and Lane, her hands clasped in front of her chest, eagerly awaiting their response.

"Maya's going to kill you for treating this like a viewing party. Again," Chanté said. But she turned to look at her with a smile. "But I really appreciate your attention to detail."

Kierra smiled. "I'm really happy *someone* appreciates my efforts."

"The broadcast is starting," Monica announced.

"Oh," Kierra said, grabbing the bag of pretzels and rushing to the middle of the table to sit next to Chanté.

"Oh now what do we have here?" Lane laughed and leaned forward in his chair.

"He's not wearing anything I set out for him," Chanté shrieked.

"He's not wearing anything," Monica said.

"Oh no, he has on underwear," Kierra corrected.

"Shame," Lane breathed.

"He better at least be wearing the cologne or I am going to kill him."

"Assuming he doesn't die of happiness," Kierra said. "They look very comfortable right now."

"Hi guys," Maya said on the screen, reclining between Kenny's spread legs. His hands rested on her thighs and his nails scraped over her skin lightly.

That point of physical contact struck Kierra as intimate and easy. She'd never seen Maya look as comfortable with anyone she'd dated. She made a mental note to bring this up when they spoke next.

"So my boyfriend had so much fun on Tuesday that he let me convince him to come back," Maya said with a sly smile and a wink. "And it seems like you all had fun too."

"Yeah they did," Chanté announced. "Viewership is already double what she pulled in on Tuesday. My girl is about to get *paid*."

"Any sign of Mehmeti?" Monica asked, reminding them all why they were all here.

"Not yet," Chanté announced. "But I'm pulling IPs from all of the users just in case."

"Good girl," Lane said.

Chanté winked, "Say it again."

Lane barked a laugh.

Monica's eyes lifted from her tablet and crashed with Kierra's gaze. Kierra winked in return and felt her nipples harden as she licked her lips. Monica's eyes tracked the movement.

"He's here," Chanté shrieked. They turned toward her.

"And the Setter brothers are here too. Right on time," Chanté added, her hands beginning to fly over the keyboard on her laptop. Kierra leaned back and peeked at the screen. It was full of code and looked like something out of *The Matrix*; all gibberish to her.

She shifted her eyes back to the smart screen and smirked. Kenny's hands were lightly caressing Maya's arms, his fingers grazing her sides, while one of Maya's hands was playing over her mound, peeking through her thighs.

"It's probably a good thing I'm staying over," Kierra said. "I doubt I'd get any sleep at my place tonight."

Lane chuckled, his head bent over his tablet, "You're not gonna get any sleep here tonight either."

In hindsight, Kierra knew she'd walked Lane right into that one. She'd have thought something was wrong if he had responded any other way. She made eye contact with Monica and her cheeks warmed. Yeah, she'd practically begged for that retort. And she'd do it all over again.

Chanté loved computers in the way she loved everything: completely.

She still remembered the first time she'd been shuffled into an aged computer lab in the fourth grade for an afterschool technology camp that was really just a program for the poor kids in school who needed to be supervised in the gap of time between when school ended and their parents got off of work. Well, those kids and the foster kids, like Chanté.

She'd always made sure to sign up for every extracurricular activity that would keep her brain occupied but wouldn't cost her any money, because she didn't have any. It was her social worker, Tamra Bryan's most useful advice. "You might get adopted, you definitely might not. So plan as if you're going to walk out of some group home at eighteen with the clothes on your back and no one to call when you need to be rescued."

Chanté liked Tamra. Of all the social workers she'd had, Tamra was her favorite. The young white ones tried to fill her head with hopes of an adoption she didn't want and the older ones – Black and white – tried to criticize and berate her into feeling grateful for every foster care placement she got, because at least it got her out of the group homes. Even though Chanté had long since learned from her own parents that gratitude, like love, had to be earned.

Tamra on the other hand was real with her. She understood that Chanté was unfortunately wiser than some other kids her age. She'd spent her entire childhood, stunted as it was, being passed back and forth between a mother and father who loved her, but couldn't afford to care for her and who hated each other just a fraction more than they loved their daughter. And that fraction, for a neglected kid, was huge. It could be the difference between her parents pooling what little money they both had to buy her a warm winter coat or both buying her the cheap, thin coats they could afford separately. Because the point was to frustrate each other, not take care of Chanté. That fraction of an inch felt like miles when they refused to communicate about her and confused the dates when she would be at one house or the other. That fraction was how Chanté ended up spending days, one time almost two weeks, alone in her father's cold apartment because he thought she was at her mother's. And her mother, taking advantage of her "week off," had refused to answer the phone when Chanté called because she didn't answer a call from her ex-boyfriend's house; not even if the person calling might have been Chanté.

After years of that, the group homes had been a relief. Full of kids her own age, loud but not in the parents arguing and fighting in the kitchen loud; just kids being kids loud. Tamra had immediately picked up on Chanté's relief. She didn't want to be adopted, she was wary of a foster home since she no longer had any illusions that "home" was a safe space. And she wasn't necessarily in a rush to be reunited with her parents either. So Tamra told her to make the most of her education, because the only person she could count on was herself.

Maybe that's why computers always made sense to her. From the minute she'd sat down in that old computer lab full of desktops that were either dead or had stopped working, she'd known she was home. They, unlike people, followed patterns that made sense. Computers, unlike people, could be fixed. Chanté had learned how to build, break down and rebuild a computer from the trash heap of old parts. Tamra had given her a very rare smile and said it could be a metaphor if she wanted. She could deconstruct and rebuild herself. When she was eighteen, she could become someone completely new if she wanted. And she did.

"Okay, I've got good news, bad news and meh news," Chanté announced to the room.

"What is 'meh news'?" Lane asked.

Chanté shrugged but kept typing. "Not good or bad. It just is."

Monica exhaled, annoyed.

"Meh news first, please," Kierra chimed.

"Okay, just as I suspected Mehmeti's using an IP scrambler."

"What's the bad news?" Monica ground out.

Chanté exhaled. "His IP is in a different location every seven minutes but I need at least nine minutes to track his actual server down. And *then* I'd have to hack into it."

"How long would it take to hack?" Lane asked.

Chanté shook her head. "There's no way to know that before I locate the server. Who knows what his security is like."

"So we need to stick with our original plan to get him into a private session to give you more time," Monica announced. "What's the good news?"

Chanté smiled but kept typing for a few minutes. The briefing room was quiet but for the tapping of her long acrylic nails on her laptop and the faint sounds of Maya's moans from the live broadcast. Finally, she smiled and looked up at

Monica, "The good news is the Setter brothers aren't nearly as cautious. I'm downloading their hard drives remotely as we speak and they get off," Chanté said, nodding toward the screen.

Monica didn't smile but Chanté could read her approval in the gentle nod of her head.

Lane exhaled. "So now we just need to get Joseph Mehmeti to request a private session with Maya and soon?"

They all turned toward the screen where Kenny was rolling Maya's nipples between his fingers as her pussy spasmed around her internal vibrator, her orgasm close.

Monica tapped at her tablet. "I don't think we'll have to worry too long about that," she said. "He's already tipped her close to five hundred dollars and she still has another twenty minutes left."

"So we wait," Kierra breathed.

Chanté chuckled and started tapping at her computer again. "Ooooh I don't do patience well."

"Are you going to start sifting through the Setters' hard drives?" Kierra asked.

"Nah, I created some code to sort what we're looking for: bank accounts, correspondence, passwords, etc. While I'm waiting, I thought I might see what Asif's up to. And maybe buy myself an early early Valentines present."

"It's September," Lane said with a chuckle.

"I said early *early*," Chanté replied.

Monica turned to her and squinted. "You two have such a strange relationship."

Chanté raised her eyes and both eyebrows, but Kierra replied before she could, with a reassuring pat on Chanté's arm.

"We've fucked in every room of Command and Maya and Kenny are fondling each other for all of the internet to see. Let's just all agree that no one else's relationship is up for discussion."

Monica smiled and went back to her tablet. Lane reached across the table to snag Kierra's bag of pretzels and sat back to enjoy the rest of the broadcast.

Chanté turned to Kierra, who smiled at her with a wink. "Wanna steal a purse?"

nine

Maya ended the broadcast by pushing the power button on her camera's remote and toeing her laptop closed with one shaky foot. In fact, her entire body was shaking with the aftershocks of her orgasm. She stretched out and lifted her arms over her head. She grasped Kenny at the crown of his head with both hands and held onto him for dear life. Kenny fought against that touch, her fingernails scraping along his scalp. He bit back a groan and tried to still his hips – he wanted desperately to pump into her. He wrapped his arms around her, pulling her close instead.

"Touch me," she begged in a tight, strained voice that wreaked havoc on his resolve.

He moved his hands to her breasts and began to knead gently, the soft flesh spilling out of his palms. When he moved his thumbs to her nipples she groaned and gasped and arched her back in beautiful distress. He focused on touching her in just the right way – just the right pinch of her oversensitive nipples, his mouth pressed to her temple. He ignored his own physical needs and the signs of his arousal; his hard dick in his underwear, his rapid heart rate, his panting breaths.

"Oh fuck, I'm coming again," she groaned, convulsing in his arms.

"I've got you," he whispered directly into her ear.

She planted her heels onto the bed and lifted her hips, her thighs shaking, her labored breath filling the room. His dick pulsed, wanting her. He held her through this final climax. It took a few minutes for her hips to lower back to the bed, and her breathing to slow.

"Please," she whispered, exhausted.

He reached for the remote control for her vibrator and shut it off. Her body sagged against his. The room filled with the beautiful tinkling of her post-orgasmic laughter. He groaned. She gently stroked the backs of his hands on her chest. Kenny was still painfully hard but this moment was beautiful; intimate. Even more intimate than everything they'd shared so far.

"Are you close?" she whispered after a while.

His body was still rigid with his own lust. He nodded.

She turned slowly in his arms and he moved so they could make eye contact. She sucked her bottom lip into her mouth.

"Can we wait?" he whispered back.

She raised an eyebrow. "Wait for…?"

"After our date," he said and felt his cheeks warm.

The smile that slowly spread across her face was surprised at first and then dirty. "You're a sweet one, Kenny," she said.

His blush was intense. "Not really. I'm just selfish. I want to be the one to get you this hot before I fuck you."

She smiled wickedly, "We'll see." And then she moved away from him, crawling from between his legs. When she stood she turned and her eyes trained on his hard dick. "Are you sure?" She asked, her eyes never leaving his lap, her tongue swiping across her lips.

"Don't tempt me," he said in a strained voice.

"That's kinda my job," she shrugged. "But if you're sure."

"I am," he said and then mumbled, "unfortunately."

She moved into her bathroom and he had to avert his eyes from her retreating form. He looked around her room for his clothes before remembering he'd followed her across the hall nearly naked without thinking about his return journey. But as he thought of his short walk back to his apartment, it wasn't his exposed skin that occupied his mind. It was leaving her.

"Hey, Maya," he called to her.

She appeared in the bathroom door, "You change your mind?"

"Do you want- I was thinking maybe we could watch a movie?"

He was becoming addicted to her easy smiles and knowing that they were for him – only for him – in real life. "Does this count as our first date?" she asked with a suggestive purse of her lips.

He laughed. "Yes. If you want it to."

She licked her lips, her eyes falling to his dick again. "I do," she whispered, each word dripping with lust.

He ducked his head and smiled. He remembered what she'd told him and lifted his head to make eye contact. "Okay. I'm just going to run home and..."

"Relieve some tension," she offered helpfully.

"Some of it at least. I'll be back in a bit."

"Okay. Oh wait," she said before he could even turn to go. She sauntered across her bathroom and he gulped at the soft shimmy of her fleshy thighs and hips. When she was right in front of him, she leaned forward to press a kiss softly, chastely to his lips. He smiled and moved his lips against hers. It was innocent but it still made his body tingle.

"I was already hot for you, by the way," she whispered against his lips.

AFTER KENNY LEFT, Maya took a quick shower and changed into her favorite pair of baggy sweatpants and a tank top with a shelf bra that gave her the illusion of support without the restriction of an underwire. The lack of actual bra or the equivalent was usually how she demarcated the space between work and relaxation. That and the glasses she shoved onto her face after she took her contacts out.

She walked to the kitchen, trying not to overthink her current situation as she waited for Kenny to return by keeping her hands busy. She started rummaging through her cupboards pulling out every kind of snack she could find. But then she remembered that he didn't snack – and didn't like candy – and she put them all back with a frown.

Finally, she gave up on being a good hostess and grabbed her phone from the charger on her nightstand, thinking she might check her chatroom or text Kierra. But when the knock came at the door, Maya was standing in the kitchen, staring off into space, thinking about Kenny's groan in her ear. She took a deep breath, gave herself a hard mental shake and walked across the living room on legs that felt like jelly. Just before she pulled the door open she took another deep breath, straightened her back, pressed her chest forward and fixed her mouth into her sexiest smile.

The pizza delivery woman's eyes widened as her mouth fell open. "I… I..." she said, her eyes trained on Maya's chest.

Maya squinted her eyes. "What the hell?"

"I got it," Kenny yelled from down the hall, jogging the delivery person and Maya out of their stasis. "Got it," he said again, waving the money in his hand. "Here you go."

There was a moment where Kenny tried to negotiate handing over the money in one hand and grabbing the pizza with the other. It shouldn't have been an ordeal, but the poor woman was flustered and Kenny, actual spy, seemed to be an adorable, gangly mess. Maya had never thought he might be so physically awkward while they were chatting or in the few days they'd known each other offline. She was charmed.

Her eyes zeroed in on his lean waist and she licked her lips.

"Maya," he said, pulling her out of the trance his body had put her in.

Her cheeks warmed at the realization that he'd caught her ogling him. But when she raised her eyes to his face and found him smiling warmly at her, they warmed for another reason.

"Sorry," she said and backed into her apartment to let him in.

He moved into the living room and set the pizza on the coffee table.

"Um, I'll get plates," Maya said, closing the door and turning the locks, ignoring the way he already had her hands shaking. "Do you want something to drink?" she called from the kitchen.

"Just water," he said.

She grabbed plates, napkins, the pitcher of water and two glasses, turned, and almost dropped them all. Kenny was standing in the living room, his hands in the pockets of his sweatpants, his hard chest pressing through his tight Henley, his eyes raking over her.

She gasped and blurted out the first thing that came to mind. "How do you know what I like on my pizza?"

He grinned, "You told me."

She squinted at him. "I did?"

He shrugged and lifted his eyes as he very clearly quoted her, jogging her memory. "Extra cheese, meat, lots of meat, veggies but only like the right veggies: peppers, onion, mushroom, ugh so many mushrooms. I'll slap someone for putting fruit on my pizza. Hard."

She giggled.

He smiled at her and inclined his head. "Come on. Let's find something to watch."

She put the water and glasses onto the tray in front of her and walked toward him.

He extended his long arms across the couch and grabbed the tray from her hands.

"I've got it," she laughed.

"I know," he said, pulling the tray from her anyway.

Maya sat down on the couch, a respectable distance away from Kenny and navigated the TV to the on-demand schedule. "Are you in the mood for anything in particular?" When he didn't answer she turned to find him staring at her. "What?"

"You're so far away," he said in a voice that felt like velvet as it washed over her.

She shivered, stood from the couch and moved to sit next to him at the center. There were still a few inches between them. Kenny bounced along the couch and pressed his side against hers.

She tried to stop the smile from spreading across her lips, which only made her cheeks puff out more. "Close enough?"

"For now," he said. "I love your dimples."

She raised her eyes to his. "You have beautiful eyes," she whispered.

"They're just brown," he said around a laugh.

She leaned forward and pressed a kiss to his neck.

He froze.

"Beautiful," she whispered against his skin. They were so close that she felt the shudder that rocked his body in hers. Maya was in no rush to move. "I don't like horror," she said.

They both laughed. She sat back to watch the way the smile brightened all of his very serious features.

He nodded. "I don't either. Wanna watch a romcom?"

Maya sat back in shock and raised her best and second best eyebrows at him. "Are you just saying that to butter me up?"

"I like romcoms," he said defensively. And then, "But is it

working?" He laughed, and Maya tried not to get lost in the deep lines bracketing his mouth or the flutter of his eyelashes. It was all too much.

She turned to the television, toggled to a romantic comedy she'd been waiting weeks to watch. And then she turned to him. "Yeah. It's working," she whispered. She lost the internal battle she was fighting and leaned forward to kiss those laugh lines to the right of his mouth. "Definitely working."

Kenny blushed and looked away from her to open the pizza box. "This wasn't the dinner I'd planned when I asked you out." He dished a slice for her onto a plate and handed it over.

"What did you plan?"

He laughed, "I hadn't thought that far ahead yet." He grabbed a slice for himself.

Maya smiled, her lips pressed together, and she ducked her head. She poured them each a glass of water and then pressed play on the movie. As it began, they both settled back onto the couch in a deep recline, as if they had synchronized it. It might not have been the date he would have planned, but as far as Maya was concerned, it was the best date of her life.

HIS APARTMENT WAS dark and quiet when he let himself in. And it felt cold, much colder than Maya's warm apartment and her body wrapped along his side on the couch, her cheek smushed into his shoulder and her soft snores drowning out the audio of the movie that had put them both to sleep. He smoothed his hand over the back of his head and let his smile fully form in the dark where no one else could see it. The kitchen light flickered on. When Kenny turned, Chanté was glaring at him.

"And where have you been?" she asked in a deep, serious voice before dissolving into giggles.

Kenny rolled his eyes.

"Tell me everything," she screeched.

"Why are you up? Why are you here?" Kenny said irritably, breezing past her into the kitchen.

"I had an early shift. I woke up to get some water and then I heard you trying to sneak in."

He pulled open the refrigerator door, "I wasn't sneaking in. I don't need to sneak."

"Sure, sure," she said, grabbing two glasses and setting them on the counter between them.

Kenny pretended to concentrate on pouring the water, hoping Chanté would drop the subject, even though he knew she wouldn't.

"Was it good?" Chanté whispered.

His hand slipped and he spilled some water onto the counter. Chanté cackled loudly. Kenny grimaced and reached for a paper towel to clean up the mess he'd made.

He shoved a glass into Chanté's hands. "Drink."

"That good, huh?" she whispered over the rim of the glass and took a sip.

Kenny ignored her question again, turning back to the fridge.

He drank his glass of water slowly, trying to avoid Chanté's raised, nosy eyebrows. She put her glass of water on the counter and had opened her mouth wide to harass Kenny some more – he rolled his eyes preemptively – when a small shuffle from the hallway leading to their bedrooms interrupted them.

Kenny's eyes widened as a tall woman with dark brown skin and long dreadlocks came into view. She was slipping a leather coat onto her shoulders.

"Oh no. Did we wake you up?" Chanté said in a soft voice that made Kenny turn to her with his own nosy, raised eyebrows.

He watched her walk across the kitchen and meet her…

friend in the living room. And then he watched them embrace with needy hands grabbing at exposed flesh and hungry, wet kisses. Kenny smiled in shock. The woman was whispering to Chanté too low for Kenny to make out her exact words, but whatever she said made Chanté laugh and growl at the same time.

Kenny cleared his throat.

Chanté came to herself and pulled slightly away. She had a shy smile on her face. "Kenny, this is Tracy," she said, while clutching the other woman's arms and bouncing up onto the balls of her feet – a move Kenny recognized as her adorably smitten pose. "Tracy, this is my roommate and best friend, Kenny. He's just getting home from his girlfriend's apartment and I'm interrogating him."

Kenny rolled his eyes as he walked toward them. He extended his hand and grasped Tracy's. "Nice to meet you, Tracy. She's not my girlfriend. It's complicated."

Tracy laughed a husky, deep breath that Kenny knew had probably turned Chanté's knees to jelly the first time she'd heard it – she had a thing for great laughs.

"Nice to meet you. You two are definitely best friends," Tracy replied. "Don't let me interrupt."

"No. Please. Interrupt," Kenny said.

"Yeah stay," Chanté breathed.

Tracy turned to Chanté and smiled. "I'd love to, but I need to go home and get ready for work." She wrapped Chanté more fully into her arms and pressed a kiss against her cheek. "When can I see you again?"

"Whenever you want," Chanté said. Kenny smiled in shock and his eyebrows rose even higher than before.

"Alright. I'll call you later today," Tracy said with a broad smile.

"You better," Chanté giggled.

Kenny watched as Chanté walked Tracy to the door and they kissed goodbye. "Nice to meet you Kenny. I hope it gets uncomplicated with your girl," Tracy called one more time before Chanté closed the door.

When Chanté turned around her brown cheeks were flushed and she wouldn't meet Kenny's eyes.

"Okay, first of all, you need to marry her. Second of all, WHO THE FUCK WAS THAT?!" Kenny yelled.

Chanté, who never got shy, like ever – Kenny wasn't even sure if she understood the concept – began to fiddle with the hem of the long shirt she wore and mumbled her answer. "Just someone I met at the club."

"Is she another dancer?"

"No. She works security sometimes for extra money."

"Well, I like her already," Kenny laughed.

Chanté raised her eyes and smiled at Kenny. He exhaled sadly. He could already see the questions building there and they had a silent conversation made possible by over a decade of friendship.

Did he like Tracy better than Asif?

Fuck yes.

Was Asif really so bad?

Worse.

Why can't I move on from him?

No idea. But he's not worth it.

It was a heavy moment between them. Too heavy for three in the morning. So Kenny changed the subject, he hated fighting with Chanté about Asif.

"We didn't have sex," he said.

Chanté's face lit up immediately. "I told you to wear the outfit I picked out."

"I wore the cologne, chill. And it was my decision not to have sex yet."

"What is wrong with you?" Chanté spat in disgust.

"I asked her out on a date," Kenny said, yawning. "And then we had pizza and watched a bad romantic comedy."

Chanté smiled and jumped up in excitement. "Fucking

adorable. They literally don't make men like you anymore, Ken Doll."

He shook his head at her compliment. "I'm tired. I need to sleep," he said as he walked away from her toward his bedroom. She followed him on her short legs, probably prepared to annoy him some more. But he turned to her, his hand on the doorknob. "There's no one else like you," he said sincerely. "You should be with someone who appreciates that."

Her smile faltered and she frowned for a second before she forced herself to nod and smile at him. He smiled back, walked into his bedroom and closed his door softly.

MAYA WOKE up with a crick in her neck, a vague throbbing in her sex and Kierra's frowning face staring at her.

"So you flubbed it?" Kierra said with a disappointed shake of her head.

Maya turned on her back and stretched slowly like a cat. "Flubbed what?" she asked around a loud yawn.

"Kenny obviously. And not in the good way."

Maya pushed herself up to sit and stare at her friend. "What the hell are you talking about?"

"I'm talking about you having the entire apartment to yourself and not fucking the guy you've been pining after for months. Not even after that broadcast. Oh, Lane told me to tell you that he nominated you for ChatBot's broadcast of the month."

Maya smiled. "Oh my god! Tell him I said thank you."

Kierra brushed her reply away. "Explain yourself."

Maya rolled her eyes. "Okay, so I wanted to."

"Duh, I have eyes and ears and an internet connection," Kierra said.

"But he wanted to wait until..."

"Until what? Until we catch this Albanian mobster? Life is too short."

"No. He wanted to wait until after our first date," Maya mumbled, her eyes focused on her fingers as she played with a frayed seam on her sweatpants.

Kierra moved from her perch on the coffee table and fell onto the couch next to Maya. "Holy shit, he's a unicorn."

Maya nodded. "I know."

"If his dick is as good as his head, you'll have to marry him."

Maya grabbed the pillow next to her and slapped Kierra in the face with it. They laughed. "My mama told me to never marry a man for good sex."

"Preach that," Kierra said.

"If I get married it'll be to a man who makes me laugh and is kind and blushes at the drop of a hat and treats me like a queen and remembers how I like my pizza," she whispered.

Next to her, Kierra whipped out her phone and began to type.

"What are you doing?" Maya whined.

"That got oddly specific at the end, so I'm assuming you were talking about Kenny. I'm gonna start looking for bridesmaid's dresses. I don't want you putting me in some ugly ass mermaid cut monstrosity when the time comes."

Maya pushed off from the couch. "Oh my god. You're like a relationship evangelist ever since you started banging your bosses."

Kierra laughed wickedly and didn't bother to reply. But she hopped up from the couch and followed Maya down the hall.

"Leave me alone. I have work to do," Maya yelled, yawning again.

"Sure Jan," Kierra called. "Anyway, do you think you want a spring or summer wedding?" she asked.

Maya squinted her eyes and glared. "I hate you," she said and then slammed her bedroom door.

Kierra's loud cackle filtered through their thin walls.

A COUPLE OF HOURS LATER, Maya sat down at their dining room table with her laptop in front of her. She pulled up her monthly earnings spreadsheet and was ready to input last week's figures. She was preemptively frustrated that the spikes from Kenny's appearances on her weekly broadcasts were going to ruin the bar graph for this month. But she took some solace in the fact that their missed Thursday private session would even things out.

She logged into the ChatBot site and pulled the information she needed. As expected, her income jump from last week and the week before was the highest week-to-week increase she'd ever seen. She frowned at her computer, saved the file and closed it. Maya didn't want fluke success. She wanted to grow her channel and online presence sustainably so that cam modeling would be there for her for as long as she wanted to do it. When it was time to move on, Maya wanted to make that transition because she was ready, not because she had to. Yet another unintended long-term consequence of this rash decision. But there was nothing she could do about that now.

She clicked around the ChatBot site for other work admin. She responded to a few private messages; just a little bit of dirty talk in her email. Her analysis had shown that for every ten horny men in her inbox wanting some free chat, three of those men would ask for a private video session and at least one of them would become a regular client.

As she was sifting through her emails she gasped and clicked on the email from the site administrators.

To: ThickaThanASnicka
Subject: Daily Rankings

Congratulations ThickaThanASnicka!

We are pleased to inform you that last night you placed sixth in the Top 10 BBW cam rooms. As you know, placing in the Top 10 in your category-

MAYA WAS TOO OVERCOME to read anymore. She jumped up from her chair and started screaming, "Oh my god. Oh my god," at the top of her lungs.

"What's wrong?" Kierra asked, rushing out of her room.

And then there was loud knocking on their front door.

"What?" Kierra asked as Maya continued screaming. The knocking on the door became louder, harder and Kierra rushed to open it. When she did, Kenny burst into their apartment, a gun in his left hand and Chanté at his heels.

"What's wrong?" Kenny asked, his eyes efficiently scanning the room.

Kierra raised her arms in bewilderment.

Finally, Maya blurted out, "I made it to the Top 10 list in my genre!"

"Oh my god," Kierra and Chanté exclaimed and rushed toward her. They all jumped around in happiness until Kenny's voice cut them off.

He was reaching to put his gun into the waistband of his jeans, hard eyes on Maya. It was a different intensity than when he was turned on, but not unwelcome.

"One, congratulations," he said, holding up his index finger. "Two, please refrain from yelling that loud unless it's a real emergency. Three, I'm sorry about the gun." He walked toward her then, Kierra and Chanté moving out of his way. He grabbed Maya's face and pulled her into a kiss. His tongue licked just at the edges of her mouth. She thrust her tongue forward, wanting to taste him, but his own tongue blocked her invasion even as he moved his lips against hers roughly. It was a maddeningly intense tease of a kiss and it drove Maya crazy.

"You earned it," he whispered against her lips.

A soft chime emanated from her computer. It took Maya a few seconds to realize that it was another ChatBot email and a few more seconds to tear her eyes away from Kenny's to look at it. What she saw there made her pulse quicken, but not in a good way.

"Fuck," she said.

Kenny moved to her side and read the email she'd just opened.

"What's wrong?" Chanté whispered.

"It's Mehmeti," Kenny said as they scanned the email quickly. "He's requesting a private session with us." He turned back to Maya and dropped one arm to her waist to squeeze her close to him. "Looks like your plan worked."

It was a compliment that didn't suffuse her with warmth. Instead it made her shiver in his arms. Finally, Maya had found a compliment she didn't enjoy.

Chanté's voice interrupted the apprehension blossoming in Maya's chest. "I know this is all about to get very serious in a second, but can I just say that you two are really adorable together."

"I'll second that," Kierra chimed in.

Kenny didn't roll his eyes, they stayed trained on Maya's face as a ghost of a smile played at the corners of his mouth.

ten

Maya was shocked at how quickly they went from celebrating her first time in the Daily Top 10 rankings to that kiss to emailing Joseph Mehmeti back to scheduling his private session to today. The Day. That's what she was calling it in her head.

She wanted to slow down the passage of time, and rewind it back to that kiss, not just because it was sensual and teasing and it made her stomach clench, but also because in the last three days that was as close as Maya had gotten to Kenny. Ever since then, he'd been secluded in Command, planning for what to do when Chanté got the information they needed from the private chat – and Maya guessed, what to do if they didn't. These were conversations Maya didn't have clearance to hear. And what little access Kierra did have, had kept her best friend away nearly night and day for the past three days as well. Which meant that Maya had spent most of that time alone. This normally wouldn't have been a bad thing, except that she was bored. And it was Thursday.

Usually she wouldn't have been able to schedule a private session today, because today was MasquerAsiaN's weekly appointment. And Maya normally treated it like a holiday.

She slept in late to make sure she looked rested. She lounged around the apartment with various masks and scrubs on every part of her body. She showered and shaved and contoured and curled and mascara'd herself into perfection. Then she artfully arranged herself into position and signed into her ChatBot account ready to have the best hour of the week as far as she was concerned; so good she would have paid for it herself.

Maybe that was what was stressing her out this morning. For the past five months every Thursday had been Their Day. It felt wrong to lose that and replace it with an appointment for someone she didn't know and wasn't worth all of the extra effort she used to put into preparing for Kenny. But Kenny would be there, with her. So maybe the real issue was that she felt alone.

Maya was in the kitchen staring into the refrigerator even though she didn't really want anything and they didn't have anything anyway. She sighed to herself just as the front door opened.

"Kitchen," she called out, assuming it was Kierra, hoping it was Kenny.

"I brought ice cream," Kierra yelled back.

Maya pursed her lips. Her best friend definitely knew how to soften the blow of her disappearing act. Maya raised her eyebrows as she walked out of the kitchen. "What kind?"

Kierra simply held the white bag up for Maya to see. She would know that bag anywhere.

"Bananas Foster?"

Kierra actually stopped walking and gasped. "Of course. What kind of friend do you think I am?"

Maya put her hands on her hips, "Hopefully the kind of friend who brought me a waffle cone on the side since she's been MIA for days."

Kierra rolled her eyes, reached into the bag and pulled out

a waffle cone. "Like I *said*, what kind of friend do you think I am?"

Maya smiled and clapped her hands. "The best, obviously. I'll get the spoons."

They settled onto their couch, each with a pint of ice cream in hand, Maya's bananas foster and Kierra's berry crumble. They ate in silence, staring at the TV, which neither of them had the desire to actually turn on. Maya broke the silence only when they switched pints.

"So what's the deal?" She asked and shoved a spoonful of the second-best ice cream ever into her mouth.

"I can't tell you much." She turned to Maya and rolled her eyes. "Clearance."

Maya sighed. "Is that why you've been staying away, so that you don't spill classified info?"

Kierra smiled, "Actually no, but that would have been a good plan." And then her face dropped and she frowned. "Lane's gone."

Maya's eyes went wide, "Oh my god, you three broke up?"

Kierra quirked up an eyebrow. "What? No. That would take much more than ice cream to fix?"

"Like wine and sushi, a lot? Or are we talking tequila and tacos and maybe a public drunkenness charge?"

"Probably all of the above," Kierra said. "He's on remote assignment." She shoved more ice cream into her mouth and sighed.

"Where?" Maya said and then, "Oops, sorry."

"Don't worry, I wouldn't have told you that. It's soo boring. Anyway, Monica and I just miss him."

"Damn girl, you've got it bad."

Kierra's sad face lit up momentarily, "Monica's really strict when she's sad."

"When did you get this freaky?" Maya asked, truly astonished that this woman in front of her was ever that sad girl in the back of their college auditorium.

"When you meet the right people." She let that sentence trail off and Maya had a hard time not letting her thoughts wander to Kenny. Who she hadn't seen in days.

"So what's up with you and Kenny? What have I missed?"

Maya exhaled a frustrated breath and leaned over to set her pint of ice cream down. "Not a goddamn thing. I haven't seen him in days."

"Oh, that makes sense," Kierra breathed.

"How?"

"He's heavily involved in the US side of the arms deal. Lane's gone to work with one of his former partners and he's been trying to facilitate that from here. And he's been working some contacts in Interpol too, I think. Dude is connected."

Maya pursed her lips, "And what the fuck does any of that have to do with me?"

"He's busy," Kierra said around a laugh. "And you don't care. I can definitely relate. It's weird. I know that Lane and Monica have dangerous jobs, but I don't really think about it. All that matters to me is that they come home. It was like that even when I was just their PA. I didn't give a shit what dangerous thing they were out there doing, just as long as they showed up in the office every morning. When they didn't, I was pissed."

"And horny as hell?"

"To be fair, I was always horny then."

"Then?" Maya turned to her. They both laughed.

"So this is normal, him being out of touch for a while?"

Kierra put her ice cream down and shrugged. "Can't say. Every assignment is different, and every agent handles the absence differently, I guess. That's not any less true because they're… you know…."

"James Bond?"

"Yeah, but much hotter."

They both sat back. "So much hotter," Maya breathed.

"You and Kenny need to talk," Kierra said after a bit of silence.

"This isn't the best time for a 'where do you see this going' kind of heart-to-heart."

"True, but take it from me," Kierra said as she stood, "the girl who only finally admitted that she wanted to fuck her bosses in a Serbian fetish club. There is no good timing."

Maya's mouth fell open and she only found the words to speak after Kierra had closed her bedroom door behind her. "A Serbian what?!"

KENNY WAS TIRED; the kind of mentally drained that always seemed worse because of how hard it made processing very simple things. He was lucky his drive from Command was short. He pulled his car into the parking garage under the apartment building and took the elevator instead of the stairs. He'd spent the last two days in the briefing room trying to work through the intel on the Pendleton Patriots, looking for any links to the Mehmeti family's offshore bank accounts. He was also monitoring Lane and Lamont's op in Ohio. All night, whenever there was any mental downtime, he spent it dreaming of getting back to his apartment, showering and crawling into bed. But his feet stopped in front of Maya's front door instead of walking the few feet to his own. He realized why he hadn't gone to his apartment; he didn't want to be alone like he was on every other mission he'd run. He'd spent a lot of his childhood playing by himself, the perpetual new kid in town, or the only kid in the sleepy retirement village where his grandparents lived. It was the thing he hated most about his job actually, how much time he spent on solo surveillance missions or operations where he was alone in a room full of people who didn't know his real name. As he stopped in front of Maya's door, his body had understood before his exhausted brain that he didn't *have* to be alone. Instead of logging into her private chat, he could see Maya in person. He knocked. If it were possible for a knock to sound weary, his did.

Kierra answered the door. He exhaled loudly.

"No need to be rude," she said with a smirk. "Maya, your boyfriend's here," she called out, her eyes still on him.

"Kierra, shut up," Maya said.

Kenny considered himself to be a smart man. But every time he got even a glimpse of Maya he felt at least half of his brain simply give up and his entire vocabulary narrowed to one word, 'beautiful.'

"Hi," she whispered, shock and he thought happiness lighting her face.

"Hi."

"Are you okay?"

She was fucking adorable, in her glasses and a pair of baggy sweatpants that hung off of her hips nicely. She was wearing a white tank top that made her tits look great. Her hair, which was normally straight and beautifully styled for her broadcasts, was piled on top of her head, messy and curly. He was starting to see how different she looked offline. He was becoming just as infatuated by her leggings and baggy sweats as the sexy lingerie. It thrilled him to realize that he wanted Maya no matter how she presented herself.

"I'm tired," he said. And maybe if he hadn't been quite as exhausted, he might have second-guessed himself. But the fatigue he felt was bone deep. "Will you take a nap with me?"

The smile that spread across her face was slow, sweet and charming as fuck. She nodded and he could have fallen down right then and there, but the thought of climbing into her bed was too tempting to miss.

"Well, I'm wet," Kierra breathed.

"Kierra, go check on your girlfriend," Maya hissed.

Kenny didn't take his eyes off of Maya, but he heard the

excitement in Kierra's voice. "Oh my god, is Command empty?"

She didn't wait for Kenny to answer. But before she left she said, "I have condoms in the linen closet if you need them."

Kenny turned to glare at her.

"Go, tiny terror, oh my god," Maya said.

When the door closed Kenny turned around and smiled at her. She rolled her eyes and held out her hand to him. He felt an amazing sense of relief when their palms finally touched.

He followed her to her bedroom and pushed the door closed. Her bed looked inviting, but he cringed. He'd been at Command for twelve hours straight. He should have gone home to take a shower.

"Wait," he said.

Maya was bent over to pull the covers down. She turned and looked at him.

"I should go home and shower first. I'll be- I'll be right back."

He turned and reached for the doorknob when her voice stopped him.

"I have a shower here too, you know."

Kenny gulped.

"Do you want to take a shower with me, Kenny?" she purred.

He recognized that voice. It was the one she used when she knew she had him. The one that usually pushed him right over the edge in their private sessions. His throat was thick. He could only nod in reply.

MAYA HAD ABSOLUTELY HAD a dream like this once. In fact, she'd dreamt of taking a shower with MasquerAsiaN so many times it hardly felt like a fantasy anymore. But this was different. So deliciously different.

She'd thought from all of Kenny's blushing that he would be nervous. He wasn't. He locked his eyes on her as he stripped his clothes off in the middle of her bathroom. His gaze was intense and her skin tingled under his watchful glare. When he finally released her eyes, the electricity coursing through her only increased as he raked his gaze over the rest of her.

"I love your body," he whispered. More to himself than to her.

"Clearly," she said, her eyes on his dick; thick, heavy and hardening between his legs.

She moved past him to step into the shower and turned it on. She looked at him over her shoulder. He stood in place, watching her and waiting, she realized, to be invited inside. Jesus, she didn't think they still made men like him.

She sucked her bottom lip into her mouth and extended her arm again. He clasped it and stepped into the shower. She smiled when he moved between her and the spray, grateful that she didn't have to explain that her hair would not be going under the water.

He ducked under the shower head and she grabbed her loofah from the hook on the shower door. She poured her favorite lavender-scented body wash into her sponge. It was not cheap, and she usually reserved it for days when she was at her most tired or stressed. To use her good bath products on Kenny was special, but he didn't need to know that. She started rubbing the loofah, followed closely by her bare hand, across his chest and down his arms. His eyes were on her as she did this. Maya had been in a lot of relationships before, but she thought this was the single most intimate act she'd ever shared with someone. She pushed his arms up over his head and ran the loofah up his side and into his armpit.

"I'm not ticklish," he said, his intense gaze still on her.

She frowned and tried the other armpit. He didn't laugh but the amused smile playing on his lips made her smile back.

"Really? You're not ticklish at all?"

"Sorry," he said.

She sighed, "Turn around then."

His back was big and broad and muscly and while Maya believed that all bodies were great bodies, fuck if Kenny's body wasn't making her clit jump. "Jesus," she breathed before she could stop herself, her fingers ghosting over every ridge and plane.

"Do you like what you see?" he turned his head to say. Her hands stilled on his waist.

"Are you flirting with me?" she asked, a smile pulling her lips apart.

"Seems like as good a time as any," he said and chuckled.

She moved forward and pressed her body against his back. He stifled a groan.

"True. Your timing is better than mine normally is," she said into his ear.

"You mean there's a worse time to flirt than in the middle of a mission to bring down an Albanian crime syndicate?"

"I don't want to brag but I once flirted with my waitress while my boyfriend sat across from me. I'd just told him that I wanted to see other people."

Kenny turned his head quickly, "You didn't?"

She cringed and resumed washing his back. "I was a mess in my twenties. Ask Kierra." And then her hands stilled over the globes of his ass. He lifted an eyebrow. "Actually don't ask her. She'll tell you."

"Got it. Ask Kierra," he laughed.

"Turn around," she instructed.

"Whatever you want."

She rolled her eyes and looked at him very seriously. "I'm going to bend down to wash your legs. I don't want any funny business. No trying to angle your dick near my face and absolutely no touching my hair. Am I clear?"

"Crystal," Kenny said quickly, "But…"

She arched her second-best eyebrow at him. "But what?"

"But when do I get to clean you?" he asked in a very serious voice.

She didn't bother to hide the shiver that went through her body. She kept her eyes trained on his as she squatted down to wash one leg and then the other. His hips didn't move but she saw his dick jump as he stared down at her.

When his legs were clean, she stood back up and hung her loofah back onto its hook. She reached around him to grab more body wash. She kept her eyes on him as she poured it into her palm. His eyebrows were on high alert. She moved forward, their mouths so close. He gasped when she grabbed his dick tight in both hands.

She stroked him slow and held him tight.

"Fuck," he breathed as his eyes closed and his head dipped back under the shower spray.

He was a fucking work of art.

"Does that feel good, baby?" she whispered.

He righted his head and wiped the water from his face. He smiled at her. "Good wasn't ever going to be the right word to describe you."

"You're trying to soften me up," she said with a grin and a firm squeeze of his dick.

He grabbed her waist roughly and squeezed. "You're already soft, Maya."

Maybe it was the way he said her name or the feel of his fingers digging into her flesh or the fact that his beautiful cock was hard and pulsing in her hands. Or maybe it was the fact that they'd both been waiting for months for this and so much more. Or maybe it was the way his head dipped and his mouth found hers. Or maybe it was the gentle pressure of their tongues sliding against one another's as his come spurted onto her belly. But Maya felt softer than ever before.

KENNY'S entire world was an overpowering lavender-scented happiness. He and Maya had washed soap and his come from their bodies and she'd kept an arched eyebrow on him while he washed her, making sure he didn't get nearly as familiar with her pussy as she'd gotten with his dick. On the one hand, he wanted to touch her, but on the other hand, his dick seemed to enjoy tickling her toes as he washed her feet almost as much as the flash of pink he got of her pussy as he raised each leg. It wasn't nearly the same, but it wasn't bad at all.

Their hands had lingered as they'd used the same towel to dry off and then put lotion all over their bodies. The slick glide of their hands over each other's skin was quickly becoming a happy and familiar experience at this point.

"Is lavender your favorite scent?" he asked, amused.

"And what of it?" she said, playfully annoyed.

"Nothing," he replied as he rubbed lotion along her lower back. "I just don't think I'm going to be able to smell a relaxing candle without getting hard ever again."

The sound of her laughter made his dick jump. Again.

In her bedroom, they moved to her dresser.

"I don't have anything to wear," he said.

She raised an eyebrow. "Is that a problem?"

"It's not for me. You?"

She pulled a pair of yellow lace underwear and a matching bra from the top drawer. "Not a problem at all," she said, pushing her panties toward him. He smiled and kneeled down. She ran her hands along the back of his head and he tried not to moan at the intimacy of that touch. She settled her hands on his shoulders and stepped into her underwear. He pulled them up her legs and over her hips. He nipped at her left thigh, his teeth sinking briefly into her flesh. She moaned and scraped her nails along his shoulders. He smoothed her underwear into place and took the opportunity to palm the large globes of her ass.

"Leave the bra?" he breathed into her collarbone.

She nodded.

He took her hand and walked back to the bed. They pulled down the sheets together and she crawled in first. It was disorienting how well their bodies fit together. He moved one arm under Maya's shoulders and the other over her waist, his palm splayed over her soft middle.

"Do you have any brothers or sisters?" she asked out of the blue.

"No," he said. "I'm an only child. My parents were in the Army."

She moved her hand to entwine their fingers above their heads. "That must have been lonely."

He kissed her shoulder in response. "What about you?" He knew, but he wanted to hear it from her.

"Little one of each. Pains in my ass. Perfect."

He smiled, his mouth still pressed to her skin.

"My mother died a few years ago. They're all I have left."

"I'm sorry," he breathed, knowing that it wasn't nearly enough.

"Thanks."

Kenny could feel his body relaxing into hers each second they held one another in silence. But adrenaline was still thrumming through his veins. He knew what he wanted; what would put him to sleep.

"Can I?" He didn't know how to finish the sentence, but thankfully Maya understood.

She lifted her left leg for his thigh to push between. His dick had already begun to harden but he shifted to move it away from the apex of her legs. He squeezed her stomach and she giggled.

"Fuck," she breathed.

"So you are very ticklish," he said and nipped at her earlobe.

"I have no idea what you're talking about."

He kissed her pulse as his hand traveled down her stomach and over her mound, the pads of his fingers enjoying running over the lace. "You have the best fucking underwear."

"Is that your thing?" she whispered. Her breath hitched when he circled her clit.

"You," he whispered back. "Everything about you is my thing."

She moaned as he moved his hand to the top of her panties and then slipped inside.

Her pussy was softer than the expensive lace and his fingers glided across her moist lips. She sucked in a harsh breath and moved her ass back to grind into his body.

"Be careful," he laughed. "I'm not wearing any underwear, remember."

She growled at him and grabbed at her left breast. He laughed. He'd never seen her frustrated, that was literally the exact opposite of their previous relationship. And it made his heart and dick swell in equal measure.

"Kenny," she whined.

"I know. I know," he said, kissing her cheek and pushing his middle and ring fingers down her lips and into her pussy.

She sighed. And that breathy exhalation was everything.

He stroked her gently, slowly, and moved his hips with hers. She rolled her nipple between her fingers before she lifted her heavy breast to her mouth. He added a third finger and gave her harder strokes, his eyes riveted to her tongue on her dark nipple.

"Fuck, Maya," he said.

She turned a wicked eye on him, "I only do this for you." And then her long tongue snaked out of her mouth and flicked her nipple.

He moved onto his elbow, her hand still clasped in his, and he stroked her harder, their eyes still locked. When his thumb found her clit, she groaned and dropped her head to the pillow.

"Maya," he whispered, as she clenched around his fingers. "Maya."

"What? Fuck, right there," she breathed.

"Look at me, baby."

"Why? Oh my god, harder."

"Because. I want to look at you when you come. Without a computer between us."

She opened her eyes just as her hips jerked and her pussy shuddered around his hand. He continued to pump into her until she begged him to stop. They licked every bit of her from his hand before turning over and falling asleep. Best nap of his life.

mission prep #1

Kierra was sitting on the conference table next to Monica's chair. Her boss was pretending she wasn't eyeing her legs bared by the khaki shorts she was wearing. Since Lane wasn't around, she'd been tailoring her outfits to Monica. Instead of a pair of impossibly tall heels she was wearing a pair of platform wedges with a peep toe and ankle straps. She was also wearing a tank top with spaghetti straps and she might have forgotten her bra. Or at least that's what she planned to say when anyone asked her. No one had asked her yet, but Monica might later when she was lifting Kierra's shirt over her head. For now, Kierra crossed her legs and bumped her shoe into the side of Monica's chair rhythmically, waiting for her to get annoyed enough to do something about it.

Or for Maya's broadcast to start. Whichever came first.

"So do we think they finally had sex or…?" Kierra asked.

"God, I hope so," Chanté breathed as she tapped at her computer. "They're cute together. And my boy needs to get laid."

Kierra leaned back, resting her palms on the table, angling to see what Chanté was doing. "So does Maya. She's got every toy known to man, but sometimes you just want another body."

"Or more," Chanté added with a wink.

"To mix it up a bit," Kierra finished, her shoe still tapping rhythmically against Monica's chair. "Whatcha doin'?" she asked Chanté.

Chanté lifted her head and smiled. Kierra knew this would be good.

"When I was buying my early birthday present from Asif," she started.

"I thought it was Valentine's?" Monica said, not lifting her head from her tablet.

"No, yeah, I bought that present. But I hate when Asif misses my birthday, so I thought I should go ahead and grab something for that too."

Finally, Monica lifted her head. "I've read your asset file a number of times and I don't ever remember seeing a birth date listed."

Chanté grinned, "Exactly. So I make sure that Asif never misses it. Whenever it is."

Monica lifted one eyebrow but eventually went back to her tablet.

Chanté turned back to Kierra. "So anyway, when I was budgeting for my birthday present in Asif's bank accounts, I realized that he's been sending a bunch of money to England."

"Okay?"

"And I want to know why," Chanté said matter-of-factly.

"Doesn't he get mad when you snoop in his accounts?"

Chanté put her hands on the table and leaned up, her face inching closer to Kierra's. Kierra's eyes dropped to Chanté's adorable lips. "Really mad," she said and giggled.

Monica's hand snaked around her ankle.

The phone rang.

"It's Kenny," Monica announced, reaching toward the

center of the table to the secure office phone placed there. She answered the line and routed it to the intercom. "We're here. Go."

"We're set up," he said. "Is Chanté ready?"

"I'm always ready, thank you very much."

Kenny sighed. And then he spoke but his voice was muffled for a bit. "Maya wants to speak to Kierra. Is she there?"

"Here," she sang, but almost choked on the note when Monica's hand began to slide up her calf. Kierra turned to make eye contact with Monica who had seemingly gone back to her tablet. And yet, her fingers were grazing up Kierra's leg, tickling her.

"Small fry," Maya said.

"What's up?"

"Okay so look, I'm *not* freaking out or anything, but just in case I die I need you to watch out for Kaya and Jerome."

Monica's hand stilled on her leg and all three women turned to look at the phone as if they could somehow see Maya's face there.

"I'm sorry, what the fuck is happening?" Kierra breathed.

"Nothing I'm just not freaking out a little bit."

Kierra opened her mouth but the only thing that came out was a squeak.

And then Monica spoke, "Maya, I realize that you might only just now be realizing what you've gotten yourself into."

"You got that fucking right."

"But I want you to know that you're safe. Chanté has been encrypting your IP address since this mission started."

"Um," Chanté said, with wide eyes and an innocent smile on her face, "I might actually have been doing it a bit longer than that."

"How long?" Kierra and Maya asked at the same time.

"Oh…" Chanté said with a shrug, "Not *that* long. Just you

know, once I saw that Kenny was visiting you on ChatBot. There are a lot of bad people on the internet."

"Your best friend is scary and great," Maya said, clearly speaking to Kenny.

Kierra giggled at Kenny's loud sigh.

"And you're with one of our best agents right now. You are safer today than you were two weeks ago."

"Do you promise me that?" Maya asked.

"I do," Monica said, her hand stroking Kierra's calf lovingly.

Maya exhaled loudly. "I want hazard pay."

Kierra smiled, very proud of her friend.

"How much?"

Kierra butted in, "Standard hazard pay for regular Agency independent contractors." She and Monica locked eyes.

"Ooh girl, that's good money," Chanté said to Maya.

"I'll say yes on one condition," Monica said.

"I'm listening," Maya replied. Kierra lifted her eyebrows.

"You move in with us when Lane gets back, not when the mission is over."

"Oh you're talking to Kierra," Maya said. "We agree."

"Girl, you can't accept these terms on my behalf."

"Yes, I can. Besides, I love you, but I need a roommate who cooks," Maya said.

"Kenny's a great cook," Chanté offered helpfully.

"Oh, would you look at that," Maya said. "My alarm is going off. Gotta get ready for show time."

"I don't hear anything, Maya," Kierra ground out.

But she'd already hung up.

"They're so adorable," Chanté said before turning back to her laptop.

"That was underhanded," she said to Monica.

"More or less underhanded than you coming to work without a bra?"

"Well she's got you there, girl," Chanté mumbled.

"Say yes, Kierra." This wasn't a request or a demand. This was a plea. And if Kierra were the type of woman who cried over romantic gestures she would have crawled into Monica's lap and bawled. But Kierra didn't cry, she got dirty. She leaned forward and moved her hand to the base of Monica's throat. "I want you to fuck me with your strap tonight."

"Anytime, sweet girl," Monica breathed.

"This is romantic as fuck," Chanté sighed.

eleven

Kenny was trying to focus on what Maya was saying. But he was having a really hard time since, when Maya spoke, she moved her hands which made her breasts jiggle over the tops of the bra cups on yet another lace teddy that made his heart race. He felt certain that one or both of her breasts would spill out and he didn't want to miss it.

"Are you listening to me?" Maya asked.

Kenny shook his head. "I'm trying but fuck Maya, what's your lingerie budget?"

Maya was perched on her knees on the bed, her hands on her hips. She smiled. "It's as big as it needs to be," she whispered. "But actually I got this on sale! You like it?"

He raised his eyes to hers, "I've already told you, 'like' isn't a strong enough word."

She leaned forward and crawled across the bed toward him. He'd sprinted across the hall after their nap to grab some clothes. But since he was once again stripped down to a pair of boxer briefs and his dick was already growing heavy, he wondered why he'd even bothered.

He sucked in a breath and held it. Maya was just about to press her lips to his abs when the alarm on her phone began to blare. She sat back on her heels. "Ugh, it really is time to get to work."

Kenny put his hands on either side of her face gently and kissed her hard, his tongue delving into her mouth. And then he pulled away to whisper to her, "I promise I won't let anything happen to you."

She smiled and licked his lips.

MAYA LOGGED INTO CHATBOT. She was taking deep breaths and trying to calm her nerves as she checked the angle of her camera one more time to make sure the shot got as much of Kenny's hard abs as possible while still hiding his face. Also she needed to make sure her tits looked great at this angle. Check on both accounts.

King_Maker has requested a private chat.

MAYA ROLLED her eyes at his username. She accepted his request and then set her rates. She usually gave new customers a discount to encourage them to keep the appointment and come back, but Kenny and Monica had decided she should raise her rates. Based on everything they knew about the Mehmeti family, and Joseph in particular, being able to splash out on their niche pleasures was a favorite pastime.

She doubled her rates. "Are you sure about this?"

"Send him the quote, sweetheart."

Maya sighed and pressed send. She held her breath and waited for his reply. He accepted.

She tossed her hair one more time in the reflection and

put her best come-hither smile on her face – lips puckered and slightly parted as if she were in the middle of a moan.

When Joseph Mehmeti came on the screen Maya was shocked, but she hid it. She'd just assumed that the youngest son of an international crime syndicate, using the site to run guns *wouldn't* show his face during their private chat. But apparently, gun runners were fucking dumber than she'd thought.

"Hi, love," she breathed.

"Well hello," he said, leaning forward toward his camera, ogling her.

She moved her hand to play at one of the straps on her teddy. His eyes followed the movement. "I don't know if you've done a private chat before…" Maya said in her breathiest voice.

"Loads," he said and laughed.

Maya's eyebrows rose and her head tipped downward. Lord he's one of those, she thought to herself. In Maya's two years as a cam model she'd classified all of the patrons she'd had into a few categories. Most were horny and grateful; easy to manage. An unfortunately sizeable population was horny and bitter that no one in their real life would fuck them; Maya usually blocked those men – always men – immediately. The women were few and far between but most of the ones she'd met were either active duty military and/or in a long-distance relationship. They usually liked to spend their private chats talking about their girlfriends for half an hour or so and then in the last fifteen minutes watching Maya fuck herself to a quick orgasm before they ran out of time. There were the outliers, like MasquerAsiaN: respectful *and* great tippers. And then there were the Bart Simpsons – that's what Kierra called them – immature bros who made unfunny dick and pussy jokes ad nauseam. Those guys grated Maya's nerves, but they were generally harmless and money was money.

Apparently Joseph Mehmeti, gun kingpin, was a Bart Simpson. Sigh.

"Be that as it may, I just want to run over my rules before we get started," she said in a pleasant voice.

"Rules?" He sat back in his chair and frowned. He looked as if he were in an office.

"Rules," she said again and waited. This was always a tricky part of the negotiation, but necessary. Maya liked ChatBot and she liked being a cam model, but she wasn't interested in letting some old white man call her a nigger while he beat off to an antebellum plantation fantasy. So she waited, seeing if he was going to bail.

He didn't. He nodded minutely and she launched into her practiced speech.

"I don't mind cursing, but no derogatory language of any kind. No recording this chat. And if you want any anal play you'll have to let me know now so I can send you a new quote." She was sitting between Kenny's legs, her legs demurely to the side, her hands in her lap. She waited. She could feel the tension rolling off of Kenny's body behind her, but she didn't look for him in the laptop screen. She was certain she would lose her nerve if she did.

Finally, Mehmeti nodded once, again. "Deal."

"Great," Maya said and crawled to her knees. "So tell me how to get you off," she whispered as she leaned toward her new camera, giving him a great view of her breasts just almost about to spill out of her teddy.

"I wanna watch you suck him off," he said simply.

Maya kept her face open and seductive, but her mouth had gone dry. She raised her eyebrows and smirked, "That's it? Really?"

"A good blowjob is worth every penny," he said, like a man who'd either never had one or had only had a great one once. She shrugged and turned around to Kenny. She leaned forward and gave Mehmeti a great view of her ass.

He groaned and she heard the rustling of cloth on his end.

Kenny grabbed her camera's remote and pressed the button to mute the microphone. "You don't have to do this," he whispered.

She leaned forward, her hands on his shoulders. "You don't want me to?"

"Of course I do. But you don't have to do it for him."

It was sweet, she thought. A little condescending and tiresome, but sweet. "Babe, you're literally paying me for this. And *he's* paying me for this. I was gonna suck your dick at some point." Her eyes darted to his lap. She licked her lips. "Why not now?"

His brows had bunched together, but he didn't answer.

"Unless you think there's something wrong with us doing this? Something wrong with *me* doing this."

He shook his head. "I don't. I swear. I just wanted to make sure."

"Of?"

"That this is what *you* want," he said.

"Hello?" Joseph Mehmeti called.

Maya grabbed the remote and unmuted the mic. She turned toward the camera and smiled. "Just a second, sweetness. This is his first private chat."

"Oh, am I breaking his cherry?" he exclaimed.

"You sure are." She winked at him and muted the mic again.

She turned back to Kenny. "Okay, we're running out of time here, honey. If I didn't want your penis in my mouth, it wouldn't be heading there. These are the fundamentals."

His face turned a beautiful shade of red.

"But as it happens, I've been dreaming of sucking the life out of you for months, so why not now?" she asked again.

Kenny choked out a laugh. He grabbed her face and pulled her over him, kissing the life out of her.

"Aw yeah," Mehmeti said. "That's right."

"This guy's a douche," Kenny whispered against her lips.

She laughed and nodded. "Huge dick. Now lie back, put your hands behind your head and let me give you the best blowjob of your life." She unmuted the mic and crawled down his body.

ABOUT A MONTH after Kenny first started visiting Maya's public chatroom regularly, he'd been in China on a covert mission to track a Saudi prince. His target had recently been indicted by The Hague for human rights offenses ranging from religious persecution to torture and supporting slavery-like conditions for refugee populations. He'd been captured by the prince's security detail, which was part of the plan, and tortured for almost a week, not part of the plan. The goal had been for him to be in custody no more than three days, understanding that he would likely be tortured. The extra days had threatened to unravel him. But the thought of Maya had surprisingly pulled him through.

It was so odd. He didn't know her. They hadn't even had a private session yet. But in the midst of the waterboarding and sensory deprivation, he did what he was trained to do. He kept his mouth shut and thought of his family – his grandparents who had long since passed, his parents who were happily retired in Florida, Chanté and Maya. Maya's smile. Maya's giggle. Maya's pursed lips when she was frustrated. Maya's soft thighs jiggling as she came, Maya's coy smile. Maya.

By the time his team had located him at a black site they'd thought was abandoned, Maya was the only thing keeping him lucid enough to slip his arms through the heavy iron bars, grab his guard's neck and twist. When Asif had finally busted the door open, Kenny was barely hanging on. But he remembered the sound of Chanté's voice coming through a SAT phone and the memory of Maya turning to the camera, her pupils wide and mouth open in a gasp, her skin flushed in her post-orgasmic haze. Her smile. Until now, those semi-lucid memories had been some of the best moments of his life. But the last two days had pushed all of that aside. Because Maya's taste on his tongue, her pussy convulsing around his fingers, her soapy hands on his cock, her warm delicate fingers rolling a condom down his shaft and her wet mouth chasing her hands were better than he could have imagined. Better than he'd ever dreamed, even when his life was on the line.

They were technically performing for Joseph Mehmeti. Kenny tried to keep his mind on the mission. But he failed. He failed so badly. His hand was in Maya's hair – she'd kept it curly tonight just for him – and their eyes were locked on one another as she sucked and gripped and twisted her mouth and hands around his dick.

"Fuck," he breathed, even though he was supposed to be silent. He couldn't help himself. And he honestly didn't care. "I'm close. Fuck, I'm close." His voice was a strangled cry.

He couldn't be sure, but he thought she smiled as she sucked him over the edge. It took every bit of his self-discipline to gently pull his hand from her hair. He grabbed his own head as his abs tensed, hips arched up from the bed and he groaned wildly through his release.

She opened her mouth so that he could see his come fill the small reservoir at the tip of the condom. And this time he didn't have to imagine her smile. He was panting, groaning, his heart racing, his eyes wet and his fingers twitching to touch her again when they both started at the familiar chime from her computer; the private chat was about to end.

Maya sat up and smiled at her camera. "Was that good for you too?" Maya asked, her chin wet with her own saliva. Kenny could feel his dick trying to harden again and failing.

Joseph Mehmeti only groaned in response, the sound of his orgasm almost ruining Kenny's mood.

"Bye, love," Maya breathed and wiggled her fingers at the screen.

He heard the sound of the chat screen closing. He'd lived and died by that sound for months. Maya leaned over, tapped at her laptop and folded it shut. She grabbed the remote and powered her camera down. She turned to him with a smile on her face.

Whatever she was about to say was interrupted by his phone ringing. He pushed out a breath of air and leaned over to look at it. "It's Command."

He tapped at the phone to answer and put it on speaker. "How'd it go?"

"We've got bad news," Kierra said in a small voice.

Kenny sat up immediately. "What?"

"Get down here," Monica said.

"No. Tell us."

There was a moment of silence and Kenny was certain that the whispered negotiation between the three of them was fierce because Chanté's voice was tense when she spoke.

"I couldn't get into his computer without alerting him to my presence."

"So, we got nothing?" he said, his hands raking over his head.

"Actually, no," Kierra said. "Chanté broke through his IP scrambler and figured out where he's located."

"Where?" Maya breathed.

"San Francisco," Monica said.

"He's in the States?"

"Yes," Monica breathed.

"Is that a good thing?" Maya asked him.

But before he could answer, the ChatBot app on her phone chimed. She tapped the screen and navigated to it. "It's Mehmeti," she breathed. She turned the phone to Kenny so he could read.

"What does it say?" Monica's voice was urgent, hard.

He wrapped an arm around Maya's waist to reassure her as he read.

Dear ThickaThanASnicka

May I call you Maya? I thoroughly enjoyed our date tonight.
You and your lover were worth every penny.

"BLECH, 'LOVER'," Chanté breathed.

It has been hard for me to find a couple that satisfies me.
But tonight I am very satisfied. My dick is still hard thinking
about you.

"HONESTLY, SAME," Kierra said.

Maya rolled her eyes.

If you are amenable, I would like to invite you both to my
private club in California.
So that we might play together.

MAYA TURNED to him and frowned, "This sounds like a bad European porno. Why?"

Kenny smiled, trying to hold back his laughter.

"Oh girl, preach. What's with this corny ass dialogue? Remind me to tell you about that Serbian club!"

"Aw, I like the cheesy dialogue," Chanté said. "Very 1970s, hairy chest porn."

"Yes," Maya said. "That's the problem."

Kierra giggled.

Monica's voice was exasperated, but affectionate. Kenny could imagine her running a hand up and down Kierra's back. He squeezed Maya's side.

"Kenny, I need you to come back to Command," Monica said.

"Tonight?" Kenny had never once ignored a direct order, but he was considering it.

"No," she breathed. "This new development means tonight wasn't a bust after all. First thing in the morning though, I want you here."

"Yes, boss," he breathed, his eyes on Maya.

He hung up the phone and tossed it onto the mattress. She sucked her bottom lip into her mouth and smiled. There was so much happening and on any other mission he would have gone into the office to debrief immediately. But like every other mission since he'd discovered Maya, the job mattered so much less than being near her. And now that he was near enough to touch, he had no plans to leave.

He lifted his eyebrows and smirked, "Wanna watch another romcom?"

Maya's face lit up and she squealed, "I have ice cream." She bounced from the bed and headed to her bathroom door. "Oh," she said. "You don't like sweets."

He smiled, his heart swelling. "I'll lick it off your lips," he said, his entire body hot at the sight of her. This was more than he'd ever dreamed.

KENNY WAS TIPTOEING into his apartment once again. He and Maya had fallen asleep on the couch again. But this time he let himself carry her to bed. He'd sat on the edge of her mattress, stroking her arm for a few minutes before he'd finally decided to leave. He hadn't wanted to presume that she wanted him to spend the night. Sure, they'd had that nap, but that was a far cry from a season pass under her sheets. He wished he'd asked her if he could stay before they'd started watching that two-star *Bodyguard* knock-off.

"Was it good?" Chanté asked, her voice full of glee.

He sighed and turned toward her. "Why are you up? Again?"

"Waiting for you," she said with a shrug.

"Are you serious?"

She managed at least ten seconds of seriousness before she dissolved into giggles. "I'm kidding. I'm packing."

Kenny's frown froze on his face. "What?"

Her smile widened at his question, but he knew Chanté well enough to recognize the tension at the corners of her eyes. And for the past five years he'd associated that look with Asif.

"What did he do?"

"Nothing," Chanté said. "But he's coming."

He put his hands on his hips and began to pace the length of their living room. "Why?"

"With Lane in West Virginia, you need someone else who can help with infiltrating Mehmeti's club."

"You're an actual dancer," Kenny droned.

"A dancer with a schedule so packed I'll be flitting around the world for the next year," she said with a shameless smile and flip of her long, curly hair. "Say it."

He rolled his eyes, "No. Okay, maybe we need Asif, he's pretty good on surveillance."

"He's great at surveillance, you know that."

Kenny ignored her, "Don't we still need you to hack into the computer?"

"Well duh," she said. "But I can do that from anywhere once you all give me direct access to his machine. When it's time, Monica knows how to get ahold of me."

Kenny shook his head and stalked into the kitchen, standing across the island, glaring at her, "But isn't being with Asif what you want?"

She seemed to think about that for a few seconds. She walked around the island to stand next to him. She put her head on his bicep, since she was too short to reach his shoulder. "I don't know why I can't get over him. He's not worth my time."

"You got that right," Kenny breathed in aggravation.

"But I love him," Chanté whispered. "I can't help it."

"So why are you leaving?"

She sounded so impossibly sad when she spoke, "Because now's not the time for us. And I'm not willing to let him hurt me again."

Kenny's breath was hard and he was frowning down at the marble countertop, not wanting to frighten Chanté with his fury. But fuck if he didn't hate Asif for pushing his tiny but larger-than-life best friend to such a sad, whispered admission at two in the morning. She deserved so much more than that and Kenny could hardly contain his own frustration.

"Ken Doll," she whispered, her hands settling on his forearms. "Look at me."

When he did, he saw her the way he always did, as that round-faced first year in short shorts and glasses with a Capri Sun in her hand and a mischievous glint in her eye.

"Where are you going?" he finally asked.

She smiled. "Tracy wants to take me to Mexico."

He smiled in spite of himself. "I like her for you."

She shrugged, "Don't get attached. I don't."

Except the one time she did.

He leaned down and pressed a kiss to her hair. "Hey, can you do me a favor?" he asked.

She smiled. "Anything. You know that."

He went to the refrigerator and took out a near empty bag of sugar. Chanté frowned at him, confused. He reached inside and pulled out a plastic bag with a charred cell phone inside and handed it over.

"What's this?"

"Last month, I was on a job that went left. I don't know why and that's all I have to show for it. I've been waiting to give it to you. Whatever you can get off it would help," he finished.

"You know I love riddles," she breathed, turning the phone over in her hands.

"I know."

"Why me? Why not one of the hackers The Agency *officially* employs?"

"Because you're better," Kenny said honestly. Chanté smiled up at him. "And also because no one should have even known I was there. It was a nothing job."

Chanté's face cleared and she nodded. "Got it."

"How much?"

She patted him on the cheek, "How many times do I have to tell you that you can't afford me."

He covered her hand on his face. "Don't get arrested," he implored her with a smile.

"I'll try," she giggled. And then she leaned back to look at him. "Next time I see you, you and Maya better be Instagram official."

"I can't have an Instagram, Chanté." He rolled his eyes.

"It's a turn of phrase. You know what I mean. Lock that down."

"Ew," he said. "Come on, let's get you packed." He offered her his arm and she took it.

“I really like Maya,” she said as they walked toward her bedroom.

“So do I,” he breathed.

“Well, fucking duh. Who wouldn’t be head over heels for a girl with an ass like that? I’ll marry her, if you don’t.”

He exhaled, “You really can’t stop yourself, can you?”

She shrugged, “I don’t even try.”

“I hope you bought yourself something really big with his money,” Kenny breathed.

Chanté’s smile was dangerous and expensive, “It’s really small actually. He’s gonna be pissed when he gets that receipt.”

twelve

Kenny was starting to regret leaving Maya's apartment last night. It was the right thing to do, he knew that. But Chanté had kept him up half the night packing a surprising amount of clothes and tech for what had only been a few weeks' pit stop. By the time she was on her way, he decided to go for his regular run and head into Command. His eyes lingered on Maya's front door each time he passed. But he had a smile on his face that lasted right until he walked into Monica's kitchen.

"Kenny," Asif called as if they were old friends.

Kenny stopped short and frowned. "You're here already?"

"I was in the neighborhood actually," he said, his thick Boston accent grating on Kenny's nerves.

"Why?"

"I've been tracking some suspicious purchases from my account. Have you seen Chanté?"

Monica and Kierra both sipped their cups of coffee as they watched the exchange. Monica's eyes were blank, but Kierra's jumped excitedly between the two men.

"Not in months," he said with a shrug.

"Sure about that?" Asif's eyes narrowed suspiciously.

"Last time I saw Chanté she hadn't slept in almost three days from crying because you left her in Berlin without even bothering to say goodbye," Kenny ground out. "I'm very fucking sure."

Asif at least had the almost decency to look embarrassed, but almost was all Asif could manage and it was never going to be enough as far as Kenny was concerned. Not enough for Chanté. His hands flexed at his side.

"Well then," Kierra cut in, "I'm gonna go pick up Maya and uh, hurry back here for the briefing."

"Good," Monica said. They all waited as Kierra scurried from the kitchen. When she was gone, Monica spoke, "Is this going to be a problem?" She gestured between them.

"I'm fine," Asif said, his voice light and airy as usual.

"So am I," Kenny hissed.

"Perfect. Now let's get this mission underway," she said, walking toward the pantry.

Asif grinned at him, big and confident and smug. Kenny glared and clenched his fists.

He marveled that it had only been a few hours since he'd woken up with Maya's head on his shoulder and her body curled into his side. It felt like weeks had passed and he missed her.

He should have grabbed a pillow and hunkered down on the floor next to her bed, he thought, hating himself for not thinking of it sooner.

ASIF KNEW KENNY WAS LYING. There was no fucking way someone buying designer purses and size five-and-a-half shoes (Chanté's exact size!) in the same city where Kierra, Monica, Lane *and* Kenny were currently set up could ever be a coincidence. He knew his pint-sized pickpocket was somewhere nearby, and he was going to find her. But in the meantime, he was perfectly willing to bring down the Albanian mob. It sounded fun!

"So what you're telling me," Asif said, cutting into Monica's brief of the mission thus far, "is that Captain America over there catfished this Amazon – who's way the fuck outta your league, by the way," he leaned across the table to hiss at Kenny. "And you're not going to report him? *And*," he yelled, "she gave him a world class blowjob last night, but nobody recorded it?" He laughed while shaking his head, "This place is bizarro world. You're all gonna get fired for fraternizing with *yet another* civilian, and that woman is a saint."

"I'm gonna break your nose," Kenny hissed.

"Is that a threat?"

"It's a fucking promise."

"Oh," Asif sat up straight in his chair, a broad smile on his face, "I like new Kenny."

"Will you both shut the fuck up," Monica yelled. She might not have actually raised her voice, but it definitely boomed.

They sat back in their seats like chastened children. Asif turned his head to smile at Kenny, who glared back. Oh good, he thought to himself, this is far from over.

"As I was saying," Monica continued, "Now that we know where Joseph Mehmeti is and we have an invitation inside his club, we need to move forward as if we're only going to have one shot inside."

"One shot inside to do what?" Asif asked.

"Our orders are to apprehend Joseph and turn him over to a black ops team for interrogation."

Kenny exhaled an angry breath. For once Asif agreed.

"So this fucker has been buying guns from terrorist cells in Russia and selling them to white supremacists and they're sending us in to *arrest* him?" Asif scoffed and dropped his head to inspect his perfectly manicured nails. "On second thought, I might actually be busy."

"We also need to clone his hard drive so we can track his global contacts. We need to know exactly who he's been arming."

When Asif looked up, Monica was watching him. She'd said those words to pique his interest; dangle the hope of Chanté. It worked. "We'd need a hacker for that," he breathed.

"We will."

He clapped his hands together and stood. "Well fuck, why didn't you say so. Count me in." He put his hands in his pockets and leaned across the table to whisper to Kenny, "Tell my little rabbit that I'm coming for her and I hope she bought a very slinky dress to match those shoes."

Kenny pushed up from the table and Asif laughed. There were few things more exhilarating than pissing Kenny off. Well, at least when Chanté wasn't around.

Kenny's face was red with fury and he was taking deep breaths to calm himself. When he finally spoke, however, Asif's glee seemed to seep out of his pores. "I wonder," Kenny said in an eerily calm voice, "if the person making those suspicious purchases from your account has bought anything recently."

Asif's entire body stilled. Dread washed over him. He tore his eyes away from Kenny and pulled his phone from his pocket. He logged into his banking app, which Chanté always found a way to hack no matter how many times he changed his password or how random the string of numbers, letters and symbols, and not even now that he'd instituted a two-factor authentication system with a biometric screening. All of which he'd changed almost a week ago after a very expensive pair of shoes had been bought by someone in New Jersey from a custom boutique in Milan. The shoes were neon pink with crystals up the ankle strap. He'd seen a picture. They were absolutely Chanté's style and they would look fucking fantastic on her.

"What the fuck?" he yelled. He looked from Kenny's smiling face to Monica's impassive glare. "She bought a diamond encrusted thong!?"

Kenny fell back into his chair howling with laughter.

Monica locked eyes with him, "Please never tell Kierra or Lane that's a thing, said seriously.

MAYA THOUGHT she'd be waking up to Kenny's arms wrapped around her. Not Kierra leaning over her with a smug smile on her face.

Maya rolled her eyes and ducked her head under her covers. "Go away!"

But Kierra just plopped down on the bed and stretched out next to her. Her friend's short body was a poor replacement for Kenny's. Maya peeked over the edge of her comforter and glared.

"Was it so good he put you to sleep or were you two up all night going at it like rabbits?" She raised her hands and crossed her index and middle fingers, "I know what I'm hoping for."

Maya growled and threw the covers off of her. "If you must know, we watched a romcom and ate the rest of the ice cream."

Kierra sprang up and glared down at Maya, "Bitch, if you ate my berry crumble-"

Maya smirked, "All gone."

The two best friends had never really fought, but Kierra's eyes were full of murder. She was so small. If forced, Maya was certain she could take her. They were both momentarily sizing each other up when Kierra seemed to think better of her odds and pushed from the bed, staring down at her friend. Her arms were crossed.

"I'm going to let that slide," she said in a restrained voice, "but only because I'm moving out thanks to you."

"No one told you to start banging your bosses and fall in love, little bit." Maya yawned and stretched. "How soon?"

Kierra shrugged, "Don't know. Lane's gone silent wherever he is. At least with me."

Maya sat up in bed, "Is everything…"

She shrugged again, "Monica says he's fine. But I don't really know."

"I'm sorry, short stack."

"It's okay," she breathed, and turned away with a surreptitious swipe of her hand along her cheek. She turned back to look at Maya with a raised eyebrow, "I mean, it would have been nice to eat my feelings in ice cream this morning-"

"But you can't. Oh well."

"You're terrible, you know that?"

"I try. Why are you in my room?"

Kierra's eyes lit up, "Oh yeah, I'm here to get you for a briefing."

Maya lowered her eyes and tried to sound nonchalant. "Why'd they send you?" She whispered.

Now a good friend might have been sympathetic and answered Maya's question directly and lovingly, noticing the apprehension in her voice. And Kierra was a good friend. But Maya could accept that she *had* eaten the rest of her pint of ice cream. So really, when Kierra started cackling, she guessed she deserved the response she got.

"I fucking knew you liked him! That blowjob last night must have been damn good. Girl, maybe you should teach a class!"

Maya threw one of her pillows at Kierra's head. It made contact. Kierra did not stop laughing.

Not at all the morning Maya had been expecting.

MONICA HAD LED lots of different kinds of teams on all kinds of missions. The trick, she'd learned over time, was not to choose the best technical agents or the agents who always got along. Her style had always been to construct her teams based on who was willing to do exactly what she said, when she said it. It was too much to hope for the kind of devotion Lane gave her, but he was her benchmark. Would an agent run into a burning building if she told him to? No? Then he could fuck off and work with someone else. Yes? Great, now listen up: she would never send anyone into a burning building unless she went in first. She needed people who could follow her orders and watch her back until the bitter end if necessary. This kind of leadership had inspired an incredible amount of loyalty over the years.

But she had also come to realize that the people who had proven to be loyal to her were not particularly loyal to one another, or at least not in any demonstrable way other than as a mission imperative. So her best team was usually a sarcastic comment – probably from Lane – away from a full-on implosion at the best of times. And this did not feel like the best of times, she thought as she glared across the conference table at Kenny and Asif. Both great agents and both utterly useless if one of them decided to shoot the other.

"We're heeeere," Kierra called from the foyer as if they weren't spies planning a secret mission. She stopped in the doorway and fixed Monica with an impish smile and fluttered her eyelashes.

Monica sighed, "Is your skirt shorter than when you left?"

Kierra smiled and clapped her hands, "I hiked it up, thanks for noticing." Monica really missed Lane in that moment.

"Move, smurf," Maya said from the hallway and Kierra pitched forward.

As soon as Maya stepped into the doorway Kenny stood

up, his ears reddening and a stupid grin spreading across his lips.

"Hi there, sweet girl," Asif said to Kierra as she bounded across the room to Monica.

She stopped in her tracks and frowned down at him. "If you call me that again, I'll have Chanté buy a small island with your money," she hissed. And then collected herself, "Wherever she is." She walked to the front of the room to plant a small kiss on Monica's cheek, her hand slowly stroking Monica's clenched fists, urging her to relax.

"Hi," Kenny breathed.

"Hi," Maya said with a blush.

"Well, isn't this sweet," Asif said with bared teeth.

Kenny's back stiffened but he kept his eyes on Maya as she walked toward him. She turned to Asif.

"Who are you?" Maya asked.

"My name's Asif," he said reaching his hand across the table.

Kenny slapped it away, but Asif was unfazed.

"And I know who you are," he said with a wink. "They got me caught up on your work for us and can I just say, I really hope you make it to the site-wide charts for that performance a few days ago."

Monica smiled warmly, "Thank you. I really put my all into that."

Kenny swallowed loudly.

"It showed," Asif said. "I heard there was a blowjob last night. Sorry I missed that. You ever think about doing a tutorial?"

"That's what I said," Kierra chimed in.

Asif turned and nodded at her before returning to Maya, "It'd be a hit. Trust me."

Maya sucked her bottom lip into her mouth, and they all pretended not to hear the muffled groan Kenny tried to pass off as a cough.

"I guess I could think about it."

"I hope you do. And if you need a volunteer-"

"Don't make me shoot you," Kenny said as a wicked smile spread across Asif's lips.

"Who are you exactly?" Maya squinted.

"Asif works for The Agency," Kenny ground out, his dislike for his colleague dripping from every word. "He's here to help us infiltrate Mehmeti's club."

"I'm also looking for someone who's been robbing me blind. You haven't run into a computer whiz with big curly hair, full mouth, great hips, sometimes exotic dancer with a laptop attached to her too-long acrylic nails, have you? About this tall," he said, his hand hitting around mid-chest. "She might have tried to get you into bed or maybe left a pile of glitter in her wake?"

Everyone held their breath as Maya stared at Asif. She pursed her lips and shook her head. "Nope. But if I see her," Maya said, leaning across the table toward him, "she wouldn't have to work too hard to get me anywhere."

Asif's mouth fell open.

Maya turned toward Kenny and smiled, the wink implied. And then she turned to Monica, "So does this mean I get hazard pay *and* a field bonus?"

"That's my girl!" Kierra exclaimed.

Monica missed Lane.

THE PLAN WAS SIMPLE. Not simple to execute, but direct. There was a chance she was overestimating Mehmeti's security, but she felt certain she was giving the man far more credit than he deserved. Any idiot smug enough to conduct business on the site where he jacked off and video-chatted with total strangers to get his rocks off, was not someone who was likely to be particularly stringent about things like computer passwords. It seemed possible that he relied on his security to keep people out and that's it. Monica was betting this mission on the hunch that once Mehmeti invited someone inside his club all bets were off. And with Maya in front of him, Monica felt certain that what few defenses he had left would melt away. Maya was their honeypot Trojan horse.

"We'll leave first thing tomorrow morning," Monica announced to the room. "We'll have a few hours in San Francisco before you arrive. All you two have to do is pretend to be a happy couple on a vacation paid for by an eccentric mobster who maybe just wants to watch you fuck."

"I've always wanted to do that," Kierra whispered.

"You have?" Maya asked.

Kierra winked at Maya but turned to Monica to answer, "I have a very active imagination."

"I missed this horny bunch," Asif chuckled.

"Anyway, once we get to San Francisco, we can't have any direct contact with you just in case Mehmeti is watching but keep an eye out for one of us just in case. Is that clear?"

Kenny and Maya nodded.

"Once we're all in the club on Wednesday night-"

"Wait, how are you three getting in?" Maya asked.

"No idea," Asif said. "We'll figure it out."

Kierra smirked, "I've got this dress. It's all mesh and-"

"Let's stay on track," Monica hissed. "That should leave you and Kenny to deal with Joseph and his personal guard."

She turned to Kenny, "I thought you all were supposed to be super spies. This plan sounds thin as hell."

"Preach, girl," Kierra mumbled under her breath. Monica glared at her, but she just shrugged. Shameless insubordination. When Lane returned, Monica started to think, but had to nip that thought in the bud. They didn't have time for her to be distracted. More distracted than normal.

"It's best you don't know any more than is necessary," Monica said. "Just know that we'll all be there on Wednesday night. We'll do our jobs and you do yours. Asif," she said turning to him. "We'll need an exit strategy that will have to get past the security system since we can't hack into it remotely."

"And how do you know that?" Asif asked, fishing for more information on Chanté, which Monica was absolutely not going to give.

"We have intel."

"What do you think security will be like?" Kenny asked. Finally, a mission-related interjection.

"We can't know for sure. The Mehmeti family has lots of money to splash around and lots of enemies. Let's plan to be outnumbered."

Kenny nodded.

"Our hacker-"

"Whose name is?" Asif asked.

"Steven, he's new," she answered automatically. "Our hacker tells us that the club is in a warehouse in Hunter's Point. It used to be a poor neighborhood. It's gentrifying, but not gentrified. Hopefully we can use that to our advantage." She tapped the smart screen and brought up schematics for the building. "The bottom floor seems to be a sex store."

"Smart," Kenny said.

"Will I have time to shop?" Maya interjected. Monica pretended again that she didn't hear Kenny's gasp. Maya did not. She smiled and ran a nail down the back of his hand.

"The second and third floors are the dance club, but we don't know much more than that. The fourth floor is some kind of meeting space, the local ATF thinks, but again we don't know much more than that. And then Joseph occupies the top floor."

"Where he jacks off to cam models all day and sometimes sells guns to terrorists," Kenny said.

"Fun," Asif interjected.

"When you make it here," Monica said, speaking specifically to Maya and pointing at the top floor on the schematics. "You need to distract Joseph and any of his personal security. Kenny will locate the computer. Is that clear?" She made sure not to blink. This was all fun and games and flirting and blowjobs until it wasn't. Kenny was too besotted with Maya to scare her, and Kierra didn't have a clear sense of danger, especially not when she was horny – which was at least 90% of the time – so it was up to Monica to impress upon her the seriousness of their situation. "Joseph can't suspect anything is out of sorts at least until you three are alone."

"Monica," Kenny started, but she cut him off with a raised hand.

"I've seen you on camera. You put on a great show. You make everyone watching think you're performing just for them." Maya's eyes cut to Kenny, who sucked in a sharp breath. Monica brushed the awkwardness of their relationship aside, that was none of her business. Apprehending Joseph Mehmeti and keeping them all alive was her objective. "Think of this trip as the performance of your life. If you succeed, we bring down a spoiled international arms dealer and you earn enough money to make sure that your brother and sister can afford to finish college without student loans. But if you fail, we all pay the price."

Monica watched as the realization of what she was saying washed over Maya. Kenny's hands were clutched into fists on the table, but they were all quiet, even Kierra and Asif.

Eventually Maya nodded, sitting up straight in her chair. Monica watched Maya put a gentle hand over Kenny's before she spoke. Her voice was strong, even though she was clearly nervous, "How much is the field bonus?"

Monica smirked, she agreed with Lane, Maya was something else. But she tamped down on her approval. "That depends on the hazard rating."

"What's that?" She turned to Kierra for help.

"Agency standard hazard rating," Kierra nodded proudly.

"There's a whole complicated grid about approved weaponry and personnel and percentages of total expenditures." She rolled her eyes.

Monica nodded, happy to see that Kierra *had* been studying for her Classified Materials exam. "Until we can gather more intel, this op has been rated a level five hazard. The higher the danger, the lower the number."

"Not that you want a level one," Kierra whispered across the table with a smile, "but if it happens, you won't ever have to work again a day in your life." And then she sat up straight, "Assuming you survive."

"Nice one," Kenny said.

Kierra cringed and mouthed, "Sorry."

Maya nodded at Monica, "The performance of my life. Got it."

"What about Lane?" Kierra whispered.

"I talked to Lane this morning. He's in West Virginia."

"You talked to Lane?" Kierra asked, her voice brightening with excitement but also his name was strangled with worry as it fell from her lips.

Monica moved around the table to stroke her shoulder tenderly.

"He checked in. He's fine. The rest is classified," she said. She knew that wouldn't be enough, but right now it would have to do.

"So what's the name of this club anyway?" Maya asked excitedly.

Monica moved back to the smart screen and tapped it, revealing a series of surveillance images they'd received from the ATF office in San Francisco. Apparently, the club was under surveillance as a potential site for trafficking already. The ATF didn't seem to have any idea that it was an Albanian mobster's front, but these were all things Monica thought they could use to their advantage if the mission spiraled out of control.

"LICK." Maya read the signage above the otherwise nondescript brick building that still looked like an abandoned factory from the exterior.

Kierra groaned. "Dear lord, not again."

Monica couldn't help but smile.

"What do you mean, 'again'?" Maya asked.

Kierra looked at Monica before she answered. Monica nodded.

"Okay, so basically European sex clubs are somehow cheesy as fuck, with the worst names, and also a bit wild. I know from experience," she said as she widened her eyes and nodded sagely at her friend.

"You don't have to do this," Kenny interjected quickly, turning to Maya.

"Actually, you do," Monica corrected.

Kenny opened his mouth to protest but Monica silenced him with a look. While she could understand his impulse to provide Maya a way out, this was what she'd signed up for. This was what they'd all signed up for.

Maya turned to Kenny and put a hand on his face tenderly. "You'll be with me, right?" She whispered.

His eyes softened, and he nodded. "Every step of the way."

"So fucking sweet," Kierra whispered.

"Very," Asif breathed and leaned forward. "You know, if you two are ever looking for a third-" he started.

Kenny turned to glare at him, but it was Kierra who replied.

"Hey," she said in a sharp tone to get Asif's attention. They all turned to look at her. "I know I seem very meek and calm." Everyone at the table squinted at her in disbelief, but she kept going. "But if you don't shut that fucking leering at my friend all the way down, I really will stab you. Don't sully the cute shit they have going on over there."

Maya exhaled around a smile at Kierra, who smiled back.

"Besides, if her and Kenny decide they want to get a little freaky, *clearly* it'll be with us," she said gesturing toward Monica.

"You really don't know when to stop, do you?" Maya breathed, an annoyed glare on her face.

Kierra leaned forward and shook her head, "Not a clue."

Monica sighed. It would be a miracle if they even made it in the club's front door.

mission prep #2

"Is there anything I can get you?" Kierra asked as she shimmied onto Monica's desk.

"No," Monica said, pretending to pore over the trip manifest in front of her.

"Are you sure?" Kierra leaned down to whisper the words directly into Monica's ear.

"I have a lot of work to do before we leave." Monica looked up. "And so do you."

Kierra smiled smugly, "I've pulled all of the hardware you requested on the mission manifest and packed it for transport. All you have to do is approve it. I've contacted the safe house in the Mission district, and I've scheduled our transportation to the airport. We take off just before dawn tomorrow. I'm just waiting for Maya and Kenny to finish up in his office so we can head home and pack." As she spoke, Kierra pushed the papers in front of Monica out of the way and settled herself on the desk in front of her, her legs demurely to one side, knees together.

"How do you manage all of this?" Monica asked as she looked up into Kierra's bright eyes, her own gaze warm and her body tingling.

"All of what?"

Monica shook her head and almost lifted the side of her mouth into a smile. "How do you do your job and still have time to proposition me? All of our previous assistants were junior agents and they could just barely keep up with our needs."

Kierra's smile was instantaneous and dirty; she loved awe-filled compliments. She moved to spread her legs in front of Monica and lifted her skirt up her thighs. "I'm a very motivated person," she said, a hand traveling between her legs. She rubbed along the front of her panties. Monica's eyes followed the movement.

She had a lot to do between now and take off. But when Kierra pulled that little scrap of wet cotton aside, she knew she would just have to make it all happen with a bit less time at her disposal. She ran her hands up Kierra's thighs and gripped her hips, pulling her ass closer to the edge of the desk. Closer to her mouth.

"You promise that Lane is okay?" Kierra whispered, her eyes soft and fearful.

Monica lifted one hand and stroked her thumb lightly across Kierra's bottom lip. "I promise, sweet girl. And he gave me a message for you."

Kierra smiled minutely, "He did?"

Monica slipped her thumb between Kierra's lips. The tip of her tongue brushed the pad of her finger. "He told me to tell you not to behave."

Kierra's mouth widened into a full-fledged smile and she nipped at Monica's finger. "Never." Monica knew *that* was a promise.

When she lowered her mouth to Kierra's pussy, licking and sucking at her with firm pressure, she didn't gentle the strokes of her tongue or her fingers as they sawed into Kierra's cunt. Her thrusts were strong, just the way they liked. Because this, too, was a promise. A promise that Lane would be back soon and they would all make it out of this alright.

"I won't let you out of my sight," Kenny said, not for the first time.

"Mmmmhmmm," Maya mumbled.

"I might have to carry a gun," he mumbled, "I'm sorry."

"S'okay," she said, breathless. "Just don't shoot me."

He pulled back from her with a stricken look on his face. "I would never. I'm always safe."

Maya couldn't help but smile, "I was joking. I assume you all have to go through some kind of gun safety training… workshop?"

"We log thousands of hours and have to record every time we fire our guns at the range. You're completely safe with me."

She smiled, shocked to find that she believed him. Completely. And she told him so. He visibly relaxed.

"Now if we could get back to business," she said, squeezing his dick. He groaned and his back bowed. She guided his mouth back to hers and gasped against his lips as his fingers began to move inside of her again. Maybe it was the adrenaline of the upcoming mission that made everything around them seem so real all of a sudden. Or maybe it was just they could sense that whatever was coming would put them on display in a way that was both familiar, but also brand new. And they wanted something that was private to ground them in the fact that they were real. That they had been something before this operation.

Or maybe it was just months of pent up sexual frustration still rearing its head and the few stolen kisses and soft touches and a stellar blowjob just wasn't enough. This quick mutual masturbation wasn't going to be enough either, but it was all they had time for. And it was all theirs.

"Fuck," Maya breathed as he slipped his tongue into her mouth. "I'm so happy you're a good kisser," she mumbled.

He pulled back, "Huh?"

"I said I'm so happy you're a good kisser. I was afraid you wouldn't be."

He smiled. "I'm good at a lot of things, Maya."

There was something about the way he said her name that made her heart swell and throb right along with her clit. Well, the way he said her name and the way one hand was working her pussy over and the other was pinching her nipples and the way his dick was swelling in her palm. It was all so much and not enough at all.

"I want to wait," she whispered.

His brow furrowed. "Wait for what?"

"I want to fuck you so bad," she said. "But not until the mission is over."

She wanted to explain herself, but the hormones flooding her veins made complex sentences difficult to come by. But when he moved his hand from her breast to gently grip the side of her neck, stroking her jaw, she knew that he got it. She wanted them to have something to look forward to. She wanted them to survive.

They kept their eyes locked together and stroked each other purposely to beautiful, gentle and just a little bit dirty orgasms. He moved his mouth over hers, panting into their kiss, "So we'll wait."

Asif was pacing around the living room, his cell phone pressed to his ear. Chanté's phone rang and rang until her voicemail picked up again.

"I'm booked and busy. Leave a message."

He huffed out a breath. This was the third time in a row he'd called her phone. She hadn't picked up. Not even when he went anonymous. He finally decided to leave a message.

"Chanté," he said her name in his sweetest voice, but then descended into frustrated snarls. "Where are you? I came all the way to New Jersey for you. New. Jersey. Pick up." He practically barked the last two words.

And then he took a deep breath. "I'm sorry." It wasn't the first time he'd said it. It wouldn't be the last. He didn't even bother to apologize about a specific hurt anymore. There were too many. Sometimes the words were less an apology than an admission. He didn't deserve her. He knew that. He'd always known. He'd tried for a time to ignore that yawning pit of inadequacy in his gut, but he knew who he was. He was the kind of man who ruined everything he touched. He didn't know any other way to be.

Once the realization hit, he'd run away from her, from himself, from a future where he would only hurt her more. And he kept on running, returning for a bit every now and then and always when she needed him most. He meant well, but he was also selfish and could never quite see how his leaving hurt her; each disappearance dimming just a bit of the light in her eyes; doing the exact thing he was always trying so hard not to do.

It was proof, wasn't it? That he was right. That he was always going to fuck up. He'd been telling her that for years, but she never got it. Or at least she hadn't until Berlin. Now she didn't reach out to him anymore. She used to drop everything to answer his calls, to run across the world just to be with him. Not anymore. She was hiding from him and it broke something inside Asif's stunted heart to realize that she'd finally seen the truth of who he was. He'd always known this day would come, but deep down he'd hoped that no matter what he did, Chanté would always love him. She'd never get tired of him. She'd always be there.

But she wasn't. Not anymore. Not like she used to be. She left breadcrumbs: a fraudulent purchase here, a trace on his location there. But it wasn't the same.

"I'm sorry," he said again and then hung up.

thirteen

"I've never flown first class before," Maya said excitedly, practically bouncing in her chair.

It was adorable. She was adorable. So much so that Kenny was having a hard time focusing on their surroundings, scanning the other passengers as they filed down the aisle to their seats. He was certain that Mehmeti would have placed someone on the flight with them and he wanted to figure out who it was. It wasn't strictly necessary; he and Maya had already agreed to hold their cover from the time they left their apartment building this morning until Joseph Mehmeti was in Agency custody. But a good spy knows that you can never have too much information.

Still, his eyes kept drifting to his left to look at Maya as she marveled at how much leg room she had to stretch out. He only wanted to look at her and that was a problem.

"Champagne?" The flight attendant leaned toward them, taking advantage of a break in the onboarding traffic to serve the premium passengers. Kenny started, he hadn't heard her approach; he was very focused on the hem of Maya's dress and the expanse of her thighs.

"Yes, please," Maya said, reaching across Kenny's body to grasp the small plastic flute.

"And you, sir?"

He was about to shake his head when Maya elbowed him. He smiled and reached for the glass instead, opening his tray table to set it down.

"I can't drink while we're away, Maya," he whispered as the flight attendant moved on. Away meaning on the mission.

She took a sip of her drink and nodded as she swallowed. "I know," she rolled her eyes, they'd been over this. "That's for me."

He raised his eyebrows at her.

She put her glass down on the tray beside his and leaned over their armrests into his side. The heavy weight of her breast made his throat close and every muscle in his body tensed in the best way. Maya's lips almost touched his before she moved her head and skimmed her lips along his jaw, his teeth clenched.

She whispered to him, "If we were a young couple being flown out to San Francisco first class by a billionaire paying us a bunch of money to let him watch us fuck, we'd be celebrating, right?"

He nodded once, unable to speak now that the scent of her soft floral perfume was filling his nostrils; gently pulling him under. Not that he was resisting.

"I'll drink the champagne so you can focus on the spy stuff," she whispered, and then because she was evil or perfect or both, her tongue snaked out to wet the inner shell of his ear. He couldn't help but dip his head and smile.

"You're a natural," he said.

"Natural what?" She leaned back in her chair and smiled at him. A soft smile, curious, beautiful. She was so fucking beautiful.

Everything, he wanted to say. "The spy stuff," he whispered instead.

Maya reached for her glass of champagne and winked at him as she took a sip.

He smiled back at her, glad that the tray would hide the gentle mound of his erection. This was going to be a long trip.

"THERE'S something wrong with the flight attendant," Maya whispered over the rim of the second glass of champagne, her eyes trained on the front of the airplane.

They'd just reached the cruising altitude and the flight attendants were up preparing for the drinks service. After being on high alert during boarding, Kenny had finally relaxed. Well, he was as relaxed as Maya had ever seen him when she wasn't touching his dick.

"What do you mean?" Kenny turned to her.

"I said there's something wrong with the flight attendant."

He rolled his eyes, "Yes, I heard you. What's wrong with her?"

She chewed on the question for a bit and then frowned, "I'm not sure. But something."

Kenny exhaled and sat back in his chair. She turned to him and watched as his shoulders sagged. She was momentarily distracted by those shoulders, big and strong and certain to look great between her thighs.

"Maya," Kenny said, pulling her out of her reverie. "Please don't look at me like that."

She tilted her head to the left and smiled at him, "Like what?"

"Like you want me to fuck you in the airplane bathroom."

Her nose wrinkled and she shook her head. "First of all, that's disgusting. Those things smell like industrial strength disinfectant and urine. Second of all, I can barely fit in there alone, so you're certainly not coming in with me. And thirdly, with all of this leg room we could just throw a blanket over our laps if we want to fool around." She shrugged.

Kenny made a choked sound and grabbed the inflight magazine, putting it over his lap. She couldn't help but smile.

"There's nothing wrong with the flight attendant," he said, red-faced.

Her smile slipped and then she remembered that that's what they'd been talking about. "Oh right. Yeah there is. Trust me."

He leaned toward her, their arms touching on the armrest between them, "I thought you were going to leave the spy stuff to me."

She leaned forward, their mouths were so close. "I am. But I can help, can't I?"

"Of course you can." He held her gaze and when he spoke, his soft breath tickled her lips. She wanted to lean forward and lick him again. She was finding it hard, harder than she'd expected, to keep her tongue off of him. Well, at least anyone watching would think they were definitely a couple.

Or very affectionate friends?

"Okay," she said, "then in the name of help, something ain't right with her ass."

He exhaled again.

"Stop the dramatic sighs and listen to me."

"I'm listening-"

"More champagne?" The flight attendant asked. They both jumped in their seats and turned toward her.

"Fuck, you scared me," Maya breathed.

She only smiled. "I'm so sorry. Would you like more champagne?"

They both shook their heads. She nodded and moved to the next row. "More champagne?"

When she was out of earshot Maya turned to Kenny and traced a finger across his jaw, "Come on. Tell me."

She watched his strong muscle tick underneath her touch, which unexpectedly made her nipples hard.

"Something *might* be up with the flight attendant," he whispered, placing heavy emphasis on the word 'might'.

It wasn't a full admission of her correctness, but she'd take it. And make him pay. She smiled and leaned forward, pressing her lips to his. She wanted to slip her tongue inside his mouth and pull another groan from him but she didn't. "Maybe I am a natural at the spy stuff," she whispered against his lips. She pulled back and smiled at him.

He rolled his eyes, but smiled as well. She moved her hand to his cheek, "You have a tiny dimple. Right here," she said, brushing her thumb over the barely noticeable indentation.

His breath caught and then he whispered, "What should we do for our next date?"

It was her turn to gasp. She closed her eyes as his hand touched her arm and moved over her stomach, around her hip and settled on the curve of her ass. She chewed on her bottom lip and smiled, her eyes still closed, as his breathing became labored. When she opened her eyes, he was looking at her as if he was cataloguing every minute detail of her face. He probably was.

Her thumb moved back and forth over the place where his dimple had briefly appeared. There was something about knowing it was there that made Maya's heart race.

"I guess a dinner and movie would be too normal," she said.

His lips curved slightly into a smile.

"I've always wanted to go to Hawai'i," she said.

He smiled fully, "Yeah?"

She shrugged and dropped her eyes. He moved his free hand under her chin to lift her head. She blushed and nodded.

"Then I'll take you to Hawai'i," he whispered and leaned down to kiss her. He didn't hesitate to use his lips to pry hers open and slip his tongue into her mouth. This kiss was slow and tender and full of promise that everything would be just fine. She hoped.

MAYA WAS PASSED OUT, her head resting on Kenny's shoulder. On the one hand, he thought that was probably a great development. Maybe now he could focus on figuring out if there was a Mehmeti plant on the plane. Or at least in first class. But on the other hand, Maya had practically wrapped herself around his side and one of her arms was flung across his waist. He still might have survived that, except she'd wriggled her fingers just under his shirt.

And as much as he was trying to focus on the flight attendant and the mid-forties businessman two rows ahead who kept looking back at them – both likely candidates for Mehmeti plants – his brain refused to let him stray too far away from how perfect her skin felt against his.

The flight attendant caught his eye as she walked down the aisle toward him. He smiled, tensed, and prepared for anything.

"Hello sir, would you like a blanket?" She gestured toward Maya.

"Yes," he said, trying not to think about what Maya had said about them fooling around.

The flight attendant moved to the overhead compartment just behind their seats. When she returned, she unfolded the blanket and tossed it over them.

"Mr. Mehmeti is looking forward to meeting you both," she whispered.

Kenny's eyes widened, because his cover demanded it, but he schooled his body not to tense as if in preparation. He wanted to look shocked, not deadly.

"When we land, there will be a car to take you to your

hotel. You'll receive further instructions there. In the meantime, if there's anything else you need, please let me know."

Kenny gulped and nodded.

Her eyes shifted to Maya and she licked her lips. "I look forward to seeing you both tonight," she said before she walked away.

Kenny watched her go, his eyes wide, his heart racing and his hands clenched under the blanket.

Maya shifted against him. She rubbed her face into his chest and snuggled closer.

"Told you," she mumbled and then fell back to sleep.

THEY WERE STARTING their descent into SFO. Maya was awake and looking somehow both grumpy and smug. The flight attendant was fluttering around them, preparing the passengers for landing and also sending hungry glances their way.

Maya turned to stare out the window, looking down on the city as it appeared. She melted when Kenny wrapped his body around hers from the back. He placed a small kiss on her shoulder. "Welcome home," he whispered.

She smiled, "You remembered."

"I remember everything you ever told me," he whispered. "Also there's a file on you at The Agency because of Kierra. It's pretty thorough."

She turned to him with pursed lips. He cringed and shrugged.

"Say less," she hissed.

He smiled.

A man stood in the aisle in front of them. "Yes?" Maya said.

Kenny's entire body tensed as he turned.

The man was kinda cute, just below middle-aged maybe,

with some nice gray in his beard and beautiful dark brown skin. "I'm sorry but are you," and then he leaned forward to whisper, "ThickaThanASnicka from ChatBot?"

Maya raised her eyebrows. "I am," she replied warily.

The man smiled and clapped his hands. "I knew it." And then he looked at Kenny. "Oh man, you must be the boyfriend." He reached out to shake Kenny's hand and then Maya's. "I'm a *huge* fan. Your last broadcast," he said, shaking his head and pressing his palms together as if in prayer. "Fantastic. You totally deserved to make the daily rankings. Congratulations!"

Maya smiled her best, biggest smile, "Thank you."

"Um… yeah, thanks?" Kenny said, his body still tense but confusion dripping from his voice.

"Sorry to interrupt. I've just been trying to figure out if that was you the entire flight. Oh my god, wait 'til I tell my wife that I met you. She's going to be *so* jealous."

"You watch me with your wife?" Maya asked.

He nodded vigorously.

She narrowed her eyes and chewed on her bottom lip, "I wonder how many other couple viewers I have." The wheels in Maya's brain were turning. She whipped out her phone and opened the notes app.

She looked up, "What's your screen name?"

"Uh, Big Keith underscore 01," he said.

She nodded as she typed, "Would you and your wife be interested in dedicated couple content? You think there's a market for that?"

His eyes and mouth yawned wide and he looked shocked even as he nodded, "We'd love that."

"Interesting. Let me give it some thought and I'll contact you. Maybe I'll do a focus group for couples."

BigKeith_01 looked like he was ready to melt, "My wife is going to give me the best head of my life when she hears this."

Maya's smile brightened. "Do you guys use flavored lube?"

The person in the row in front of them started but Maya didn't pay him any mind.

"Nah," Keith said, "She can't find a flavor she likes. We manage though."

Maya nodded, "If you go on the shop on my ChatBot page, I have a link to a store where I sell my favorite products."

"Wait, you do?" Kenny asked.

"Yes, oh my god, I need to make sure I advertise that better. Anyway," she turned back to Keith, "Try the lube I have there. My favorite flavor is vanilla. And when she's sucking you," the man in front of them started again. Maya ignored him again, "Tell her to use lots of lube, a firm grip and tongue. Less work for her, better feel for you."

Kenny started.

Maya's smile widened, "It's what he likes." She tilted her head toward Kenny. Out of the corner of her eye she could see that his face had gone completely red.

"I-I'll tell her," Keith said, a slight sheen of sweat developing at his hairline.

"Excuse me sir, you need to return to your seat," their flight attendant said, eyeing them warily.

"Oh. Okay, sure." He turned back to Maya, "Oh my god, I can't believe I met you."

"You're the first viewer I've ever met in real life. Thanks for being totally cool and not creepy," she said sincerely.

"Yeah, thank you," Kenny repeated.

"Oh absolutely. You literally make my wife and I very happy. You deserve to know that," he said, before waving and turning away. After he was back in his seat he turned and waved at them again.

"That was so cool," Maya said.

"Yeah," Kenny breathed, "Except he wasn't the first viewer you've met."

Maya turned to him, confusion surely written all over her

face. And then her mouth opened and she nodded, "Oh god, I totally forgot." She laughed.

"How could you forget? I'm right here," he frowned.

She laughed a little louder. "No," she said reaching out to cup his cheek. "I meant I forgot that you were a viewer. I haven't thought about you like that for a long time," she admitted.

Maya watched the words settle over him. She laughed as he reached for her face and pulled her mouth to his. Out of the corner of her eye she saw their flight attendant smile their way. It sobered her for that half a second before their lips touched. This would be great for their cover, but the kiss was all real. And that was difficult for Maya to reconcile; how something so real could have blossomed under such odd circumstances.

KENNY WALKED down the aisle first, his hand outstretched behind him holding Maya's tight.

"Thank you for flying with us. I look forward to seeing you again," their flight attendant said to Kenny, as her eyes turned to Maya, lustful. Maya tried not to shudder.

She'd felt fine the entire flight, but there was something about being on solid ground again that shook her. Was she really doing this?

"You're shaking," Kenny whispered.

"I think I might be freaking out."

"It's okay. I've got you. And the rest of the team is here… somewhere?"

She didn't know if he meant at the airport, in the city or just on this plane of existence, but either way she was not comforted. He squeezed her hand in his.

"Tell me this is all going to be okay," she breathed.

"I promise that we'll get through this and I'll take a vacation for the first time ever. And we'll go to Hawai'i for our second date."

She didn't smile but she wanted to.

"Why Hawai'i by the way?"

She turned to him and smiled, surely sadly, "My mother always wanted to take us there, but she couldn't afford it. So close, but so far away. She never got a real vacation in her entire life."

His eyes were serious and intense and she believed every word he said as they fell from his lips, "I'll buy you every souvenir we see."

She giggled, "I really could use a refrigerator magnet."

He let go of her hand to throw an arm around her shoulders, "Anything you want, it's yours."

"Oh my god, this is so fucking sweet," someone said.

They both started.

"What are you doing here?" Kenny hissed.

"Duh," Kierra said with a roll of her eyes, even though she didn't turn to look at them. "Delivering info. Meet me in the women's bathroom." And then she sped away.

"I don't think I've ever seen her in tennis shoes," Kenny mused.

"Wow, this is real life spy shit," Maya breathed.

At the bathroom Kenny brushed his mouth against her temple. "Make this quick. Someone's waiting for us at baggage claim."

She smiled up at him and winked.

The bathroom was packed. Kierra was at the farthest sink from the door applying mascara. They locked eyes in the mirror as Maya put her purse on the counter and leaned forward, pretending to check her reflection.

"Oh my god, your purse is so cute," Kierra said in a cheery tone that sounded saccharine sweet, very unlike the teasing flirt she was.

"Thanks, I stole it from my roommate," Maya responded with a wide, genuine smile.

"I thought it looked familiar," Kierra mumbled under her breath.

Maya smirked.

Kierra began to rummage in her own purse, speaking casually, "I hate flying. It's havoc on my skin."

Maya wasn't certain exactly what was happening, but she knew that was bullshit. Kierra's skin was flawless, not a bump or scar in sight. "It's the same with me."

"I have this serum," she said. "You should try it." She pulled a small bottle of Maya's favorite serum from her bag. Maya squinted her eyes.

"I stole it from my roommate," Kierra said with a smug grin on her face. And then she laughed.

Maya laughed, it sounded artificial and threatening. Kierra ignored the danger. As usual. "That's so sweet of you," she said through gritted teeth.

Kierra's face lit up. "Actually, you should try these wipes I have as well."

Maya watched her fish a small plastic container from her bag. She was certain there wouldn't be one wipe in the entire thing.

"Oh my god you're so generous," Maya said.

Kierra shrugged. "There's nothing better than passing on skincare tips, right?"

As soon as Kierra placed the containers in her purse, Maya snatched it up and put it over her shoulder. "I completely agree."

"I hope those work for you."

"Thanks, so do I."

"Nice meeting you," Kierra said and moved toward the exit without a backwards glance.

Maya leaned over the sink to wash her hands, slowly, and

dried them just as slow. She felt it in her bones that it was best to put a little distance between herself and Kierra.

Outside of the bathroom, Kenny was leaning against an airport map. She lit up when she saw him and hurried across the human traffic to get back to him. He grasped her hand immediately and they resumed walking toward baggage claim.

They stood to the right on the people mover. He turned to her and kissed her softly. "What'd she want?"

"She gave me a package. Don't know what's in it?"

"Okay," he said simply.

"She also might have stolen some of my skincare. The little thief," Maya pouted.

Kenny smiled, "She *has* been spending a lot of time with Chanté."

They stepped off the people mover and were at baggage claim quicker than they expected. They spotted the chauffeur with a sign in his hands immediately; Maya's name printed on it. "This is about to get so real," she mumbled under her breath. He squeezed her hand in his.

reconnaissance

They hit the ground running. They had barely six hours before Kenny and Maya's commercial flight landed and they had to make the most of that lead time. Asif was up and out of his seat as soon as their jet hit the tarmac.

"Are you sure you don't need backup?" Monica's voice was tight.

"I like working alone," he said easily as he went over his small pack. He pulled the gear he needed for this job from his larger duffel. They could take the rest of his stuff to the safe house.

"Be that as it may, wouldn't it be better if someone went with you?"

Asif raised a skeptical eyebrow at them. "Not to be rude, but you two are the opposite of conspicuous."

Kierra perked up, "Thank you."

Monica let out an exasperated sigh.

Asif smiled, "We're light on personnel at the moment." He heard the ground crew working on the plane. He wanted to be ready to go as soon as the door opened but then he turned, one hand on his hip. "Unless you want to call in some backup. I could sure use a hacker right now."

Monica's face didn't flinch. She held his gaze and they stared at one another in a standoff. "No."

Asif huffed a breath of something like laughter. "Then let me do my job." He grabbed his pack and turned toward the door.

"Be careful," Kierra said. Asif was happy she didn't finish her thought. He didn't know Kierra well but he could practically hear the words she'd left unspoken. *"Chanté would be crushed if you died."* He wasn't sure if that was true since she wouldn't even return his phone calls. But he hoped.

Asif had a few areas of expertise, but surveillance and small explosives were his favorites. Mostly because he liked to be nosy and blowing things up was fun. Usually. He'd offered to just topple Mehmeti's club when they knew he was inside and shoot anyone who made it out, but apparently that sounded "messy" and "abhorrent" to Monica and Kierra had gaped at him as if he were a monster. Which he wasn't, by the way. He was, however, impatient. He needed to find Chanté. If he'd known leaving her in Berlin would be her last straw, he liked to think he'd have turned around. Unfortunately, he wasn't completely sure. Either way, he couldn't have missed her in Jersey by more than a few hours and he needed to get back onto her trail. Sure, Monica had said they'd need a hacker on this job, but he wasn't an idiot. The only reason he was here was because if he wanted to find Chanté, staying close to Kenny was as good an idea as any.

So even though he'd signed onto this mission, he wanted it to be over as soon as possible. Especially right now as he was shimmying into the basement of Mehmeti's building through a window that was barely big enough to admit his body. He was also covered in spider webs. Disgusting.

He swiped as much of the debris from his body as he could, stooped down to unzip the duffel bag he'd thrown in ahead of him and set to work.

"Report." Monica's barked through the transmitter into his ear.

Asif jumped. "Can I get a warning next time?"

"No. Report."

"I miss Lane," Asif muttered.

"Join the club. Report."

Asif exhaled as loudly as he dared. "I'm in. I'm going to set some explosives down here."

"Asif."

"Just in case," he hurried to add. "You never know when you might need a distraction." He took Monica's silence for acceptance and continued. "I don't want to risk going into any of the upper floors blind so I'm going to send some probes through the air vents."

"Good. If nothing else, getting some footage from the building's interior is better than nothing."

"I agree."

"You have one hour. If you don't check-in then, you're on your own."

"I'm always on my own," Asif said as he attached a small pack of explosives behind a load-bearing brick column. He surmised that this old building wouldn't take much to bring it down so he surmised that would be enough. Besides, if worst came to worst, he could use a small blast as a good enough distraction to get his people clear.

"Only because you want to be," Monica said and his hands stilled. She hung up before he could respond. Not that he could think of a witty retort for the truth.

Monica shifted the car to park in a basement parking lot of a building that looked like an old school residential hotel on the outside, but was really a safe house. She pressed the button to open the trunk and pushed her door open. She stood and stopped in her tracks. Walking toward her across the garage was a lanky body with a cocky strut she'd recognize anywhere.

Monica thought she'd conquered her fear of sending Lane out on a mission years ago. This was their job. This was what they'd signed up for. But she realized, only as his face was illuminated under a row of track lighting – that damn smile aimed right at her – that Kierra changed everything. The gush of air that left her lungs and the relief she felt as she ran into his arms and he held her close wasn't just for herself.

"Does this mean you missed me?" Lane chuckled as he planted kisses in her hair.

"You have no idea," she whispered. His lips grazed her cheek. "No idea."

He laughed, a deep rumble in his chest, "She's been keeping you up all night, hasn't she?"

Monica laughed and nodded. "And not just with her mouth."

Monica looked over Lane's shoulder as a tall Black man she recognized as Kenny's former partner stood awkwardly looking on. "What's he doing here?"

He raised his eyebrows and then his eyes lifted over her shoulder. His brows bunched together and he frowned. His voice was shaky with fear when he spoke again, "Where's Kierra?"

Kierra didn't want to be a spy. She had absolutely no interest in the part of the job that involved guns or broken bones or anything gross like that. She wasn't trying to break an acrylic nail. And from what she'd glimpsed in Europe and in the aftermath of Monica and Lane's missions over the years, the gun parts were either a lot or a whole lot. And nope, Kierra was too pretty to risk getting shot.

But the other stuff… she knew she'd be fantastic at that.

She'd heard that from Lane and Monica enough to be sure. She was a great liar, fast on her feet in a chase (so long as she immediately ditched her heels, of course), and she could manage a pretty solid French accent. But most importantly, especially right now, she could sense danger. Once she'd left the airport bathroom she'd known something wasn't right.

Monica had once forced her to take a self-defense class that she'd kinda bombed because she'd been too worried about her very expensive manicure to hit her pretend attacker too hard. But she had absorbed all the useful information the class had to offer. For instance, if she was ever being followed, she was supposed to go to a public place. She could practically hear her former instructor saying that very sensibly, albeit forcefully, inside her head. But that voice of reason in her head started screaming when she turned down a hallway, *away* from the very heavy flow of human traffic.

The sound of the flight attendant's heels sounded like gunfire as she stepped off of the airport carpet onto the tile flooring. Kierra had spotted her as soon as she'd left the bathroom. She was hanging back, watching Kenny. He looked up and nodded minutely at Kierra. It was barely noticeable. Someone passing by wouldn't have even registered the movement of his head. But the flight attendant was so focused on him that she had. The sudden movement of her head caught Kierra's attention and they'd locked eyes. She didn't know who the fuck this woman was, but Kierra knew in that moment that this development was not good.

She slowed her steps in the hallway. They were alone. The flight attendant sped up.

When she was close Kierra turned, a huge smile on her face. "Oh my god, I think I'm lost?"

The flight attendant's steps faltered for a second, which was all Kierra needed. She reached out and grabbed the flight attendant by the shoulders, pulling her close. Most self-defense assumed that the assailant was a man and rightly so. But what to do when it wasn't? Or more accurately, what to do when the assailant presumably didn't have a dick to smash with your knee? This had actually been Kierra's singular obsession while she'd been failing that class. She'd posed it to Monica over and over again, the other woman – only her boss at the time – had been exasperated until finally she'd yelled, "Aim for the gut. When they're doubled over, aim for the nose. And then run." Made sense. So Kierra did exactly that. Well, except the running part.

"Who do you work for?"

The woman was wailing, blood pouring from her nose. It was all a bit too loud and messy for Kierra's liking; she'd add that to the list of reasons she was unsuited to the life of a spy. But later. Right now, she didn't have much time.

She leaned down, but well out of the woman's reach. "I said who do you work for?"

The woman spat at her. "Bitch, are you trying to get kicked in the face?" Kierra hissed as she jumped back from the spray. "Gross."

Monica's advice had always been practical; she urged Kierra to do whatever it took to break free and get to safety. Lane was a bit more confrontational, especially after Berlin. "If you think your life is in danger, you have to neutralize the threat."

Kierra assessed her position. A strange woman had maybe been following Kenny and Maya and then had followed her. If her instincts were right this woman worked for Mehmeti and once she recovered, she'd run straight to her boss and the mission would be fucked. And worse yet, she, Kenny and Maya's covers would all be blown.

She pulled her cell phone from her back pocket. Chanté picked up immediately.

"What's up, sexy?" Chanté said. She sounded happy.

"I've got a problem," Kierra breathed.

She heard Chanté speak to someone. After a few seconds she was back. "What do you need?"

Kierra explained her situation quickly and waited. She heard the tapping of computer keys.

"Okay I'm in the airport security system."

"Okay?"

"Take a picture of her face. Get as close as you can."

The flight attendant had stopped wailing, but she was still clutching her face.

"Um, I think I broke her nose," Kierra said apologetically.

"Look at you! Does she have a security badge or something?"

Kierra scanned the attendant quickly. The woman's bag had fallen to the ground in their scuffle. She inched toward it, keeping the woman in her line of sight and rummaged through it. Thankfully the badge was near the top. "Got it."

"Okay, send a picture and your location," Chanté said.

Kierra complied and then waited. The hallway was barely off of the concourse but it was so eerily quiet back here. The flight attendant had stopped wailing and was simply glaring at Kierra over her bloodstained hands pressed to her face.

"Okay, I've marked her as a high security risk. Potential terrorist threat. Security is on their way to you right now and the FBI has been notified."

"Shit, you can do that?"

"Shockingly, I can," Chanté said, almost regrettably. "Now get the fuck away from there."

"Okay," Kierra breathed. "Thanks, girl."

"Oh, any time," Chanté trilled. "Just," she hesitated for a second. Kierra was already backing away from the flight attendant who'd begun to stand. Bloody handprints stained the floor. "Make sure Asif doesn't get himself killed, okay?"

Kierra turned and took off running. She wanted to tell Chanté that right now she was trying to save her own hide.

But she knew that if the tables were turned and Chanté was on a mission with Lane or Monica, she'd say the same thing.

"I'll try, girl. Gotta go," she huffed, sprinting back down the hallway toward the concourse. She could hear the flight attendant's heels clacking behind her.

Just as she burst into the concourse, a security guard grabbed her. She shrieked. And then she put on the performance of her life. "Oh my god officer, she attacked me."

Maybe under normal circumstances this man would have questioned her intensely. Certainly he might have wondered how, if the flight attendant had attacked her, Kierra didn't have a scratch on her but the flight attendant's face and uniform were painted with blood. But whatever national security protocol Chanté had put out on that woman had security pushing Kierra to safety and drawing their guns.

When the flight attendant burst into the concourse, she pulled to a stop quickly.

"Hands in the air," one of the guards yelled. She complied. Kierra hung around just long enough to see them order her to lie face down on the ground and to watch them secure a pair of handcuffs around her wrists. And then she slipped away as if nothing had happened.

She hailed a cab and thought to herself that in another life, she'd be a great fucking spy. Kierra kept turning around in the cab, peering out of the back window, making sure she wasn't being followed. It certainly made her conspicuous as hell, but whatever. She tipped the cab driver way too much and crawled from the cab four blocks from the safe house. She called Monica once the cab had turned onto a major street and she verified she was alone.

"Where are you?" A voice that was not Monica's asked.

Kierra shrieked. "Oh my god! You're here?"

"Where are you?" he asked again, rudely.

"A few blocks away," she said and started running toward the safe house.

Lane stayed on the phone with her the entire short trip. And he was standing outside of the safe house, very dramatically, his phone pressed to the side of his face, turning in a circle, waiting for her. She ran straight into his arms.

Lane pressed his mouth against her cheek, which wasn't nearly enough for her. She turned her head and pressed her lips to his, slipping her tongue into his mouth greedily. She'd missed the taste of him.

"Are you three always this dramatic?" A strange voice said.

Kierra lifted her eyes and took in the tall, built body, the smooth dark brown skin, the perfect cheekbones. "Hi," she breathed at him.

"Jesus," Lane muttered.

"How'd it go?" Monica asked, stepping into her line of view. She reached up to cup Kierra's face. "Are you alright?"

Kierra smiled down at her. "Yeah, I'm fine. I think I broke some woman's nose though."

"What?" Monica and Lane shrieked.

Kierra leaned around Monica. "You've got great lips, by the way," she said.

"I'll take that as a yes," the stranger breathed.

All Kierra could do was laugh.

fourteen

On the drive from the airport, Maya realized that it was entirely possible to be in the lap of a tiny bit of luxury and also scared shitless. It kind of ruined her experience in the back of the chauffeured town car.

Chanté had discovered that Mehmeti owned a number of properties all over the city so they weren't surprised when the driver pulled the car into one of his hotels. As soon as the car stopped moving, Kenny pushed his door open and crawled out. He bent down to reach for Maya. She scooted across the seat and took his hand. The chauffeur took their slight in stride and pulled their baggage from the trunk. A porter met them and placed their bags on a trolley. Kenny tried to tip the chauffeur.

"No sir. Mr. Mehmeti has paid me well. Please enjoy your stay."

They both smiled and Maya tried not to fidget out of nervousness. They followed the porter into the lobby and straight toward the elevator.

"Don't we need to check in?" Kenny asked.

"No need, sir. You are guests of Mr. Mehmeti," he called over his shoulder as if that explained everything.

Kenny clutched Maya's hand tighter in his.

The elevator ride to the penthouse was silent. She could feel sweat collecting at her hairline and she hoped her palm wasn't also sweating. Kenny's body grew ever more tense as they ascended, his hand tightening around hers. Maya could barely breathe. She wondered if it was too late to back out of this. She wished she and Kenny were back in her living room snuggled together on her couch.

When the elevator stopped Maya closed her eyes. She had no idea what was on the other side and found that she was terrified to find out. But when she opened her eyes she exhaled, "Oh shit, this place is amazing!" She tried to let go of Kenny's hand, wanting to dive into the room, but Kenny held her fast. Thankfully, he was much less awed by the spacious living room, floor-to-ceiling windows, full size kitchen. "Is that an infinity pool?" she screamed.

"It is, ma'am," the porter said.

"Oh, I'm fucking skinny dipping in that bitch," she exclaimed.

Kenny couldn't hide the choked gasp. As they followed the porter around their hotel suite, Maya's mouth and eyes were wide open in shock. Kenny's body was tense and alert. The porter bowed – actually bowed – as he turned to leave. Kenny tried to tip him, but he refused as well. They stared at the elevator doors for at least a full minute after it closed.

"So like…What now?" Maya said turning to Kenny.

Kenny turned to her and slipped a hand behind her neck, pulling her close. Just before their lips touched he whispered, "Assume the room is bugged." And then he kissed the fuck out of her. It was hard and insistent with lots of tongue. He grunted when her teeth grazed his lips. It was a perfect kiss. So perfect she almost forgot he'd warned her someone might be spying on them.

When she remembered, she broke the kiss, but Kenny kept her head close to his. So they could talk, she realized.

"You think he's spying on us?"

"I think he's a creepy fuck who flew us out here first class to watch us have sex in person."

"Great point," she breathed. And then, because his mouth was so close, she kissed him again, smiling as their tongues danced. He backed her against the wall, lifting one of her legs around his waist. She groaned when he ground his hips, and his semi-hard erection, into her.

"So what do we do?" she whispered when they came up for air with panting breaths, their mouths still close.

He trailed kisses across her face. "We go about the rest of our day as if we're being watched."

"That doesn't help," she hissed and then moaned when he sucked the sensitive skin under her chin into his mouth.

"We know the mission. We're going to Mehmeti's club tonight. There's nothing to do until then. If you need to tell me anything, find a way to say it without saying it." He licked at her pulse. "Or text me."

"Or kiss you?" She giggled, arching her back to press her breasts into him.

"Or kiss me," he said. "But feel free to do that whenever you want."

He lifted his head and smiled down at her. A shocked smile spread across her lips. "Fuck, are you really flirting with me now?"

He laughed and kissed her again.

She moved her hand over his on her hip and then dragged them both between her legs.

He groaned and broke their kiss. They pressed their foreheads together. "Why aren't you wearing any underwear, Maya?" he croaked.

"Better question," she whispered, using her hand to grind his against her very wet core. "What are you going to do now that you know I'm not wearing any underwear?"

She'd barely gotten the question out before two of his

fingers curled inside of her, stroking her slowly. Their breaths became pants and moans as his fingers skimmed along the sensitive flesh. But when he added the heel of his hand to put delicious pressure against her clit, they both turned into writhing, groaning messes.

Kenny undid his pants, licked her palm and she snaked her hand inside his boxers. She'd just gotten a slow and steady rhythm, pumping him into a frenzy, when his fingers pulled her over the edge. She shuddered and shook, her head listing forward onto his chest. She smiled and laughed. And then drooled onto the head of his cock.

He groaned, his hips jumping. She was barely conscious, but her body knew exactly what to do. Exactly what she wanted. She stroked him slowly to orgasm, his fingers still inside her, her pussy clenching around his digits as he sprayed over her hand and their clothes.

She lifted her head to meet his eyes.

"He better give you a bonus for that," Kenny said and then crushed his lips to hers.

"I'll split it with you," she laughed.

He shook his head, "I'm happy to donate all of my time to your business if you make me come like that."

She kissed him gently and whispered, "Deal," against his lips.

KENNY WOKE to the sound of his phone chirping. He and Maya had stumbled to the closest bedroom, stripped off their clothes and fallen immediately to sleep. He crawled from the bed and pulled his cell phone from the pocket of his pants.

The text message was a series of numbers. A cypher. He knew exactly who it was from and what it said. The knowledge made his pulse quicken and not in the way Maya did. He wanted to crawl back into bed with her, wrap his body around hers, let every possible inch of his bare skin touch hers and never leave. But this was not her bed. And however great that orgasm had been, he reminded himself that this was not real life. But he did something he'd never done before her; he put the mission aside for a moment, because there was something more important. He crawled onto the bed and kissed her softly on the cheek.

She stirred, smiled, but she didn't wake up.

"I love you," he whispered, even though it was too soon and they barely knew each other and they were on a mission. He traced his thumb over the curve of her chin. It was cowardly, since she wasn't awake. But it felt right.

His phone chirped again.

He took a quick shower and rummaged in his suitcase for workout clothes. Just before he left, he grabbed the pad of paper on the bedside table and scribbled a quick note to Maya. He called the elevator to their floor. He hated leaving her, he'd promised her that he would stay by her side, but this message would not wait.

He used his room keycard to let himself into the hotel gym. His eyes drifted to the row of treadmills. He was desperate to hop on one and run a few miles to expel the frustrated energy coursing through his body. But he couldn't. He walked through the regular gym and headed into the locker room tucked behind it. He grabbed a towel from a well-stocked cabinet and headed to the closest empty locker. He toed his shoes and socks off and deposited them in an upper locker. There was no one else around so he pulled his shirt off and shorts down. He wrapped the towel around his waist and pushed the locker closed, pulled the key out of the lock and headed to the sauna.

He tried not to look directly at Lamont. He wasn't sure if this was a good or bad omen, but either way, there could be cameras here. He sat on a bench across the sauna from Lamont and avoided looking directly at him. They both kept the door in their peripheral vision. Kenny began to sweat immediately. But this was a good sweat. His muscles ached from the prolonged tangle of fear, worry and sexual arousal. His body needed this break, even though he wanted to run back upstairs to Maya.

After a few minutes of silence, Kenny leaned forward and ran his hands over the crown of his head. "What are you doing here?"

Rather than answer, Lamont stood up and poured more water onto the coals.

Kenny exhaled loudly. "What's going on?"

"We have the Setter brothers in custody."

Kenny almost laughed from relief. "That's fucking great. Isn't it?"

"We have two of the Setter brothers," Lamont said, his lips barely moving.

"There are only two," Kenny breathed. His eyes moved in Lamont's direction but didn't land on him. "Aren't there?"

"That's what we thought. But then we found a mole. Two moles," he quickly amended.

Kenny's head snapped to the side. If they were being surveilled, there was no way to take back that movement. He cringed at his misstep. "In what agency?"

Lamont gavc a frustrated grunt, "Mine."

"The ATF has two moles? For who?"

"Had. And so far as we know they were working for the Setters."

"You're certain?"

Lamont nodded once. "As certain as we can be."

"Who?"

"One was passing himself off as an agent in my office. He was the other Setter brother."

"How did we not know there were three?

Lamont shrugged. The movement would have seemed nonchalant if not for the rigid set of his entire upper body.

"And the other mole?"

Lamont's jaw tensed even more, which Kenny wouldn't have thought possible. "Neutralized."

"What the fuck is going on in Columbus?" Kenny exclaimed, not bothering to hide the whip of his head or avert his eyes from Lamont's face.

Lamont inhaled and exhaled slowly. He was always so measured. Kenny had enjoyed that about him during their brief time as partners.

"Once I clean house, I'll let you know."

"What are you doing here, Lamont?"

For the first time, Lamont turned to look at him. "I worked with this asshole for over a year. I'm here to arrest him and take him back to Ohio so he can be prosecuted. He'll be put on trial with his brothers and the rest of their white supremacist cell."

"We could have done that," Kenny said lamely.

Lamont laughed bitterly, "The Agency doesn't give a shit about anyone else's directives but their own. When we find him, I'll put a bullet in his forehead or arrest him." And then his eyes settled on Kenny's. "I won't get in your way so long as you don't get in mine."

"You alright man?" Kenny asked, his eyebrows furrowed.

"I'm fine. Did the PA deliver the package?"

"Yeah," Kenny breathed, surprised that he'd completely forgotten about the bathroom exchange. "I haven't looked at it yet," he admitted.

"There's a comm piece for you and the USB device you need to let your hacker into the computer when you find it."

Kenny nodded. "Weapons?"

"I'm in locker fifteen. When I leave, there'll be a package for you there." With that Lamont stood and headed toward the door.

"It's good to have you watching my back again," Kenny called after him.

Lamont didn't hesitate as he pushed the sauna door open without a word.

MAYA WOKE up to her phone ringing.

"Shut up," she mumbled in her sleep. "Go away."

The phone kept ringing.

She pushed the covers off of her body and sat up in bed. She was naked, groggy and confused. She looked around her at the bedroom, with its wall of windows behind the headboard. She wasn't sure where she was.

Her phone stopped ringing.

She stood up, stark naked, and looked around her. When she saw Kenny's suitcase open next to hers, a pile of their clothes next to it, she remembered where she was. And more crucially, why she was here.

Her phone started ringing again. It was coming from the pile of her clothes. She had to squint at her phone to read the name on the screen. She'd fallen asleep in her contacts.

"Short stack," she croaked.

"How's the penthouse?" Kierra asked in a giddy peal, as if this was a normal part of their day. And then Maya realized that actually, maybe this was a normal part of Kierra's day.

"Fucking gorgeous. Huge bed, softest sheets."

"You nervous?"

Maya moved back to the bed. Her eyes caught on the pad of paper. The note read: Sauna. Back soon. She nodded, filing away how stupidly happy Kenny's neat script made her as she crawled back into bed.

"So fucking nervous," she finally answered. "What am I doing? I shouldn't be here." Thankfully, she wasn't so tired that she forgot Kenny's warning. She wasn't sure if the room was bugged – which was an incredibly ridiculous thought to even have – but just in case it was, she chose her words carefully. "What if this was a terrible idea?"

Kierra laughed. Because she was Kierra. "Of course this is a terrible idea. You and me should not be living the lives we're living right now. I'm a poet and you're a CEO in the making. And yet here we are."

Maya couldn't help but smile as she burrowed deeper into the incredible bed. "Here we are."

"Kenny will keep you safe," she said reassuringly.

Maya nodded even though Kierra couldn't see her. She bit back her smile and felt the rightness of what Kierra said. She was safe with Kenny. She knew that. But where was he?

It was as if Kierra could read her mind, "He's meeting with another agent for intel. He should be back soon."

Maya let out a sigh of relief and laughed. She sounded near hysterical. "I feel like I'm living in an alternate universe," she breathed.

"Let's imagine that you are."

"What?"

"Look," Kierra said, sounding much more serious than she normally ever did. "For the rest of this whole experience, why not just imagine that you're living in some alternate universe. You're not a kindly cam girl with hella debt. You're La Femme Nikita."

"I fucking love that movie."

"Good. So your mission – and you've already accepted it so let's just go with the flow – is to make this Albanian mobster want to give you all of his money. You need to make it so that he can't see anything past you and your fucking amazing boobs. Got it?"

As Kierra was speaking, Maya found herself sitting up in the bed, her back straight and her head held high. She smiled to herself, "So you're finally admitting that my titties are the best?"

Kierra hung up the phone. That was all the answer Maya needed.

She read Kenny's note a few more times before finally crawling out of bed and heading to the bathroom. She showered, brushed her teeth and padded across the penthouse, still naked. She walked to the sliding glass door off of the living room and the open plan kitchen and peered out at the pool and the hills beyond. When she walked outside, the late afternoon air was colder than she'd expected. But she didn't care. She kept her eyes on the crystal blue water as she took a running start and canonballed into the pool with a laugh.

When Maya came up for air, Kenny was calling her name.

"Maya," he called again, kneeling at the edge of the pool.

She swam over to him and smiled as he tried valiantly, but very unsuccessfully, to keep his eyes on her face and not the hazy outline of her naked body in the water.

"You're back," she said.

He smiled, his eyes finally lifting to hers. He nodded. "I'm back."

She put both of her hands on the ledge and lifted her body up. Kenny's eyes widened and he choked. She could only imagine what she looked like, water cascading over her full breasts and round stomach as she moved her mouth to his. She kissed him quickly. "Everything okay?"

He nodded, his mouth slack with desire.

"You sure?" While she loved the effect she had on him, this moment was important. So she leveled her eyes with his and stared at him intently as she lowered her body back into the water.

He nodded. "Everything's okay," he breathed.

She smiled, "Good," and pulled him into the water. Because right now she wasn't Maya, cam girl, great friend, and loving sister. She was La Femme Nikita and she had a mission.

mission brief

Asif just wanted to shower and change and maybe call Chanté a few dozen times before they headed to Mehmeti's club tonight. He approached the safe house from the rear through a deserted alley. At the service entrance, he knocked three times on the door. Nothing happened. He knocked again as he turned to peer left and right down the alley to confirm that he was still alone. Again there was no answer. This time he pounded on the metal security door with one hand and reached for the gun in his bag with the other. When it began to creak open, he put his thumb on his gun's safety and waited.

He let out a tense breath of air as Lane's face came into view. That damn smile and a soft chuckle.

"Hold your horses, I'm coming," Lane drawled.

Asif rolled his eyes.

"Ugh, what happened to you?" Lane scrunched his nose up at him and Asif was reminded of how much he wanted that shower.

"Move," Asif said.

Lane stepped back into the utility room. Asif turned to watch Lane scan the alley again. And then they walked to the elevator. On the third floor, Asif followed Lane to one of the corner units. The hallway was dingy with dim lighting, but the electronic biometric lock was state-of-the-art.

Lane punched in a code and nodded his head for Asif to place a finger on the keypad. They waited as his fingerprint scanned and the door unlocked. Lane followed Asif inside.

"Honey, I'm home," Asif called out.

"Good, you're alive," Monica deadpanned.

"You look terrible though," Kierra added helpfully, perched on the arm of the couch next to her.

"Who are you?" Asif said, a rakish smile on his face. He knew he looked dusty, but he had long since tested the theory that a good smile and a lot of nerve could seduce anyone already willing to be seduced.

"He's Kenny's…friend," Lane said from behind him.

Asif frowned, "Never mind. Where's the bathroom I feel disgusting."

Kierra nodded gravely at him, as Lane walked around the couch and pressed a kiss against her temple.

Asif rolled his eyes.

"Last door down the hallway," Monica said with a dismissive nod of her head. "And hurry up. We only have so much time. We need to be ready to go as soon as the sun sets."

Asif walked across the living room, but Kierra stopped him in his tracks.

"I talked to Chanté," she called.

Asif turned quickly. "When? Where is she? What'd she say?"

Kierra's smile was predatory. She looked as if she liked thinking she had him on the hook. And considering that she had the two best agents he'd ever met at her beck and call, maybe she did. "Earlier. Not here. She told me not to let you get yourself killed."

Asif sucked in a harsh breath. He didn't cry. He wouldn't

cry. That was not who he was. But he felt the pressure of phantom tears at the back of his eyes.

Kierra's grin melted away and she frowned at him. That look was full of pity. He thought maybe she would say more, but she didn't. Instead she leaned forward and kissed the crown of Monica's head gently.

Asif turned and walked to the bathroom. He tried to tell himself that he wasn't running away from the judgement in her eyes. But running was what he did best.

"Kierra and I will arrive together. Lane will arrive separately. Lamont," she said, turning toward him. "Once you locate the other Setter brother you'll have to stay on him, but you can't take him down until I give the word. Understood?"

Lamont frowned and shifted uncomfortably in his seat. "Understood."

"What about me, boss?" Asif asked.

"We'll need you watching the exterior," she said.

"Wait, what?" Asif breathed. "I don't even get to go in? It's a sex club. How can you not take the sexiest person on this mission inside?"

"Take it back," Kierra hissed, her eyes shooting daggers at Asif.

Asif lifted his eyebrows. "Make me."

Lane laughed out loud, "I really missed you idiots."

Monica locked eyes with Lamont. He seemed appalled and shocked at their behavior. "We're much better behaved in the field."

"We'll see," he said gravely.

"Anyway," Monica continued, "Kierra and I will shadow Maya and Kenny in the public areas. But from all of our intel, everything about the fourth floor is heavily restricted and we might not be able to breach their security easily or at all."

"Don't worry. I left my probes in the air vents. That should give us some cover."

Monica nodded at him.

"Kenny and Maya won't have any tech on them besides a comm piece. We can communicate with them, but let's assume that Mehmeti or his bodyguards will be close at all times, so keep the chatter to a minimum."

"We should be on radio silence unless absolutely necessary. After Kierra's run in with the flight attendant, we should assume that everyone is a potential Mehmeti operative," Lane offered.

Monica nodded in agreement.

"So what's the plan?" Lamont asked.

"It's simple," Monica said, even though simple was relative. "Once we confirm Mehmeti's identity, and locate your ATF mole, we take them down quietly if we can."

"And loudly, if we can't," Lane breathed.

"Maya and Kenny will handle Mehmeti, with Lane as floating backup. Our job is to make sure they can do their jobs."

Lamont nodded. "Sounds half-baked and like a probable death trap."

Kierra perked up, "That's kind of our style."

Monica eyed her warily. She wished they didn't have to take her to the club. She wished they could leave Kierra at the safe house, especially now that she knew how close she'd come to danger at the airport. But they didn't have a choice. They needed Kierra now for the same reason they'd needed her earlier. Even with Lane and Lamont's arrival, they were still down an agent in the field. And like in Berlin, Kierra was a magnet for attention. If Maya could hold Mehmeti's attention and that of his inner circle, Kierra would hold everyone else's. They would never know what hit them. But that didn't mean Monica had to like it.

"So now we wait?" Lamont asked, tearing Monica from her fear spiral.

"When Mehmeti contacts Maya with details, we head out."

Asif stood from the couch, "Sounds like a plan to me. Now, if you'll excuse me, I have a hacker-dancer to hunt. Call me when it's go time."

Lamont checked his phone again. No new messages. He hadn't expected that there would be. If his office needed to contact him, they'd call. And his ex-boyfriend was completely unlikely to send him another message since he'd kicked him out of their condo.

He leaned against the window and looked out at the street below. There was nothing to see, nothing out of the ordinary. But he couldn't believe how much had happened professionally and personally in such a short period of a time. Even though he would be best served by staying focused on the professional changes and preparing for the mission, his mind kept straying back to the only thing that wouldn't help him right now: Caleb.

He looked down at his phone and opened the text message from an unknown number.

Maybe one day.

He stared at the short message. Just three words. He knew they were from Caleb. He wanted more. But he'd been right to push him away in Cincinnati. Even if it had felt completely wrong at the time and had only felt more wrong each day since he'd watched him drive away.

Kierra's giggle tore his attention away.

Lamont stared at Woodhouse…Lane, trying to reconcile

the FBI agent who'd shown up in Columbus – all flirty and cryptic and, when necessary, deadly – with the man cuddled up on the couch with his wife, their girlfriend between them. He'd seemed in control and at ease during their op in West Virginia, but now that he saw him actually relaxed, he noted the subtle differences.

Kierra turned her head and brushed her lips against Lane's. Their eyes were intent on one another as they kissed lightly. A pit of jealousy opened up in Lamont's stomach that only made him miss Caleb more. He turned away when he saw the pink flash of their tongues between their lips.

The street was still quiet.

"Okay, let's get down to business," the new agent, Asif, said as he walked into the room. "Oh, unless we're doing something else?" He aimed the question at the tangle of bodies on the couch.

Kierra pushed up from the couch. "You wish," she said.

"I do," Asif replied.

Lamont watched as Lane and Monica rolled their eyes, but Kierra raised a suggestive eyebrow at Asif. Or at least Lamont thought she did. It was hard to tell. If he'd thought Lane was a flirt, Kierra was a tsunami of innuendo that stirred something in Lamont's chest. Something that was mostly a longing for the hacker he'd let get away.

His phone chirped.

He looked down, expecting – hoping – to see another anonymous message.

Instead, it was a text from Kenny. He looked up and everyone had turned toward him. "Mehmeti wants them at the club at midnight. We have three hours."

Kierra squealed. The entire room turned toward her. "Wait until you all see my outfit," she screamed and practically ran from the room.

Lamont and Asif watched as Monica rose from the couch and followed her down the hall.

Lane stood and smiled at them. "We'll try to keep this brief," he said apologetically over his shoulder. "But maybe you two should go over the plan a few more times. Together."

Lamont frowned in confusion. He turned to Asif who was shaking his head.

He laughed, "They're going to fuck, new guy. Wow, you really are Kenny's friend."

"My name's not new guy. It's Lamont."

Asif raised an eyebrow at him and smirked. "I'll call you new guy until you give me a reason not to."

Lamont shook his head and turned away. "Is The Agency just a clearinghouse for spies who want to fuck each other?"

He jumped as Asif's breath tickled his ear, "Shhh, don't say it too loud. That's our best kept secret."

Asif's hand trailed lightly down Lamont's back as he moved away.

Fuck, he missed Caleb.

fifteen

"This is really romantic," Maya whispered. "Completely fake, but romantic as fuck."

Their chins were resting on their folded arms at the edge of the infinity pool as they watched the darkened city below them light up. They could see brief snatches of lights at the docks bouncing off the inky water and taillights lit the path of the city's streets.

"If this were our second date, it would be great," he said.

He saw Maya turn to him in his peripheral vision.

"If you brought me to a hotel like this on our second date, we'd be having the filthiest sex right now," she said in a husky voice.

He turned to her and smiled. "How filthy?"

She moved toward him in the water and slipped her leg between his. He swallowed a groan as her thigh came into contact with his dick, which hadn't had a chance to deflate since he'd found her making good on her promise to go skinny dipping.

She ran her hands up his chest and bit her bottom lip, fluttering her eyelashes at him seductively. "Spoilers."

His chest ached at how she could bring him to his

metaphorical knees so easily. She abruptly pushed away from him with a laugh, floating in the water, the beautiful rise of her breasts and stomach just visible above the water. He would have fallen to the actual floor if he weren't floating. And thank god he was floating, because his entire body felt as if it were struck with electricity as Maya climbed out of the pool. The water dripping off of her body was literally the most beautiful thing he'd ever seen. And she knew it.

She turned to look at him over her shoulder and sucked her bottom lip into her mouth. He knew exactly what that look meant. He couldn't swim to the edge of the pool fast enough.

Maya laughed as he hopped from the pool and wrapped his arms around her. "Be careful. Didn't you ever learn not to run by a pool?"

He cradled her neck in one hand and pulled her mouth to his. He tasted the last remnants of her laughter and happiness and he couldn't help but wonder if this was what it would be like between them. She smiled against his lips and pulled back. As she looked at him, her eyes were bright, sparkling in the dusk and he almost forgot where they were or why they were there.

And then her phone chimed.

She'd dropped it on a deck chair and they both looked down at it.

Maya leaned over to pick it up. The short gasp of breath told Kenny all he needed to know about who had messaged her.

"What's it say?"

She read the message to him, "Maya. Welcome to California. I look forward to meeting you and your boyfriend tonight. A car will arrive to bring you to me at midnight."

Kenny checked the time on her phone. They had three hours.

"Please accept these small tokens of my appreciation and enthusiasm."

"Huh?"

She shrugged and turned to look at him. "That's all it says."

The elevator dinged as it opened. Maya dropped her phone and grabbed the beach towel next to her, throwing it haphazardly around herself. Kenny grabbed another towel and wrapped it around his waist as he stepped back into the sitting area. The elevator doors opened, but no one entered.

"Hello," he called.

"May I come in, sir?" The porter from earlier projected the question into the room in his crisp, formal accent.

"Yes."

When he walked into their room, he had two large boxes in his hands. Behind him, another porter held two garment bags in his outstretched arms. They put the parcels onto the coffee table and draped the garment bags over the couch.

"These are gifts from Mr. Mehmeti, sir."

"Is it clothes?" Maya gasped from the deck.

Kenny turned to her, she was still outside, craning her neck around the sliding glass door, trying to hide her nakedness.

"Yes, ma'am. Mr. Mehmeti has very particular tastes. He hopes that you will enjoy these tokens." He nodded and walked back to the elevator.

"Thank you," Maya called after him.

"Uh, yeah," Kenny stumbled. "Thanks. Oh wait."

The porter turned, "Yes, sir."

"Can we um, can we have some food sent up?"

"Yes, sir. Absolutely. The menu is just there," he said, indicating a desk near the couch. "Instructions are inside. I will bring you whatever you like."

"Oh, okay. Great. Thanks," Kenny stammered.

They stepped into the elevator and were gone. As soon as

the coast was clear, Maya walked into the room and tossed the beach towel over a chair. She walked naked to the desk and picked up the menu. "Great idea. I'm starving."

He gulped, "Yeah… I…I thought you'd be."

He tried not to stare, but not that hard. Not as hard as he'd wished.

Maya cleared her throat. His eyes shot up to her face. She was smiling smugly at him. "I'm not distracting you, am I?"

He furrowed his eyebrows. "No, what would you…?" And then he remembered and blushed. "I'm uh…gonna wring out my clothes and shower."

He walked back to the pool and picked up his phone, happy that it had fallen out of his hand before Maya pulled him into the water.

He tapped out a quick message to Lamont and then wrung his sopping wet clothes out on the concrete deck. He slipped back into the sitting area, his eyes flying to Maya, still nonchalantly and nakedly perusing the menu.

"What do you want to eat?" She asked him.

"I'll eat whatever. You choose," he said, turning his head to keep her in his line of sight as he walked across the room.

"Great, I want the pasta and the salmon. We can share," she mumbled to herself.

He couldn't help but smile. By the way she said the word "share" he assumed that whichever dish Maya liked least would be his. Just before he walked down the hallway to their bedroom, he turned to look at her once more briefly. This time, his eyes lingered on her face.

His cell phone chirped. It was Lamont. He knew that. And he knew he would have to shut off the part of his brain that was distracted by Maya soon – which was his entire brain along with his body – so he let himself look his fill. And even though he wasn't the kind of man who prayed, he sent up a silent prayer that they would make it through this. Because he desperately wanted to take Maya on another date. She could have his entire meal, tonight and every night for as long as she wanted him around. Straight-laced, by-the-book Kenny had finally found something more important to him than his career. And it would fucking suck to lose her now that they had a real chance together.

"IS THIS *TOO* SHORT?" Maya asked. "Or *too* tight?"

She turned her torso left and right, admiring the open expanse of her chest, exposed by the bustier top of her mustard yellow dress, the hem just barely longer than the length of her arms. "This color looks fucking fantastic on me," she said as she turned around to admire the way her ass looked in the tight dress. "And my butt," she exclaimed. "Although I probably shouldn't bend forward. What do you think?" It took Maya a second to take her eyes off herself and realize Kenny hadn't answered any of her questions. When she finally looked at him, she understood why.

She smirked and nodded, "I look great, right?"

He swallowed loudly and nodded.

Kenny didn't look bad either. The dark blue suit and matching tie were casual, but there was something about the way they hung off of his body that made him seem sharper, a little more severe, sexy. Maya liked the look on him. A lot. She walked in bare feet toward him and ran her hands up his chest.

He hissed at the contact but immediately wrapped his arms around her waist. "You look perfect in everything," he said.

She dropped her head and blushed. "You should see what I wear when I clean the oven at three in the morning," she joked.

Kenny moved his hand under her chin and tipped her head back. They looked into each other's eyes. "I can't wait."

Maya would not have considered herself a romantic or the kind of woman who could be wooed by romantic gestures. And yet, there she was, looking deep into Kenny's eyes and wondering how long she'd been falling for him.

His thumb caressed the soft, rounded curve of her chin as his eyes bored into hers, calm and uncomplicated; somehow completely uncomplicated even though the world around them was absolutely not. Anything could happen tonight and Maya's stomach wanted to tie itself into knots at the fear of the unknown. But Kenny's eyes telegraphed a million promises to her. And completely unlike herself, she believed them all.

Kenny's phone chirped.

He sighed and rolled his eyes. Without even looking at his phone, he bent forward to press a gentle kiss to the tip of her nose. It made her smile. He pressed his mouth against hers. She smiled wider. He slipped his tongue past her lips. The kiss was quick, hot and fast and another promise of all that was to come.

"I'll be in the other room," he whispered against her mouth, "whenever you're ready."

She nodded as he released her. She turned and watched him walk out of the room. "Holy shit," she whispered to herself after he closed the door. She snatched up her phone and began to text Kierra, but decided to text her brother instead.

What do you do when you like a boy?

JEROME'S RESPONSE WAS IMMEDIATE.

How would I know? I've been crushing on my lab partner all semester.
I think we're best friends now.

MAYA RECEIVED another message in her sibling group chat from Jerome.

K, M likes a boy. Help her.

THE BUBBLES INDICATING that Kaya was typing popped up quickly, but Maya grew impatient waiting for her response.

Hurry up, I have places to be.

JEROME MESSAGED QUICKLY,

Where you going? You don't have a life.

MAYA SCOFFED. "RUDE," she breathed to herself, even though she had to admit that he unfortunately was not wrong.

Kaya finally responded.

You're both absolutely pathetic.

I'm glad you're finally admitting that you need my help.

JEROME BEAT Maya to the punch.

I'm just here to get Maya some help.

MAYA COULD PRACTICALLY SEE Kaya's rolled eyes.

Sure, hon.

MAYA'S EYES flitted to the time at the top of her phone's screen. She needed to put her shoes on and go.

Hey, don't have time for this. Gimme a three sentence crash course on what to do!!

JEROME,

No really girl, what is up? You barely leave the house.

KAYA,

Clearly she's going on a date, doofus.
My god, you're gonna need a multi-week seminar.
Cashapp me $29.99 and I'll happily Cyrano your life.

MAYA SNORTED A LAUGH.

Take the deal, J.

JEROME,

Is there room in my budget??

MAYA,

For this and ONLY this. Now HELP ME, KAYA!

KAYA,

I've taken a screen shot of that sentence and will be using it for blackmail purposes.
Okay, here ya go.

You like a boy… Tell said boy that you like him.

MAYA'S MOUTH fell open with shock. The group chat went quiet. Finally, Maya typed back,

Save your money, J. She's scamming.

JEROME SENT A FROWN EMOJI,

I already paid her.

MAYA ROLLED HER EYES.

Both of you need to stay in school. Goodnight.

KAYA GOT one last text message in,

Well good luck girl lmao

EVERYONE SIGNED OFF. Maya fought the urge to chew her bottom lip to shreds; she didn't want to ruin her makeup. She looked at the phone again. She was out of time. What a waste, she thought. She sat on the bed and slipped into her shoes.

When she walked out into the living area, her phone clutched in both hands, Kenny was pacing, texting furiously. She knew that whatever he was doing was spy stuff and the thought of it only added another knot to her anxious gut. But when he looked up at her and smiled, she decided to let that go and to forget, momentarily, the budding feelings for him that had only seemed to grow over these past few days, weeks, months.

Tonight, she had a job to do. She would help Kenny and Kierra, Monica, Lane, Asif and Chanté catch Joseph Mehmeti by doing the thing she did best: making a rich man want to have sex with her and convincing him to give her all of his time, attention and money. She could do that in her sleep.

Maya smiled back at Kenny and took the hand he extended to her. They walked to the elevator and waited. She looked over at him and then she got it, what Kaya was saying.

"I think I really like you," she whispered.

She watched as his right ear and cheek turned red. He turned to her and smiled, "I've been waiting months to hear you say that."

sixteen

Kenny kept at least one hand on Maya during the entire ride to the club. Their fingers interlaced, his hand on her thigh, and now as they approached the front of the building, his palm pressed flat against the small of her back. He hoped that it helped to calm her the way it calmed him.

Maya gasped as she looked up at the neon sign lit up, flickering between pink, orange, green and back. The word LICK hovered above a tongue. Based on the smile on Maya's face, Kenny assumed she liked it.

She turned to him and smiled, "Do you think they have a gift shop? 'Cause I need a shirt with that sign on it."

He smiled. Okay, he corrected himself mentally, she liked it a lot.

Kenny was surprised to find that there was a line to get into the club. All of their intel said this was an exclusive experience and yet their driver was leading them past a queue of scantily clad people shivering as they waited to be admitted. His eyes caught on a dark, shiny head. When it turned, Kenny made sure to look away, not wanting to linger on Lamont for any longer than necessary.

At the door, the driver motioned for them to stop as he

whispered with the bouncer. Both men nodded. Their driver turned to Kenny and Maya and nodded again. "I'll be here when you're ready to leave." And then he walked away without another word.

The bouncer opened the velvet rope and motioned for them to enter.

"I feel so fancy," Maya said with a giggle. She winked at the woman at the front of the line. Her mouth gaped.

The woman turned to Kenny and smiled. "If you two are looking for a third…"

Kenny smiled back at her, because it seemed like the right thing to do.

Just inside the door was a set of metal stairs. They climbed them quickly and entered a sedate room with a coat check, two security guards and a black curtain that one guard pulled aside. Beyond that partition, Kenny's senses were bombarded with… a million different sensations all at once. The track lighting hanging from the ceiling was turned low and cast shadows all over the dancefloor in front of them.

Maya turned to him. He couldn't see her face clearly, but he could hear the frown in her voice. "This isn't what I was expecting," she said.

Kenny was just about to respond, when he spotted a man walking toward them. He was tall and bulky and Kenny knew that taking him down without a weapon would be a challenge. He leaned down to brush his lips against Maya's cheek and whispered, "Incoming," into her ear.

She didn't flinch or look around, she simply smiled up at him as if he'd whispered the most romantic declaration of love to her. God she's a fucking natural, Kenny thought to himself.

"Excuse me," the tall man said loud enough for them to hear over the music.

Maya jumped, as if she didn't know he was approaching,

and plastered herself to Kenny's side. He wrapped an arm around her waist.

The man looked at her and nodded, "Maya," he said.

"Y-yes," she replied.

"I am here to bring you to Mr. Mehmeti. Please come with me." He turned on his heels and walked away. They followed him, Maya's head swiveling to look around her and Kenny's body tense.

As they walked, Maya reached back for his hand. Their fingers laced together and he squeezed her palm. Here we go, that squeeze said. There was no turning back now.

MAYA WAS PREPARING her rant to Kierra as she walked through the lower floor of LICK. Kierra had promised her a bit of wild debauchery but all Maya could see was a regular old dance club with a shitty DJ at that. Her first time in a sex club was very disappointing so far and a waste of her A+ makeup.

But then the security guard who was built like a bald brick wall led them to an elevator. When the doors opened onto the fourth floor, Maya's eyes widened in shock and excitement.

"This is what the fuck I'm talking about," she breathed as they stepped into a room that looked like a decadent French salon. Couches and chaise lounges were scattered around the room with pillows and silky throws thrown artfully over them. There were two bars – one at each side of the room – and waiters and waitresses, in very small bathing suits, traversing the floor, serving guests.

"Please follow me," the guard said.

Maya nodded and walked gleefully into the room, craning her neck trying to see all there was to see.

And then she saw too much.

When she turned her head to the left her eyes caught on

Kierra in a nude lace teddy, a very short black leather skirt and sky-high heels that Maya wasn't sure her friend could actually walk in. She was leaning back on a couch, her legs spread obscenely wide, Monica and Lane on either side of her talking calmly to one another, each with a hand under her skirt.

Maya's mouth gaped. "Girl…" she whispered under her breath.

Kenny squeezed her hand and leaned down to whisper to her again. "Don't look at her."

She turned to him and frowned. "Everyone's looking at her. I'd be stupid not to." When she turned back to Kierra, she caught her roommate's eyes. She smiled and raised her eyebrows. Kierra smirked and raised one eyebrow before her head fell back and her mouth opened. Maya couldn't hear the moan across the room but based on the way every head nearby turned toward her and a few men reached to adjust their dicks in their pants, Maya could guess that it had been a good one.

"You will wait here," the guard said, taking Maya's attention away from her best friend.

She nodded and sat down on the empty couch, which had clearly been reserved just for them. Kenny sat down next to her and settled his hand high on her bare thigh. The guard motioned to a waiter who rushed over with a bucket of champagne and two glasses.

"Courtesy of Mr. Mehmeti. He will be with you shortly," the guard said to them, turned and walked away.

"So when does the sex start?" Maya asked as she looked around, nervous excitement coursing through her veins. Most of the people clustered around them had turned to stare, clearly wondering who they were. And besides Kierra, Monica and Lane, the room was generally PG-13, except for the revealing clothing.

"What?"

She rolled her eyes at him. "Sex. When does that start? Is someone going to ring a bell and then everyone strips down? What's the timeline here?"

Kenny's mouth gaped. "Maya. Focus."

"I am focused. On the lack of sex in the *sex* club."

"We have a job," he whispered through clenched teeth so no one nearby could hear.

She smiled at him and leaned forward to swipe her tongue along the seam of his lips. "Your job is to take down the bad guy. My job is to distract him so you can," she whispered against his mouth. "Do I have that right?" she asked.

He swallowed hard and nodded.

"I thought so," she said and stood from the couch. She poured herself a glass of champagne, bending over in front of Kenny. He let out a strangled cry as her thighs and the soft globes of her ass were bared to his eyes underneath her very short dress.

When she sat back down, Kenny's eyes were on her and so were the eyes of a small cluster of older, elegant women behind them. Maya smiled and they smiled back, one of them waving hello. Maya winked in return.

"Are you wearing underwear, Maya?" Kenny asked.

"Of course I am," she said, her eyes shifting to a man lying on another nearby chaise. She watched as he slowly unzipped his pants, his eyes aimed their way.

"I didn't see any," Kenny said.

"They're there," she replied as the man slipped his hand though the zipper. Maya moved one leg onto Kenny's lap. "Why don't you find them."

His hands were on her thighs, trembling. "I can't," he said.

She shifted her eyes to him. She was surprised to see his face flushed but not surprised when she dropped her eyes to the large bulge in his pants.

"Why not?"

"I need to concentrate," he ground out. "And I can't concentrate on anything else if I touch you."

His words made her feel sexy and powerful. God he's wonderful, she thought to herself.

"Babe," she said and kissed him gently, just the soft pressure of her mouth on his. "I thought you were a professional."

"They don't train us for this kind of situation."

"Lane and Monica seem just fine," she said.

He rolled his eyes, "They're different."

"How?"

His brows furrowed. "I don't like putting you in the middle of this," he finally admitted. And then she saw the fear in his eyes.

She put her champagne flute down and softly touched his face. They made eye contact and she smiled at him. "I trust you," she whispered. "If I didn't, I wouldn't be here."

He inhaled sharply and huffed out a breath. Kenny covered her hands with his and leaned forward so their foreheads touched.

"We can do this," she said.

"We," he whispered back.

She raised his head and smiled at him. "We," she said again with a smile.

As the smile spread along his mouth, Maya watched his eyes light up with something soft that chased the look of fear away.

"Now touch me quick, the sex is finally kicking off," she laughed.

He furrowed his brow and looked around. On the nearby couches their unexpected audience had begun to shift clothes to the side or were in the process of taking them off all together.

"You did this," Kenny said with a smile.

"I am *very* good at my job," she smirked. "And you know I love an audience."

When he turned back to her, she raised her eyebrows at him in challenge.

He smiled at her and then his eyes darted around. "Keep your eyes open," he said, reaching for the strap of her dress. He pushed it over her shoulder with her bra strap. His fingers traced the skin across her chest and then dipped down into her dress. He pulled her breast free and began to roll her nipple between his fingers.

She whimpered.

He dipped his head and swiped his tongue across her nipple and then began to gently pinch the sensitive flesh.

She groaned and her eyes drifted closed.

"Maya," he said in a hard tone that made her clit jump.

She opened her eyes.

"You watch my back and I'll watch yours."

She frowned and let out a harsh breath of air. But she did as he said, alternating her gaze between his face and the room behind him. There was so much to see, people touching themselves and each other, some watching them, some in their own little world. But she didn't care about any of it; none of it was as interesting as Kenny's intense stare or his fingers on her. So she only looked away when he did. As soon as she verified there were no more human walls headed their way she hurried back to his eyes.

She could feel her sex weeping at his touch. It wasn't enough. Maya spread her legs and licked her lips. His eyes settled on her mouth. "Touch me," she whispered.

His eyes darted to her legs and the hem of her tiny dress. He looked up, scanning the room.

She could have jumped when his hand landed on her knee. He squeezed her there and then began the slowest path up her leg toward her pussy.

"Faster," she breathed.

He turned to follow the movement of a waiter and laughed. "It's my turn to tease you."

She growled, "Didn't take long for you to get cocky." Her eyes darted to his lap. His erection was a large mound and her mouth watered.

"Maya."

Her eyes flew to his. "I was just looking for a second," she said and then shifted to check the room behind him.

His fingers touched the crotch of her underwear.

"Huh," he said. "You are wearing underwear."

"Not for long," she mumbled.

He huffed a laugh.

She didn't know what he thought was funny and she would have said that except he started to rub her clit through the wet patch at her crotch.

"Fuck," she said, fighting to keep her eyes open. And a good thing she succeeded, because she saw the moment the elevator doors opened and the human wall returned, Joseph Mehmeti behind him.

"Incoming," she breathed and then let her head fall back.

"Him?"

"Yes," she hissed and settled her eyes on him. "Please, make me come before he gets here. I might have a hard time concentrating now." She could see Mehmeti walking leisurely toward them but she didn't care about him right now.

He laughed. "How the tables have turned," he whispered and then did as she asked.

His touch transformed in an instant from light and airy to hard and needy. Maya's body shivered with an onslaught of so many emotions as he pinched her nipple with one hand and slipped two fingers around the scrap of fabric and inside of her wet sex quickly. He turned his hand, sawing his fingers in and out of her, rubbing along her most sensitive spot and then settled his thumb to rub her clit.

"Fuck are you ambidextrous?"

He laughed and maybe he answered but she was too overcome. Her head fell back and she opened her mouth to let out a loud moan as her body shivered and her sex clenched and gushed around Kenny's fingers.

The orgasm made her back arch and the rest of the room disappeared around them. That was probably a bad thing considering an Albanian mobster was stalking toward them. But in that moment, Maya truly did not care.

"YOU HAVE STARTED WITHOUT ME," Mehmeti said. In his peripheral vision, Kenny watched a waiter bring a chair for Mehmeti to sit on. Another waiter brought him a glass of dark liquid. Mehmeti crossed his legs at the knee.

Kenny's body tensed, but he kept his eyes on Maya, letting the beauty of her orgasm calm him so he could focus on the job at hand.

He could tell when she came back to herself. She lifted her head and looked at Kenny, a filthy smile on her face. He recognized that look. It was the one she gave her viewers after a show, just before she signed off. He marveled again at how natural this all came to her.

He reluctantly took his hand from between her legs and helped her straighten her dress. When they turned to Mehmeti, Kenny stuck the fingers he'd buried inside Maya into his mouth and sucked her essence from her digits. She tasted wonderful.

He could tell by the smile that spread over Mehmeti's face that he enjoyed the sight. Maya pressed herself against Kenny's side and laid her head onto his shoulder.

"I am already so pleased," Mehmeti said, his eyes feasting on her.

"I aim to please," Maya said.

"Yes," Mehmeti said hungrily. "I've noticed." He obscenely adjusted his erection.

"May I touch you?" Mehmeti asked.

Kenny's mouth turned down into a frown and his fists clenched.

"No," Maya said, squeezing his bicep reassuringly. "You haven't paid for that. And my boyfriend is very," she turned to him, kissing his cheek sweetly, "possessive."

There was a tense moment of silence and Kenny's body coiled tightly in preparation for any kind of response. But then Mehmeti burst into laughter and turned to his guards. "Do you see?" he asked them. "She is perfect."

Maya turned her head and smiled at the mobster.

He licked his lips at her. "Maybe next time the three of us," he said and turned to Kenny, licking his lips again, "Can come to some agreement?"

Maya leaned forward, catching Mehmeti's gaze again with her chest. She grasped her champagne flute. They all watched as her soft lips rested on the glass and she took a small sip. She kept her eyes on Mehmeti, flirty and distracting. "Let's not get ahead of ourselves," Maya said. "One night at a time."

Mehmeti nodded and sipped his own drink.

"Yes," he breathed, his eyes trained on her mouth. "We can stay here, if you would like. Or we can go to my private rooms."

This was it, Kenny thought to himself, working not to show his interest. Chanté hadn't been able to hack into Mehmeti's computer remotely. They needed to locate his computer and Asif's intel from earlier in the day indicated that the most likely place for it to be was in his private rooms on the fifth floor, the most heavily guarded floor of the entire building.

"Well, that's up to you," Maya said, her hand rubbing across Kenny's chest. "You've paid all of this money to watch us fuck," Mehmeti's body jumped at the word, "Do you want to share that with everyone here? Or are you going to be selfish?" She whispered the last word against Kenny's jaw before nipping at him gently.

Mehmeti adjusted his erection again before standing up quickly and heading back toward the elevator without a word.

They both turned to watch him, confused.

"Please," the guard said. "Follow me."

They stood from the couch and Kenny grabbed Maya's hand.

As they walked out of the room, he cut his eyes to look at the couch where Monica, Lane and Kierra had been sitting. When he looked, there was only Kierra straddling Lane's lap. They were staring at one another lovingly, but Lane's eyes moved to Kenny's. His nod was so small it would have been imperceptible.

Maya whispered to him, "I thought he'd be taller."

Kenny turned to her, a startled smile forming on his lips. She smiled up at him and winked.

He squeezed her hand in his.

Lamont

Lamont hated clubs. He'd never been the out all night at a nightclub kind of person. His ex always said he was too serious for that. And he was. His grandmother had worked herself to the bone to get him through high school and into college. She'd taken him as far as she could and had always made clear that he would have to take himself the rest of the way – with her cheering him on from afar, of course.

While his friends were out getting drunk and skipping classes and failing exams, Lamont had been in the library. When he joined the ATF it had been the same. While his recruitment class had been out drinking and fucking each other in the name of bonding and good morale, Lamont had been memorizing his new recruit manual cover-to-cover. It might not have made him the most popular person, but it had made him damn good at his job.

He tried to remind himself of that. Even though the past week had felt like a terrible nightmare where no one was who they seemed to be – because they hadn't been – he was still a damn good detective. And he had a job to do.

"Can I buy you a drink?"

He turned and blinked at the woman standing next to him

at the bar. He hadn't noticed her before; he was too busy scanning the crowd for any sign of Travis Keeler. But he smiled down at her and shook his head, lifting the glass of tonic water in his hand. "Thanks, but I'm okay."

She frowned slightly. "What about my boyfriend?" She tipped her head to the left and he followed the movement.

The girl was definitely no more than five feet tall and she was wearing sky high heels so Lamont's eyes widened to saucers when he spotted the tall, round man with a handlebar mustache dressed in head-to-toe leather staring at them. He was clutching a bottle of beer in one hand and had looped the thumb of the other through a belt loop on his leather trousers. Lamont turned back to look at her to confirm that yes, she was dressed in Sailor Moon cosplay. They were an odd pair.

"Um," he started, genuinely at a loss for words.

She took that moment of hesitation as an invitation and leaned into him. "We're a *great* time," she promised with a dirty smile on her face.

Lamont laughed. This was another reason he didn't like clubs. There was something about strangers propositioning him that turned him right off. And this was the second time in two weeks he'd had to let himself be propositioned in a nightclub to catch a criminal. Not for the first time since his ex kicked him out of their house, he wondered if it was time to retire and do something different with his life. Weren't these signs that it was time for him to move on?

"I bet you are," he said to the girl. "But I'm actually waiting for someone."

She frowned slightly but then rallied, trailing a hand over the hair on his forearm. "Well if you and your someone are looking for a couple of someones… Like I said we're-"

"A great time," Lamont finished for her. "I'll keep that in mind."

"You do that."

Lamont watched as she tottered away on her platform

heels to rejoin her boyfriend. He watched as the man had to nearly double over to kiss her in greeting. And then he watched as they both turned their attention back to him to smile and wave.

He smiled and waved back. "Get me the fuck out of here," he whispered to himself through clenched teeth.

His eyes caught on sandy brown hair and he pushed away from the bar without a second thought.

He moved through the crowd carefully, without watching where he was going. He could almost hear his covert operations instructor yelling at him, "You know how many ops tank because some idiot takes their eyes off the mark?" Lamont had actually never gotten a solid figure on that, but he still took the advice to heart and kept Travis Keeler in his sight. The man was milling at the edges of the dance floor and he seemed to be waiting for something. Based on the intel they'd gathered from Ruiz's interrogations so far, they knew that Travis had been the one to broker the deal between the Pendleton Patriots and the Albanian mob. He was connected, but just how connected? That remained to be seen.

Lamont moved to a hidden alcove under the stairs to watch and wait. It only took a few minutes before a man who was clearly part of security approached Keeler. Lamont held his breath. If they headed upstairs, he was screwed. He'd been watching the security guards police elevator access for half an hour. As far as he could tell, passage required at least two people and possibly a special wristband. He wasn't sure how the others had gotten upstairs but given Kierra's lack of clothing, Lamont assumed they'd stumbled upon an unadvertised third way to go to the more private areas of the club. And he was no Kierra. Or Maya. Or Lane for that matter.

He watched as the security guard led Keeler away from the elevator down a hallway that Asif confirmed led to the bathrooms and then beyond to the club's storage rooms.

Lamont exhaled. He could work with this. They had prepared for this.

"They're heading back," he said.

"Roger that," Asif's voice filtered through his earpiece.

"What?"

Lamont turned and jumped, staring at two women slunk so far under the alcove that he hadn't seen them.

"Shit, I didn't see you there," Lamont breathed.

One of the women shrugged and moaned. Lamont backed away apologetically.

"Hey, you're welcome to join us," the other woman called after him.

He turned on a sigh and just saw Keeler's head disappear down the hallway. All he wanted to do was get Keeler and take him back to Ohio. He wasn't a spy and he was more than ready to get this operation over with and go back to his real life. Because this spy shit had been nothing but trouble.

But as he pushed through the crowded dance floor his mind suddenly reminded him of a sardonic grin and long eyelashes and perfectly tailored slacks. And the suggestion of a promise he knew he couldn't keep.

"There's an office at the end of the hallway," Asif was saying in his ear. "I'm pretty sure that's where they've gone."

Lamont was standing casually near the mouth of the hallway, waiting. He would have loved nothing more than to rush into the back office and take Keeler down, but they were outnumbered and Monica hadn't given him the signal yet. This operation was a finely, albeit thinly, arranged web. Now that he'd found Keeler he just needed to keep an eye on him and stay out of his line of sight. If he was spotted before everyone was in place they could all miss their chance to bring down Mehmeti's operation.

"Can you move your probe there?"

"How are the drinks?" Asif asked in response.

Lamont exhaled. "Don't chatter over the connection. I don't want people thinking I'm talking to myself."

"Everyone in that club is probably flying higher than a kite right now. Who cares what they think?"

Lamont turned to look out at the club. The music was something bass heavy and annoying in its persistent thumping beat. All around him he saw bodies grinding against each other, mostly on purpose. His eyes caught on the girl from the bar and her hulk of a boyfriend. They waved. Lamont smiled and waved back, but quickly looked away, hoping they didn't take that as an invitation to come and talk to him. Just as the thought crossed his mind, he watched as they put down their drinks on the bar and seemed determined to do just that.

"Fuck," he breathed.

And then they stopped.

"Looks like you have two admirers," Monica whispered into his ear as she pressed her body against his side.

Lamont's mouth fell open as he looked up at her. He was not into women at all, but if he were, she would be his type. Tall with a strong jaw and a severe mouth that never seemed to smile except when she was looking at her husband or girlfriend. Tonight, she looked amazing in a kind of tailored suit in the darkest black with a crisp white shirt and long black tie.

"They're just horny," Lamont said.

Monica's smile was almost imperceptible. "If my husband were here, he would say, 'Aren't we all?'" She asked the question in a decent imitation of Lane's accent.

Lamont tilted his head trying, not for the first time, to work her out. After working with Lane to bring down the Pendleton Patriots, he thought he understood the man, even if he was still adjusting to using his correct name. But the women in Lane's life, he didn't get.

"And what would Kierra say to that?" Lamont asked.

Now Monica's smile was big and bright enough to be seen. Monica leaned forward and brushed her mouth against his cheek. "She would be the reason Lane said that. Now let's go get your man."

Lamont raised his eyebrows at her as she straightened. "You're going to help me? I thought you were going to stay upstairs near Mehmeti."

"There's only one way for us out of here and that's through that door," she said indicating the entrance. "Every other exit is heavily guarded by a mountain with a gun."

Lamont laughed.

"Kenny and Lane will keep Maya safe," she said even though he could see some conflict in her eyes. "I'm here to make sure that our exit route is clear when it needs to be. And that means getting your rogue agent and clearing a path."

"Sounds like almost a plan."

Monica smiled at him. "Almost," she said before kissing him.

He started and tried to push her away. "Shut up. It's Keeler," she whispered against his lips. Out of the corner of his eye he saw his target walk directly past him. He seemed calmer than he had earlier, relaxed and sauntering. Whatever had happened in that back room had been good for him, which meant that it was bad for Lamont. But the good news was that with Keeler happy, he was also sloppy. He'd walked right past Lamont without noticing him, a man he'd sat across a desk from for almost a year. He settled into a VIP booth across the dance floor. Lamont guessed that, while it might not be easy, the mission to bring down his mole might just go smoother than he'd thought. Thanks in no small part to Monica.

As their lips parted, he looked at her seriously. "What do you need me to do, boss?"

Monica nodded. "Asif," she said. "Did you come up with a distraction?"

Asif's chuckle was almost apologetic. "A few actually."

"Good, get ready."

Lamont didn't know the other man well at all, but he felt certain that he could hear the smile in his voice. "On it," he said, quickly and efficiently.

"Now you," she said, focusing on him, "need to go make some friends." She tilted her head and they both turned to see the couple still staring intently and happily at him.

"Fuck," Lamont breathed again as he began to push through the crowd. The short woman and her tall boyfriend tried in vain not to register their shock and excitement as he approached.

seventeen

There's surprisingly little training to teach an agent how to be calm in the field. The Agency had training programs for everything else: weapons, surveillance, evasion. But none of that was any use if you couldn't keep your brain clear when there was a gun in your face and bodyguards the size of small mountains blocking your exit. And that was the thing that mattered. That was the dividing line between a field agent and an intelligence specialist or, more often than not, someone who signed a one-hundred-page NDA and lived out the rest of their life with a great story of how they were almost a spy – a story they could never tell.

But keeping calm had never been a problem for Kenny. He was focused, efficient and effective. Those words had always been at the top of his performance reviews and he'd come to take those qualities in himself for granted. Unfortunately, right now he felt none of those things. He had no coping mechanisms to calm himself, because he'd never had to even think about it before. And if he couldn't calm himself, he, Maya and this entire mission were screwed.

He suddenly remembered a speaker from his new recruit orientation at The Agency. Most of the scheduled speakers at the three-day-long event, including Monica, had given practical and generally inspiring information about the job they were all walking blindly into. But one agent was on the program specifically to make them shit their pants. For his entire ten minute talk he'd basically just unbuttoned and rolled up various pieces of his clothing to show off his many scars and share war stories.

Kenny hadn't been fazed by the increasingly gory details, but the guy next to him had excused himself to the bathroom never to be seen again. Right at the end of his speech, before he limped off stage, the old guy had leaned over the podium and whispered in a harsh voice, "None of you is as smart or capable as you think you are. The sooner you realize that, the better. And as soon as you realize that your next day isn't a given, the more effective you'll be in the field. We're not meant to do this job for too long. Remember that." Kenny had nodded sagely at that advice all of those years ago and then promptly forgotten it. But there was something about the warmth of Maya's hand in his and her taste still lingering on his tongue that plumbed that advice from the deep recesses of his brain. And he was scared shitless.

As if she knew he was silently freaking out, she moved in front of him as soon as they'd stepped onto the elevator, standing between him and the bodyguard who was currently escorting them upstairs to Joseph Mehmeti's private quarters. They didn't know what they would find there and Kenny needed to think. And because she really was a natural at this, Maya leaned back against him and began to chatter at the bodyguard, who didn't answer her. She pulled all of the focus onto herself.

The elevator ride was no more than a handful of seconds but Maya gave Kenny the space to reset and focus. She pressed her ass into his groin, squeezed his hands in hers. He breathed in the floral scent of her hair and he found his center: her. He wondered if this was what Monica and Lane felt when they were in the field together. Did they remind each other that there was more than this job? Did they provide each other with a point of focus; a port in the storm where the stakes were always clear? If so, he thought he finally understood. He dipped his head to place a small kiss behind her left ear. She kept talking to the bodyguard about eyeshadow on camera, but she squeezed his hands.

The elevator dinged.

The bodyguard walked out into a sitting room, the entire far wall was a large mirror.

Kenny moved his hands to Maya's waist and squeezed gently to reassure her.

If she was nervous, she hid it well. She was doing more than her part and he wasn't going to let her down.

"Mr. Mehmeti is ready to see you," the bodyguard said, opening a door to their right.

Just as he said that, the first bodyguard they'd met came out of the door to their left. Kenny turned his head and caught a brief glimpse beyond the guy's insanely broad shoulders and his breathing settled. He caught a glimpse of a large oak desk cluttered with papers and a computer monitor atop it.

He turned his head and followed Maya into Mehmeti's bedroom, not at all shocked at its close proximity to his office. It was finally show time.

IT'S funny the things Maya had been totally fine with up until now. Best friend works for spies? Okay. European arms dealer in her chatroom? Believable. Sex club in an old factory across the Bay from her hometown? Ah gentrification. Arms dealer wants to pay her to have sex with hot spy of her dreams? Hello savings!

She'd rolled with all of that with ease. But there was something about stepping into Joseph Mehmeti's bedroom that made her completely freak out. Maybe it was the fact that they were in a room with a guard out front, and more guards throughout the building, that tipped the scales from plausible to too much. Or maybe, she thought to herself, it was the fact that Mehmeti's large four-poster bed was covered in sheer drapes and velvet pillows. The over-the-top décor had worked for her downstairs, but not up here. In Mehmeti's private room the gaudy furnishings only reminded her how absurd this entire situation was. Irrationally, she was also freaking out that the first time she and Kenny would have sex would be in front of this creepy, shorter than she expected, criminal. Also, she amended with a tilt of her head, the fact that there was a throne, like a large, gaudy, golden throne set at the foot of the bed, didn't help her nerves. Because who the fuck has a throne in their bedroom?

She hoped she survived long enough to tell Kierra that the throne was the thing that sent her over the edge.

"Please," Mehmeti said, gesturing toward the bed. "Sit."

Maya wanted to shake her head and run, but Kenny squeezed her waist again. The small gesture helped to calm her a bit while also making her legs turn to jelly. He stayed close to her side as they walked to the bed and sat. She put her purse next to her and tried to regulate her breathing.

"Would you like some champagne?" Mehmeti asked, like this was all so normal. Maybe because it was for him.

Kenny shook his head.

"I don't drink while I work," she said and then took a deep breath. She smiled and batted her eyelashes. "In fact, that glass of champagne downstairs went straight to my head." She giggled.

She was completely clearheaded, but the words had the desired effect. She saw Mehmeti's hand tighten on the glass of dark liquid he held and his pants slowly tented as he stared at her. Maya was still freaked the fuck out, especially when he lowered himself into the throne, but she started to regain control of herself in that moment. As she'd told Kenny downstairs, her job was to keep his attention on her, to distract him. That she could do. And according to the daily ratings on ChatBot, she could do it better than thousands of other cam models on the site.

"So," she said, licking her lips. Mehmeti's eyes followed the movement before his gaze slid down Maya's body. She moved her hand to rest on Kenny's thigh. Mehmeti grunted. "How does this work?"

Mehmeti kept his eyes on Maya's hand on Kenny's leg. "I like to watch."

Maya had to force herself not to roll her eyes. Duh, she wanted to say, she paid her rent on just that reality. She began to move her thumb in circles. "What would you like to watch us do?"

Mehmeti set his glass down on the table next to him and began to undo the knot of his tie. "Strip."

Maya squeezed Kenny's thigh and stood. "Before I take this off," she whispered in a sultry tone, "Don't you want to admire the way your dress looks on me?"

Mehmeti grunted. His eyes devoured her body, his gaze clouded in lust. He grunted again as he followed her hands to the straps of her dress. She hooked her thumbs underneath them. He gasped.

Maya wasn't certain if he noticed Kenny stand from the bed. But just in case he did, she slid her dress straps over her shoulders. Mehmeti leaned forward to focus on Maya. The dress gaped at her chest and Mehmeti stood.

She wanted to stop him, remind him that he hadn't paid to touch her. But he was so focused on her that he seemed not to have noticed that Kenny was reaching toward his back. Mehmeti stepped closer to Maya, his eyes trained on the slowly bared flesh of her chest. His breathing was labored. He took another step forward. Her nipples were almost in view.

His eyes opened in shock as Kenny pressed the muzzle of a gun to Mehmeti's head.

"If you move or scream, I'll kill you where you stand," Kenny said in a hard tone that Maya tried not to focus on too much because it kind of turned her on. "Maya, move to the other side of the bed."

She didn't need to be told twice. She righted her dress, grabbed her purse and stepped away from Mehmeti, whose eyes were now slitted in anger. He glared at her.

"How did you get these weapons in my club?" Mehmeti whispered.

"Hate to break it to you, but security in this place is garbage."

"What do you want? Money?"

"Stop talking," Kenny said.

"I will make sure they torture you before they put a bullet in your head," Mehmeti hissed at her.

Kenny pushed the barrel of the gun harder against Mehmeti's skull. "Threaten her again." Mehmeti pressed his lips shut.

Kenny moved his free hand to his ear. "We're in."

Maya knew Kenny was talking to the other spies so she kept her eyes on Mehmeti. When the mobster looked as if he was about to make a move on Kenny, she opened her purse and pulled out the small pistol she'd packed there. She aimed it at Mehmeti. His hands stilled.

"Don't do that," she said.

Kenny put his gun back into his waist holster and pulled out a set of zip ties. "Hands," he said.

Mehmeti moved his hands to his back. Kenny restrained him quickly. Maya kept her gun on Mehmeti as Kenny patted him down, pulling a number of knives from various parts of his body. Kenny threw the weapons onto the throne, pulled more zip ties from his jacket pocket and then restrained Mehmeti's ankles.

Only then did Maya realize that Mehmeti was oddly calm.

"You won't get out of here alive," he said and laughed mockingly.

Kenny put his hands on his hips and looked down at Mehmeti, "You don't want to know who we are?"

"I know who you are," Mehmeti spat. "An internet whore and her boyfriend trying to make it rich. You have taken me for a pathetic mark."

Kenny rolled his eyes, "Joseph Mehmeti. Youngest and dumbest son of the Albanian mob. Does your father know what you're doing with your spare time?"

As he spoke, Kenny nodded his head at Maya to move behind him, out of the line of sight from the bedroom door. He motioned with his hand for her to squat down. Belatedly, she wished she'd taken her shoes off. What if she had to run?

Once again Maya saw surprise wash over Mehmeti's face as he processed what Kenny was saying. "Who are you?"

Kenny pulled his gun from the waistband of his pants, "You should have asked that before you threatened my girlfriend. I might have told you." And then he shot Mehmeti twice in the shoulder.

Maya jumped and yelped at the loud blast.

Mehmeti screamed and fell back onto the bed, writhing in agony.

Kenny spun away from Mehmeti and was ready when the guard rushed stupidly through the door. He barely made it into the room before Kenny took him down with a headshot.

They waited for a beat, Maya crouched in the corner, Mehmeti whimpering on the bed, and Kenny's gun trained on the door. The hallway was silent, but still they waited. The elevator dinged and they heard the doors open. Maya clutched the gun tighter in her hands. She had no idea how to shoot it, but she reminded herself of Kenny's advice not to put her finger on the trigger until she was ready to use it.

They heard footsteps in the hallway. Cautious. And then a whistle.

"We're here," Kenny said, finally relaxing his arm.

"Clear," Lane called.

Kenny moved to the door and kicked the gun near the bodyguard's hand away. He used his foot to turn him over.

"Who's that doing all that crying?" Lane asked as he stepped into the room.

"Mehmeti," Kenny said. He was moving around the room opening the door to the closet, his gun in one hand. "Clear." He moved to the only other door, the bathroom Maya guessed. "Clear," he said again.

"You shot him?" Lane breathed as he leaned over Mehmeti, who'd gone mostly quiet. Maya saw his body wracking with pain or sobs. "The mission was to capture him unharmed."

"No," Kenny corrected. "We're supposed to bring him in alive. He won't die."

Lane stared at Kenny and then he turned to see Maya, still crouching in the corner. "You okay there, honey?"

She frowned at Lane and turned the gun in her hands toward him, "I told you not to call me anything but my government name."

Lane laughed, "God, you're great."

Kenny walked across the room toward her. He gently took the gun from her hands and placed it onto the dresser next to him. He offered his hands to help her stand and gripped her shoulders. "Are you okay?"

She took a deep breath, her eyes darting around the room, settling on Mehmeti and then the dead bodyguard. He moved his hands over her shoulders, up her neck and stroked her jaw. She could smell something like smoke. She wasn't sure if she was going to scream, but she thought she might.

"Maya," he said her name in a soft whisper.

When her eyes settled on his he took a deep breath and

she mirrored him. They inhaled and exhaled together a few times.

"Maya are you okay?" he whispered.

She kept her eyes on his and considered the question. It took her brain a second to kickstart. She nodded. "Does this mean I get hazard pay?" she whispered.

The left side of Kenny's mouth lifted and the sound of Lane's laughter filled the room.

"We're almost done," Kenny said. "Just do what I say and stay close."

"Okay," she said. "Kiss me." She expected Kenny to tell her they didn't have time for this. That this moment was life or death. But he didn't. He pulled her face to his and crushed their mouths together.

Maya's brain came fully back online with that kiss. It was all a lot. The feel of his tongue, the lingering taste of champagne and her sex. The slightly metallic smell of Mehmeti's blood in the air as it mingled with the scent of gunfire.

Lane coughed.

Maya and Kenny broke their kiss slowly. They opened their eyes and smiled at each other.

Lane coughed again. "Far be it from me to stop this really touching moment, but we do have a job to complete."

"Almost done," Kenny whispered to her. He turned to Lane, but his right hand moved to grasp hers. He snatched her gun from the dresser and led her toward the bedroom door, through the hallway and across the hall.

Maya made a mental note to ask Kierra about that kiss. Was it the adrenaline? Endorphins? Dysfunction? Were butterflies in her stomach after Kenny shot a man in the shoulder for threatening her supposed to feel good?

Because they did.

Kenny and Lane cleared the office while Maya shuffled from one foot to the other at the threshold, wary eyes on the elevator. Mehmeti moaned pathetically on the ground at her feet.

"Clear," Lane said.

Maya jumped over Mehmeti and moved to the couch. She put her foot onto the coffee table and began to unbuckle her shoes.

The sound of snapping fingers caught her attention.

She looked up and found Kenny glaring at Lane.

"Let's stay focused," Lane said around a laugh.

Kenny looked as if he was seriously considering shooting Lane, but his ears were also red. He blushed when he turned back to Maya. She smiled, her entire body heating.

Lane chuckled again, ruining the heated moment between them. "Okay, I think I get why people are annoyed by us."

Kenny turned to the desk and tapped the computer keyboard.

"Chanté," he said and then he went quiet; listening. "It's locked."

Maya watched as he straightened and reached into his pocket. He pulled out what looked like a USB stick and put it into the computer. And then they waited, Kenny and Lane staring at the computer.

Maya unbuckled her shoes and stretched her toes. She padded across the room and moved behind the desk.

"Oh," she whispered as she looked at the computer screen. A bar in the middle of the screen indicated that Chanté was already downloading Mehmeti's entire hard drive.

"Yeah," Lane said. "She's good."

"She's great," Kenny said. And then he sighed. "Shut up or I'm never complimenting you again." He was talking to Chanté.

Maya found herself smiling at him, lost in the way annoyance looked on his beautiful face.

Lane's whisper in her ear startled her, "I'm gonna tell Kierra about this."

She turned to him with a glare and then frowned. “Where is my miniature bestie?”

Lane smiled as he spoke into his own ear piece. “We’re downloading the hard drive now. Clear a path.” And then he smiled down at Maya, “Doing what she does best.”

Maya’s frown deepened, “Wearing very little clothing?”

Lane laughed, “Yeah, exactly that actually.”

They all stilled when the elevator dinged and they heard the doors slide open.

the honeypot

For the second time today Kierra was giving some very serious consideration to becoming a field agent. She wondered if she'd *have* to handle a gun. She wondered if she'd be allowed to train under Monica and Lane. Oh, and then her brain just drifted off at the thought of that. All of a sudden the crush of people she'd been pushing through disappeared and there was her mark.

Agent Travis Keeler, the third Setter brother that no one had known about until Lane had gone to Ohio, was sitting like a king on his throne in a booth at the edge of the dance floor, surrounded by a group of women who were clearly enjoying the bottle service if nothing else. There was a bottle of some dark liquor that looked expensive on the table in front of him. It looked like the kind of liquor you were supposed to sip slowly. But Keeler was throwing it back in shots. Kierra wanted to shake her head and frown because one of Monica's bedrock rules was to never get drunk on the job. When you worked with people who used guns as a negotiating tactic, the workday was Russian roulette at the best of times. Add in alcohol or any drug and your chances of survival dropped precipitously.

So either Keeler was not as meticulous about his job as Monica was about hers or he was just a fucking idiot. Or both. Kierra watched as he threw another shot of liquor down his throat. But instead of swallowing it, he grabbed the girl next to him, tipped her head back and dribbled the liquid in his mouth down her throat.

Kierra gagged and turned away, plunging back into the dancing crowd. "Nope. Nuh-uh. Can't do it."

"Kierra." Monica's voice came to her through her ear piece.

She shook her head harder. "Absolutely not. Did you just see that sick shit?"

"What happened?" Asif said.

"It *was* gross," another voice said, she assumed it was Lamont.

"Tell me," Asif whined.

"Shut up," Monica demanded.

"You're not going to convince me to go over there," Kierra cut in. "I don't care what you say. We have no intel on his oral hygiene so I'm assuming the worst. That was rank."

"Kierra." Monica's voice was hard. "I know that was off-putting."

Kierra scoffed.

"But, I need you to do this, sweet girl. We need to give Lane and Maya a way out."

Kierra's mouth fell open at Monica trying to guilt her into this so brazenly.

"You don't have to touch him," Monica continued. "Just distract him and his bodyguards."

"And what will I get for this? It's not *technically* part of my job."

"Shake her down," Asif whispered.

"What do you want?" Monica asked. "And before you tell me, I want to remind you that you have maxed out all possible bonuses for this quarter. Anymore and The Agency will be on our asses."

Kierra smiled wickedly, "Don't worry, I don't want another bonus."

"Then what do you want?"

"A vacation."

She could hear the confusion in Monica's voice. "You have lots of vacation time. You can take it whenever you want."

"No," Kierra said. "I want the three of us to go on a vacation. No guns. No ear pieces. No cheesy European sex clubs. I want us to sleep in in the morning, no technology and *classy* sex clubs." Kierra's eyes caught on a figure at the edge of the dance floor across the room from Keeler. A body she would recognize anywhere because she knew every plane of it by touch and taste.

When their eyes met, Monica's tongue darted out and she licked her lips. Kierra raised one eyebrow and waited.

When she spoke again, Monica's voice was thick with lust and emotion, "Anything you want, sweet girl."

The smile that spread across her face was dirty and triumphant.

"I would have asked for a new car," Asif said. "You need it."

"Shut up," Kierra and Monica said at the same time.

Kierra took a deep breath to gather her strength and turned on her very tall heels back through the crowd. When she made it to the other side of the room, she felt powerful and without inhibition. She could see why Monica didn't drink on the job. Why bother with alcohol when the heady rush of adrenaline was such a better high?

She walked with an exaggerated strut and caught Keeler's eyes immediately. She stopped at his table and held his gaze as she grabbed the neck of his liquor bottle. The women at the table grumbled, but Keeler smiled, waiting for her next move. She tipped the bottle to her mouth, the taste smooth and harsh as it hit her tongue, which she pressed against the bottle to stop it from flowing into her mouth; just enough to taste, but not nearly enough to even get her buzzed. She made sure to keep Keeler's eyes on hers so he wouldn't notice. She tilted the bottle down and eyed him across the table.

She licked her lips. His eyes followed the movement. She put the bottle back on the table and turned to the poor girl who'd been on the receiving end of his bird feeding. Her eyes were wide and locked on Kierra's. Kierra sucked her bottom lip into her mouth and smiled at her. She crooked her finger and beckoned her forward. She didn't know if the girl scrambled to stand because she was so desperate to get away from Keeler or because she was interested.

It didn't matter.

What mattered was that when she grabbed the girl's hand and pulled her toward the dance floor, by the time she turned back, Keeler was already moving to follow them into the crush of bodies. Away from his security detail.

Undercover operations were Lamont's specialty. He liked to think that given enough time and preparation, he could blend into any group for any length of time. But he was struggling trying to keep his eye on Keeler and follow what the short girl, Sarah, and her tall bear of a boyfriend, Kay, were saying. This should have been easy. He only needed them to provide a cover so he could keep his eye on Keeler without being spotted. But his brain kept stuttering over their words.

"Wait," Lamont said, his eyes darting over Kay's shoulder briefly to make sure Keeler was still in his booth. "So you're saying that the wolf has magical powers, but only on the blood moon?"

"No!" Kay and Sarah screeched before tripping over each

other to explain the plot of the obscure anime they were obsessed with one more time.

Lamont had assumed he would only have to flirt with them and maybe dodge some inappropriate touching. He'd been shocked to find that the couple were quite polite and more comfortable wooing a third with their geeky interests rather than sexy talk. It was throwing him for a loop.

"Okay so the wolf can shapeshift into any animal," Sarah began. "But he can only become a human again during the full moon."

Lamont nodded.

"Which means he can only be with the person he loves when the moon is high," Kay added.

"Okay, I got that." Lamont watched Kierra approach Keeler's booth again. "Then what about the blood moon?"

"The entire show is the wolf searching for a spell that will turn him into a human full time. When he finds it, he has to say the spell under a blood moon for it to work," Kay said.

"But he hasn't found it yet," Sarah said excitedly.

"Five seasons, more than one hundred episodes and he *still* hasn't found it!" They began to bounce on the balls of their feet.

Lamont turned to them and his mouth fell open. He could not, for the life of him, understand why this was supposed to be entertaining. Out of the corner of his eye he saw Keeler rise from his booth, so it didn't matter.

"Yeah…" he said, "I don't think this show is for me."

Sarah and Kay's faces fell.

"I'm sorry," Lamont said, already moving away. "I see my friend finally. I have to go."

"No wait," Kay said. "Do you like space operas?"

Lamont had no idea what that was and he thankfully didn't have time for them to explain. He was already enmeshed in the crowd, his eyes on Keeler's sandy brown hair. He pulled the metal cuffs from his pocket, which were wonderfully easy to bring into the club as part of his outfit. He opened the bracelets and held his breath.

Keeler was too drunk to understand what was happening when Lamont slapped one cuff on his wrist. But when Lamont grabbed his other wrist and locked his arms behind his back he straightened, "Wha-"

Keeler whipped his head around and he looked as if he might shit himself when he saw Lamont behind him. He started to struggle and Lamont wrapped a hand around his neck, applying gentle pressure, just enough to put him to sleep. He struggled for a second and Lamont strengthened his hold. He finally went limp and Lamont dropped to the floor with him.

He looked up and Kierra was whispering into the girl's ear and slipping a set of car keys to her. Lamont furrowed his brows. The women straightened and Kierra nodded just before the girl ran back toward Keeler's booth screaming. No one on the dance floor noticed, the music was just loud enough to drown out her cries. And everyone was just high enough not to wonder what the hell was going on next to them.

Monica appeared out of the crowd. She slipped zip ties around Keeler's ankles and then she and Lamont lifted him up. "Distraction, Asif."

"Way ahead of you, boss," he said just as the music was almost drowned out by a fire alarm and the sprinklers erupted. The crowd went wild.

Lamont looked over his shoulder. He could see Keeler's bodyguards behind them in the crowd, heading toward where they'd taken Keeler down, but with the alarms, the water and the hysterical crowd, their progress was slow. They moved toward the bar.

"Wait," Monica said, her eyes on the small hallway where Keeler had disappeared earlier.

Lamont followed her line of sight. He saw Kierra talking

to the guards clearly explaining from her hand movements his takedown of Keeler.

"So this is what you're into?"

Lamont startled and turned to see Sarah and Kay staring at him. "Um… yes?"

Sarah frowned at him and Kay put their arm around her. "I guess we wouldn't have meshed."

"Move," Monica said.

"Sorry," Lamont called back at them. "I hope you find what you're looking for."

Kierra was running down the hall in front of them, the sound of her heels clacking against the concrete spurring him on.

They moved past the closed doors and the line of people waiting for the bathrooms. No one seemed to register any of the commotion. At the end of the hall, Kierra pushed open the emergency exit, the light above it began to whir and a new siren joined the fire alarm. Lamont turned as they exited, shocked that no one had even blinked twice at the three of them high-tailing it out of there with an unconscious, restrained man. He was ready to go back to Ohio.

They carried Keeler down a set of brand-new steel steps. Lamont found himself in another alleyway, stuffing another unconscious man into another vehicle. "This is the weirdest fucking week of my life," he said out loud to no one in particular.

"You gotta get out more," Asif said and then slammed the van's back doors closed.

"Lane," Monica said, her eyes unfocused, the sign that she was speaking into her ear piece. "Report."

They waited in silence for his reply. It didn't come.

eighteen

Kenny's hand was on his gun before he heard the elevator doors fully open. He pushed past Lane and moved Maya quickly back. There was a bathroom behind them and he motioned for her to go there. Immediately. She was already halfway there before they even made eye contact.

Mehmeti was squirming weakly, hogtied just inside his office.

"What's going on?" Chanté said, breaking the silence and alerting whoever had arrived that something was up.

Lane reached for Kenny's phone and hung up, slipping it in his pocket. They needed to give Chanté at least ten more minutes to finish downloading Mehmeti's hard drive. They could even afford to leave the physical backup behind if need be. It wouldn't be ideal, but if Kenny had to choose between grabbing that USB stick and getting Maya out of here quickly, it wasn't a choice.

They waited in silence, Kenny crouched beside the couch and Lane behind the desk, their guns trained on the doorway. Two full minutes passed. The good news at the moment was that as soon as someone stepped into that doorway, they would drop; Mehmeti's body worked as an unexpectedly useful obstacle to slow their approach. Since they were stalling for time, this worked to their advantage. But as soon as the download was complete, the odds would flip. The longer they waited, the more time for reinforcements to arrive, and the harder it would be to get them all out of here in one piece.

"Hello," someone called from the foyer. Kenny recognized it as the voice of the first, and biggest, bodyguard who'd met them downstairs.

Fuck, he mouthed silently.

"Howdy," Lane called back.

Kenny turned to look at him; Lane was laughing silently.

"I don't know who you are, but this will not end well for you," the bodyguard called.

"I was gonna say the same thing to you, hoss."

Kenny rolled his eyes at Lane's impossibly thick Texas accent. He silently willed Chanté's download to speed up so he could escape this deathtrap and that fake drawl.

"What do you want?" the bodyguard called.

Kenny spotted a shadow near the door.

"Thank you for asking," Lane said in an excited tone. "No one ever asks me what I want and Christmas is coming. So first, I really want a pair of those running shoes that look like Flintstone feet. I don't run, but they'll annoy the shit out of my wife."

Kenny groaned.

"I want a new pair of cowboy boots and a ten-gallon hat for the exact same reason."

Kenny saw the shadow move again. He moved his finger to the trigger and tried to ignore the sound of Lane's voice, something he was becoming adept at. He was ready when a hand shot out and tried to grab Mehmeti by the shin. He let off two rounds. One shot was aimed at where the hand was, he didn't hit his mark, so he pulled the trigger one more time, grazing Mehmeti's thigh. The man screamed loudly and began to writhe again. Kenny's point was clear: he had no problem riddling their boss with bullets if they tried to rescue him.

Lane started talking again as if that exchange hadn't just happened. Although he did have to speak a little louder to be heard over Mehmeti's whimpering cries.

"I really want a vacation. It's been a long year. I'm not as young as I used to be. I want to just sit on a beach somewhere and drink some fruity drinks. That'd be nice." There was a moment of silence. Kenny almost turned back to look at Lane, the seemingly uncomfortable honesty of that wish catching him off guard. It made him think of Maya, cowering in the bathroom alone.

Lane's voice brought him back to the crisis at hand. "But I guess what I really want right now is for you to go ahead and threaten my life again or whatever, so we can get this show on the road."

There was silence from the foyer but Kenny heard the muffled movements of many feet on the carpet. He didn't know how many people were out there, but he felt certain that the odds were not in their favor. They never were.

"I will give you the chance to surrender, old man. You and whoever is in there with you," the bodyguard said.

Kenny turned to Lane. The man had a large smile on his face. Oh, he thought, that's why he talked about being old. Lane was older than Kenny for sure, but so was Monica. And an agent didn't get to their age with the personnel records they had without having been consistently effective and deadly. Regardless of age, annoying twang or not, there were few people Kenny would have trusted Maya's life with in that moment. Making the bodyguards think he was older and less effective was potentially a great way to get them to make a mistake. He was suffused with a begrudging respect for the man. It didn't rival the adoration and near hero worship he felt for Monica, but it seemed like a significant shift in their relationship nonetheless.

"Do I have to decide right now?" Lane asked.

"I will count to ten," the bodyguard said.

"Can you make it twenty?" Lane asked. There was a soft knock on the desk.

Kenny turned and Lane motioned toward the bathroom.

The bodyguard started counting.

He moved to the door, opened it. Maya was crouched across the room, near the shower. Kenny motioned for her to come close. She knelt down near him.

"When I give you the word, you stay behind us at all times."

She nodded.

"And if we get separated you get the fuck out of here as fast as you can."

She shook her head. "I'm not leaving you," she hissed.

"Nine," the bodyguard yelled.

"Yes you are. And you're going to take the money The Agency gives you, get out of debt, and take care of your brother and sister."

She frowned at him.

"Eight!"

"Look asshole," Maya hissed. "You don't get to catfish me in my own cam room, burst into my apartment, tell me you're a whole ass spy and then get me caught up with the Algerian mob."

"Albanian," Kenny corrected.

"I don't give a shit where they're from," she yelled.

"Seven!"

Kenny's eyes darted to the door briefly before coming back to Maya's beautiful face.

"The point is," Maya continued in a more reasonable tone, "that you've caused me a lot of fucking hassle and now I'm invested. Also, you don't get to die on me before we go to Hawai'i like you promised. So we're getting out of here together. Period."

"Six!"

Kenny stared at Maya, the rest of the room – and the dire straits of their situation – falling away. He blinked. Her face had flushed, her breathing had escalated and her pupils were wide with anger and he realized that he was going to fall in love with her. Life-threatening endorphins aside, he was halfway head over heels in love with her already.

"Okay," he breathed simply. Because he would give her anything she wanted. Even if the thing she wanted was as far-fetched as them getting out of this situation alive and together.

The computer chimed.

Kenny nodded and Maya crouched back into the bathroom. When he turned, Lane had already stood and was pulling the USB from the computer monitor. And like a fucking idiot that big bear of a bodyguard had thought that moment was the time to rush into the room. Forgetting, apparently, that the door was a bottle neck.

Kenny stood and put two rounds into his head; there was no reason to aim anywhere else on a man that big. A kill shot was the only way to go. He fell backwards as another man entered the frame. But with Mehmeti and that big corpse blocking the doorway he didn't make it far. Lane took a shot, the guard yelled and retreated. They couldn't hear anything in the foyer, which didn't mean the coast was clear, just that the few security guards left were smarter than the ones they'd picked off.

They waited, but now time was not on their side. The same things that had made the doorway a bottleneck for security were also going to slow them down, especially now with more bodies cluttering the floor. And on top of that was Mehmeti. They'd need to carry him, which would mean they'd need to put their guns away. That was a death sentence. And Maya had said that was not an option.

"Get ready," Asif said, his voice bursting into their ears.

"For what?" Lane said just as the fire alarms started to blare. A few seconds later the sprinklers turned on.

"Son of a bitch, Kenny said, wiping at the water droplets on his eyelashes.

But then they heard it, the shuffling of feet in the foyer. It was barely perceptible and if they'd been still moving stealthily, Kenny wouldn't have heard it. But they were freaking out. He and Lane advanced on the door. Kenny pressed himself against the wall and inched forward to look at the mirrored wall at the back of the sitting area. From that vantage point he could see three guards at the elevator; two facing the door and one pressing the elevator button, clutching at his throat as blood poured over his fingers. Kenny assumed he was the one Lane shot.

He turned to Lane and relayed that information silently. And then he crouched down, grasped Mehmeti by the ties at his ankles and dragged him quickly out of the way. His moans were barely audible over the alarm.

An errant shot from the foyer splintered the wood of the doorframe.

Lane moved to the bathroom and Maya followed him out into the office. Kenny moved to her and handed her his gun.

"Anyone you don't recognize, you shoot them here," he told her, pointing at his gut, "or here," he pointed at the center of his forehead.

Her eyes were wide but she nodded.

He turned, grasped Mehmeti and picked him up, throwing him over his shoulders in a fireman's carry.

As soon as the elevator dinged, Lane moved in a rush into the foyer. There was a hail of gunfire. When Kenny moved to the door, he saw Lane across the hall in the bedroom doorway with a smile on his face. "Did I ever tell you I was a top-rated marksman when I went through the Academy?"

Lane moved into the foyer, his gun still at the ready.

Kenny inched to the doorway, leaning around to survey the damage. "Clear?"

Kenny heard a groan and then one more shot. "Clear."

"Move now," Kenny called over his shoulder.

He stepped into the hallway and nodded Maya into the elevator. She was quick in her bare feet, her heels and purse clutched in her hands and pressed tight to her chest. Kenny held his breath as they crowded inside. He lowered Mehmeti to the floor and the man wailed. Fresh blood began to pour from his wounds.

Lane pressed the button to the second floor. The exit they needed was at the back of the club and they'd have to cross the main dancefloor to get to it. He wiped his wet hands on his pants and grasped the gun from Maya. He held it at his side, waiting as the elevator descended slowly.

On the fourth floor, the elevator doors opened to the private salon.

Kenny and Lane raised their guns at the two men standing there kissing. They barely seemed to notice that the elevator had opened. Lane pressed the button to close the door and they moved on.

"Damn, I really liked this place," Maya whispered from the back of the elevator.

"You and Kierra really are the same person," Lane chuckled.

Just before the door opened on the main floor Kenny handed the gun back to Maya and hauled Mehmeti over his shoulders again.

Lane's gun was aimed high, unsure of what to expect. But when the door opened all they encountered was the thumping bass of an EDM song and a packed dance floor in front of them.

"Does no one hear the fucking fire alarm?" Kenny hissed.

"Is that the name of this song?" Lane laughed as he lowered his gun to his side and led the way.

Kenny motioned for Maya to go before him so he could keep an eye on her.

He kept waiting for someone to realize that he was carrying a bloody, near-unconscious man on his shoulder, but no one did. The lights were low and the intermittent spotlights that moved around the space made it harder for him to see much beyond Maya's frame in front of him. So he guessed that worked in their favor.

When they entered the back hallway, he was even more alert. The line to the restrooms was long and he held his breath, but again no one noticed them. In what felt like less than a minute but also an hour, they were pushing out of the emergency exit and there was the rest of their team. They hustled down the stairs in relief.

"I said report," Monica yelled at Lane, rushing toward him and pushing against his chest.

"We were in a hairy situation," Lane said with a laugh, grabbing his wife's wrists.

"I don't give a fuck if there's a gun to your head. When I say report, you better at least cough."

Kenny could see the shine of tears in her eyes and he got it. For the first time, he got it.

His eyes shifted to Maya who was hugging Kierra tightly. The two of them clutching at one another.

"Are you all always this emotional in the middle of an op?" Lamont asked.

"Yes," Asif said. "They are." And then he shifted, looking deeper into the alleyway. A dark van Kenny hadn't noticed was idling there. The passenger door opened. "Carlisle," he said in a hard tone at the man who stepped from the vehicle.

Kenny recognized the black ops agent he'd seen exactly once, when a job in Italy had gone really fucking wrong.

Qualifying for the black ops division of The Agency was near impossible. Or at least it was shrouded in the kind of mystery that made it seem near impossible. Because the goal for that division was to be nearly invisible. If black ops showed up, something was very wrong, you were very much fired, or they were taking someone some place where they would never be seen again.

"Asif," Carlisle said with a grin on his face. "How's the shoulder?"

Asif scoffed, which made Carlisle smile. He turned to Kenny and his face sobered into clear professionalism; all business. "That my transpo?"

Kenny nodded. "He's got a few holes?"

Carlisle nodded, "I'll alert the medic."

He turned with a tilt of his head. Kenny followed. The back of the van opened up, another agent who Kenny didn't recognize jumped to the ground and helped him toss Mehmeti inside. The other man jumped back into the van and pulled the doors closed behind him. Quick. Easy. Professional.

Carlisle turned toward them with a smile. They all stopped as the sound of police sirens and the horn of a fire truck sounded. "Looks like it's time for us to get the fuck outta here." He saluted them, Asif scoffed again, Carlisle laughed as he jumped into the already moving van.

"He's right," Monica said. "Let's go."

They all crawled into their own cargo van with Asif at the wheel.

"I'm sorry, who the fuck is this?" Maya asked, looking down at Keeler.

"He's mine," Lamont said.

"Your *what*? And also who the fuck are you?"

"He's Kenny's old partner," Kierra said helpfully.

"And this guy is going to jail for a very long time," Lamont said not helpfully.

Maya stared at all of them before turning to the front passenger seat where Monica was sitting.

"So what's-"

"Yes, I know. You want more money. It'll be in your

account in three to five business days," Monica said, cutting her off. She turned to the back of the van and eyed Kierra. "They're going to audit us after this mission. I don't think anyone has ever managed to so effectively shake The Agency down." And then she smiled.

Kenny turned as Lane pressed a gentle kiss to Kierra's temple, "That's our girl."

Maya nodded and turned to Kenny. They locked eyes but didn't speak. The ride in the back of the van was bumpy and uncomfortable, especially with an unconscious Keeler between them. But Kenny had had worse rides in worse transportation. This trip felt like a limousine ride in comparison, especially when Maya curled herself against his side and laid her head on his shoulder.

"Thank you for not dying," she whispered eventually.

He brushed his lips against her forehead in answer.

scatter

Lamont always preferred to work alone. Especially in the last few years. But as the van pulled into a remote cargo hangar, he was willing to agree that maybe this one time, not working alone had been worth it. But that didn't mean he was looking to stretch this mission out any longer than necessary. As soon as the van pulled to a stop, Lamont pushed the back door open and hopped out.

He turned around and offered his hand to Kierra. She smiled down at him and took his hand gently. He blinked as she hopped delicately to the ground.

Lane followed her. "Don't mind our sweet girl. She gets a little keyed up when the mission is over and we're all safe." He wrapped his arm around her waist and picked her up, whispering into her ear.

"So we're pretending like this only happens when the mission is over?" Asif asked from the driver's seat.

Lamont shook his head and turned to offer his hand to Maya, the last person in the back of the van. But Kenny slapped his hand out of the way and reached up to lift Maya down himself.

"I was just being a gentleman," Lamont said with a roll of his eyes.

"Be a gentleman with him," Kenny said, gesturing toward Keeler who seemed to be coming back to consciousness.

"Fuck," Lamont breathed and reached quickly for the man's legs before he was awake enough to start kicking.

"Can I get a gag or something?" he yelled.

Before he could get the sentence out completely, Monica had crawled into the back of the van to shove a piece of cloth into Keeler's mouth to muffle his screams. The man's eyes went wide with fear. They settled on Lamont and he began to buck, trying to free himself. He thought he'd escaped and would get away scot-free after years of infiltrating the ATF and a year sabotaging Lamont's case against his white supremacist gang. Lamont felt a deep sense of relief and satisfaction that he was wrong. And he looked forward to being able to finally close the Pendleton Patriots case as soon as he made it back to Columbus.

"So how are we doing this?" he asked no one in particular.

He was surprised when Asif came around the side of the van and answered. "We've got a cargo plane in the next hangar that'll take us to Columbus."

"Us?" Lamont said.

"I'm following a lead." Asif turned to Kenny, "So you got the hard drive?"

Kenny's jaw ticked, "We did."

"Who hacked it?"

Kenny pressed his lips shut, refusing to answer.

Asif laughed and pulled his phone from his pocket. He pressed a few buttons and they stood there as the line on the other end rang.

"Mabel's Pies," a voice Lamont didn't recognize said. Kenny's hands flexed.

Asif smiled wider with every word, "Thank you for picking up this time."

"Well, I mostly wanted to confirm that you were alive," the woman said.

"I am and so is everyone else."

"Well now that we've handled that, take care of yourself, Asif."

Lamont wondered if he was imagining the sadness in Asif's eyes.

"Where are you?" Asif asked in a soft voice, his eyes dipping for the first time to stare at the phone in his hand as if he could see her through it.

She didn't answer.

"Chanté," he breathed as the call disconnected.

Lamont's entire body went rigid at the name. "Chanté?" he asked looking around. "That was Chanté?" He looked at Asif but the man was still staring despondently at his phone. He turned to Kenny.

"It's a long story," Kenny said.

"Caleb's Chanté?" Lamont asked.

"The one and only," Lane said, coming around the van flanked by Monica and Kierra.

"What am I missing?" Kenny asked.

Lamont wouldn't have told him if he could have found the words. He pressed his lips shut.

"We had our own adventure if you must know," Lane said. "And as dramatic as it was, we've all gotta get a fucking move on."

That snapped Asif back to reality. He turned away from them without a word and crawled back into the van.

Lamont turned to Kenny.

"You alright?" Kenny asked.

He wasn't. Maybe he would be some day, but he wasn't right now. He shrugged and stuck out his hand. "I guess this makes us even," he said.

Kenny's mouth tipped up into a smile. "I am sorry about last time."

Lamont huffed out a laugh, "And it only took you three years to apologize." He squeezed the other man's hand firmly. "Water under the bridge." And then he turned to Lane, "Thanks for the assist."

Lane's eyebrows lifted in shock. "There are direct flights from here to Hong Kong, fyi."

Something deep in Lamont's chest came to life at those words. He smothered it. "Got a prisoner to transport. I've got a job to do."

Lane shook his head. "Job can't be all there is."

Lamont took a deep breath into his nose and exhaled from his mouth. He nodded at Monica, Kierra and turned to do the same to Maya before walking to the passenger side of the van.

Mercifully Asif didn't speak to him on the ride to the other hangar or on the flight halfway across the country. They traveled in near silence; both men somewhere else, with someone else. People they felt certain they could never have.

"Alright let's get the hell out of here," Lane said, turning toward the jet.

"We're not going with you," Kenny said.

"We're not?" Maya asked.

"You're not?" Kierra echoed.

Kenny turned to Monica, "I know I just started working with you and you might not even want to work with me after…" his eyes darted to Maya, "Everything. But I've never taken one day of vacation in almost six years with The Agency."

Maya gasped. Kierra's eyes bounced between them. Kenny's red face and Maya's shocked smile were all she needed to know that whatever was happening here was special.

"If it's alright with you," Kenny continued, "I'm requesting three weeks of vacation starting right now."

When he stopped talking they all turned to Monica. She was eyeing Kenny with a shrewd stare. "No," she said, and Kierra's mouth fell open.

"Now hold the fuck up," Maya said.

Monica's eyes were trained on Kenny, "Your personnel records indicate that you have almost four months of vacation time. And since we're probably going to be audited soon, you should use your time before they take it. I don't want to see you before the new year."

Kierra felt herself smiling as a warm feeling of love spread through her veins.

"Does that…does that mean that you still want me to work with you?"

Monica almost smiled, "We could have gotten Mehmeti without you. I offered you the job because you're a good agent. And I can make you better."

Monica nodded and turned toward the plane. Their eyes met briefly and the right side of her mouth lifted up just a fraction of an inch. She enjoyed ruffling all their feathers sometimes.

Lane's smile as he watched Monica walk onto the jet was a pure and unceasing adoration. Kierra could absolutely relate. When he turned to Kierra, his eyes were dancing. "Say your goodbyes. And you two have fun," he said to Maya and Kenny, handing over the other man's phone before he followed Monica onto the plane.

Kierra turned to Maya, a smug smile on her face.

Maya rolled her eyes in annoyance. "Don't."

"So you Pretty Woman'd your life, huh?"

"I said don't."

"When have I ever listened to you?"

Maya huffed a laugh and she stepped toward her. "Great point, tiny Tim."

Kierra smirked, "Technically in my heels we're almost the same height."

"You're like a baby giraffe," Maya said.

"A baby giraffe with a great ass."

Maya burst into laughter, "What does that even mean?"

Kierra laughed and shook her head, "No idea."

They grabbed each other then, pressing their bodies together in a tight hug. "I'm glad you're okay," Kierra whispered. "I was worried for a few minutes there."

"I was worried for hours," Maya laughed. "I'm glad you didn't die, short stack. You still owe me a month's rent."

Kierra laughed, and they squeezed each other tight before pulling away. She moved her hand to grasp Maya's and they both turned to Kenny. "If anything happens to her annoying ass, I'll kill you."

He nodded gravely but smiled, "That sounds fair."

Kierra lifted her eyebrows at Maya, "When you get back we'll have a very long and thorough discussion about you two in the salon."

Maya gasped, "Jesus you saw that?"

Kierra turned to her and smiled, "I tried to record it for your channel but Lane wouldn't let me."

Maya rolled her eyes, "There is truly something wrong with you."

Kierra lifted onto the balls of her feet and brushed her mouth along Maya's cheek. "Truly. Have fun, babe. You deserve this and more." With a final wink at Kenny, she turned and walked up the stairs onto the jet.

She found Lane and Monica sitting in their normal seats and she sat across from them, crossing her legs slowly. The cabin door closed and the skeleton crew began to prepare to taxi out of the hangar.

She locked eyes with Lane and then Monica, a slow smile forming on her lips.

She uncrossed her legs and their eyes settled on the crease

of her thighs. "Is there anything I can get you two before takeoff?"

There was barely a moment of silence before Lane launched himself at her, pulling her across the aisle to settle between them.

The sound of Kierra's laughter mixed with Monica's sighs and Lane's grunts as their plane moved slowly toward the queue of departing planes.

Maya turned to Kenny as Kierra disappeared into the jet. It was odd to feel shy after all they'd been through, but she did. And then she felt tired, so tired all of a sudden. "Are we going back to the hotel for our stuff?"

Kenny shook his head, "That would not be smart. Besides, I asked the porter to send our stuff to the airport before we left."

Maya's eyes widened, "That's not suspicious at all? Won't Mehmeti's men look for us?"

Kenny shrugged. He walked toward her and gently grabbed her hand, "Eventually. Once they realize that their boss is gone and contact his family. But when they go looking, they'll discover that our bags were rerouted through Oregon and Alaska but lost somewhere in Iceland. I hope there was nothing in those bags you needed urgently."

"I mean a change of clothes and some tennis shoes would be great right now," she said gesturing to her bare feet with their joined hands, her heels and purse clutched in her free hand. She did not relish having to put those heels back on.

"Let's get to the main terminal and I'll buy you the best this airport has to offer," he said. Maya wanted to tell him that sounded like a terrible fashion look in the making. But she didn't. She was too distracted by the smile on his face, the way the dim light in the hangar danced in his eyes, which seemed light and playful for the first time since they'd met in person.

She could hardly believe that had only been a couple of weeks ago. It felt as if they'd lived a lifetime since then. And she guessed on some level – with all of the strange things that had happened since he'd strolled into her apartment, ashamed and nervous – they had.

"I have big feet. You better pray they have something in my size or I'm never going to let you forget this."

They walked to a golf cart at the back of the hangar and he helped her in. "You can needle me about this for as long as you want. Forever even."

Maya gasped and Kenny took the opportunity to brush his mouth against hers, his tongue swept inside and coaxed hers forward.

When he pulled back she felt as if she was still in a daze. They were driving across the airport before her brain rebooted enough to form a full sentence. "Fuck that was smooth," she said.

His laughter was music to her ears.

nineteen

"Are you sure you're not mad?" Jerome asked. Again.

"She said she's not. Chill dude. You get to hang out with your boyfriend with no beakers involved. Don't ruin it," Kaya huffed.

"He's not my boyfriend," Jerome corrected. Maya could hear Jerome's blush in his voice.

"Leave him alone," she breathed. "We don't tease you about being in a full-on relationship, so don't tease him."

"I'm not teasing him," Kaya said, sounding to Maya like she used to when she was a pre-teen and their mother told her to clean her room. "I just want to get to the good stuff."

Maya frowned. "What good stuff?"

"Whatever it is that has you so deliriously happy that you're apparently just fine with the three of us not spending Thanksgiving together for the first time since mom."

Maya had her siblings on speaker phone so she could lotion her body while they talked. The way Kaya said "since mom," but not "since mom died," stilled her hands. She wondered if she was making the right decision.

She and Kenny had arrived at a private villa in the mountains on the outskirts of Oahu in the afternoon and immediately passed out for the rest of the day. Now that they were awake, showered and had even eaten, Maya was beginning to feel like herself again. But her real self had two younger siblings who needed her. Or at least, they used to need her. She'd been shocked to turn her phone on for the first time in at least a day to find text messages from her siblings independently asking if she would be mad if they didn't come to New Jersey for Thanksgiving. Kaya wanted to go to New Mexico with her new special friend. And Jerome's lab partner had invited him to stay local and spend the holiday with his family. Maya was shocked to realize that her shoulders had relaxed as she read those messages.

Kaya was right. This would be the first time they wouldn't spend the holiday together since their mother had died and maybe that was a good thing. Maybe, she thought to herself, that meant they were finally healing. She certainly felt that way; as if she could let go of them just the tiniest bit and watch them become their own people. And maybe this was her time to take control of her life again.

There was a splash in the pool outside.

Maybe it was time she lived for herself again.

"Does this have anything to do with you asking us how to tell someone you like them?" Jerome asked carefully.

Maya grabbed her phone and moved to the window. It looked down on the pool. "Yeah," she breathed.

"Well look at us," Kaya said. "Us misfit orphans aren't doing so bad on the relationship front this year, huh?"

"I- I'm not in a relationship," Jerome breathed self-consciously.

"Not yet," Maya said, as her eyes tracked Kenny's body cutting gracefully through the water.

"So are you going to tell us anything else?" Kaya asked.

"No," she replied. "It's too soon." She tore her eyes away. "The point is that it's completely fine that you two spend the holidays with your boos. I'll miss you, but we deserve to be happy together and apart."

Her siblings were silent for a few seconds before they burst into laughter.

"How corny," Kaya breathed.

"Okay, Maya Angelou," Jerome said and Kaya cackled loudly.

Maya rolled her eyes and smiled. "You two are the biggest dicks," she breathed. "You're very lucky I love you."

KENNY LIFTED himself from the pool, planted his foot on the edge and stood. He ran his hands over his head and stopped. Maya was standing on the deck, just outside of the house, staring at him. Wearing a very small pink bikini with white polka dots.

His eyes raked over her body, from her curly hair to her softly rounded chin, to the gentle drooping mounds of her breasts, across the slope of her stomach that hung just over the top of her bikini bottoms. His eyes darted to the sides, something about the ties at her hips made his throat go dry. His eyes kept traveling down, over her thighs and folded flesh of her knees and then her adorable toes, painted a bright white that caught his attention.

"Haven't you had enough of just looking at me?"

He huffed a laugh and stalked toward her. When he was close, she turned around and ran. The way her soft flesh moved gently with each stride made his heart beat faster and he groaned, running after her, but not fast enough to catch her. At least not yet.

She looked over her shoulder to made sure he was following. She took the stairs and the view of her ass above him made him almost double over in pain as his dick hardened in his swim shorts.

Just inside their bedroom he sped up and grabbed her from behind. She yelped and giggled. He'd never felt anything so perfect as her body in his arms. He pressed her gently against the wall just inside the room. She turned her head to look at him over her shoulder, panting.

He moved his mouth to her jaw, licked at her flesh, until their mouths met.

"Condoms?" she whispered into his mouth.

"Boxes," he whispered back as he gripped her waist and ground his erection into her ass.

She groaned and he could have lost it right there.

"What are you waiting for?" she whined.

He slipped his tongue into her mouth as his hands played with those ties at her hips. She suckled on his tongue slowly and he pulled those ties apart just as slow. He increased the pressure of his lips against hers and slid their tongues together. She moaned into his mouth. He might have said that he'd never tasted anything as sweet, but he could still remember the way her pussy tasted on his tongue. And he wanted to taste it again. But there would be time for that.

When he had her bikini bottoms untied, he moved his foot between hers, spreading her legs apart. She smiled against his mouth as they kissed. He palmed the wide globes of her ass, rubbing and squeezing, until eventually he slid one finger down her crack. She arched her back and moaned as that finger came in contact with her sex. He slipped his hand between her legs, turned his arm and cupped her.

"Oh my god," she breathed into their kiss.

She was already wet. His balls were heavy in his shorts. He wanted her to touch him desperately. And just as he thought that, her hand snaked around and she cupped his sex through his shorts.

He laughed in pure, debilitating, wild lust. She sucked his bottom lip into her mouth.

Kenny drew his fingers along the cleft of Maya's sex, her

wet folds felt like velvet. He circled her clit and their tongues tangled as she managed to maneuver her hand into his shorts.

She grunted in frustration. He smiled and used his free hand to help her push his shorts over his hips. They fell down his legs and he stepped one foot out so that he could widen his stance, open his legs further and give her access to his cock. His hand was wet from her pussy and he moved it to his dick, using her juices to lubricate himself.

"Oh fuck," she groaned, putting her forehead against the wall as she started to stroke him slowly.

He grabbed her chin and turned her head so he could kiss her again as his hand went back between her legs. He used the pads of three fingers to rub her clit, slow and firm, like he always saw her do when she wanted to get herself ramped up quickly. Her keening whines let him know he was doing it right.

"Please," she mumbled awkwardly, unwilling to move her mouth too far from his.

He shivered at the way that word tasted on her tongue in his mouth and slipped a finger into her cunt.

They both groaned and stilled. Their panting breaths filled the room. Their bodies were hot, all of the water from the pool on Kenny's body had evaporated, but sweat was building at the places where their skin touched.

Kenny registered in that moment that Maya smelled like sweet peaches and his hips jerked when he realized that he would smell like that soon. He slowly added a second finger into her pussy. He wanted her scent all over him.

Her hand started to move as their kiss resumed. But this time everything was less measured. They had wanted to tease each other before; get one another worked up. But now the pressure was building and they wanted to come; wanted to make each other come. Their hands moved wildly, their tongues slid together, their lips crushing and sliding.

Kenny moved his hand from her chin to her chest. He

wanted to grope her breasts and pluck at her nipples, but there would be time for that later as well. He pulled her body back toward his so he could run his palm over her belly and between her legs.

"Oh god," she moaned as his fingers settled over her clit.

Her orgasm was wild and wet and shuddering, but her hand didn't stop jacking him off. Not until he came in his own shuddering mess over her palm and on her hip.

"Maya," he mumbled against her lips.

"Yeah," she said with a laugh, "I know. I'm great."

Their laughter was thin and reedy; they were out of breath. It was perfect. But it wasn't enough.

EVEN BEFORE SHE knew his real name or what he looked like or how wet his deep voice could make her or what his dick felt like in her mouth, Maya knew that the first time she had sex with MasquerAsiaN it would be like this. She was on her back on the bed, her legs open for him, one hand squeezing her left breast – her thumb running over her hardened nipple – and the other massaging her pussy. Kenny was standing over her, his eyes drinking her in as he rolled a condom down his shaft.

"Hurry," she said and laughed. "Or I'm going to charge you."

A ghost of a smile crossed his lips. "I think we've already established that I'll pay whatever price you set."

Her hands stilled and her heart swelled. "Fuck that was smooth too. Where did all this game come from?"

He ducked and shook his head and then gripped her behind the knees, pulling her closer to him. They both held their breath as he lowered his hips and slid his dick along her lips. When the head of his cock came into contact with her clit she jumped and he moaned. He sunk into her slowly. Too slowly. She wanted to tell him to hurry it up. She was horny. Very horny. This was months of anticipation and she wanted him fast and hard and now. But this was months of anticipation, so she got it. He wanted to savor every second, every inch, as he slid into her. They held their breaths. When he was fully inside, he stilled. He leaned over to run his tongue over her thumb and suck it into his mouth along with her nipple.

"Oh fuck," she whispered in a strained tone.

He sucked on one breast and palmed the other as he began to move out of her just as slowly as he slid in.

"You've gotta be fucking kidding me," she growled.

He laughed and lifted his head. He pulled out almost to the tip and then began to sink into her again. Just as slowly as before. Apparently, he was not kidding. He lowered his head to her other breast.

"I'm never going to come like this," she whined.

"I know," he mumbled against her skin.

She pushed at his shoulders until they were eye-to-eye. His gaze was playful, bright, and mischievous. Her mouth fell open in surprise and she shook her head. How did he seem to remember every conversation they'd ever had? Even in a moment like this. She pushed him off of her.

"Get on the bed," she demanded.

"Whatever you want," he said.

There was a moment when Kenny was just her client. They'd once had a marathon chat session about exactly how he would fuck her if they ever met. It was pure fantasy. She had one of those chats with a different customer once a month at least. Except it wasn't. She didn't know how to explain it then, but every word she'd typed to him had been exactly what she wanted. From him. Especially after he told her that the only thing he wanted wasn't to fuck her, but to let her fuck him. He wanted her to take control. That was her catnip.

Kenny sprawled his body on the bed, stacking two pillows

under his head so he could watch her. His dick was standing up at attention. From this angle she noticed that it curved slightly to the left. It was perfect. She crawled between his legs and then grinned. She turned away from him, maneuvering her body over his in reverse cowgirl. She lifted one knee, tossed her hair over her shoulder and turned to look at him as she settled slowly onto his dick. She'd see how he liked being on the receiving end of that, she thought to herself.

Of course he loved it. She shook her head and turned from him. She placed her hands onto his impossibly muscled thighs and started to ride him. Slowly at first; nice and gentle. But then his hands began to roam over her ass and hips and back and then around to palm her breasts and she lost control of herself. Soon enough she was rubbing her clit and bouncing on his hips while he smacked her ass with just the right amount of pressure, it was everything she'd ever dreamed of and more.

The room filled with the sound of flesh on flesh and their moans and curses. And when she came with a high-pitched scream and her body wracked with tremors, he didn't miss a beat. He moved her forward and rose up to his knees behind her. There was no slow entry this time, thank god. He pushed into her smoothly and then fucked her face into the bed, his fingers digging into her hips and her name on his lips. She came again and again and still he rode her, all of those months of need and frustration and longing finally evaporating now that they were together. Truly together.

But the best part of it all. The part that she would tell him about when she woke up from the nap they would surely fall into after they were done. The thing Kierra would absolutely ask about. The best part was when he came, her name on his lips, and she came one more time with him.

"Kenny," she breathed in exhausted glee directly into the comforter underneath her. "Kenny."

Epilogue

Asif very rarely felt fear while out in the field. It was such a sporadic emotion for him in general that his training agent had actually recommended he *not* be allowed to run his own operations. "Likely to get himself, other agents, and civilians killed," had been the exact wording on his performance review. Asif had lodged an official rebuttal of that assessment, pointing out that he loved himself too much to be reckless with his own life. Vanity wasn't the expected defense in such a situation, but it had worked. The Agency approved him for field work, Asif turned out to be a great provocateur and a year later his training agent was discovered to be a mole. So really it all worked out in the end.

After almost a decade in the field, Asif had proven that base self-preservation was actually a really wonderful trait for a spy. Fear could be paralyzing. Fear could get you killed. But self-preservation reminded you to run, to yell, to fight, kick, scream, bite. So it wasn't fear that made Asif slip his cell phone from his pocket and make that phone call. It was self-preservation. He'd go to his grave making that distinction clear if need be.

"Pearl's Soul Food," a feminine voice said when the line connected. He exhaled in relief.

"It's me, Chanté," he said, hoping his voice didn't betray the worry – not fear – that she wouldn't accept his phone call.

"Oh," she squealed. And then in a wary tone, "Oh. Have you checked your bank accounts lately?"

"No," he hissed, "Why?"

"No reason," she said, sounding light and bubbly again. "What accent is this now?"

He should keep asking questions about what sum of money she'd stolen from him recently so he could add it to the mental tab he kept in his head. But in this particular moment her theft felt like the least important thing in the world. The most important thing was wringing the pleasure of simply hearing Chanté's voice; a pleasure he'd spent years denying himself.

It used to be that he would ration the joy of one short conversation over months for endless hours of recycled ecstasy, dodging her calls until he needed another fix, because he'd been too afraid to let her know how happy she made him. But times surely had changed. Now it was she who seemed able to go longer and longer without talking to him. She didn't even call anymore. And she only picked up sporadically. He hadn't even seen her since Berlin. But he didn't think she was rationing their connection; he was terrified that she was weaning herself off of him. But terror, like fear, was a new companion for Asif. He tried not to let the unusual taste of it color his words when he answered her question. "I'm trying for an Australian-Kiwi mix," he answered. "I've got a complicated backstory."

"Oooh, I'm listening," she trilled.

He smiled in spite of himself. A real genuine smile that felt as rusty as it had when they'd met almost eight years ago and she'd pulled that first unexpected tilt of his lips from him. A loud shout from downstairs reminded him that now was not the time for nostalgia.

Asif was skirting through the shadows in the balcony above a luxury private casino for the rich and corrupt. It was all very reminiscent of spy movies from the 1970s. The building used to be an opera house and it still held a bit of the elegant ostentation of its former life. But apparently the arts were no match for the caprices of capitalism and greed. Or at least that's the kind of thing his mother would have said, her glasses perched precariously on the tip of her nose as she drank a delicate cup of tea. His father would have nodded and hummed his agreement as he turned the pages of his morning newspaper.

Asif slipped further into the shadows and lowered his voice. "Can't talk much right now."

"Well then why'd you call? Or do you need me to hack something?" She sounded giddy at the prospect.

"No, no I don't need you to hack anything. You're a little too subtle for my current situation," Asif said as he reached the door at the end of the hallway. It led to a stairwell that ran along the eastern edge of the building. "I just wanted to hear your voice," he admitted.

Chanté's breath hitched and his hand stilled on the doorknob. He wanted to ask her to make that sound again, but the rising volume of the escalating argument downstairs once again pulled him back to reality. "Tell me a story," he whispered as he slowly turned the knob. He inched into the stairwell cautiously. If he headed down, he could be out on the street in a few minutes, hail a cab to the airport and be in another country in a few short hours, scot-free.

"I got a package of this great biodegradable body glitter today," Chanté started.

Asif smiled and headed up the stairs. Where was the fun in scot-free?

"So you're probably thinking, 'Chanté, don't you have

enough body glitter?' right now," she said, in a terrible imitation of his Boston accent.

As it happened, he was thinking exactly that.

"But this is special glitter," she said conspiratorially.

Asif moved swiftly up the two flights of stairs and pushed open the door to the roof. The night air was almost painfully cold. Late fall in Russia felt like full-blown winter back home. He wished for the perfectly good winter coat he'd surrendered at the door of the club, but making a detour to coat check would have been like a neon sign, broadcasting that this Australian was up to no good.

He focused on the task at hand. At least out here on the roof he could respond to Chanté. "What's so special about this glitter?" His teeth began to chatter. He walked to the northeast corner of the roof and knelt down. The bundle of explosives was right where he'd left it earlier this morning.

"I'm glad you asked. This glitter looks plain and boring in the tube. Just regular, shiny, vegan glitter, no parabens, no sulfates, no whatever else is de passé these days. Nothing to write home about."

"You would write home about glitter," he said, laughing, and then wishing he hadn't as his throat seized on the inhalation of the bitterly cold air.

"I have an entire blog about glitter, thank you very much," she said haughtily.

He laughed again. It hurt. He didn't care.

"But *this* glitter, Asif. It is everything. Because it glows in the dark," she whispered that last sentence.

"Okay," he said as he pulled the detonator from his pocket, disguised as a pack of cigarettes. If this place had a halfway decent security system, or even just a metal detector, they would have discovered it. But as Lane never missed an opportunity to point out – correctly – rich criminals were dumb criminals.

He'd just attached the detonator to the bomb and was setting the timer when Chanté responded.

"Okay? Asif, think. Imagine. Me, naked on stage, my body covered in pink, glow-in-the-dark glitter. All of the lights in the room turned off," she said in the sultry whisper that he always found terrifying in its ability to bring him to his knees – even if he didn't always show it, especially not to her.

He opened and closed his lips. He couldn't tell if his mouth was dry because of the cold or because of the image she'd put in his head.

"Yeah," he croaked. "Okay. Got it."

She giggled. "So, what are you doing at the Imperial Soviet Casino?" she asked nonchalantly.

"What? How do you-"

"One," she said, and he could just imagine her lifting a delicate finger as she said it, "Your Australian-Kiwi accent is good, but not good enough to fool a native. Two, I could have sworn I heard someone yelling in a Russian accent earlier. That didn't necessarily mean that you were in Russia, but it was a clue. And then three, you sound cold. You need a coat."

"I have a coat. Had. It's a casualty of the mission at the moment," he said defensively. "Anyway, I refuse to believe that's how you know where I am."

"Oh no, I started tracing your call as soon as I picked up. The other clues were just fun breadcrumbs."

Asif exhaled as he set the timer for twenty-five minutes and walked back toward the door. "You hack my accounts, trace my calls and bug my apartment. It's starting to sound like you love me," he said, a rakish smile on his face that she couldn't see, but he knew she would hear in his voice.

"I only bugged your hotel room one time. Get over it." He heard the eye roll in her voice. But she stopped him dead in his tracks, his hand stilling on yet another door handle, "And you already know that I love you." She said the words 'I love you,' as if they weren't as explosive as the bomb he'd just armed. As if that feeling was so simple. She always had.

The problem was that he couldn't say them back. "I'm...I should go. Things are going to get loud here in a minute," he said.

He could practically see the sad smile spread across her lips. He hoped she wouldn't cry this time. He hated when she cried. Especially when she cried over him; he was absolutely not worth it.

"Always keep your eye on the exit, right?" His heart broke at how bitter his own words sounded coming from her mouth. "Don't die, Asif," she said and hung up before he could respond.

He slipped down the staircase and back onto the balcony. The fight below had escalated into a standoff, at gun point no less. He guessed finding a marked card in your hand would cause any gambler to leap to the conclusion that the house was cheating. And he guessed that when accused of cheating, any casino owner would pull a weapon. And definitely if someone aims a gun at your head, you have to aim one back, right? That's how these things worked with the rich and idiotic at least.

But since most casinos were rigged and all of the players in this casino were wagering the equivalent of a working-class family's annual gross wages on each hand, cheating seemed a strange hill to die on. But Asif had never presumed to understand the rich, he simply used their greed against them. It had barely taken two hands for the already suspicious gamblers to notice the small marks on the presumably fresh pack of cards he'd planted at the table before the games started.

He stepped back onto the casino floor and checked his watch.

"Kareem, there you are," Asif's asset said, sidling up to him. "Where have you been?"

Asif smiled his best, most charming smile that made

everyone on the other end of it weak in the knees. Everyone except Chanté, his brain shouted at him.

"I had to make a phone call," he said slowly, trying to ease himself back into the Australian-Kiwi accent the target recognized. He'd accidentally slipped out of it on the roof while speaking with Chanté. Or more accurately, she'd pulled him out of it as she always did, tugging him toward the real and authentic at every turn. He hadn't fully descended into the Boston accent he used so infrequently these days, since they hadn't been on the phone long enough, but he'd come close.

"I had to make a phone call," he said again. "Business," he added vaguely. The target nodded and the tension in his eyes melted away as he happily accepted Asif's lie and filled in the many holes in his story. Something Asif had known well before he'd joined The Agency was a useful truth in this line of work: the best lie is the one with as few details as possible. "Now what's this?" Asif asked, gesturing toward the standoff.

"Apparently," the target said in his crisp upper-class British accent, his eyes dancing with mirth, "someone's been stacking the deck." They both turned to watch the two Russians pointing guns and spitting threats at one another in their native language.

"What are they saying?" Asif asked, even though he was fluent.

"I've no idea. But this is awfully exciting. Don't you think?"

Asif smiled and placed a hand on the target's back. He turned to Asif, his cheeks already flushing. "This isn't the kind of excitement I prefer," Asif replied in an intimate whisper.

He watched as the target gathered all of the suggestions he'd laid out before him. They were out on the street – bundled in their coats, waiting for the valet to return their car, the target's hand stroking Asif's crotch – in no time. The asset leaned down to whisper something dirty in Asif's ear. Asif raised his hand to grasp the target's neck and surreptitiously check his watch at the same time.

"*Don't die, Asif,*" Chanté's voice whispered in his head.

Finally, the valet arrived. Asif grabbed the keys and jumped behind the wheel. They had five minutes to get as far away from the casino as possible. When the target leaned over to unzip Asif's pants and lower his mouth to Asif's lap, it was a blessing honestly. He was so focused on sucking Asif's dick that he didn't even register the loud bang of the bomb detonating behind them.

The explosive pack was strategically placed at the building's weakest structural point to crumble the roof and collapse inward, keeping the damage fairly contained. He watched the building partially cave into itself in the rearview mirror.

Likely no one had been killed. That wasn't the point of this mission anyway.

"See Chanté, I didn't die," he murmured to himself.

"What?" the asset asked, lifting his mouth from Asif's wet cock.

"I said that feels amazing," he responded with a smile. The asset smiled back and lowered his head again.

Acknowledgments

This story means a lot to me. I originally thought Pink Slip would be a standalone, but then I wrote Maya and fell in love with her. I wanted to write a love interest who loved her even more than I did and then I fell in love with Kenny. Even when it was painful, writing these two made me happier than I can tell you. It's really warmed my heart to see people loving Maya and Kenny in all their glory. Thanks, Kai, for encouraging me to continue with this story even when it kept growing and Agata for loving Maya's fatness just as much as I did.

If you liked this story, I hope you'll keep reading in the series and recommend them to a friend. I'd also really appreciate it if you could leave a review on whatever site you feel comfortable with. And please come talk to me on twitter @katrinajax!

Other books by
KATRINA JACKSON

<u>Welcome to Sea Port</u>

From Scratch

Inheritance

Small Town Secrets

Her Christmas Cookie

<u>The Spies Who Loved Her</u>

Pink Slip

Private Eye

Bang & Burn

New Year, New We

His Only Valentine

Bright Lights

<u>Erotic Accommodations</u>

Room for Three?

Neighborly

<u>Heist Holiday</u>

Grand Theft N.Y.E.

<u>Love At Last</u>

Every New Year

<u>The Family</u>

Beautiful & Dirty

The Hitman

Bay Area Blues

Layover

Back in the Day

standalone stories

Encore

Office Hours

The Tenant

Sex Toy Soldier

Made in United States
Orlando, FL
02 June 2023

33738905R00228